THIS SIDE OF THE GATE

A novel by

JOHN P. JOHNSTON

author**HOUSE**™

1663 LIBERTY DRIVE, SUITE 200
BLOOMINGTON, INDIANA 47403
(800) 839-8640
WWW.AUTHORHOUSE.COM

First published by AuthorHouse 10/20/05

ISBN: 1-4208-8866-8 (e)
ISBN: 1-4208-8865-X (sc)

Library of Congress Control Number: 2005908866

Printed in the United States of America
Bloomington, Indiana

This book is printed on acid-free paper.

This book is dedicated to Jamie, my loving wife and companion, without whom it would not have been possible.

TABLE OF CONTENTS

PROLOGUE

OMES NOW THE time to galvanize the emotions and awaken memories long since recorded in the halls of eternity. Comes now the time of recollection, for some a time fraught with danger, but for others the blessed age of revelation. Comes now the era when the scales of justice are balanced, a time when everybody is held accountable according to the sins of the past. Comes then too the final chapter, when rewards long since forgotten arrive on wings of glory.

The age of revelation is upon us and our tale unfolds in order to prepare the way for the coming of the Light. It is an ancient tale, one that both awakens the past and summons the future. It is a tale of good and it is a tale of evil; however, do not expect to readily distinguish one from the other, because the distinction is not always apparent.

Thus do I bring you the saga of one Soul who has been bound to the Wheel of Rebirth for thousands of years. Mark it well, because many there are who are similarly trapped in the world of flesh. Know that this is a tale of two worlds, one on this side of the gate, and one on the other side of the gate; so take care that you do not mistake the meaning of the gate. Truly, it is the portal between the two worlds, but then few things are what they appear to be, least of all what is commonly called life and death.

LIFE ONE
The Boy And His Master

L ONG AGO IN the depths of man's beginning, there was a continent the size of Australia off the coast of present day Florida. A highly cultured people inhabited the island and, while they never landed men on the moon, their technological achievements rivaled those of the modern world. Most notably, they created a science based on natural rock crystals. Those crystals empowered their nation with all manner of marvel, not the least of which was an unlimited supply of energy. The continent was Atlantis and, despite the fact that the entire continent sank to the ocean floor approximately 12,000 years ago, many of those crystals still radiate energy into the atmosphere.

The crystals were natural formations, just like those admired and collected in modern times, but with one major exception. These crystals were cut, polished, and then placed in the sun, sometimes absorbing the sun's energy for months, if not years. Meanwhile, large groups of devotees, frequently numbering in the thousands, bombarded the crystals with preselected thoughts and images. Whole libraries, as well as enormous data bases, were painstakingly projected into the atomic structure of carefully chosen crystals. The crystals were selected according to size and color, with special attention paid to their crystalline structure. Some of them had very specific uses, while others were amenable to almost any type of data storage. For example, some crystals readily accepted programming, but just as readily surrendered their data; while others resisted programming, but once programmed required the modern equivalent of a password to both enter and retrieve information.

The science of crystal technology was founded upon the discovery that everybody radiates energy into the environment. When that energy is scattered and misdirected it presents as confusion and lack of motivation. When focused and directed it manifests as willpower. Thus when a dedicated group of people sharing a common purpose come together they have the power to set a mighty force in motion. The larger the group, the greater the force, and when the group numbers a thousand or more the power is tremendous. Imagine the great good that could be accomplished when an entire nation embraces such a principle, and sets its will to the achievement of a lofty purpose. In fact, large groups of people aligned with the spiritual truths of the age elevated Atlantis to the status of a great culture. It wasn't until much later that the masses succumbed to the influence of the Black Lodge, otherwise known as the Dark Forces.

During its heyday Atlantis rode the crest of the wave and, while the glamour of the world may have captivated the masses, their society achieved a balance between the high and the low. The upper echelon of society led the way, and its vision invariably embraced both science and religion.

The pinnacle of Atlantean science resided in a program dedicated to exploring the feasibility of space travel. Mars was the targeted destination because they were convinced that life existed on the red planet. In point of fact, life did at one time exist on Mars; however, the Martians atomized themselves in a planetary nuclear war approximately five million years ago. Science will eventually discover the remnants of Martian society, but for now the Martian world remains the butt of endless jokes. The Martians do not find the situation the least bit humorous, even though they now inhabit a different planetary system. The Atlantean space program was never launched, ostensibly due to the lack of funding; however, the truth be known, it failed because the glory of Atlantis subsided long before the continent actually sank into the ocean.

Most Atlanteans embraced religion with unbridled passion, rendering them susceptible to trancelike states of mind. Mental passivity opened the door to psychic intrusion, sometimes originating in the subconscious mind, sometimes appearing from the depths of the collective unconscious. Even worse, earthbound spirits, ever vigilant for unwary prey, attacked anyone susceptible to their influence, sometimes with cataclysmic results. Large numbers of Atlanteans suffered nervous breakdowns, while many others lapsed into deep depression. The effects generally wore off over time; however, many thousands were permanently disabled.

And so it happened that during the latter days of Atlantis the agents of good had their backs to the wall, while the forces of evil steadily accumulated unprecedented power. The nefarious work of the Black Lodge was such that many perished, and in the end Atlantis sank into the ocean, leaving but a few small islands to bear witness to her former glory. One day humanity will find a way to reconstruct its past; however, until that day arrives Atlantean karma will continue to influence every aspect of modern society.

Now the reason I bring you this bit of lost history is to set the stage for the tale to come. It's the life of a boy, later grown to manhood, who flourished in the latter days of Atlantis under the care of one of the principal agents of good. This is his life and, should you question its relevance, you should know that many in the world today have lived such a life.

Except for one notable feature, nothing remarkably distinguished this twelve-year-old boy from any other Atlantean child. And while his most distinguishable feature was not uncommon for an Atlantean, it should be understood that his gift was not entirely the product of his culture, but derived from his rather unique spiritual background. That background is best kept secret for now, but suffice it to say that the boy had the mind of a genius.

The boy's genius did not manifest along the lines you might suppose, because like most Atlanteans he was polarized upon the emotional plane of life. And while that might seem to imply a lack of intelligence, that isn't necessarily the case. It's a little known fact that the emotional brain, an aspect of the subconscious mind, does in fact have the capacity to think. When highly refined the emotional brain manifests a type of logic that obeys not the formulas of the logician, but the principles of Universal Beauty. Such was the nature of the boy's gift.

Being of sound mind, the boy realized that his parents would never endow him with a meaningful life. They, like so many others, were completely consumed with greed, and therefore exhibited little interest in their parental duties. Atlantean children were raised without the benefit of parental guidance, and yet strict obedience to parental authority was demanded. The expectations placed upon their children contrasted sharply with their own behavior, which resulted in thousands of children fleeing their homes. Some fled in search of a higher moral standard, but most simply sought the right to accumulate their own horde of possessions. As children they had no property rights, but as emancipated teens they were entitled to rights generally reserved for adults in Atlantean society. And so the boy abandoned his home, not in rebellion, and not to accumulate property, but in the pursuit of higher ideals.

The Atlanteans were fascinated with beauty, and in the end that fascination led to an obsession with material possessions, ultimately creating a society of thieves. They stole everything they could carry, and then stored the bulk of their plunder in warehouses. The warehouses were heavily guarded and, although they were recognized for what they were, the sanctity of private property overrode any possibility of ever exposing the practice to the light of public scrutiny. Stealing was a national pastime, and the problem was so far out of control it's a wonder traffic police weren't required to work through the night. They saw no conflict with their God, because in their minds they were only seeking beauty. And beauty was their God. Truly, Beauty is an aspect of the Godhead; however, Beauty does not exist apart from Love. In the distant past the people of Atlantis had in fact balanced Love and Beauty, the twin sisters of spiritual life, but that time had long since passed into history when the boy took up his journey. Beauty was no longer being sought in the Spirit of man, but in man's creations. One is the true expression of a spiritual life; the other is what the Old Testament refers to as the worship of idols.

During the time we now visit, the Black Lodge, black as in the absence of light, was hard at work planning the downfall of Atlantean society. Its members swore allegiance to Satan, an ancient concept, but a figment of the imagination, nonetheless. That being said, ancient evil from another time and place does in fact haunt the world of men. Ancient evil is but an aggregation of energy, comprising the evil of Mars, as well as other societies that have existed in our solar system at one time or another. Those energies are capable of manifesting form when invoked by the misguided, and once the connection is made the chains that are forged are nearly impossible to break in any given lifetime. Belief is a powerful force, powerful enough to validate moral corruption as nothing more than viable choice. In truth, choice is a very small part of the seduction, because once the Dark Forces take over there is nothing left but bondage.

The masses never saw it coming, but the Masters of the White Lodge, white as in the presence of light, understood every nuance of the problem. They recognized man's vulnerability, and knew that the Black Lodge had launched an all-out attack. The Black Lodge sought to enslave humanity, but the guardians of civilization, the Masters of the White Lodge, thought it entirely possible to save the continent with the help of their students. In the end the Black Lodge won the battle for Atlantis; however, the devastation wreaked upon its legions was so extensive that it ultimately lost the war. Atlantis sank beneath the sea, and with it went any hope the Black Lodge had of controlling the planet.

The leaders of the Black Lodge relied upon crystal technology, first infusing their crystals with massive doses of hate, and then placing the likeness of their intended victims within their circle of evil. Their attacks focused on judicial officers and political leaders, and were capable of causing serious injury, if not death. The general public was attacked through the creation of free-floating clouds of negativity, and anyone vulnerable to their influence almost never failed to feel the effects. Some sank into depression, while others resorted to suicide. Only those who wrapped themselves in Light were immune to the attacks, and even they had to maintain a state of constant vigilance.

The Black Lodge boasts several million lost souls who are either currently incarnated in the world, or awaiting the opportunity to do so. They are literally possessed by the inanimate forces of evil in our solar system, and constitute a brotherhood of men and women intent on destroying humanity. They include all races and creeds, and can be found in every nation on earth. They have a plan, and that plan is even now at work. Most of them have no conscious awareness of their roles; however, the leaders of the Black Lodge are fully aware of their purpose. They almost always attack humanity through the baser emotions, constantly trying to lure the unsuspecting onto the lower levels of the astral plane; hence, the caution to align oneself with the highest and best in any given situation. Currently, the Black Lodge has extended its influence to the mental plane, hoping to entice world leaders to embrace mass destruction.

Under the influence of the Black Lodge Atlantis plumbed the depths of depravity. For example, sexual violence was so extreme that a significant number of people evolved into sexual psychopaths who murdered their victims for no other reason than the sexual arousal it occasioned. Other forms of sexual perversion included self-induced comas that lasted anywhere from a few minutes to an entire lifetime. Specially programmed crystals discharged powerful electrical charges directly into the brain centers associated with sexual potency. Each application elicited a powerful orgasmic response, plunging the practitioner into a temporary coma. If the practice continued unabated the probability of either irreversible brain damage or permanent coma was extremely high. The karmic consequences can be found today in people who routinely masturbate throughout the day, never achieving anything more than the perpetuation of their addiction.

The Masters of the White Lodge tried to save the people of Atlantis, and even now stand between humanity and the evil intentions of the Black Lodge, hoping to prevent another catastrophe. The White Lodge was founded at the dawn of human civilization, and consists of men and women from every race, creed, and color. That being said, the Masters of the White Lodge recognize no such distinctions, embracing instead the Divine Presence within every life. Earthly existence no longer interests them, and yet they have volunteered to remain behind in order to help humanity fulfill its promise. They are capable of manifesting on all seven planes of consciousness; however, except for a handful of brave souls, they rarely walk the earth in physical form, preferring instead to serve humanity from the unseen world. They reside in Shamballa, the sacred City of Light, and they number in the tens of thousands.

After a year of wandering the boy came in contact with a teacher who was a prominent member of the White Lodge. It happened that the Master immediately recognized the boy, not because of his physical appearance, but because the Light of the Lodge radiated from his aura. To understand an experience such as that would require the release of secrets long since sealed in the sacred archives of Shamballa. Those secrets will eventually be revealed, but the time of revelation has not yet arrived, so they remain protected against the possibility of misuse.

The Master was well aware of the boy's potential, and after a period of testing and observation began instructing him in the Ancient Wisdom. The boy applied himself with a diligence far beyond his age, and soon developed a solid foundation in the metaphysical arts. He was, in short, a disciple upon the Path. When he turned eighteen he received his first Initiation, a step that formalized his affiliation with the Lodge. At present the first Initiation signifies control of the instinctual brain, but on Atlantis it represented mastery over the negative energies projected by the Black Lodge. True, those energies were directed at the instinctual brain, but the challenge wasn't to subdue the brain, rather to protect it from intrusion.

When the boy reached the age of 21 he was again initiated. The second Initiation currently signifies control of the emotions, which protects the student from the worst of his or her karmic tendencies. On Atlantis the second Initiation, rather than indicate an achieved level of emotional control, allowed the student to disengage his astral/emotional body in order to travel on the astral plane while fully conscious in the brain. The second Initiation allowed the boy to travel the astral world, but only during meditation, and only when accompanied by his Master. It may not seem much of a victory, but the ability to travel the astral world allowed him to access the realm of the deceased, thus expanding his conscious awareness to include the reality of life after death, no small thing on Atlantis.

Death terrified the Atlanteans, and many of those fears still afflict the human family. The Atlanteans believed in an afterlife, but they also believed in eternal damnation. The hell they imagined was no worse than any of the modern versions, but that was apparently bad enough, because for the Atlanteans hell was a tangible thing, made all the more real by the psychic attacks perpetrated by the Dark Forces. Those attacks combined with their misguided religious practices to create an atmosphere of terror. Consequently, the general public experienced nothing short of panic whenever the subject of death was mentioned. The afterlife became a world fraught with danger, and even those who lived decent lives feared for their safety once through the gate. Only those trained in the Ancient Wisdom truly understood the nature of life after death.

After the second Initiation the Master granted the boy additional privileges, which included the right to draw upon his energy whenever the need arose. To do so the boy either formed an image of the Master in his mind, or silently enunciated the Master's name. Whenever he called upon the Master in this fashion he invariably received an influx of energy, not unlike what he experienced in meditation. Besides the privileges associated with initiatory status, the boy enjoyed other benefits. He was, after all, not only the Master's adopted son, but his Son in the spiritual sense of the word. Sonship represents an unbreakable bond of Love, and once attained it can never be lost, even until the end of time.

The relationship between Master and student in today's world is both similar and dissimilar to what transpired on Atlantis. Students are still kept at bay until such time that they have proven their reliability, and they still have to pass all of the tests associated with any given initiation. The primary difference between ancient and modern practice lies in the realm of discipline. In ancient times the Masters favored strict disciplinary training; however, today's students are more highly evolved, and therefore more easily instructed.

Each morning the boy and his Master joined hands, and together took up the work of salvation. They began by mentally wrapping the continent of Atlantis in a cocoon of Light. Next they directed Love and Wisdom to the leaders of the nation. They always worked in conjunction with the Master's crystals, which were arranged in specific configurations according to the nature of the work at hand. Once their task was completed, they placed their effort in the Law of Right Action, an attribute of Divine Consciousness rarely invoked by humanity. Once invoked, the Law of Right Action makes corrections as needed so that only the highest and best manifests in accordance with the Divine Plan.

They never witnessed the good that accrued, but relied upon their faith to verify the fact that they had accomplished something of value. It should be noted, however, that transmitting energy never guarantees acceptance, because the intended recipients must either ask for help through prayer and meditation, or live a life so in harmony with goodness that they routinely recognize and accept goodwill.

It wasn't long before the boy was tackling the rules of logic, applying his emerging intellect to the task of conquering his emotions. He studied, he meditated, and he applied his lessons to the fullest extent of his ability. He was fast approaching the third Initiation, which in Atlantis signified control of the emotions. The third would free him from the Wheel of Rebirth, and allow him to complete his evolutionary journey on the other side of the gate. The boy was looking forward to the challenge, and had no reason to fear the tests associated with his upcoming Initiation.

In today's world the third Initiation signifies mastery of the mind. The mind is ever susceptible to attitudes and beliefs founded upon the mistakes of the past; however, those mistakes are easily overcome through the cultivation of an outlook that embraces the Wholeness of Life. Wholeness implies interrelationship, and interrelationship implies both group awareness and personal responsibility. Once placed in the context of life's inherent Wholeness, dysfunctional belief systems are immediately challenged, and ultimately eliminated.

The day finally arrived when the Master retired into seclusion. He willed his estate to the boy, and then took up residence at a mountaintop retreat. Leaving the boy behind nearly broke his heart, but he felt it necessary to dedicate his remaining years to advanced meditation. Meditation for the neophyte is little more than relaxation while communing with the Soul. That, to be sure, is a major accomplishment, but when compared to the rarified consciousness attained by a Master, whether of the fifth, sixth, or seventh degree, it pales in comparison.

The Master entered realms of consciousness so lofty as to be barely discernible from the vantage point of the Soul. In order to fully understand his state of mind it is helpful to recall that the Bible frequently refers to the Holy Trinity: Father, Son, and Holy Ghost. The Father refers to the Creator, while the Son refers to that blessed state of awareness known as Christ Consciousness. The Holy Ghost refers to the Soul, a temporary polarity holding the promise of humanity's ultimate goal of Christ Consciousness. When Jesus proclaimed Himself to be the Son of God, he was not declaring anything remotely personal, but acknowledging the Spirit of Christ, the birthright of humanity.

Despondent, the boy pined for his Master, thinking only of their joyous reunion. Not surprisingly, it wasn't long before he journeyed to the Master's mountaintop retreat. The Master had thought it best for the boy to remain behind, but immediately relented when he caught a glimpse of his radiant smile. The Master, overcome with joy, entered meditation straightaway with the boy at his side. The gods must have been smiling upon the boy, because a brilliant ray of Light flashed into the crown of his head, bestowing his first taste of Samadhi. It lasted but a few seconds, but to the boy it seemed a timeless moment in which his every care evaporated.

Although Samadhi usually manifests as a gradual infusion of Light, it sometimes bestows total illumination in a single stroke. Samadhi is most often identified with advanced states of meditation; however, the little known truth is that it can manifest at any time. It has been known to dawn during moments of relaxation, but also during the twilight between sleep and waking consciousness. It is almost never bestowed before the third Initiation, but is generally experienced after the fourth Initiation, commonly referred to as the Crucifixion.

Crucifixion symbolizes the eradication of worldly desire, not the total annihilation of the personality as is sometimes thought. The crucifixion of Jesus Christ marked his fourth Initiation, not as an ordinary student, but as an aspiring Planetary Christ. His Crucifixion did not grant personal salvation, demonstrating instead the power and presence of Unconditional Love - truly, the only salvation man will ever know. That being said, you should know that Master Jesus is immediately available to all who seek Him. He rarely reveals His presence, but never fails to give aid and comfort to those who ask for help.

Not long after the boy's arrival the Master suffered a setback. His health had finally succumbed to the effects of long hours of meditation. Meditation taxes the nerves, and every adept of the art experiences at least one, if not several, of its side effects. Those effects rarely surface in the young; rather, they generally appear late in life.

The Master was not adverse to medical treatment, so he consulted a local physician, who interpreted his loss of vitality according to the science of the day. Mainstream medicine held that poor health stemmed from wrong thinking, and consequently favored treatments more akin to psychiatry than medicine. To be sure, Atlantean doctors prescribed medications, recommended herbs, and even practiced a rudimentary system of acupuncture. Those treatments, however, were thought to be useful only when combined with psychiatric intervention. The fault, it seems, lay within the patient, and not with the fact that their ministrations were frequently of little value.

In reality physical illness is only rarely caused by the mind. Powerful emotions, on the other hand, promote cellular breakdown, rendering the organism vulnerable to all manner of disease. Emotions include both the high and the low, and either extreme can weaken the body if allowed to affect its chemistry. Of course, emotions sometimes pass for thought; however, that type of thinking originates in the solar plexus, and obeys not the rules of logic, but the dictates of the ego.

That being said, many illnesses are not related to emotion, but to genetic aberrations caused by the planet's contaminated soil. The contamination is largely due to the millions of diseased bodies that have been absorbed into the soil. Burial is hazardous, and cremation will have to become the law if the planet is to reverse the effects of extensive contamination.

The Master's condition almost immediately worsened, so he began making preparations for his transition to the other side of the gate. The prospect of losing his Master nearly unbalanced the boy, until he remembered his lessons - lessons long since inculcated into his daily life. His balance restored, the boy dedicated himself to the task of caring for his Master. When the Master asked for help he ran to his aid. When the Master requested privacy, he was quick to remove himself, only to stand at the ready just outside of his chamber. He was determined not to fail his Master in his final hour.

Early one morning the boy knocked at the Master's door. Hearing no response he quietly entered the room. He was carrying a cup of hot beverage generally considered good for the nerves, but in fact possessed no value beyond the warmth it infused. But, the thought was good and the intention was pure. The Master liked to see the boy happy, and bringing him his morning cup of beverage certainly seemed to please him.

The boy recognized the indications at once and immediately despaired. The Master's pale blue eyes revealed the vacant gaze of the dead, his jutting jaw announcing the fact that he had been calling out for help. To his everlasting shame the boy realized that he had been sound asleep when his Master called for help.

Overwhelmed with grief the boy immediately entered meditation. He first relaxed his body, followed by several rounds of alternate nostril breathing, thereby achieving a state of mental relaxation, completely free of internal dialogue. Then he visualized an outpouring of radiant White Light descending from the heavens, wrapping his body left to right in a cocoon of living substance. Next he radiated Light from the Center of his Being, thereby elevating his consciousness, achieving a sense of Oneness that included the Wholeness of Life. Finally, he began purging his grief. Utilizing the inherent power of happy memories, he created a mental checklist of every joy he had ever shared with the Master. The effect was nothing short of miraculous. His heart center, that sacred source of abundant life, poured forth a veritable ocean of Love. Thus did he recapture his balance and accept the fact that his Master now resided on the other side of the gate.

The following day, while comfortably ensconced in meditation, what remained of his grief suddenly and unexpectedly zigzagged across the surface of his mind, but he paid it no mind. It never established a beachhead, but simply flitted through his awareness with no urgency attached. At that precise moment a descending ray of Light illuminated the area just above the crown of his head, ultimately penetrating the very core of his brain. Samadhi dawned just when his grief was attempting to attract his attention.

It rarely happens, but sometimes a life is destroyed in less time than it takes to form the thought, which is what happened to the boy. His life was forfeit the moment his grief was denied. Generally speaking, it is certainly advisable to turn troublesome thoughts and feelings over to the Soul, allowing it to purge the psychic landscape during the hours of sleep. And yet, there are those times when it is necessary to address head-on the slightest evidence of emotional turmoil. The boy was no psychologist, so he really can't be blamed for what happened next.

The Law of Energy is not a science known to man; nevertheless, the Law applies just the same. The Law dictates that energy applied to a self-contained unit of consciousness uniformly multiplies everything contained within that consciousness. And that's what happened to the boy. His grief was magnified a thousand-fold by the Light of Samadhi. Under ordinary circumstances the result would not have been so disproportionate, but this was no ordinary circumstance, because the boy was being tested. It was the final challenge standing between him and the third Initiation, and subsequent release from the Wheel of Rebirth. Had he but directed Love and Light to the source of his grief, things might have turned out differently. But, he never thought to pay close attention to the details of his mind, especially then, when it seemed he had transcended his sorrow. Little did he realize, but it's the details that separate the novice from the adept.

Events moved quickly from that point forward. Consumed with anguish, the sound of his pounding heart accompanied the avalanche of grief that buried his rational mind. The sheer velocity of the debris caught up in the maelstrom somehow reduced his bodily mass, and like a feather caught in gale force winds he was carried away, landing on the face of a cliff some distance from the retreat. Mindless and totally numb with shock, he hurled himself into the void, coming to rest a thousand feet below upon a tumble of rocks that had once adhered to that very same cliff. Broken bones protruded from his flesh, while the fragments of his shattered mind littered the landscape of his tortured human soul.

The pain he experienced seems unbearable even now, as I, the Soul, reveal the ancient tale of the boy and his Master. His love for the Master was unfathomable, based as it was, upon their mutual commitment to God's Plan for Humanity. His love for the father who had adopted him was equally profound, founded as it was, upon one of humanity's worthiest emotions, the love of a parent. The depth of his love for a true friend and confidant was itself enough to drive many a soul to destruction once lost. He was so completely destroyed that one would have thought him a victim of the volcanic holocaust that would ultimately submerge the continent of Atlantis.

He was an empty shell when he made that leap, which is why he transitioned to the other side of the gate in a state of witless confusion. For the longest time it appeared as though he was going to pass the time between incarnations trapped in repetitive re-enactments of his tragic death. Just when it seemed all hope was lost he snapped out of his self-imposed horror, and was overjoyed to learn that his Master loved him still, but grief stricken all over again when he discovered that his Master had shed a tear. Know that Masters never experience negative states of mind beyond the genuine expression of sorrow, but also know that even their sorrow serves God's Plan.

Eventually, he began making preparations for his next incarnation. Atlantis was in even greater peril, although tens of thousands still carried the Light. Many thousands more conducted normal lives, not unlike modern society where the wealthy are juxtaposed with the poor and the homeless.

Such was the life of the boy and his Master.

LIFE TWO
The Counselor

A T ITS PEAK Atlantean culture was one of the finest ever produced by the human race. It scaled the heights of achievement in many areas, but none so well as the spiritual. The spiritual arena, not to be confused with the religious practices of the masses, was very much the study of Yoga. Several higher types of Yoga, each representing an aspect of the Ancient Wisdom, were offered to advanced students; however, the Yoga taught to the general public emphasized bodily postures. Those postures facilitated control of the animal instincts through the stimulation and development of the endocrine system which, when fully developed, secretes hormones yet to be discovered by modern science. Those hormones hold the secret to eternal youth, and can be used to predict the health of the organism far into the future. The postures also produced beneficial effects upon both mental and emotional functioning. This was possible because of the link that exists between mind and body through the aegis of the subconscious mind, which resides in the solar plexus, and consists of the same gray matter found in the cortex of the brain. The body is in constant communication with the subconscious mind, and that connection is of critical importance to humanity.

As a member of the White Lodge the Counselor was a student of the Ancient Wisdom. He therefore utilized a variety of techniques, ranging from behavioral to existential to spiritual. He employed standard behavioral techniques when the situation required the application of significant force to the subconscious mind, and existential analysis when facilitating the discovery of life's inherent meaning. Spiritual unfoldment was the ultimate goal, and anyone seeking to establish a connection with the Creator was eligible to receive advanced instruction.

Unlike mainstream approaches, the Ancient Wisdom places very little emphasis upon the past, focusing instead upon the art of living in the present. Psychologists remain divided over the efficacy of reconstructing the past, versus vitalizing the present with healthy attitudes and effective life skills. The educated professional understands the distinction, and makes every effort to achieve a healthy balance. The Counselor emphasized the present, and therefore expended very little time and effort exploring past trauma. The recent past, however, presented an obvious exception, because past experience lies beneath the threshold of consciousness for weeks, and sometimes months before it's stored in the subconscious mind, and even longer before it's imprinted into the cells of the body.

Left to its own devices, the subconscious mind organizes memories according to significance, and not just according to similarity of emotion. Over time those memories fuse, creating a morass of convoluted emotional reactions. If and when those memories are activated, the personality is confronted with a volatile situation, because what was once dormant now requires significant resources. Consequently, the distant past is best left to the Light of the Soul. There is, however, one notable exception to that rule of thumb. When the past threatens the stability of daily life, it needs to be examined, and adjustments need to be made. Even so, care must be taken and caution observed. First and foremost, the patient is liable to sustain a serious setback if the therapist fails to focus on the facts, but instead relies upon emotional release. The release is only imagined, because repeated discharge does not neutralize negative emotions. This can only be achieved through the cultivation of the opposite emotion. Replaying past trauma is harmful, serving only to reinforce the perception of impotence.

The other important consideration when delving into the past is the possibility of inadvertently activating the collective unconscious, which is nothing more than a repository of human futility. It contains no archetypes as thought by Jung, and it offers no help to the suffering client. The archetypes Jung discovered are in reality thought forms created on the mental plane. They can, and sometimes do, shed light upon life's tribulations; however, many of them have limited applicability, while others are so outdated as to damage the mind that contacts them.

When the collective unconscious is activated the client frequently feels overwhelmed, sometimes experiencing a foreboding sense of inexplicable tragedy, thereby promoting psychic construction. Psychic construction accounts for those instances of recollected abuse which are later proven to be confabulated. It also accounts for many of the so-called past-life regressions experienced by sincere, though uninformed students. In such cases the ego's desire for personal glory, especially when acted out upon the world stage, activates the content of the collective unconscious. Therefore, past-life regressions should only be attempted by trained professionals; otherwise, serious complications can result.

Once aroused, memories, both subconscious and collective, are capable of triggering psychotic episodes. Psychotic episodes were common in Atlantis, where thousands were permanently disabled with serious disorders. Psychosis is typically related to difficult karmic conditions; however, that being said, it is also true that psychiatric disorders sometimes bear no relationship to personal karma. Such was the case in Atlantis, where millions of people were genetically predisposed to mania.

Atlantis seemed to spawn the manic individual and, lacking effective treatment modalities, the worst cases were housed in isolated communities where they received little or no care.

As a psychologist the Counselor was highly skilled and widely respected. He always followed the appropriate guidelines, which included instructing his clients in the proper method of meditation. He began by teaching them to relax their bodies, followed by breathing exercises known to quiet the mind. Next he taught them to use affirmations to achieve alignment with the Divine Inner Presence. Correctly applied, affirmations reorganize the subconscious mind, thereby marshaling support for targeted goals and objectives. The highest and best affirmations attract the attention of the Soul, which supports every effort motivated by Love and Service. Once attracted and drawn into relationship, the Soul not only reinforces the work at hand, but also plants the seeds of future development. In such a manner is character developed and the evolution of consciousness carried forward.

Like many of his colleagues, the Counselor could read auras. Every physical form, whether plant, animal, or human, emanates cellular energy, and that energy constitutes the health aura. The health aura consists of millions of wavy strands, each strand representing an amalgamation of radiating energy. When those strands are active and fully extended they indicate a general state of good health. Droopy, inactive strands indicate extreme fatigue. When the strands become entangled in certain recognizable patterns, death and disease can be predicted. When the strands vibrate wildly, mental health problems are present. Interpreting the health aura is a science, and while the Counselor was not an adept of the art, he was able to identify conditions likely to interfere with therapy.

Besides the health aura, the Counselor could read the astral/emotional aura. He was not an expert, but he could identify relevant conditions by virtue of the aura's coloration. Every aura exhibits multiple colors, and every color represents an aspect of consciousness. Dark colors, not the deep, true tones, but those characterized by the absence of light, indicate intense negativity. Black, especially when spattered with patches of scarlet, typically indicates malevolent intentions. Radiant colors, on the other hand, indicate purity of heart and mind.

The Counselor also practiced hands-on healing, consciously directing healing energy to his patients. Hands-on healing is not recommended for everyone because of the risk involved, namely the transference of negativity. The Counselor was a second-degree Initiate, and therefore generated sufficient energy to forestall any negative energy that might be transferred from the patient's subconscious mind. In reality nothing is actually transferred; however, dormant conditions, whether physical or emotional, within the healer are sometimes activated by the patient's condition. In such cases the transference should be purged in meditation; otherwise, the problem can become serious.

Throughout the therapeutic process the Counselor remained inwardly aligned with the Light of the Soul. Spiritual alignment is akin to magnetic resonance, and once achieved the transformation of both the therapist and the client is assured. Unfortunately, despite his training and experience, the Counselor's personal life was not similarly aligned, creating a constant state of imbalance. His work consumed everything. He had no hobbies or diversionary activities, nothing to offset his daily schedule. His life was entrenched in routine, and nobody was more surprised than he was when he finally met a woman who wasn't frightened away by the monotony of his existence. She too was a practicing psychologist and a member of the White Lodge.

Despite their divergent lifestyles, not the least of which was the fact that she traveled extensively, she experienced an immediate attraction. Like her father before her, she frequently traveled to the Indian subcontinent where, many centuries before, the Lodge had established a school on the shores of the Ganges River. Each tour of duty required a one-month commitment, although Mother Nature sometimes intervened, lengthening the stay indefinitely. In fact, she had recently been stranded in a remote location for months before being airlifted to safety. Her life was never in danger, although the experience awakened her maternal instincts, quickening her desire to marry and raise a family. Thus she married the Counselor, not only because of the inexplicable attraction she felt, and not just because she longed for a family of her own. Certainly, that was reason enough to marry, but above all she loved the Counselor because of his dedication to a life of service. The ceremony took place on the Island of Poseidon in the main temple of the Lodge.

Despite her love and devotion, she sometimes tired of her husband's unwavering routine. He never left the island and he never vacationed, but dedicated every minute of every day to either his work or his meditation. Beyond that, there was the matter of his father. Even though his father now resided on the other side of the gate, the Counselor continued to honor many of his customs. The main point of contention was his penchant for sitting down to dinner, as did his father, at a very late hour. It was a major source of irritation to his wife, who frequently retired early. They eventually sought help via marital counseling, which is how the Counselor discovered he had never grieved the loss of his father.

Grief work is generally considered essential; however, it isn't necessary to grieve every loss, because some losses are expected, and therefore accepted. Beyond that, successful grieving is almost always related to the resilience of the mourner. For the Atlanteans resilience meant a proper education regarding the nature of death. Even today many people view death as a form of punishment, both for the deceased, and for surviving friends and family. Excessive grieving disrupts people's lives; sometimes drawing the deceased back to the earth where they run the risk of becoming trapped in the lower astral plane. In the Counselor's case, he failed to grieve at all, having decided that it was completely unnecessary.

When the Counselor entered therapy he did so with the expectation that his point of view would be validated. In his mind he had every right to dictate to his wife on matters concerning his father's house. It wasn't until the third session that the telling argument was made. He was already beginning to sense the nature of the problem when the therapist pointed out that he had not only failed to grieve his father's death, but, by his own admission, he rarely even talked about his father. That was all he needed to hear. Every therapist knows that grief must be closely examined when clients either become mired in protracted mourning, or completely block all conscious thought of the deceased. In the Counselor's case, he rarely thought of his father, and yet manifested many of his attitudes. Some of those attitudes were barely discernible, although a few were so clearly his father's that he couldn't imagine how he had ever missed the dynamic at work. It was but a small step from there to the realization that his home was a veritable museum dedicated to his father's memory. In the end they sold their home and moved from the old neighborhood to a new development on the outskirts of the city, freeing both husband and wife from the unwanted influence of the past.

When he wasn't preoccupied with his work, the Counselor practiced the art of meditation with consummate skill, sometimes contemplating the Divine Inner Presence, sometimes investigating qualities universally attributed to Divinity. When contemplating the Divine Inner Presence he consciously expanded his awareness beyond the limits of the earth, achieving a sense of Wholeness that encompassed the entire Solar System, thus merging with the Life of the Solar Deity. When contemplating the nature of his own Soul, he focused his attention upon the brow, the location of an energized focal point, otherwise known as the brow chakra. When awakened, the brow chakra silences the mind, magnetically linking the personality to the Soul. From there he often contemplated the Divine Virtues, thus facilitating his journey into the world of the Soul.

Another option involved the use of the imagination. While in meditation, he both visualized and affirmed the achievement of coveted goals and objectives, knowing that a focused, directed imagination has the power to influence, if not shape the future. There is almost no limit to what can be achieved; however, there is in fact a limit. That limit is commonsense. Don't imagine what you aren't willing to work for, because the technique does not perform miracles. It simply creates a template; unless of course, you have discovered the power of Faith, in which case the template is more real than not.

Faith is without a doubt one of life's greatest mysteries. It empowers both thought and action, effortlessly aligning the personality with the Divine Plan. Once aligned with God's Plan there is no possibility of failure, because the good attributed to the Whole is automatically imbued within the individual.

The Counselor and his wife had a daughter, and had always hoped that she would one day apply for Lodge membership. But, she never expressed an interest in the rigors of discipleship. Instead, she was interested in medicine. After completing the mandatory ten years of public education, she enrolled in a well-known medical college affiliated with one of the major hospitals. Three years later she graduated with honors and joined a team of researchers dedicated to the eradication of cancer. Her area of expertise focused on the study of environmental contaminants and involved the introduction of various toxins into her subjects.

The Counselor and his family had always managed to avoid the many problems connected with the ongoing destruction of Atlantis. Still, they knew that their luck would not last forever, and they were right. It happened that the Counselor's wife was seriously injured in a plane crash while on her way to India. Although an experienced pilot, she had failed to account for the debris that cluttered the skies. The breakup of the continent was underway, and the skies were no longer safe. Because her injuries were considered life threatening, a blood transfusion was administered, despite the likelihood of receiving contaminated blood. Atlantis was rife with disease, but with no other available options, the seriously injured were routinely transfused with blood known to be infected. Not unexpectedly, the Counselor's wife contracted a deadly strain of syphilis. By the Grace of God death came quickly, thereby facilitating her smooth transition to the other side of the gate.

Repeating the same mistake he made when his father died, the Counselor failed to grieve the loss of his wife. Because he understood the nature of death, he considered himself beyond the reach of grief's insidious grasp. Thus he assured everyone that his wife had simply transitioned to a better place, and that they would be reunited when he made his own transition.

Six months later his grief surfaced in the form of a major depression, plunging him into the depths of despair. Plagued by thoughts of suicide, he thought to leap from the peak of a nearby mountain. Of course, he had no knowledge of the manner in which he had passed the gate in his previous life, so the impulse made no sense to his conscious mind. In the end his daughter dispelled the dark cloud that had engulfed his life when she insisted he seek professional help. Before long he was back at work, having learned a valuable lesson regarding the nature of grief, albeit for the second time; but not, as it turned out, for the last time.

Years later his daughter unexpectedly died of a rare disease, undoubtedly related to her work with contaminants. The loss of his father had been tough, the loss of his wife tougher still, but the loss of his daughter was more than he could bear. The suicidal ideation that had attended his wife's death had merely been a trial run. This time he really would take his own life. Many people reach that place in their lives where suicide seems a natural solution. However, self-destruction rarely provides the solace imagined, because suicides are magnetically linked to the earthbound world for the duration of their allotted time, until once again called to the flesh.

He knew beyond any shadow of doubt that suicide was wrong, but it made no difference. He was going to kill himself, and then he was going to be reunited with his wife and daughter. Once again he was entirely wrong. Suicides rarely reunite with friends and family. Once their earthbound existence is over they almost always take birth without having experienced the higher planes of consciousness. In his previous life he had leapt to his death, but the circumstances had been such that he was not heavily penalized. Things would be different this time. This time he would lose more than his life, because he was about to create some very serious karma.

Intent on self-destruction, he drove to the mountains where he located a ledge overlooking a rock-strewn valley. The scene struck a familiar chord, and he couldn't help but wonder why he had been drawn to that particular spot. In fact, the scene bore some resemblance to his previous leap. Just when it seemed a fait accompli he suddenly stepped back from the edge. Something had changed his mind, because he got back in his vehicle and drove away.

Occasional bouts of depression aside, the Counselor was possessed of average temperament, and most would have agreed that he conducted his life in a sensible manner. That temperament, however, belied an underlying tendency to make important decisions in the moment. The story behind that particular karmic tendency is well-known to the Lodge, and can be briefly summarized as follows. The Counselor's previous experience in higher realms of consciousness had left him susceptible to making decisions without taking time to think things through, believing that his actions would either be perfect, or easily corrected. It's an unusual talent, one that courts both magic and disaster. On this occasion it worked magic, transforming his state of mind in a matter of seconds. Knowing his past, you might suspect that he simply suppressed his grief. Such was not the case, because in that brief moment on the ledge he received a glimpse of the sorrow that awaited him. And for some people a glimpse is all that it takes to reorganize the psyche.

The following year the government offered him a position at Machu Picchu. Thousands had already fled Atlantis for the safety of the mountaintop community, and thousands more were preparing to abandon their homes. The move held the promise of a new beginning; besides, the continent was nearly finished, and the opportunity to leave coincided with commonsense. Unfortunately, fate entered in before his scheduled departure.

The Counselor owned his own plane and was taking one last flight over the continent, saying goodbye to the land that he loved. He was considered a capable pilot, but had, nevertheless, overlooked the federally mandated maintenance schedule for working crystals. Energy-bearing crystals required periodic regeneration in the sun; otherwise, they lost their charge, sometimes exploding into fragments. One of those fragments punctured his emergency fuel tank, instantly triggering a massive explosion.

The violent nature of his death damaged his body's etheric counterpart. The etheric body serves as both the template for the physical form, and the temporary vehicle of consciousness immediately after death. Normally, the deceased make an instantaneous transition from the physical body to the etheric body to the astral body. However, when the etheric vehicle is either damaged or depleted, the transition to the astral body can take weeks if not months, sometimes requiring several years.

Had his condition been left to Mother Nature the Counselor's transition from the etheric plane to the astral plane would have been slow and painful. As it turned out, he was admitted into one of the many etheric hospitals, where he enrolled in a Light Therapy program. Immediately upon admission the staff of doctors and nurses bathed him in a shimmering pool of radiant orange light, thereby rejuvenating the nervous system. Fully restored, the Counselor sloughed his etheric body and soon found himself alive and well on the astral plane. His discarded etheric body was allowed to drift into the void, but not before the nervous system was shattered with an application of high-pitched sound, just in case earthbound denizens should think to steal it in order to play tricks on unsuspecting psychics.

The first order of business was to conduct a life review. Life review is not mandatory, but it is highly recommended to everyone when they arrive on the other side of the gate. The process involves several hours of deep concentration, frequently becoming the basis for adjustments to be made in the next incarnation. Once the review is completed the Soul infuses the personality, lending its support to any changes that are to be made.

After completing his life review the Counselor was reunited with his wife and daughter. He was amazed to discover that they worked as hard as they ever had, and yet had ample time for friends and family. Given time to reflect, he decided against entering the work force, choosing instead the life of a student. So he enrolled in one of the universities founded by the White Lodge. Upon graduation, he was offered a promotion to the mental plane; however, not wanting to leave his family behind, he refused the offer, never realizing the significance of his decision. Because of the mistakes he had made, mistakes that had involved serious lapses in judgment, he would have received specialized training in the art of discernment. As luck would have it, discernment was about to play a very important role in his next incarnation.

LIFE THREE
The Teacher

THE GREAT PYRAMID in Egypt was not built in the manner that the experts of the modern world presume. It was, in fact, not even built by Egyptians. The Egyptians supplied the manpower, but the design and technology were pure Atlantean. When Atlantis went down those who were able fled the continent in airships. The exodus actually began a hundred years before the final breakup, so that when the end came the Atlanteans had already assumed positions of power in various places around the globe. The foremost society to come out of the dispersion was founded by the elite of Atlantis in and around the mountaintop fortress known as Machu Picchu. The Atlanteans who settled in Egypt were not nearly as enlightened, and the indigenous population suffered greatly as a result.

Relocation represented an enormous challenge for the Atlanteans, but the inevitable demise of their race was their greatest concern. Even the best of their society cringed at the thought of a weakened gene pool. Their other concern was the loss of thousands of irreplaceable crystals. Atlantis was rich with crystals, some deep in the earth, some beneath the sea. Those crystals were mined, cut, and polished with meticulous attention to detail. For example, the number of facets was mathematically derived and directly related to the crystal's intended function. Personal data crystals were multifaceted, resembling a small marble in appearance. Government agencies and national corporations used large, yellow spheres bearing thousands of facets for database storage. Hospitals preferred long, flat sheets of blue crystal, while police departments found the color green amenable to their needs. Whenever possible naturally colored crystals were used; however, dyes capable of permeating the atomic structure were frequently employed.

The largest and most important crystals formed the core of a sophisticated network. They were virtually impossible to move, both because of their size, and because of the enormous power they contained. Those seven crystals somehow survived the cataclysm, and may yet be recovered if the location of Atlantis is ever determined. Each of the seven resembles a compact car in both size and shape, and together they generate enough heat to facilitate detection despite the fact that they are deeply imbedded in the ocean floor. They should not be moved because any attempt to do so would likely shatter them into thousands of useless pieces. If they are in fact discovered, great care should be taken, because the information stored within their crystalline structure can only be retrieved with the help of psychics capable of unlocking the secrets of Atlantis.

One of those crystals, the smallest of the seven, contains a complete history of Atlantis, spanning nearly 100,000 years. Another contains the secret formulas underlying the science of crystal technology, while yet another contains a history of the White Lodge. If and when those secrets are unlocked, the future of humanity will be dramatically altered. For instance, had that information been available, humanity might have avoided the many problems associated with nuclear energy. The atom was not meant to be split, but controlled through the power of thought. The atom is responsive to the mind, and when correctly understood humanity will be in a position to eliminate both disease and disability.

Those who settled in Egypt represented the middle class of Atlantis. They possessed no great moral compass, and consequently produced few leaders of noble character. They considered themselves the rightful rulers of the planet and from the very beginning intended on enslaving the local population. To that end they anointed a king, known at that time as the Divine Man, later known as the Pharaoh. Whereas the Ancient Wisdom teaches that all men contain the spark of the Divine Being, the Atlanteans convinced the masses that the Pharaoh alone was innately divine. It was a stroke of genius, and that masterstroke tolled the bell on cultural slavery. The deception was later adopted by the leaders of the Catholic Church, who fully understood the role of the Pharaoh.

The Atlanteans chose the role of slave master over that of elder brother, and in that choosing sealed their fate. Unfortunately, they also sealed the fate of humanity. Because of that karma, mankind must endure leadership that invariably betrays the public trust. The karma is heavy and many more centuries will pass before it is finally resolved.

Under the direction of the White Lodge, Atlantean engineers constructed two major pyramids, the first being the Pyramid of Zoser. Zoser came to the throne not through heritage, but through a bit of chicanery. He assumed the identity of a Pharaonic prince and, while he was never discovered, his efforts to reform Egyptian society were defeated at every turn. The pyramid operated as a dissemination point for the White Lodge for less than five years, just barely enough time for the Masters to gain a foothold. Years later, the Light established by Zoser facilitated the construction of the Great Pyramid, which was, at that time, the only significant source of Light upon the planet.

The construction of the Great Pyramid may seem a great feat; however, the truth be known, from the point of view of an Atlantean engineer it was not all that difficult to construct. The real difficulty involved the mathematics built into the structure, most notably the inclusion of astronomical data. The precise location of every channel and chamber was mathematically derived, and if the math is ever worked out it will reveal the future of the human race as conceived by the Creator. Those secrets, however, can not be revealed at this time, lest they fall into the hands of the Black Lodge.

Once the math was worked out, construction was left to the engineers, who were as likely to sabotage the project as they were to endorse it. They had to be closely supervised, and whenever sabotage was discovered the engineer was removed and replaced by someone who in all probability was just as determined to undermine what appeared to be insanity. In the end the Pyramid was constructed exactly as planned, although a few uncorrected mistakes have survived, adding to the mystification of modern observers.

Everyday work on the project was a sight to behold. Giant blocks of stone were quarried and then transported to the construction site using dozens of large, yellow crystals. Those crystals held the power to defy gravity, and when mistakes were made, as they sometimes were, tumbling blocks of granite annihilated hundreds of workers in the blink of an eye. When the blocks arrived at the construction site an entirely different set of crystals was used to maneuver them into place. The precise fitting of each block of stone was supervised by yet another group of engineers, each with a handful of rugged looking crystals. Each crystal was programmed to a specific tolerance, and it was the engineer's responsibility to select the appropriate crystal for cutting and sanding. A study of the Record reveals that over one thousand crystals were used in the construction of the Great Pyramid. Those crystals are safely secured in Shamballa, the sacred city wherein the Masters of the White Lodge reside, until such time that humanity has once again earned the right to defy the law of gravity.

Well before its completion, the Masters began conducting classes in the shade of the Pyramid, performing healings in the Queen's Chamber, and initiating advanced students in the King's Chamber. The average student never saw the inside of the Pyramid, because entry-level instruction was restricted to the outer tiers. The students were all Atlanteans because the Masters thought it unwise to challenge public sentiment by accepting local students; however, they did offer instruction to small groups of locals in secret locations.

The Teacher's grandfather hailed from the island of Poseidon, a mountainous paradise not from the shores of the main island. With the destruction of Atlantis imminent, his grandfather had elected to continue his work in the mountains of Peru. Prior to his departure, however, the governing Council of the White Lodge had insisted that he alter his plans. The Council had argued that his services were direly needed in Egypt, that his duty to the Lodge transcended all other considerations. His grandfather ultimately agreed to change his destination, but with one condition, that the Lodge oversee two generations of his descendants, thus ensuring his family's continued participation in the initiatory process.

Many traditions have been passed down orally, taking the form of legends and myths, while others have been committed to memory, revealed only to a succession of appointees. Tradition, whether openly shared or secretly transmitted, is invariably corrupted by the personalities involved. Lineage, on the other hand, sidesteps that problem through the initiatory process. Initiation secures the Truth, and that Truth is never entrusted to anyone who has not earned the right through extensive testing.

The Teacher came from pure Atlantean stock; however, lest you think him the typical Atlantean, you should know that he never felt at home in his own culture. He loathed professional sports, even though most Atlanteans enjoyed betting on their favorite games; and he detested both the opera and the theater, despite their enormous popularity. His family didn't understand him, and especially disapproved of his affiliation with the White Lodge. Both his father and his grandfather had dedicated their lives to the Lodge, and had accrued neither fame nor fortune for their efforts; just a hard life, and an early grave. At least that's the way his family saw it.

The Teacher spent his early years studying at the Great Pyramid, attaining initiatory status after seven years of intensive instruction, thereby earning the privilege of entering the King's Chamber. His progress was rapid from that point forward, because meditation in the King's Chamber represented the fast track to spiritual development. When the time was right he ventured out on his own, eventually establishing a school for the local population. He attracted both the curious and the aspiring, and although his students would never pass for intellectuals, he counted that a plus, because all too often the intellect obscures the simple truths revealed in daily life.

His method of instruction had already undergone several transformations when inspiration finally dawned, and he knew at once that his method was flawed. Instead of relying exclusively upon didactic instruction, he would teach his students the art of meditation. First he taught them to relax their bodies, from the soles of their feet to the tops of their heads, consciously attending to each and every part of the anatomy. Next he taught them to quiet their minds through the proper use of the breath, filling first the abdomen, and then the chest, holding the breath for a half count at the top of the lungs before slowly expelling the spent air. Then he taught them to visualize White Light cascading down from above, wrapping themselves head to toe and left to right. Only then could they safely enter into deep meditation.

Beyond that he taught them that the universe was ordered according to plan; otherwise, everything in nature would be subjected to endless chaos. He taught that an ordered universe presupposes a Divine Being Who Creates and Sustains Life, and that man, being an integral part of that Creation, therefore participates in an ordered existence. His logic was sound, whereas man's logic is typically flawed. The Creator's logic exists within the context of the Whole, and not the parts. The parts are the creation of man, while the Whole is entirely the work of God.

Several years passed without incident, but that all changed when a group of his students attempted to open a public dialogue on the pitfalls of Atlantean influence. The Atlantean community, fearing widespread rebellion, nearly went berserk. They picketed the Teacher's school, and demanded that he be exiled to the island of Madagascar, home of the savage race known as Big Foot.

Big Foot was created in the labs, and was later transported to Madagascar for observation. Once on the island of Madagascar they killed every living thing, and then proceeded to starve. Hundreds died before the decision was made to continue the experiment in another location. Several hundred of the healthiest specimens were relocated to North America, where they were promptly ignored and soon forgotten. Had it not been for the extreme difficulty of childbirth, Big Foot might have overrun the entire continent, thereby creating a serious menace to the survival of the human race. The last of them died out approximately 3000 years ago, although their etheric shells can still be seen and smelt through the use of the etheric senses. The shells are basically harmless, and the best way to handle an etheric sighting is to immediately focus upon the details of the surrounding environment, because prolonged attunement to something so evil can adversely affect the mind.

The Pharaoh, swayed by the protestors, closed the Teacher's school. It was a serious blow, but rather than admit defeat, the Teacher petitioned the Pharaoh for an audience. The Pharaoh was not so inclined; however, when he learned that treasure was being offered in exchange for the restoration of the school, he experienced a sudden change of heart. The Teacher had in his possession one of the anti-gravity crystals used in the construction of the Great Pyramid. The Masters of the White Lodge had released it into his care in order to facilitate an important construction project at his school, whereupon it was to be immediately returned. He had no authority to alter the conditions of its release.

Displaying the crystal, the Teacher proceeded to demonstrate its power. The Pharaoh nearly suffered a heart attack when the Teacher levitated high above the Royal Court. Having secured the Pharaoh's attention, he offered to hand over the crystal if the Pharaoh promised to reopen his school. Having reached an agreement, he surrendered the crystal, trading it for a lifetime charter.

The Pharaoh was thrilled to death, and in fact death was near at hand. Weeks later, while demonstrating his newfound ability, the Pharaoh spun out of control. When his minions saw how hard his head slammed into the towering ceiling of the royal palace they immediately began currying the favor of his successor. Fortunately for everyone concerned, the crystal shattered when it fell to the floor.

Meanwhile, the Council of Masters summoned the Teacher. Should he be dismissed from the Lodge, or would a severe rebuke be sufficient? The vote was split in his favor. He would be held accountable for his actions; however, his membership would not be revoked. The majority opinion held that he had violated his oath, not for personal gain, but to ensure the continuation of the Lodge's work. Besides, the Lodge had made a promise to his grandfather. And a promise was a promise. The dissenting opinion held that no one should be allowed to betray the trust of the Lodge and remain a member.

The consequences would be severe. He would be allowed to resume his work at the school, but his next incarnation would be dictated by the Lords of Karma, a fate certain to reflect the gravity of his error. He would be bound by their decision, and would receive no help from the Brotherhood for as long as it took to win back their confidence. As it happened the Lords of Karma were persuaded by the fact that had the crystal fallen into the wrong hands, the havoc wreaked would have outweighed any good accomplished by his school. And so they rendered their decision. He would take his next incarnation in the lowest manifestation of human genetics. He would enter the world of the Cro-Magnon.

The Teacher reopened his school to a flock of eager students. He carried on for years, until one day they found him sitting in his favorite chair with his hands strangely configured, as if conveying a message. That particular hand signal is no longer practiced, but at that time it was meant to deliver the deceased into the care of the Creator.

Little did he know, but the ruling set forth by the Lords of Karma went into effect the moment he passed through the gate. Neither friends nor family members greeted his arrival, and his Beloved Atlantean Master was nowhere to be seen. He walked the astral world for decades, until at last he was drawn into a vortex of energy anchored in a Cro-Magnon fetus. He took birth in the body of a savage.

LIFE FOUR
The Caveman

L ONG AGO, AT the dawn of modern civilization, there
existed a society of cavemen who lived in an area not
far from the western shore of the Black Sea. By that
time the continent of Atlantis had sunk into oblivion, and
the remnants of that once great civilization had dispersed to
other parts of the globe. When Atlantis went down mankind
stood poised at a major crossroad. On the one hand villages
and seaside communities were thriving, but on the other hand
the light of Atlantis no longer illumined the collective mind
of humanity. When Atlantis sank humanity shuddered, and
the Cro-Magnons, long since abandoned by evolution, were
temporarily revitalized.

Atlantis ruled the globe for thousands of years, sometimes
ignoring the rest of the planet, sometimes subjecting the world
to its whim. At its peak Atlantis respected the autonomy of
lesser societies; however, during its waning years, under the
influence of the Black Lodge, terrible depredations were
perpetrated against humanity. Their scientists were tasked
with the creation of a new race, a breed of subhuman warriors
possessing limited intelligence. At first they restricted their
research to apes, but when that proved unsuccessful they began
experimenting with the lingering population of Cro-Magnons.
They ultimately bred them with other segments of humanity, but
because of the innate disparity in consciousness their creation

never achieved significant numbers. The few that survived to adulthood appeared to meet their objectives; however, they eventually turned on their masters and annihilated an entire team of scientists.

The clan we now visit preferred living underground. Their underground den provided needed security, not only protecting them from inclement weather, but from the marauders who wandered the land. They showed almost no inclination to guile, but fought face-to-face with gnarled clubs and makeshift knives. There was, however, one amongst them who wielded a self-made club that featured two sharpened rocks wedged into knotholes at either end. Once constructed, the club was immersed in water until completely saturated, and then baked in the sun, thereby creating an indestructible bludgeon, no matter how hard the skull it encountered. The other members of the clan could not comprehend the nature of his invention, but clearly understood that in his hands it was as deadly as a saw-toothed prairie lion.

His club would have been lethal in anybody's hands, but in his hands it was literally a weapon of mass destruction, partly because he could strike with either hand. His group had never before encountered anyone who was left-handed, let alone a warrior capable of wielding a weapon with equal facility in either hand. Not surprisingly, at a very young age, even for a Cro-Magnon, he claimed his rightful place as the undisputed ruler of the clan.

The entrance to their underground dwelling was concealed from sight by an enormous tumble of rocks, creating the illusion of an impassable barrier. The entrance branched into a network of pathways leading down into the heart of the lair. The three largest dens housed the males, each with a narrow passage leading down to the women and children, reaching depths of 60 feet or more. When they ran out of usable space they simply expelled the old, the lame, and the sick. Conversely, when attrition took its toll, they stalked the land in search of other clans, intent on abducting their children. Their captives were raised as full-fledged members of the clan, and consequently suffered no prejudice at the hands of their abductors. They always chose young girls, and they always placed them in the care of women who had no children of their own. When they came of age, pregnancy became a fact of life, thus completing the process of assimilation into the clan.

After a particularly harsh winter, when the lower levels of their underground dwelling flooded, they had no choice but to abandon their ancestral home. Some of the cavers, however, were reluctant to exchange their home for the life of an itinerant clan. Their leader resolved the dilemma when he applied his deadly club to the skulls of several troublemakers who wanted to remain in what was now a subterranean pool. Having settled the matter to his satisfaction, he led them south, away from their homeland.

They eventually reached the Mediterranean, where they happened upon a small community of fishermen. Threatened by the manmade structures they encountered, the cavers wanted to flee, and the sooner they returned to their ancestral home the better. Their leader, however, wanted to stay, and barely worked up a sweat convincing the rest of the clan that they too wanted to stay. Those who remained unconvinced were buried there next to the sea.

The leader of the clan was determined to learn what he could from the strangers who had somehow altered the shape of the world. He harbored no fear regarding their fighting potential, and therefore saw no reason to launch an attack, let alone run for home. Choosing coexistence, he set up camp right next to the community of fishermen. For their part the fishermen feared for their lives, but hoped to live through the ordeal by maintaining an attitude of watchful cooperation.

Conflict seemed inevitable, but then inevitability isn't necessarily the best predictor, because life doesn't always obey the will of man, but sometimes reflects the Will of

God. Nevertheless, no one was surprised when the tension between the two groups reached the point of aggression. The cavers were fascinated with the possessions of their newfound friends, and couldn't help but carry off whatever attracted their attention. The fishermen understood the precarious nature of their survival, but that in no way included kowtowing to savages. Eventually, violence erupted, and the only thing that prevented a murderous rampage was the sudden appearance of the clan leader, who surprised everybody when he turned his legendary club against his own, thereby saving the fishermen from certain annihilation.

After much discussion and long hours of fretful planning, the fishermen decided to pack up and move out during the night. The stakes were high, and even the slightest miscalculation would likely precipitate their destruction. So before implementing such a desperate plan of action, the local leaders approached the head caver, now known as the Club. In addition to the recent altercation, they had witnessed the Club brain a few laggards with lightning speed, and had rightly concluded that he alone conducted negotiations for the clan. Making the sign for talk, they approached the Club's lean-to, fully aware of the danger that lurked within.

When the Club removed the hide that normally covered his head and shoulders, the fishermen were totally shocked by his visage. Four distinct claw marks furrowed the right side of his face, extending all the way down to the jawbone. The other side his face bore similar tracks, rutting the flesh from ear to eye socket. The eyeball was intact, but rested in a hollow that looked as if it had recently served as a conduit for hot lava. Unnerved by the Club's grisly appearance, the fishermen never thought to conceal the panic that threatened their resolve.

The Club had anticipated their reaction, but took no offense, because they obviously belonged to a cowardly clan. Besides, he was utterly fascinated with their ability to make magical sounds with their mouths, sounds that granted the speaker power over others. Needless to say, power appealed to the Club. He had already mastered one of their commands, and was determined to learn more while he could. Hence an agreement was worked out. The two groups would maintain a respectful distance, and the Club would personally oversee any problems that arose.

When a band of itinerant traders unexpectedly appeared in the village, the fishermen thought that perhaps the odds had changed in their favor, never realizing the danger posed by the new arrivals. The traders were unscrupulous men who immediately recognized a golden opportunity. The Egyptians offered significant rewards for captured cavers, their offspring driving the market. Based upon their apparent equanimity, they judged the beasts compliant and ready for market.

Just when their plan seemed to be rounding into shape, the traders happened upon the Club doing what he did best - cracking skulls with his trusty club. That's when they knew that their luck had changed for the worse. He was a brute with a visage that would stop the heart of a lion. In fact, the very thought of incurring his wrath was enough to set their hearts to pounding, and yet they just couldn't walk away from the fabulous bounty offered for cavers.

They consulted and they schemed, and finally concluded that if their plan was to have any hope of succeeding they first had to kill the Club. In the end seven foolhardy traders agreed to participate in the clandestine affair, more than enough, they thought, to kill the Club if they caught him alone and asleep. Little did they know, but their plan was suicidal. They planned on surrounding his lean-to in the dark of night, and then attacking with a flurry of rocks. Surely, only a fool would attack an animal at night with nothing more than a handful of rocks, and yet that's exactly what they intended. It wasn't the first time, but it surely would be the last time that greed clouded their judgment, because this time there would be no survivors.

The Club caught their scent long before they were within striking distance. He could smell the fear that cloaked their every step, and could even smell the rocks they had gathered from the nearby shoreline. Besides the olfactory warnings, the Club's hearing was superhuman, registering sounds both above and below the normal range of perception. He heard them approaching on the balls of their feet, moving like men on a hunt. They were obviously intending to keep their distance while hurling their newly acquired instruments of death. Not fully understanding the differences in their sensory abilities, it seemed to him that the traders expected him to stand his ground and act the part of a willing target. The only explanation he could fathom was that they must be crazy, just like the ones the clan occasionally had to put down. That being the case, it was only natural that they had come to him.

Grabbing the bearskin taken from the creature that had scarred his face, and subsequently surrendered its life, the Club moved out into the night. He tied the forelegs around his neck, the remainder of the hide flowing down his back to his knees. The bearskin wasn't intended as a disguise, but was used to cover his scent.

Approaching the lean-to, the traders commenced heaving rocks. They weren't expecting any resistance, but if by some chance the Club retaliated, they anticipated a frontal assault. They never thought to establish a rear guard.

The Club was no military genius, but the fact that he was a natural born killer more than made up for that deficiency. He came from behind, lethal thunder erupting from his club as he moved undetected through their ranks, until only one of his attackers remained alive. He fell upon the hapless fool with a roar that would have made a lion proud. The sound of his roar completely unnerved the would-be assassin, who died believing that a saw-toothed prairie lion had taken his life.

Searching the area for a ready-made burial trench, the Club located a nearby depression and started digging it out until it was deep enough to receive the bodies of the dead. Next he searched his victims and found several articles of interest. He had recently been exposed to flint, and immediately began experimenting with the two stones he had discovered. Comfortably ensconced in a field of dry grass, he sparked flint, fully expecting smoldering embers to appear on the ground. He was in for a surprise, because the ensuing fire leapt to life, setting the entire area ablaze. The fire spread in every direction, trapping him in the vicinity of the dead bodies, stacked and ready for burial. Desperately searching for an escape route, he climbed atop the mountain of flesh. There was only one possibility.

He jumped into the burial trench, quickly interring himself under a mound of soil, barely leaving room enough to breathe. Every breath was choked with smoke, and before he realized what was happening he was unconscious. When he came to his senses it wasn't to the sound of fiery destruction, but to the jubilant shouts of his fellow cavers. They were rejoicing and, from every indication, feasting on the roasted flesh of their enemies. Having no desire to confront a pack of bloodthirsty savages, the Club waited until they had eaten their fill and departed the area.

Armed and ready for battle, the Club took one last look at the grizzly scene his clansmen had left behind. Cannibalism was fairly common amongst the Cro-Magnon, but for reasons unknown, the Club did not tolerate the eating of human flesh. He strode into camp just as the predawn light resurrected the day, and immediately set to killing whoever he happened upon. His rampage was over in less time than it had taken to dispose of the traders, because by the time he had dispatched a handful of culprits, everyone else had run for cover.

Having re-established control, and intent on revenge, the Club entered the village of the fishermen. Blind with fury, bolts of lightning jumped from his club, killing men, women, and children with frightening precision. At first the rest of the cavers watched the spectacle from a distance, until savagery finally claimed every last shred of their existence. They killed every living thing, and when it was over the Club turned on his own clan members, methodically eliminating potential rivals. Others would eventually emerge, but until that time arrived there would be no threat to his leadership.

The following day the cavers set out for home, carrying with them the plunder they had seized. They headed north, knowing only that their ancestral home lay in that direction. Like birds in winter, they knew that it was time to migrate to where they belonged. They moved with incredible speed, traveling day and night until at last the Club gave the order to set up camp. It was time to eat. The Cro-Magnons rarely dined on anything but raw meat; however, they were known to snack on fruits and vegetables when readily available. Meals were frenzied affairs, similar to a pack of wild dogs, each afraid of losing its share of the kill. They consumed everything, including the internal organs, because it all tasted good, and they never seemed to get enough to eat.

Several days later, back on the trail, they came across the tracks of another clan, and immediately set out in pursuit. They found them camped by the sea and, despite every effort at stealth, their quarry had already established a defensive perimeter. The young boys occupied the center of the ring, because they represented the clan's future. The young girls came next because they were needed for purposes of reproduction, and were therefore considered valuable assets. The stalwart men came next, each with a club and a knife fashioned from chiseled rock. The outer ring, as was the custom, contained the old, the lame, and the sick. There was no complaining and no thought of running. They all knew their respective roles, and they all accepted the fate that awaited them.

Surveying the enemy's defense, the Club recognized a weakness right off. They were amassed in a field of dry grass, which brought to mind his recent experience with fire.

Abandoning his vantage point, the Club descended into the field of grass where he proudly struck his recently acquired flint. Just like before, flames erupted, burning the grass around him. This time the Club ran for his life, back to the safety of his clan.

The fire consumed everything in sight, inexorably marching towards the enemy, whose only recourse was to break ranks and retreat to safer ground. Undaunted, they reformed with their backs to the sea. They knew the drill and, despite the raging fire and swirling smoke, they somehow managed to keep their wits about them.

Observing their disciplined response to the fire, the Club reconsidered attacking a cadre of seasoned warriors. His instincts clamored for blood, but his clan would undoubtedly pay a heavy price for victory. So he raised his mighty club into the air, pointing it directly into the sun. The message was clear, or so he thought. His clan would not attack out of respect for their opponent's strength. It never occurred to the Club that his salute might be interpreted as a sign of weakness.

The Club and his clan resumed their trek north. They traveled at speed, and never thought to watch their backs, until they finally realized something wasn't right. Mother Nature had failed to register a single discordant note, and yet a strange but familiar scent permeated the air that they breathed. Sensing danger, their instinctual brains had responded by producing the appropriate chemicals. The creatures of the earth are replete with early warning systems, and the Cro-Magnons were no exception. Humanity has outgrown that particular biochemical reaction; however, man's instinctual brain is still capable of responding to precipitous changes in the environment.

They were being stalked by the same clan whose backs they had pushed against the sea. They had obviously interpreted the Club's salute as a sign of weakness. Luck, however, was with the Club, because he and his clan arrived at the site of their ancestral home with plenty of time to spare. The enemy had no way of knowing, but they had cornered their prey on its home turf. Ignorant of the facts, and thinking only of the impending slaughter, they were supremely confident, having trapped their quarry on a hilltop.

Instead of the traditional ring of warriors, the Club decided to meet the threat with an entirely new defense. He put everybody to work hauling the pile of rocks that hid the entrance to their lair out to the perimeter. In no time at all a makeshift wall sprang to life. It staggered here and tumbled there; nevertheless, it definitely resembled a wall. The besieging cavers had never seen a wall built for defense, and if the Club hadn't recently seen one under construction, he wouldn't have thought of it in a hundred years.

Upon seeing the wall go up, the attackers realized that their plan was fatally flawed, so they returned the salute they themselves had received not so many days before. They headed south, determined to execute a hasty retreat. Until the wall went up they hadn't questioned the cause of the fire, having assumed it to be an act of nature. Now, however, it seemed they had narrowly escaped a close encounter with a Cro-Magnon legend. Legend had it that an evil clan of indestructible warriors roamed the land, destroying everything in its path. The Club and his clan represented their worst nightmare.

The Club was enraged. He had foolishly spared the other clan, and they had repaid him by returning to wage war. They would pay the ultimate price. Not even the female children would be exempt, because he wanted none of their kind infecting his clan.

The Club waited until nightfall approached, allowing his enemies time to flee; knowing that flight exacts an exorbitant price from the body. Pursuit, on the other hand, unleashes the magical power of adrenalin. Meanwhile, he worked his warriors into a murderous frenzy.

They ran through the night and into the day before catching sight of their prey. They never stopped to rest, but charged into battle like the hell-born savages that they were. When the battle was over the Club once again turned on the members of his clan, slaughtering anyone posing a threat to his leadership, thus preserving the unity of the clan. When the Club's reign was over, someone else would assume the role of leadership, spontaneously awakening to an ancient impulse born of necessity.

When that day finally arrived, they buried the Club right next to his legendary wall. Remnants of that wall can still be found, and if you were to dig the site you would find a club with a rock wedged into either end. The wood is still sound and the rocks are still hard, but long are the days that have carried man from clubs and rocks to guns and missiles. Things have changed for the better, and yet things have changed for the worse. Man's mental capacity has soared, and with it the sophistication of his weaponry, but let man hope and pray that another Club doesn't find his way to power, only this time possessing both a mind and a nuclear arsenal.

And so it ended. The Club was released from his life amongst the Cro-Magnon. However, when he arrived on the other side of the gate, his only memories were those of the savage he had been. He had no recollection of his ancient past, no memory of past accomplishments. What's more, no one dared contradict the Lodge's edict, so he roamed the lower reaches of the astral plane, bereft of friend and foe alike. He had endured a tremendous karmic penalty, and the conditioning that attended his sojourn amongst the Cro-Magnons would haunt his soul for thousands of years to come. Such is the Law of Karma.

LIFE FIVE
The Administrator

T HERE WAS A time when he would have executed anyone who dared challenge his authority. There was a time when he would have done so without a moment's hesitation, without so much as an afterthought. Those times were behind him now, because he no longer enjoyed the Pharaoh's protection. He had lost everything with the death of the Great One, and had been banished to hell, beyond even the Lower Kingdom. The successor to the throne had sent him away, and he was now the newly appointed Administrator of the Sudan. His duties included operating the royal gold mine, as well as overseeing a community of merchants who conducted trade with the African interior.

The tribesman standing before him had been caught wearing an ornament that featured the likeness of the Pharaoh. The man had no idea he had committed a crime, and therefore fervently denied any wrong doing. Seated behind his desk in the relative coolness of his adobe-like chambers, the Administrator struggled to suppress his rage. The fact that the accused was a free man, and not a slave, was bad enough, but wearing the likeness of the Pharaoh was unforgivable. And that wasn't the worst of it. What totally offended his good name was the fact that two of his aides had vouched for the man and his character.

Death was an appropriate consequence for all three. Unfortunately, now that he was merely a backwater judge, he had no such power. The dilemma, clearly more challenging than perplexing, consisted of finding an appropriate punishment, one that did not exceed his authority. Sensing the tension between the three officials, the accused brazenly asserted his innocence; but rather than advance his cause, he managed to awaken the devil in the man who was about to decide his fate.

In such matters the Administrator could pass sentence, even harsh sentences; however, his power was limited because the law had been codified in recent years, forcing him to at least give the appearance of fairness. The most he could do was sentence the defendant to three years in the gold mine. A year in the mine was unbearable, whereas three years was unthinkable. At that point madness staked its claim, and the prisoner, having observed the condition of the slaves working the mine, lunged at his tormentor. Fortunately for the Administrator, his bodyguards were quick to react, and prevented what promised to be a vicious attack.

They pummeled him to the floor, and then dragged him by his feet to the jailhouse where he was tethered to a post positioned in the center of his cell. He bled profusely from multiple wounds, but his condition went unnoticed by the bullies in whose custody he languished. There would be no appeal. His life was over, and the best he could hope for was an early death.

The two aides were totally stunned. In all their years of service they had never witnessed such deliberate cruelty. They were used to harshness, that constant companion of the cold and callous heart, but were totally unaccustomed to calculated malevolence. Having sided with the accused, they knew that they were in serious trouble, and therefore expected the worst. In the meantime they had no choice but to faithfully serve, and thereby hope to survive the ordeal.

The following morning the prisoner was found dead in his cell. The official report claimed that he had repeatedly rammed his head into the post to which he had been tethered, thereby causing his own death. It was a believable story, because black savages were known to exhibit violent behavior when confronted with authority. His body was dragged outside and tossed onto a mountain of refuse located just beyond the wall that circled the jailhouse. Eventually, the carcass was carted away to a bluff overlooking a nearby ravine and heaved over the edge. Despite the long drop to the makeshift cemetery below, the stench of decomposing flesh filled the air, forcing his pallbearers to run from the scene.

Apprised of the prisoner's death, the Administrator allowed himself the luxury of an inward smile, and reckoned that there was more than one way to effect an execution. It was then that he made up his mind. From that day forward only the meanest of the mean would staff the jail. One day that policy would boomerang, but for now things didn't seem all that bad after all.

The two aides had obviously been too long in the Sudan, and the Administrator had no intention of allowing them to remain on his staff. Within the week they were both charged with treason for having failed to report overhearing derogatory remarks made about the Pharaoh. They were sentenced to one year in the mine, but first they had to survive a night in the jail.

The chief jailer greeted the aides with a false bravado born of deceit and the love of wickedness. Denouncing the Administrator as an evil man, he assured them that he would personally see to their safe-keeping, that he had helped others in the same situation. Relieved to find someone who understood their predicament, the two aides opened their wounds and vented their rage. Having achieved his purpose, the jailer quickly showed his true colors, and announced that he had no choice but to report their conduct to the Administrator.

Feeling the need to set an example, the Administrator staked the two aides out in the noonday sun, repeatedly reviving them with buckets of water whenever they lapsed into unconsciousness. Towards the end of the day, having had his fun, and not wanting to be perceived as a brutal man, he shipped them off to the mine. They were in no condition to work, exhibiting, as it were, every indication of having gone insane. Seemingly unable to focus on anything concrete, they lived in a world of make-believe, passing their days acting out fantasies commonly associated with children at play. Not knowing what to do with them, the manager of the mine chose the path of least resistance, and allowed them to wander willy-nilly about the compound.

Meanwhile, the entire garrison, soldiers and merchants alike, was abuzz with gossip, but not to just anyone, because caution was the watchword of the day. They were at a loss to explain the brutality, but didn't dare question the Administrator's authority. That was a boundary no one was willing to cross. The Administrator, on the other hand, recognized no boundaries, save those honored by every predatory species. Thus he went to the merchants and instituted a security tax, declaring that things had gotten out of hand under the previous administrator. It was a clear case of extortion and something had to be done.

The story was all too predictable: initially moderate, the tax burden would be raised in steady increments. In the end their profits would be eaten away. The greedy grasp of the Administrator would undoubtedly strangle the business community, so the merchants conceived a plan to get the hell out of the Sudan. They would flee in the night; otherwise, they would be found out before they ever made it out of the garrison.

The Administrator, though clever, was not by nature a crafty man. Sometimes both qualities declare together, but frequently one or the other succeeds with no need of its brother. He was not; however, as clever as he thought, and was completely taken off guard when he discovered that the merchants had fled during the night. He assembled the army and personally led the march to overtake the runaways, who had foolishly packed everything they owned. He overtook them on the trail heading north, and immediately fell in alongside their caravan. Finding some measure of craftiness after all, the Administrator politely addressed the leaders of the exodus with a seemingly innocuous question. Why, in the name of the gods, were they traveling through the wild without a military escort? He explained in unctuous tones that he could not in good conscience permit them to endanger their lives, and therefore insisted upon their return to the garrison until such time that he was able to provide an armed escort.

The merchants politely demurred and asked that they be allowed to resume their journey. Having failed with lies and false charm, the Administrator ordered the caravan turned around. This accomplished, he force-marched the merchants back to the garrison at a terrible pace. They arrived in shambles, totally traumatized and bereft of their belongings, which were now strewn about the jungle. Unfortunately, their ordeal didn't end there. Displaying an official looking document, the Administrator charged them with treason for having abandoned the best interests of the Pharaoh. Then, to ensure such conduct never happened again, he ransacked their homes and confiscated their valuables.

Awestruck by the extent of their wealth, the Administrator decided to go into business for himself. He therefore summoned the garrison's most prosperous merchant, a man who traded in precious gems. By the time the meeting was over the merchant had acquired a full partner.

During the ensuing months the Administrator made a point of learning everything he could about operating the business, including how to recognize quality gems. It wasn't long before the Administrator no longer needed a business partner, having decided he could handle everything himself. Suppressing his true feelings, the merchant expressed his pleasure at seeing the Administrator prosper. He only asked that he be allowed to launch an enterprise of his own. The Administrator consented without giving the matter another thought.

Unlike the Administrator, the merchant was shrewd, if not downright sly. He had long suspected the takeover, and had concocted an ingenious plan. He had surrendered his assets knowing that the tribe he did business with was prone to violence. Meanwhile, he would invest everything he had in the cattle business. He would take advantage of the area's natural resources, which included a plentiful supply of wild beasts just waiting to be exploited. He would supply the garrison with fresh meat, knowing that the soldiers would soon come to rely upon his services.

The merchant's plan was no simple ruse, but a well thought out strategy. Patience was required while the various steps and stages unfolded, but once in full operation, the Administrator would be snared in a trap of his own making. If there was a glitch in the plan it was the fact that the cattle operation would have to become a roaring success in order to attract the Administrator's attention. Once that happened he was sure to insist upon another partnership, thereby facilitating the merchant's plan. The gemstone business would deliver the Administrator into the hands of an unruly tribe, while the cattle business would ensure his continued dependence until the trap was sprung.

Planning the downfall of an official representative of the Pharaoh was admittedly bold; nevertheless, his abhorrence of the man, taken together with his sense of outrage at the injustice he had endured, drove the merchant to gamble with his life. Besides, he knew himself to be the better man, and felt confident pitting his wits against someone who was obviously no genius at anything but evil.

The other merchants applauded the gem trader's scheme, and were careful not to whisper a word that might awaken suspicion. They hoped for the best; however, theirs was a hope born of despair, because it rested not upon their own diligence, but solely upon someone else's effort. They were content to sit the fence and await the outcome, hoping that the scheme would work to their advantage. They never lifted a finger to help, because the risk associated with collusion was terrifying, while the risk born of silence was well worth the gamble.

The merchant's plan unfolded as expected when the Administrator insisted upon an equal partnership in the cattle business. Enamored with his ability to accrue wealth with such stunning alacrity, the Administrator considered the merchant a fool. He was obviously a simpleton, and therefore deserved what he got. He, on the other hand, understood the nuances of wealth and power. He might have landed in hell, but one day soon he would be wealthy man, ready to reclaim the status he had once enjoyed.

As predicted, the negotiations between the Administrator and the African gem traders went all wrong. The merchant, much to his glee, heard all about the fiasco from the Administrator. Things were going even better than he had dared hope. The Administrator had actually forced the traders to accept half the normal rate for their gems, a very serious miscalculation. Because they were outnumbered, the traders had no choice but to accept the Administrator's terms. Still, the merchant wasn't worried about the success of his plan, because he knew the tribesmen would return. And when they did things would go much differently.

Meanwhile the Administrator twittered excitedly every time he contemplated the huge profit he would accrue when his gems were finally marketed in the Nile valley. As was the custom, he would use intermediaries, because the Pharaoh expressly forbade the upper class from dabbling in commerce.

It was a small problem, one he could easily handle. In the meantime he would guard his treasure well.

The merchant was a patient man, and well that he was, because several months passed before he received word from the gem traders. They were but a few days march from the garrison, and this time they had brought along dozens of warriors to ensure a fair price for their gems.

As if by epiphany, a brilliant idea suddenly materialized in the frontal lobe of his brain, announcing its genius in a single flash of light. Overwhelmed by its simplicity, the merchant thanked the gods for the gift of revenge, made all the sweeter by its subtlety. For what it lacked in treachery, it more than made up for in irony. He would arrange to have the negotiations take place at the mine where the gem traders would be sure to see their enslaved countrymen. Never suspecting the orchestration behind the scenes, the Administrator liked the plan at first blush, because it played directly into his notion of a proper negotiation. By his estimation there was no better way to communicate a threat than by granting your intended victim a glimpse into his ill-fated future. Needless to say, he never grasped the inherent volatility of such a foolish juxtaposition.

The merchant intercepted the gem traders well before their arrival at the garrison and arranged for the negotiations to take place at the mine. That's when he revealed the Administrator's evil intentions: he had vowed to either have his way or to enslave the entire contingent in the mine. The merchant assured them that if the negotiations went badly, a strike against the garrison would never be expected. He only asked that they take care not to harm the merchants who would be hiding out of sight.

The negotiations had barely begun when the gem traders were suddenly confronted with the terrible plight of their enslaved countrymen. Tempers immediately flared, and before calm could be restored a bloody battle was underway. Sensing the turning of the tide, the Administrator hurried back to the garrison for reinforcements. By the time he returned with more soldiers the gem traders had already fled the scene. Thinking only of revenge, he led his men in pursuit, straight into the jungle without the necessary provisions.

The further they went, the more difficult it became, until they were finally forced to turn back. Much to their surprise, when they returned they found the garrison in shambles. Obviously, they had been tracking a decoy while the garrison was under attack. The Administrator's home had been ransacked and the treasure he had so carefully hidden was gone. Out of his mind with rage, he suspected treachery; but he never suspected the merchant. Instead, he blamed the slaves at the mine.

He ordered the slaves into the mine, whereupon he collapsed the main tunnel, thereby condemning everyone in the mine to a horrible death. The soldiers were all hardened men, but even they balked when first given the order. Strange though it may seem, men capable of unspeakable atrocities quivered at the thought of burying a few dozen slaves alive. Nevertheless, they did their duty, because they didn't dare argue with a madman.

The Administrator had finally overstepped his authority, because only the Pharaoh could authorize the closure of one of his gold mines. Never a man to be troubled with thoughts of self-destruction, the Administrator immediately conceived a plan to reopen the mine. He would hunt down every last member of the trading party and enslave them in the mine, where they would spend the rest of their miserable lives.

As soon as the Administrator marched into the interior the merchant packed his belongings in a very small satchel, taking only the bare essentials. He and his guide traveled at speed, but not without incident. On the second day they were nearly trampled in the predawn light by a herd of elephants who took exception to their presence. They managed to cheat death only because of the guide's quick thinking. He led them downwind and therefore out of danger. Elephants rarely attack humans;

however, when they do it's usually because of what they smell. These particular elephants objected to the merchant's scent, having recently been occupied with the slaughter of cattle.

Meanwhile, the Administrator and his men were marching deeper into the jungle. They had been tracking their prey for the better part of a week when they happened upon a village of several hundred people. They had no way of knowing for sure, but it seemed likely that the men they were tracking had passed through the village. They were undoubtedly long gone and far away by then, but that no longer mattered. Someone was going to suffer for the misery they had endured, and they didn't care who, just so long as they were black savages. They attacked without warning, catching the villagers completely off guard. There were few survivors, barely a handful of able-bodied men, scarcely enough to operate the mine.

Whether it was luck, sheer determination, or the hand of fate, the Administrator found his way back to the garrison with his human cargo in tow. To his utter amazement he found the garrison manned by an entirely different regiment. Before he could demand an explanation, his former aides, whom he had recently observed to be insane, suddenly appeared with a contingent of soldiers. The Administrator was taken into custody, whereupon he was beaten senseless.

It seems the merchant had reached someone in authority who had the ear of the Pharaoh's right-hand man, who, for a reasonable sum, denounced the Administrator for having interrupted the flow of gold coming out of the Sudan. The Pharaoh, long since addicted to the poppy, never really understood what all the fuss was about. The powerbrokers lurking behind the throne, however, didn't appreciate being robbed, so they sent a detachment of soldiers to arrest the Administrator.

When the Administrator, trussed and tethered to a post, finally came to his senses, it was obvious to him that a mistake had been made, that the insane aides had somehow taken over the camp. That mirage-like hope promptly evaporated when the newly appointed administrator arrived. He wasn't cut from the same bolt of cloth as his predecessor, but cloaked himself in an aura of power, nonetheless. And like most people in power he enjoyed demeaning his subordinates, which is why he recounted in vivid detail the Administrator's fall from grace. He even escorted the merchant into the jailhouse so that he might gloat over the fate of the man who had stolen his livelihood. No one was more surprised than the merchant when he failed to rejoice in his triumph. It seems the Administrator had unwittingly awakened the merchant's capacity for forgiveness. However, it wasn't until confronted with his tormentor that the merchant recognized his own transformation.

When the Administrator arrived at the mine to begin his life sentence he found the mine up and running, only it wasn't manned by the slaves he had recently acquired, but by the soldiers he had previously commanded. Needless to say, the soldiers didn't look kindly upon the Administrator; rather, they relished the opportunity to mete out their own brand of justice. Killing him would be the highlight of their lives. Once in the mine there would be no escaping the fate that awaited him. Just when it looked like a fait accompli, cooler heads prevailed. Accordingly, they decided that a life sentence working the mine was a more fitting punishment. And so it was arranged, the Administrator would be the first man to enter the mine each morning and the last man to exit at the end of the day.

The first few weeks were the hardest for the Administrator. The men who toiled at his side despised him, and therefore offered no kindness. Like a cornered animal he feared for his life, reacting to every unexpected movement and to every unidentified sound. It wasn't until he finally realized that he was giving satisfaction to his enemies that he decided to show them the kind of man they were dealing with.

Given a moment's reflection, perhaps you would agree that life is not unlike a gold mine, ever holding the promise of hidden treasure concealed within a maze of possibilities. And so it was that a rare type of gold was unexpectedly struck in the mine. It was found at the very bottom of the most unlikely shaft, and it was found in the person of the fallen Administrator. He had been a tyrant when saddled with privilege, but as a mineworker he became an altogether different sort of man.

With the passage of time he came to think of the mine as a woman, ever in need of love and understanding. Each and every day he professed his undying devotion, and when she took a life, he never blamed her, but soothed her for her loss. He knew what the others thought, that he had broken under the strain, but he paid them no mind, because he had discovered something incredible within himself. Truly, the others thought that his sanity had fallen into one of the mine's many bottomless pits, never be heard from again. He was undoubtedly mad, and there was no cure to found at the bottom of the mineshaft.

A year passed, and still he survived. If anything, he looked healthier and happier than ever. He made no attempt to reassert his authority, but seemed to revel in the role of quiet acquiescence. When it became clear that he was not deranged, but a man of exceptional quality, the others finally accepted him into their brotherhood. He was eventually offered the rank of lead miner, a position that would guarantee the shortest and safest work day, but he declined the honor, claiming that he liked it best at the bottom of the shaft.

Curious about his transformation, the new administrator decided to observe his predecessor at work. The stories turned out to be true - the man actually enjoyed his work. What really stood out, however, was the fact that the other miners seemed to have adopted something of his attitude. Surely, that explained why the mine was producing more gold, and why the number of accidental deaths had steadily declined.

Finally, the new administrator asked his predecessor the question everybody wanted answered. The miner politely acknowledged his right to ask, but answered only that he found the work challenging, which made the hardship tolerable. Failing to understand, his successor forced back a smile, and wanted to know just what part of hell he found the most challenging. The legend of the mines responded with a look that might have been interpreted as arrogance, but, upon reflection, more likely communicated nothing more than forbearance. The challenge, he explained, was maintaining an attitude of self-discovery. In the depth of the mine he had discovered the power and presence of God, something he had never imagined possible. What's more, he had learned that happiness was unrelated to wealth and power, but to the daily acceptance of life's challenges, no matter the degree of difficulty. He had discovered something within himself, something infinitely more precious than the gold he extracted from the mine.

The new administrator could hardly doubt that he had witnessed a remarkable transformation of character. Nevertheless, he couldn't help but question what he had seen. Perhaps his predecessor had suppressed his identity, thereby creating a new persona, one more amenable to survival in the mine. He had seen it happen before, but the others had eventually reverted back to their old character traits. This man gave no indication of reversion; on the contrary, he gave every indication of forward thinking, ever the sign of a healthy ego.

It was during his third year in the mine that yet another administrator arrived to relieve the fallen Administrator's successor. The new administrator was a man of few scruples, and from the outset appeared to be heading down the same path that the now legendary miner had once ventured upon. The two aides, who had at one time gone insane just long enough to avoid working the mine, suggested that he visit the mine, where he would find a previous administrator. It was a casual suggestion, seemingly lacking even the slightest hint of irony. When the new administrator realized that his predecessor actually worked the mine, he thought to punish the aides, but that had been tried before, and the man who had tried now worked the mine. In the end he decided to quietly serve out his time in hell.

The Administrator had been working the mine for seven long years when fate finally laid claim to his life. He was inspecting the shoring in the main tunnel when a slave who had nothing to lose chose to settle an old score. His last earthly wish was to kill the man who had decimated an entire village. He came from behind and thrust a pike through the heart of a legend.

When he arrived on the other side of the gate the Administrator gave no thought to the transformation he had undergone, but thought only of the mistakes he had made. He had murdered every man in the mine, and had slaughtered hundreds in the African interior. Surely, he was destined to burn in hell. Instead, he was offered a choice. If he agreed to work as a spirit guide his status with the White Lodge would be restored. Otherwise, he would be banished to the lower levels of the astral plane. The lower astral is not a preferred destination, and should be avoided whenever possible. Working as a spirit guide, on the other hand, represented a golden opportunity to work off karma while serving humanity.

Spirit guides perform a wide variety of functions. The critical roles are assigned to doctors and nurses who monitor health at the cellular level. The doctors mix and dispense chemicals, pouring them directly into the etheric body, the template upon which the physical body is constructed. But for those chemicals humanity would be teeming with sickness and disease. Beyond that, etheric chemicals are critically important for anyone who meditates with depth and sincerity, because meditation overburdens the nervous system.

Prescribing chemicals is a science, and a very difficult one at that. Misapplication can result in both physical exhaustion and severe depression; however, when correctly applied, those chemicals help immunize the body against disease, while restoring its vitality. Other types of spirit guides conduct research into matters of vital importance to the people they serve. Their findings are transmitted telepathically, and are experienced by the recipients as creative ideas. Guides perform to the best of their ability and, while they receive extensive training, their abilities vary, according to their initiatory status.

The Administrator wisely chose the role of spirit guide, and was subsequently assigned to work with an African tribesman who worked in the mine.

The Egyptian Landowner

THE GREAT PYRAMID of Egypt was built long before modern science imagines. In fact, it was built thousands of years before the earliest estimates. The problem with the estimates has been the reliance upon chemical and carbon testing, neither of which is accurately conducted. In time the error will be discovered and adjustments will be made; however, until then history will continue to be compressed, thereby distorting the overall picture. The history of Ancient Egypt is a prime example, because the historical monuments of that era actually date from the destruction of Atlantis nearly 12,000 years ago.

All told, roughly 100,000 Atlanteans migrated to Egypt. Many of them arrived one hundred years before the final breakup of Atlantis, so that by the time the last wave of refugees arrived major improvements to the land had already been accomplished. Most notably, the Nile had been dredged and the desert irrigated with an elaborate system of channels. Almost overnight hundreds of farms sprang to life, and those farms supplied the influx of Atlanteans with fruits, nuts, and grains.

Our story begins centuries later, long after the absorption of the Atlantean race into the local population. It concerns the life of a landowner who managed a large, irrigated farm in the general vicinity of the Great Pyramid. The Landowner's acreage extended for miles, his principal crop a type of fruit unknown to the modern world. His crop was harvested green, and then shipped to the farthest reaches of the kingdom, ripening in transit. Timing was critical, and the best insurance against miscalculation was an abundant supply; consequently, the Landowner was always looking to increase his yield. His harvest wasn't unusual for the area; however, his principal competitor consistently achieved better results. And the Landowner wanted to know why.

All things considered, the Landowner understood his market, and had even developed an ingenious method for preserving his harvest. He stored his produce in underground warehouses, then wrapped his shipments in crocodile skins derived from a smooth-skinned species long since extinct. When tanned and stretched they reflected the sun, thereby allowing his shipments to survive for weeks under the hot African sun.

When an orchard worker owned by his competitor turned up at the local slave market the Landowner jumped at the chance. He was determined to discover his competitor's secret, and thought that perhaps the slave could help him solve the mystery. As for the slave, he had been abducted as a young boy, and by the time the Landowner's competitor purchased him, he had already endured a lifetime of hardship. And that hardship was plainly evident, because the agony of his life echoed from the depths of his ebony eyes. The eyes invariably tell a story, and the seething cauldron of emotion residing within his fiery orbs revealed a man who had seen more than his share of the whip. When his owner tired of his insolence, rather than beat him to death, he sold him to the Landowner, hoping that disaster would befall them both.

Slavery has beleaguered humanity since the dawn of civilization. The source of the problem lies in the urge to dominate, the quintessential quality of the animal soul. Egyptian slavery was one of the worst examples of the institution, and the karmic roots of New World slavery can be traced back to ancient Egypt. Some of the people sold into slavery in the Americas were former Egyptian slave owners, while some of the slave owners were former Egyptian slaves. That being said, it is also true that the vast majority of those enslaved in the New World were but innocents caught up in the karma of the human family.

Despite the size of his farm, the Landowner had no use for slavery, employing instead itinerant workers on his land. Nevertheless, when this particular slave came on the market he put his scruples aside. He was, after all, entitled to make a profit. Besides, he planned on offering the slave the opportunity of a lifetime. It would be a grand experiment, one that would benefit both of their lives. His intentions were good, though not pure, because there is no justification for enslaving another human being. Slavery is evil, and karma does not justify the existence of the institution; however, there is such a thing as making the best of a bad situation.

When the slave arrived at the farm he expected to be housed in the barn, because it was common practice to shelter the slaves with the cattle. Therefore, he was totally bewildered when given a room in the main house. And what a room it was. It was completely furnished with a closet packed full of clothes and other amenities. The slave was accustomed to exploitation, and was therefore suspicious by nature, but this exceeded by far anything he had ever experienced. Something very important was at stake, but he could not for the life of him guess what it was.

True to his plan, the Landowner was determined to provide a decent life for his one and only slave. He was, by all accounts, a man of honor, a man who practiced no deception. The ground rules, therefore, were simple and clearly stated. If the slave solved the riddle of the differing yields, he would teach him how to run the farm. He needed an assistant, and the job would be his if he proved capable.

There was no need for the slave to mull it over, because the Landowner's offer was far beyond anything he could ever have imagined. Given the choice between living with the cattle and residing in the master's house, he accepted the offer with a grateful heart. His heart was good, but the anger that simmered within the depths of his being threatened to undo the whole affair, until he finally accepted what he knew in his heart to be true: the Landowner was an honorable man. From that point forward master and slave worked together in near perfect harmony, gradually developing a relationship based upon mutual appreciation and respect.

Two years later, having improved the yield and expanded trade with the interior, the Landowner's farm was more prosperous than ever before. The improved yield resulted from the introduction of bees into the orchards. The slave, ever the student of Mother Nature, had been quick to find a solution.

The slave was a cautious man. Years of abuse had deeply scarred his psyche, so it wasn't until he had established himself as a competent assistant that he allowed the specter of friendship to enter into his relationship with the Landowner. In fact, the more he thought about it, the more he valued the Landowner's friendship. Who wouldn't respect a man who was both skillful in business and discrete in his personal affairs? Even though he remained a slave, there was no arguing with the fact that he had flourished under the Landowner's tutelage. Some might question his gratitude; perhaps even judge it nothing more than an artifact of slavery, but the fact remains he never stooped to servility.

They didn't know exactly when it happened, but master and slave had become two friends sharing a common goal. Together they had created something exceptional, and togetherness was a quality they both valued. Their relationship was all the more remarkable given the nature of their society. Times were such that slaves were bartered like cattle, and emancipation was strictly forbidden. Understandably, their partnership of the heart was never revealed in public.

The Landowner was painfully aware of his friend's predicament, and often spoke of taking a journey into the interior for the express purpose of granting his freedom. But his friend always declined the offer, choosing instead to continue on as before.

It frequently happens, however, that Life itself ordains a change in circumstances, sometimes demanding immediate action, sometimes offering ready-made solutions for problems long since overdue. And so it happened that complications arose, and the decision was made to travel into the interior in order to repair relations with a tribe that had received a shipment of bad fruit. Under normal circumstances they would have contested the claim, but this particular tribe held the promise of significant revenue, and the Landowner thought it best to personally negotiate a settlement. Besides, it was the perfect opportunity to release his friend from bondage. Their journey would put them within easy reach of his boyhood village, and this time his friend had agreed to accept the offer of freedom.

The slave enjoyed a comfortable lifestyle; nevertheless, he found it impossible to ignore the longing of his heart. Even though he enjoyed extraordinary privileges, there was one privilege he would never accrue, and that was the freedom to come and go as he pleased. And there was nothing his friend could do about it, except accompany him into the interior, and then claim that he had escaped.

After several days on the trail they encountered a tribal representative who had been sent ahead to escort them the remainder of the way. It wasn't until the next day that the slave suddenly recognized their guide's tribal affiliation. He belonged to the tribe that had abducted him into slavery. Not only was he going home, but the tribe that had enslaved him was leading the way. Had he been a vengeful man, the guide would have undoubtedly met with misfortune. As it was the slave made a conscious choice to forgive the past, and therefore never revealed the fact that he had discovered the source of his condition.

They arrived without incident, anxious to conclude their business, but determined to negotiate a fair settlement. Days later, having made reparations and negotiated the terms of their next shipment, the two friends journeyed deeper into the interior in search of the slave's boyhood village. When they arrived at the village they were surprised to find it deserted. They scoured the area, but found no sign of life. It was a baffling riddle, but they weren't prepared to leave the mystery unsolved, so they decided to keep on searching until they found an answer.

Their search was temporarily interrupted when a column of traders packing a shipment of precious gems passed through the village on their way to the Lower Kingdom. It was their first trip north, and they were anxious to receive information regarding the market. The Landowner dealt in produce, and therefore had no experience with precious gems; however, it didn't take an expert to recognize the value of their cargo. He offered to buy the whole shipment, tendering two of his camels as down payment. The traders had never seen a camel before, and after experiencing the nasty side of the beast presented for their inspection, they really didn't care to see the others.

The Landowner's potential windfall was beginning to resemble the tattered aftermath of a trade wind gone awry when the slave offered to go back to the farm and return with a caravan loaded with trade goods. The Landowner liked the plan, but reversed the roles. He would undertake the journey while his friend continued searching for clues.

When the Landowner returned, he promptly traded a shipment of tools and sundries for a fortune in gems. Exhausted from the journey, he had no choice but to remain in the village until he was fit for travel. His friend, having surrendered all hope of ever discovering what had happened to his tribe, had decided to accompany him home.

Whiling away the time, the two friends were walking along the riverbank that skirted the village when they were suddenly confronted with an angry lion. It seems they had unwittingly scared off its meal.

The lion charged at full gallop, large, heavy paws churning the earth with killer claws. Its golden eyes riveted its prey with deadly intention, while its mane, set in motion by the force of sudden acceleration, served warning that mealtime was imminent. They ran for the river, and with exquisite timing tumbled into the water at the precise moment the lion leapt. Claws fully extended, but unable to control the momentum of its mighty lunge, the lion passed well overhead, straight into the river. Caught in the current, the lion drifted downstream, eventually climbing up onto a large, flat rock. Not wanting to exhibit any trace of panic, it hunkered down for a nap.

They harbored no illusions. The lion was not about to spend the remainder of its unnatural life perched on a rock. The average lion might have forgotten the whole affair, but there were exceptions to the rule, namely the odd lion who never forgot an insult. Those lions were known to quest until the matter was settled. Fearing the worst, they rushed back to camp and started making preparations for a hasty departure.

The following day the lion announced its intentions with a thunderous roar, nearly panicking both them and their camels. By day's end they hadn't caught sight of the lion, and therefore clung to the hope that he had abandoned his quest. By morning that hope had vanished; the lion was undeniably dogging their trail.

With the approach of nightfall they set up camp within easy reach of the river, securing their camels to some nearby trees. A storm was brewing and, choosing to remain a safe distance from the trees, they unfolded their bedrolls in a field of grass. The approaching storm was a mixed blessing, because on the one hand they could lose everything, including their lives, with no help from the lion. On the other hand, lions were known to loathe extreme weather, and the storm just might force it to abandon its quest.

The unholy sound of howling wind announced the storm's arrival. Camels abhor noise, and howling wind is infinitely worse than everyday noise to their sensitive ears. They are accustomed to stone silence, and when Mother Nature made their ears she forgot to take the wind into account. Unfortunately, shrieking wind wasn't the full extent of their misery, because the force of the blow pushed them around like ships at sea. And being pushed and shoved just happens to be the other thing capable of driving camels out of their minds. Thus the improbable happened and, despite their dislike of water, the camels charged into the river where they floundered in the rising swell. Down they went, and with them went a fortune in gems.

Happily, all was not lost, because they managed to salvage a satchel full of gems from the bank of the river. It was but a small portion of their treasure; nevertheless, it would certainly fetch a tidy sum. The satchel was heavy, but not so heavy as to discourage them from packing the gems out of the jungle. Hauling a load definitely slowed their pace, but then their pace had absolutely no bearing on the lion's feeding schedule, which was the only thing keeping them alive.

Undeterred by the storm, the lion dogged their trail throughout the day, diligently protecting his next meal. He got hungry during the night and killed them both while they slept. He sliced them to ribbons and, having eaten his fill, couldn't help but recall the villagers he had recently devoured.

The Landowner died in his sleep, totally unaware of his departure. When told of his death he immediately rejected the idea, because his new environment wasn't what he expected. Instead of paradise, he found himself in a world not unlike the one he had just departed. Truly, it sometimes happens that the newly deceased assume that they are dreaming. When confronted with the truth, some of them become furious, while others recoil in shock. Still others sink into depression, unable to bear the loss of friends and family.

Death need not be a tragedy. Almost everybody is greeted by friends and family the moment they pass through the gate; however, it's not unusual for the deceased to ignore their pleas and refuse to step into the Light. So when your loved ones arrive, it generally means only one thing. The most sensible course of action is to trust the people that you love.

LIFE SEVEN
The Fugitive

WITHIN MOMENTS OF his escape he was confronted by the village chieftain. Momentarily caught off guard, he was slow to react, but then he plunged his knife right up to the hilt, catching the chieftain square in the throat, thereby silencing his voice before sounding an alarm. Blood gushed in a continuous spray, covering his meager frame in a patina of warm, sticky liquid. He had never killed before, let alone bathed in blood, and the realization that he wore another man's life upon his skin was devastating. He immediately regretted the killing, because now he had an even bigger problem. He had killed an important man, and any chance he ever had of proving his innocence was gone forever.

His ordeal began when he was falsely accused of murder. The victim, the son of the local shaman, had been found with his throat slit somewhere north of the village. Because he was a stranger, the locals had judged him guilty of the crime, and had jailed him pending further instructions from the shaman. The jail was nothing more than a hut woven from fronds, but cutting through the double-layered tight weave had proven surprisingly difficult. He had worked through the night using a small, bronze blade he kept hidden in his loincloth, and had barely managed to escape when he was discovered by the chieftain.

He had arrived at the village the day before and, even though his instinct had been to avoid the local population, his need for human contact had prevailed. It was always the same; nobody trusted him, a man who wandered the African continent alone, a man without tribal affiliation. His tribe had been decimated by disease and, rather than swear allegiance to another tribe, he had chosen the life of an itinerant, sometimes avoiding the villages he encountered, sometimes stopping for food and companionship. Predictably, the tribal leaders questioned the truth of his story, but had, nevertheless, allowed him to spend the night in a small clearing just outside of the village.

The main trail out of the village led north, gradually winding east towards the sea. The villagers would have expected him to take the northern trail, hoping to catch one of the merchant ships that plied the coastal waters of East Africa. Hence he had chosen another route for his escape. The ancient path he now traveled wound its way into the interior of the continent, eventually leading into the jungle. The coastal tribes of Africa avoided the jungle, because to venture into its grasp was to court certain death.

He had been running for hours and the sun was beating down with relentless anticipation, his sweat collecting in rivulets of impending disaster. He knew that he had to stop for water; otherwise, he would run the risk of dehydration, followed by total incapacitation. On the other hand, he was accustomed to long hours of running in the scorching sun, and was capable of sprinting with both speed and grace over terrain that would cause the average man to falter. He would stop soon, but in the meantime his confidence was growing because his endurance was proving equal to the challenge.

He felt confident that they would search the northern trail first, although it was only a matter of time before they discovered his tracks. They would come in numbers, allowing their strongest runners to slacken their pace, while the weaker runners read sign at the front of the pack. His only hope was to reach the jungle before they tracked him down, because once in the jungle his pursuers would undoubtedly give up the chase.

His plan was well-reasoned, because the ancients respected the power and presence of Mother Nature. Thus when the land conspired against them, they thought it the hand of Fate, ever the obedient servant of Mother Nature. While this might seem like superstition, it's really nothing more than commonsense. Who would deny the fact that Mother Nature expresses the Will of the Creator? And who would deny man's capacity to live in harmony with Mother Nature? Therefore when Mother Nature intervened, the ancients were quick to recognize the hand of God.

The shaman was not an evil man, but a man who lacked any semblance of integrity, ever the sign of an unhealthy ego. He was determined to avenge his son's death, and anyone who dared challenge his authority could expect serious repercussions. When his wife questioned his judgment he dismissed her concerns as idle speculation, despite the fact that someone else had been seen in the vicinity of the crime, and had quarreled with their son the day before the murder. The shaman had witnessed the altercation and had subsequently confronted the man in question. To accuse him of murder, after having accepted his heart-felt apology, smacked of his own fallibility. The stranger was obviously guilty.

The shaman's duties included ceremonial contact with ancestral spirits, a sacred event attended by every member of the tribe. The spirits of the dead guided the shaman, but only within the context of an elaborate ritual, which included the use of mind altering drugs. Hypnotic trance was, and remains, an ancient method for contacting the spirits of the dead; however, the practice can be dangerous, because passivity invites psychic intrusion, whether from within or from without. Had the shaman actually received genuine guidance from the spirit world, he would have undoubtedly been cautioned against an unsafe practice made all the more dangerous by the unworthiness of his motives.

Under the influence of a powerful hypnotic, the shaman danced until his body surrendered to the effects of the drug. There was little doubt what the outcome would be, so no one was surprised when the shaman declared the accused guilty of murdering his son. The Fugitive, however, had already escaped, having left behind the body of a chieftain as further evidence of his depravity.

Reaching the hill country, he stopped to survey the terrain, and was alarmed by the seemingly endless array of hills and valleys that lay before him. The ancient path he had been following might prove adequate, but he had already encountered sections of trail that had been overrun by Mother Nature. Guessing was dangerous, and backtracking promised certain death. Next he studied his back trail and, seeing no evidence of pursuit, he decided to pass the night on the hill. Heartened by the prospect of a hot meal and some much needed sleep, he gathered enough firewood to last through the night.

Removing a piece of quartz from the pouch attached to his hip, he dropped it onto a pile of kindling. Applying his knife, he braced the kindling with a smattering of finely shaved lignite. Next he repositioned the quartz to receive the rays of the sun, thereby generating enough heat to start a smoldering fire. Removing one last item from his pouch, he sprinkled a noxious, yellow substance over the smoldering lignite, causing the kindling to erupt in flames. The final ingredient was sulfur. The ancients discovered the process quite by accident, but once discovered it spread far and wide over Africa.

After a meal of roasted fowl, he slipped into an uneasy sleep, only to be startled awake by the sound of howling hyenas. He was accustomed to the sounds of nature, but the circumstances surrounding his presence there in the middle of nowhere had awakened ancient memories stored in his subconscious mind. He knew that no animal would approach while the fire blazed in the night, but that knowledge had proven insufficient to prevent an instinctive reaction of fear. Even though the hyenas sounded quite near, he knew from experience that they were miles away, so he drifted back to sleep. This time he entered into a dream that seemed as real as life itself.

He was flying high above the earth, and yet he was not a bird, but a man with his faculties fully intact. Above, the effulgent sun radiated its life-giving energy, and below the seemingly endless expanse of the earth passed before his sight. He had never imagined a world beyond the land that he knew, but his dream, remarkably lucid and wondrously revealing, was dispelling the illusions that attended his internal geography. The jungle was not his only option.

He awoke with a plan that just might save his life. Gathering his belongings, he set out for the secluded lake he had spotted while studying the terrain the day before. The lake sat on top of a towering hill, and could only be seen from a vantage point, and not from the surrounding terrain. It looked to be the perfect redoubt, and with any luck his pursuers would never suspect the presence of the lake.

He arrived at the base of the hill well before sundown and immediately began his ascent. He chose the only passable route to the top, and before long he was standing on the shore of the lake. He was surprised to find it smaller than expected, never realizing that when viewed at a distance in full sunlight certain shades of blue tend to distort human perception. The light was fading fast and, unable to start a fire, he had no choice but to climb a tree for the night.

At first light he descended to the trail below and continued his journey as originally planned. He resumed the same pace as before, taking care to preserve the element of desperation that had characterized his flight from backwater justice. Within the hour he reached his objective, an impassable ridge blocking the trail. The only possible way around it led north into the jungle. A reasonable man would follow the base of the ridge, hoping to find passage before venturing too far into the wild. But, the appearance of a reasonable man was the last thing he wanted to convey to his pursuers. So he climbed the ridge, giving every indication he intended to summit. When he had climbed as far as humanly possible, he stopped and rested before taking the plunge. Having determined the safest route, he threw himself down the ridge, kicking his legs and flailing his arms all the way down, thereby creating the illusion of an uncontrolled descent.

Far from finished, he climbed back up the ridge; however, rather than take another harrowing tumble, he trekked north along the perilous slope, taking care to create ample evidence of his passing. He continued his grueling march until he reached the edge of the jungle, shuddering to think what might have happened had he been forced to penetrate deep into its forbidding darkness. Crossing into the jungle, he pulled out his knife and made an incision, causing blood to gush from his arm onto the surrounding foliage. He wrapped the gash in medicinal leaves still attached to the vine, and then hurried out of the thicket.

He ran like the wind back along the base of the ridge, certain that his pursuers would track him into the jungle, but fail to pick up his trail leading back out. His blood would draw a crowd, and his tracks would be obliterated in the frenzy. If everything went as planned, his pursuers would find ample evidence of his demise.

Returning to the lake, he established a lookout post, hoping his pursuers would pass him by. In any event, he prepared for the worst and assembled a gigantic pile of rocks, positioned to create havoc upon release. Hopefully, if his man-made avalanche became necessary, his pursuers would never suspect anything other than the hand of fate. If, however, his ruse was discovered he would be forced to flee into the jungle.

Several days passed with no sign of pursuit, when, quite by chance, he heard their approach. He had given up the vigil, and had started making long-term plans for survival when the unexpected sound of human activity sent chills up his spine. His fears escalated when he saw the size of the war party. Surely, such a large party tipped the odds in favor of discovery.

Sure enough, a party of three was dispatched up the hill, leaving him no choice but to release his pile of rocks. The avalanche roared down the narrow channel, obliterating the climbers before they reached the midpoint of the passage. To his pursuers it seemed that Mother Nature had spoken, so they made no further attempts to summit the hill. Besides, the Fugitive's trail had been discovered heading out towards the unknown.

He never saw them again, and he never followed their trail to find out what had happened. He really didn't care what fate had befallen them, but suspected the worst, because there were no other trails leading back to their village.

At last his ordeal was over, and he knew that one day soon he would be able to resume a normal life. But, for the moment he was content to remain in the wild, savoring the knowledge that he had eluded an unjust fate.

Strange though it may seem, he grew accustomed to his lonely life in the bush, little by little surrendering his ties to the past. His plight was not at all uncommon, because even the most inveterate urban dweller can be seduced by the allure of the wild. Even so, as the weeks stretched into months he found himself longing for human companionship. More and more his thoughts turned to the life he had left behind, and yet he made no attempt to break Mother Nature's hold.

In the end loneliness wreaked havoc upon his mind, launching a barrage of voices seemingly located within the confines of his head. They spoke not with the comforting words of reassurance, but declared his every transgression with endless permutations. Defenseless against their incursions, and unable to ignore their allegations, he soon entered into a dialogue with the ghosts that lived within his head. He argued with the voices, sometimes passing entire days absorbed in debate. When he took steps to block them out they responded with renewed determination; when he ignored them they taunted him with vile accusations. Snared in the grip of his own mind, he became convinced that hell's own legion had camped at his door.

One day, hearing the familiar sound of human activity, he descended to the trail below, where he caught sight of a band of hunters. Immediately recognizing his instability, they fired a volley of arrows in his general direction. Totally misreading the seriousness of the situation, he ignored the warning and rushed to greet his newfound friends. A dozen arrows took flight, silently decreeing his fate.

When he arrived on the other side of the gate, rather than step into the Light, he began arguing with the voices in his head, eventually falling into a profoundly troubled sleep. Brutal memories besieged his dreams, clamoring for admission into the world of conscious reality, ever the sign of a disturbed mind. It seems he was never quite the same after his tour of duty with the Cro-Magnon.

The Whispering Dragon

THE DRAGON GLARED at the teeming crowd. They were but lowly peasants, and yet they had the audacity to block the road. This was not at all acceptable. Any delay, for whatever reason, was an affront to his lofty position, but this was so egregious as to preclude any possibility of forgiveness. As the Provincial Governor it was his duty to impose order, and this careless disregard for authority was going to be dealt with, and dealt with in a manner that would create an indelible impression. Any fool could see that order could not be established if the riffraff of the world placed their own needs above those of the Governor.

The Dragon motioned for the Captain of the guard to approach. Responding with celerity, but without the slightest hint of urgency, the Captain met the Dragon's piercing gaze. A lesser man would have been unnerved, but the Captain had grown accustomed to the expression embodied in the Dragon's eyes. He had seen that same wraith-like emptiness before, but only on the battlefield, and only amongst the dead. However, it wasn't the eyes alone that conveyed the specter of death. The Dragon's skin was coarse and dry, conspicuously highlighted by the distinctive scaling that beleaguered his face. Mutated cells were emerging, somehow evoking the image of death and decay. Taking in the scales as if for the first time, the Captain thought he knew the source of the Dragon's appellation.

The Dragon motioned for the Captain to step closer, all the while directing his gaze in another direction. Surely, it was the perfect way to communicate disdain, giving orders while looking off into the surroundings as if bored to death. And then he whispered into the Captain's waiting ear. Every word the Dragon uttered grated on the nerves, but the sound of his whisper was far worse. It was a unique sound, by all appearances gentle and unassuming, but commanding, nevertheless, a reaction incommensurate with its weight and substance. It passed from his lips bearing no evidence of evil intention, but when it arrived at its destination, the effect upon the brain, and therefore the mind, was staggering.

What the Captain heard was beyond belief, and therefore impossible to comprehend. The Dragon had ordered him to slaughter the offending throng of peasants. Hardened warrior that he was, the Captain quickly regained his composure, and then carried out his orders with practiced dispassion. His small contingent of soldiers attacked the crowd without a word of warning, cutting men, women, and children to pieces. When it was over dozens were dead; many were wounded, some writhing in pain, some dragging themselves to safety. Having slaughtered everyone within easy each, the soldiers reassembled alongside the Dragon's chair, which remained suspended on the shoulders of eight strong men.

Thereafter the Dragon became known as the Whispering Dragon, because whenever he took offense he whispered in the Captain's ear. He whispered over the slightest annoyance; always with pride, always exhibiting a sense of accomplishment. He became quite proficient at reducing the local population, and could slaughter a mob of milling peasants faster than anybody in all of China.

While the Captain was clearing the roadway, the Dragon was venting his frustration on the men who carried his chair. The chair weighed in excess of three hundred pounds and, despite the fact that his porters were all big, burly men, they were showing the strain. The work was demanding, offering little reprieve, because they passed their nights guarding the Dragon's chair, as if anyone would steal an oversized sedan chair. They were being worked to death, but they never complained, because the Dragon always chose men from the outlying districts, men accustomed to unquestioned obedience, men awed by the complexity of life near the center of the universe.

Eventually, and by all accounts inevitably, the Dragon ordered the Captain and his entire contingent of soldiers executed for insubordination. It seems he didn't like the way the Captain looked him in the eye every time he whispered in his ear. He replaced the Captain and his men with a gang of cutthroats; men suffering from the same madness he himself enjoyed, and from amongst them chose a new Captain. They were evil men, cold-blooded to the core; ever the case when the heart ceases to inform human interaction. Not that the mind ceases to interact, but the heart, that great communicator of love and understanding, remains stone silent. Thus is a sociopathic personality developed, and thus does it lend itself to the nasty work of heartless slaughter.

Of course, from their point of view they were only obeying orders. Many a villain has claimed the same freedom from accountability. Needless to say, there are those times when the shield of misplaced loyalty can be legitimately invoked, but not when obeying orders known to be morally reprehensible. In such a case, one is obligated to do something. It need not amount to open resistance, but it should entail some expression of dissent. It might manifest as a dispassionate execution of duty, or perhaps an attempt to mitigate the full impact of the deed. Whatever the action, it is duly recorded in the Celestial Record for all eternity. The Celestial Record exactly replicates all human experience, and exists in the upper regions of the mental plane. The record made by the Captain shines just a little, because he made his objections known to the Dragon in a manner that cost him his life. The record made by the Dragon, on the other hand, was growing darker by the day, casting the seeds of impending doom upon the fertile domain of time and space.

From the outset the Dragon had plotted and schemed, determined to milk each and every opportunity for whatever he could. Never realizing the kind of man that he was, the previous governor had appointed him to the office of Royal Tax Collector. Ever ready to stab a friend in the back, the Dragon misappropriated a sizeable sum from the Emperor's coffers, and later used his misbegotten wealth to purchase the governorship when his predecessor was executed for embezzling funds. Obviously, he was not only clever, but dangerously ambitious, having orchestrated the execution of an innocent man.

Not surprisingly, the Dragon aspired to the Royal Court of the Emperor. His plan was quite simple. He would rule with an iron fist and he would collect more tax revenue than ever before. It was an achievable plan on both accounts, because on the one hand he controlled the provincial army, and on the other hand he could not fail at collecting more revenue. All he had to do was prevent his tax collector from stealing as much revenue as he himself had purloined. And that he could certainly do.

Ever thrifty when it came to unnecessary expenses, the Dragon had purchased his wife for a modest sum. Despite the status bestowed by her position, she carried herself like a peasant, constantly aware of her lowborn heritage. For her there was no possibility of escape, not in that era, and especially not from him. He was a cruel man given to violent outbursts, and when the mood was upon him he raped her, not with his penis, being impotent like he was, but with those objects that best exemplified the awesome power of the dragon. He had no awareness of her pain, knowing only the joy of its infliction. Ruthless to the core, he savored the essence of his brutality: absolute power over every living thing.

The Dragon had no sense of humor, and therefore hated the sound of human laughter. Hence, many a man left this world for no reason other than having laughed in his presence. The truth be known, humor is a wonderful thing. Behind the laugh, the chuckle, and sometimes even the smile, lurk images that challenge the limits of social propriety. There is, however, another kind of laugh. It derives not from the release of tension, but from the desire to cause pain and suffering. The Dragon enjoyed such a laugh. His laugh, not unlike his whisper, terrorized anyone within its sphere of influence. When he laughed the scales that bedeviled his face sometimes fell away, conspicuously settling upon his exquisite clothing. Having lost face, literally if not figuratively, his wintry laugh quickly turned south, bringing misery to everyone in its path.

Over the years the Dragon's notoriety spread throughout the empire. The body count rose into the thousands, and still he showed no sign of relenting. He was so greatly feared that few dared appear before him, lest they leave as a corpse. Some, however, found him impossible to avoid, invariably groveling and fawning in his presence, sickening both themselves and those who witnessed their degradation. On those rare occasions when he could find no fault, the Dragon delighted in feigning displeasure for the sheer joy of watching others break into little pieces. He found it especially amusing when they stumbled over their words, and then blurted out absurd apologies for nonexistent crimes. But most of all, he savored those times when they offered their wives and daughters for his pleasure.

The Dragon's delusory thought processes sometimes settled upon issues of imperial interest, resulting in the dictation of some unfortunate letters to the Emperor. The most outrageous of the letters laid claim to provincial tax revenues, outlining his plan to build a palace equal to the Emperor's. Another offered his province as a model for the restoration of the Empire, a massive undertaking to be sure. Nevertheless, he was ready and willing to restore the Empire to its former glory.

Upon receiving the letters the Emperor erupted in a fit of rage. His first imperial order demanded the Governor's head in a chamber pot. His second decree ordered the Governor's mansion burned to the ground, along with every member of his household. His third decree rescinded the first two, issuing instead an order compelling the Dragon to appear before him at his earliest convenience. Loosely interpreted, the Dragon was to depart immediately and travel night and day until he lay prostrate before the Emperor.

When the Emperor's summons arrived the Dragon wasn't the least bit surprised, because he fully expected accolades for his brilliant suggestions. So he packed enough clothes to last a lifetime, absolutely convinced his services were indispensable. He ascended his chair, hoisted smoothly by eight of the regions strongest and stoutest, and waved goodbye to his jealous admirers. Dozens of servants trailed behind, most of them lugging baggage on their backs. Next came the reserve force ready to spell the weary. A brigade of handpicked assassins fell in alongside the caravan, looking all the better for the prospect of fresh pickings. And sure enough, it wasn't long before they dispatched a handful of troublesome creatures caught gaping at the Dragon.

Upon entering the adjoining province for the first time since his appointment the Dragon was utterly appalled by what he found. People stood and gawked, lingering on the road for such a long period of time that his carriers actually had to slow their pace. Rage corrupted his blood, while his mind, long since addicted to the hormones associated with unrestrained emotion, slipped into those old familiar grooves etched deep by unrelenting paranoia. Something had to be done, and when he reached the Emperor's ear he would demand that reparations be made.

By some miracle the Dragon arrived at the Emperor's palace without having executed anyone outside of his own province. It had been a long journey, but not quite so long as the many highways he had traversed in his mind, all of which led to limitless power. The pilgrimage, however, was not entirely uneventful, because a certain misadventure did occur. Rather than skirt the highway, one of the local teamsters had driven his cart to the far side of the roadway, allowing the Dragon's entourage to claim the other side of the road, thereby allowing both conveyances to pass alongside each other. It seemed the most natural of choices; however, as it turned out, the teamster could not have been more wrong.

The story went something like this. Angered by the driver's impertinence, the Dragon summoned the Captain of the guard and whispered in his ear. At that point the teamster realized that he had made a serious mistake, because the legend of the Whispering Dragon had reached his ear as well. Hoping to rectify the matter, he respectfully moved his cart to the shoulder of the road. When the Captain of the guard approached, sword drawn and ready to strike, the teamster hurriedly pointed to a band of pure white silk bearing the official seal of the Emperor. Comprehending the situation, but not wanting to lose face, the Captain unleashed his fury through the blade of his sword, shattering the bench occupied by the driver.

From that day forward, because he had been seared by the breath of the Dragon, the cart driver was known as Dragon's Breath. His village accounted him a brave man, even though he trembled every time he retold the harrowing tale of his encounter with the Whispering Dragon. Not surprisingly, it became a widespread joke in his village to look him in the eye while whispering into the ear of another.

The Dragon entered the Palace with all the usual fanfare, and immediately started barking orders to everyone in sight. His letters had nearly unhinged the Emperor, but being both educated and refined, and therefore the pinnacle of his society, the Emperor had managed to control his emotions. His anger, however, had persisted, simmering upon the true field of battle, ever the realm of emotion, and ever the source of man's degradation. And so it happened that the Dragon's continued effrontery ignited the smoldering embers of the Emperor's rage. The Dragon was a dead man, but first the Emperor would have a little sport at the Dragon's expense.

The Dragon arrived for dinner in a flourish, and nearly lost his life when he deigned to speak to the Emperor without first bowing to his knees. It was a serious breach of etiquette, one that unmasked the Dragon as a man bereft of both manners and culture. The Emperor's contempt was plainly visible and, guessing his intent, the dinner guests, some twelve in number, began interrogating the Dragon regarding his ancestry.

Galloping palpitations replaced the rhythmic cadence of his heart, and the Dragon suddenly found himself struggling to maintain the façade of a visiting dignitary. He could only hope that he was being tested before admittance into their society. By the time dinner was over, however, he could no longer pretend that it was all in jest. Known for his impeccable timing, the Emperor seized the moment, and asked the Dragon if he would like to whisper in the royal ear. The dinner guests broke into raucous laughter.

Resigned to his fate, the Dragon replied that when he whispered people died; however, now that he thought about it, he couldn't help but wonder what happened when the Emperor whispered. The silence that descended upon the room could not have been more deafening. The Emperor, not one to be outdone when a little drama was at hand, snapped his fingers while casually glancing in the general direction of the Dragon. A royal guard suddenly appeared. The knife was but a blur, breaching the carotid artery running down the left side of the Dragon's neck.

Blood erupted in a spurt, spraying the dinner table with bright red patches of liquid life. The guests had witnessed the same scene a time or two before, but still marveled that such a delicate incision could be performed with absolute precision. Never one to flinch at sight of blood, the Dragon announced for all to hear that it was bad taste to ruin a perfectly fine tablecloth.

Ordinarily, the Emperor would have been moved to laughter; instead, he was struck dumb by the Dragon's composure. Few could deliver a rebuke with such presence of mind while watching his life's blood amass before his eyes. Such a man was indeed a rare find. Moved by the Dragon's unexpected display of courage, the Emperor snapped his fingers one last time, this time with a slight nod of the head, thereby signaling the guard to apply a compress to the Dragon's neck. They all knew that it was too late, that the Dragon's life was forfeit.

Growing drowsy at last, the Dragon settled into his chair and waited for the end. Once again silence invaded the room. Having observed the Dragon's composure, everyone present experienced an unexpected turn of mind, and now thought the Dragon not so vulgar after all, but a man quite similar to themselves, despite his obvious lack of refinement. And so they sat in silence, and couldn't help but wonder from what heights the Dragon might have whispered had he somehow gained the Emperor's trust. Then again, perhaps it was best that he died, because had he ascended to the royal ear, they most likely would not have been long for the world.

Exiting the body, the Dragon entered the earthbound world, where he endured several decades of unrelenting misery, until at last the desire to live a decent life resurfaced. Ever willing to make allowances for the sake of economy, the Lords of Karma granted him a special dispensation, and arranged for him to pay his growing karmic debt via the installment plan.

LIFE NINE
The Sacrifice

THERE WAS A time in India, long after the inception of the Vedic tradition, when whole villages dedicated themselves to specific aspects of Deity. The Vedas, orally transmitted, but later transcribed, addressed humanity's relationship to God, the Creator and Sustainer of Life. Vedic literature inspired hundreds of religious sects, each characterized by intense devotion and an overwhelming desire to please the Creator. It was common practice for entire villages to worship a particular aspect of Divinity, ultimately creating an organized sect around the object of their devotion. A sect is not unlike a cult, and cults become a problem when dogma supersedes commonsense. Beyond that, the human ego needs to arrive at its own conclusions through the exercise of free will if it is to have any hope of a healthy development. When free will is surrendered the ego breaks down, invariably slipping into passive states of negativity. Negative states of mind can be extremely difficult to overcome, and the only practical solution is to ground one's awareness in every day life, thereby awakening the ego to its rightful role as sole arbiter between man and his environment.

Our story unfolds during a time of unrest, a time when India was struggling to find her identity. It concerns a young Hindu boy forced to take control of his life, not because he appreciated the significance of free will, but because he wanted to decide his own fate. He was sold into bondage to a traveling merchant; however, the merchant was not the man he appeared to be, but was secretly in league with a gang of marauding bandits. The bandits were the descendants of an ancient warlike tribe that had degenerated into an assemblage of rogues and scoundrels led by an established hierarchy of villains. They were exceedingly strange in appearance and were easily identified because of their unusually large eyes. Because of their appearance they avoided direct contact with the local communities, relying instead upon a network of spies for the intelligence they needed to conduct their raids.

They headquartered in the Punjab, and for centuries their reign of terror threatened every village that had ever hoped to establish a center of culture and commerce. Villages were driven to the brink of destruction, and the people lived in constant fear of the next attack. Having no recourse but to fend for themselves, the villagers deployed their resources as best they could, but never succeeded in stopping the incursions. They organized militias, but the bandits proved superior at military tactics. They concealed their valuables, but the bandits invariably discovered their secret hiding places. They negotiated settlements, but the bandits held all the cards, and no treaties were ever fashioned that weren't immediately broken. In the end, they bargained with God, promising to feed and shelter the homeless if only the bandits were eradicated.

During the time we now visit the threat posed by the bandits was dwindling, not because the villagers had collectively outwitted the bandits, and not because God had facilitated their annihilation, but because the bandits had so impoverished the area that they were forced to look for greener pastures. It was, therefore, a time of relative peace, which gave the villagers an opportunity to recover. As a result, religious fervor reached unprecedented heights. Of course, each sect credited the region's good fortune to the intercession of the Deity they happened to worship.

As for the boy, he was virtually homeless. He grew up scrapping for a living, receiving what assistance he could from a distant relative who, though poor, tried her best to feed and clothe him. She had no room in her shed-like home, so he slept wherever he happened to lay his head. When he turned twelve, the very age when his rapidly developing body demanded more nourishment, his would-be guardian sold him to the aforementioned merchant.

Slavery was not at all common in ancient India; however, children were sometimes sold into bondage in order to better their prospects. Such was the case with the boy. His guardian believed that her decision would provide him with an opportunity to learn a trade, thereby ensuring his survival. The boy, however, took the news badly, because like most boys entering puberty, he had a girlfriend in the local village. His first thought was to flee, but there was nowhere to run to, not if he ever hoped to see his girlfriend again. His second notion was to run away with the girl, but she came from an established family, and would never agree to abandon her home. In desperation he pleaded with the old lady to rescind the sale, but his plea fell on deaf ears.

The villagers had no knowledge of the merchant's deceit, for he took great care to conceal his true occupation, which was supplying intelligence to the very bandits they feared and hated. Given the nature of his work, the merchant needed a boy with few connections, and even fewer expectations; making exploitation all the easier without any fear of discovery.

In his youth the merchant had himself been a bandit, until age and infirmity had obliged him to seek other means of earning a living. He was able to work as a spy because he lacked the distinguishing features characteristic of his tribe. By the time he purchased the boy he had been in business for years, and was universally accepted as a man who could be trusted. He had become part of the scenery and, while his trade was not absolutely essential, he added spice to an otherwise dull day whenever he arrived in a village. The bandits, on the other hand, relied upon the information he supplied.

The merchant was intent on abusing the boy, just like he had so many other boys. He counted his victims nothing more than chattel, deserving only what was absolutely necessary to sustain life. He routinely assaulted his victims with blows about the head and body, all the while working himself into a sexual frenzy. He rarely attained orgasm, but managed to do so just often enough to never stop trying. He had been roughly treated as a child and, having given up all hope of ever forming a meaningful relationship, had long since concluded that love was for fools. Hence he took a vow to never play the part of a fool. He kept his vow, and never developed an attachment to another human being throughout his life. Scarred beyond any hope of recovery, he descended into a life of violence and perversion.

The merchant was completely unaware of his faults, and thought himself a good man who was forced to satisfy his needs as best he could. He would have been shocked to discover that he was in fact an evil man. He was an atheist who believed that man had created God in his own image in order to satisfy his need for hope. He frequently cited the numerous tragedies that befell the innocent as proof that God did not exist. If there was a God then surely He was a tyrant who trifled with the lives of His victims. That being the case, he quite naturally concluded that he had as much right to play god as anybody else. Strange though it may seem, he was correct in a way, but not in the manner that he supposed.

The boy was completely ignorant of the merchant's evil ways, but was determined, nevertheless, to resist. So when his new owner arrived to collect his chattel the boy picked up a rock and hurled it in his direction. The merchant stood a fair distance away, and the likelihood of hitting him seemed remote, if not virtually impossible. As if guided by angels the rock struck the merchant square in the forehead, knocking him out cold. He was seriously hurt, and lay in a coma for several days before finally giving up his hold on the body. In the boy's defense, he never meant to harm the merchant. Nevertheless, the local headman took him into custody.

Upon hearing of the merchant's death, the villagers descended upon his belongings in hopes of inheriting something of value. They stole everything they could carry, but after lugging it home discovered evidence linking the merchant to the bandits. The news of the merchant's betrayal made a hero of the boy, who quickly took advantage of the situation, claiming that he had seen the evidence for himself. He hadn't revealed the merchant's true identity because he didn't expect anyone to believe him. It was a plausible story, one that would alter the course of his life. To be sure, he lied about his motivation, but then a lie is only harmful when it visits pain and suffering upon others, not when it uplifts the human spirit.

After the bandit's fortuitous demise, the boy embarked on an amazing journey of transformation, beginning with an offer of employment from one of the local merchants. He had risen to the status of local hero, and the villagers never tired of hearing his account of the heroic deed. The boy relished the role, and was more than willing to elaborate on the finer details of his plan to take down a bandit. His listeners relished his stories and, while they may have doubted some of his more outrageous claims, it was an incontrovertible fact that he had single handedly killed the bandit. He even attracted the attention of the surrounding villages, and over time converted his notoriety into business relationships, which proved advantageous to the merchant who had hired him.

The employer came to look upon the boy as the son he never had, and eventually shifted responsibility for running the business onto his shoulders. When his employer passed away the boy was not at all surprised to learn that he had inherited the man's business. He had a natural talent for brokering lucrative business deals, and was particularly skilled at mediating disputes. He became quite successful by local standards, but never forgot his humble beginning, frequently employing those who had nothing in life, lest they succumb to life's inherent misery.

Given his change in status, he was now viewed as a suitable match for the girl who had inspired his rebellion in the first place. Despite the opportunity to marry almost any of the local girls, his heart belonged to his first love. She was older than he, but age and custom had no bearing upon his heart. As for the girl, she too had passed up offers of marriage, hoping that one day her family would consent to a marriage of the heart.

The girl was drawn to a quality in the boy that was difficult to explain, but a quality, nevertheless, there to behold. It wasn't his physical appearance, and it had little to do with his personality. It had to do with the joy that she felt whenever she was in his presence. There was no rational explanation, but the yogis who traveled the countryside had a word that described her experience. That word was 'karma'. They shared a karmic connection that was both positive and unique.

It seems they had been friends and lovers in prior lifetimes, creating a natural rapport that could not be denied. They were physically compatible, mentally attuned, and spiritually aligned, giving them three levels of consciousness in near perfect harmony. That left only their emotional natures in need of alignment. Despite their history together, emotional harmony had eluded them, not because they harbored any degree of animosity, but because the emotional body is inherently volatile. Thus their marriage was destined to harmonize all four levels of consciousness: physical, emotional, mental, and spiritual.

His dream at last fulfilled, the groom spared no expense, graciously inviting the neighboring villages to the wedding ceremony. Their vows were traditional, requiring the bride to swear obedience to her husband. It was a time-honored tradition, accepted even today, but only by the unenlightened, because even when mutually agreed upon, the resulting imbalance invariably breeds resentment. Their union, however, was not destined to be such a marriage, because they both understood the higher meaning of matrimony. For them marriage wasn't meant to define their respective roles, nor was it meant to make one of them happy at the expense of the other. Rather, marriage represented a commitment to their mutual happiness.

They recited their vows with sincerity, expressing a degree of tenderness that escaped the notice of all save the lovers themselves. True love illumined their eyes, revealing the most cherished gift of the heart: the gift of intimate wholeness. Truly, when the Love of the Soul infuses the personality, it attends not at all to the needs of the ego, but seeks only to serve the Soul of Humanity.

They anticipated a lifetime together, but destiny had other plans. He died while still a young man, the victim of a rampaging lion. His death came as a great shock, not only to his wife, but to his friends and associates, who mourned the loss of an uncommon man. The unenlightened, however, thought it likely that God had punished him for some hidden flaw. Perhaps his life had been a sham. Perhaps the village had been saved from his devious plans. If he was so good, why had God taken him so young?

Nonsense such as that never touched the heart of his grieving widow. She knew beyond any shadow of doubt that worldly conditions stemmed from causes long since set in motion. She therefore graciously accepted the notion of a karmic reason behind her husband's death. Knowing this, however, was not enough to prevent her heart from breaking, ultimately attracting the attention of her departed husband.

When he arrived on the other side his Beloved Master, fully ascended and forever beyond the gate, greeted him for the very first time since their association in Atlantis. Love thrilled every atom of his heavenly body, and he looked forward to taking his place at his Master's side. The Master, however, recognized the depth of his love for the woman he had left behind, and therefore granted him permission to walk the earth unseen at her side.

Ordinarily, the Law requires everyone to move on to other realms of consciousness from the moment of death. Of course, that requirement does not apply to those who have passed their lives in darkness. They remain earthbound, consumed by the fire that resides within their lower natures, be it a year, a decade, or a century. The exception to the rule allows the deceased to make occasional visits to friends and family. Rarest of all are those exceptions that allow the deceased to remain behind so that they might ply the earth unseen in the service of a loved one. It is a rare dispensation, one that is only granted to satisfy the love of the Soul, and not the longing of the personality.

So he came back through the gate, taking his place alongside his wife, only not in the flesh, but upon the etheric plane. He walked at her side for decades, forever wrapping her in love from the other side of the veil. This alone sustained her. The consequence for him was a life filled with excruciating pain, because the walk of the dead is ever so when bound to the physical world. There was no avoiding the throbbing ache that permeated every atom of his being, and yet he endured, taking solace in the comfort and joy he was able to impart to his beloved.

He cherished their time together and, even though he was not permitted to reveal himself, he knew that she was aware of his presence. It was a lonely time, because aside from those who are granted special dispensations, only the wicked and the deluded walk the earth so close to their former haunts. Not unexpectedly, there were times when he pondered what he had lost, most notably the opportunity to be reunited with his Beloved Master.

When at last she made her transition to the other side of the gate he was released from the earthbound world. His etheric body was dangerously depleted, requiring immediate care in one of the many etheric hospitals. As for his wife, she sloughed her astral body in a matter of hours, and then ascended into the realm of the Soul. Knowledge of his sacrifice affected her profoundly, setting in motion a chain of events that ultimately culminated in her final Initiation. She never saw her husband again, because the call to the flesh comes quickly for those who walk the earthbound world. Consequently, he was no sooner released from the hospital than he fell into a deep sleep, and next awakened as a babe in the arms of his dying mother.

LIFE TEN
The Psychic's Son

URING THE EARLY years of the Persian Empire, before the ascendancy of the Greeks and Romans, there was a group of men who wielded political power in a nation of perhaps half a million people. A king ruled the nation through the aegis of various regional tyrants who acceded to his authority only because it served their own interests. Once entrenched, they ruled corruptly, but soon discovered that neither gold nor sexual excess cured the emptiness of their lives. They were perverted men whose life styles were extravagant and sexual practices repugnant. They gave no care to their nation, and showed no concern for the people whose livelihoods they controlled. They crushed what opposition they could, and sought alliances with those they could not. They corrupted the principles that normally govern a healthy society whenever it suited their needs, and used their own peculiar brand of logic to invalidate commonsense. It was an age when reasonable men hid from public view; a time when superstition held sway over the imagination, allowing all manner of evil to creep into the minds of men.

Amid that setting there was a man who had attained fame and fortune through the use of his psychic ability. His talent was a legitimate gift, and when used for good he was able to help others in need of guidance. When misused, however, he cast a shadow over the lives of people who already lived in darkness. In the beginning he applied his talent wisely, using his psychic ability to help his clients make needed adjustments. Unfortunately, as the years passed his desire to help himself gradually replaced his desire to help others.

He never adequately understood the world of psychic phenomena, and therefore could not know that his ability was a function of his solar plexus chakra, one of seven major energy centers found in the body's etheric template. Each of those centers has a specific function, and together they condition human awareness, connecting mind and body to the surrounding environment. As its primary function, the solar plexus chakra processes the emotions, which necessarily distorts psychic perception. Within the solar plexus chakra, however, there exists a relatively unknown epicenter. That epicenter processes the loftier emotions, and produces psychic gifts born of love and service. Psychics steeped in dark motive invariably utilize the lower faculty, while the pure of heart employ the higher of the two. This particular individual manifested both the high and the low.

All that he really understood was that he could see into the future when he placed himself in an altered state of consciousness, which he accomplished by staring into a mirror. It was a dangerous practice that rendered his mind passive, thereby allowing the subconscious mind to intrude unimpeded. But that wasn't the end of the confusion, because, oddly enough, psychics are not only susceptible to intrusion from their own subconscious minds, but are also receptive to the subconscious minds of others. Had he truly aspired to a life of service he might have found a way out of his predicament, because selfless service invariably protects those who love their fellow man. On the other hand, the fault was not entirely his, because he served a community of lost souls fixated on the demands of their egos. They cared not at all for the truth, preferring instead the illusion of inflated self-esteem.

Having long since discovered that power and position rendered most people vulnerable to manipulation and intrigue, he lusted after absolute power. Both his wealth and his fame bequeathed a certain kind of power, but not the kind capable of crushing his enemies. For that he needed to be king. Only then could he fulfill his destiny.

The would-be king had a son, who he trained in the psychic arts. The son possessed a loftier nature than the father, and endeavored to apply his talent in service to others. The father had once pursued that same ideal, but had come to view public service as totally pointless. He therefore encouraged his son to employ his talent in the pursuit of fame and fortune. They fought bitterly over the issue of right and wrong and, as so often happens when clashing wills converge, one shattered, while the other grew stronger.

With the passage of time the father's obsession intensified, until he finally surrendered every last shred of his integrity. He began fabricating psychic phenomena in order to further manipulate of his clients, adding fraud and trickery to the gift he had already debased with unworthy motives. Weaving lies and half-truths into the fabric of his deceit, he seduced his followers with visions of greatness, pitting neighbor against neighbor whenever it suited his purpose. Lives were destroyed, but still they trusted him, insisting on the privilege of continuing to pay the inflated fees he demanded for psychic consultations. It made no logical sense – unless you consider the logic of deception. His clients accepted whatever he proffered because he always baited his hook with the worm of seduction. Each and every client was first soothed, then flattered, and finally exalted. In such a manner were they rendered ripe for intrigue.

The son was the better man. He knew in his heart that his father was wrong, that he had forsaken his principles for the glitter of gold, whether that gold ultimately landed in his purse, or upon his head in the form of a crown. He understood the difference between right and wrong, and yet he gave in to his father, and chose a path he knew to be wrong. Following his father's example, he embraced his lower nature and started using his psychic gifts to further his own agenda.

It wasn't long before the son's mental health deteriorated. The persistent violation of what he knew to be right carried him to that place where sanity gives way to the chaos of a mind in tatters. Little did he know, but unrelenting guilt eventually assumes a life of its own, ultimately taking full possession of the mind.

Some people violate their principles with impunity, apparently without consequence, while others suffer terrible anguish in the unforgiving grasp of their conscience. The lack of conscience, frequently characterized by the absence of both remorse and compassion, is most often associated with sociopathic personalities; however, it is also indicative of those who tread the Path of No Return, having consciously made the choice to violate the Soul of Humanity.

Given his karmic history, it should not surprise you to learn that the son started hearing accusatory voices, seemingly arriving from somewhere outside of his head. He immediately suspected the people he had defrauded and deceived. They were obviously retaliating, intent on driving him mad. He knew that he had to stop the charade, that his sanity was at stake, but he blamed his father instead.

Terrorized by the prospect of insanity, the son begged his father for permission to retire from their loathsome occupation. Unmoved, the father denounced him as a worthless ingrate. They had, he pointed out, achieved both status and privilege well beyond the reach of all but the very few. Besides, events were unfolding according to plan, and he would soon be wearing a golden crown upon his head. He would be king, and no son of his was going to interfere with such a lofty plan. Once ascended to the throne his cooperation would no longer be needed, but until that day arrived he demanded absolute obedience.

Insanity beckoned, its hand firm but alluring, as if promising release from unbearable suffering. The son awoke from his dream knowing that it was his father's hand that had beckoned. He had blamed his father and, on rare occasions, had even denounced him, and yet he had never acknowledged the fact that his father was an evil man. So evil, in fact, that he was willing to sacrifice his son.

Truly, his father was a predator who hunted by the light of the moon, always lusting for the next feeding frenzy, always careful to pick the bones clean, lest the scavengers share in his delight. However, nothing lasts forever. Beneath all that evil something finally snapped, precipitating a dream so terrible and so evil that the father awoke permanently insane. He raved at the top of his lungs; he destroyed valuable furnishings accumulated through years of avaricious living; he rammed his head into the walls, staining valuable tapestry with his blood. They had no choice but to lock him in a barren room with guards at the door.

It sometimes happens that the death of a parent releases the child from psychological bondage, but in this case insanity served the same purpose. The tables had turned, and the father had descended into hell in place of the son, who had no sympathy for the man who had knowingly led him to the brink of insanity.

The son immediately canceled all of his appointments, and announced that for reasons of health he was no longer granting psychic consultations. His relief was overwhelming, immediately arresting his descent into madness. Surely the nightmare was over. Why else had the accusatory voices miraculously ceased? Such miracles do occur, but the truth of the matter is that miracles are rarely bestowed unless karmic conditions demand relief. His karma made no such demand.

The citizenry refused to accept his retirement. He had provided a valuable service, and they expected him to continue his work regardless of the fate that had befallen his father. Intent on having their way, they camped at his door and clamored for his presence. He had hoped to avoid being unmasked, fully expecting the mob to tear him to pieces if the truth was ever revealed, but they gave him no choice. Trembling with fear, he faced the crowd and confessed his sins. He revealed sexual encounters with their loved ones, and admitted to pitting neighbor against neighbor. Last of all, he confessed to no longer possessing a shred of valid psychic ability.

Expecting the worst, he made ready to dash back into the house, but instead froze in his tracks when the crowd implored him to take up his work exactly as he had in the past. They simply could not accept the fact that he was a fraud, because in their estimation everything he had ever told them had been entirely accurate. From a certain twisted point of view they were absolutely right. He had, after all, validated their most cherished beliefs, thereby fueling their every fantasy. Perhaps the biggest surprise of all was the fact that the entire population wasn't certifiably insane, although maybe they were, given their propensity for self-deception.

Late that night the crowd stalked its prey, having decided that he had in fact deceived them. Otherwise, he would have agreed to their demands.

At first it seemed as though the noise was coming from the street, but upon closer inspection it became apparent that the clamor originated not in the street, but at his front door. An unruly crowd had surrounded the building, some wielding firebrands, others urging them on. They set fire to the house, driving the inhabitants into the street, except for the father, who was left behind in the rush. By the time anyone noticed it was too late. Suffice it to say, the father's death was not an illuminating experience, despite the blazing inferno that enveloped his departure from the world.

They dragged the son into the street, kicking and screaming every step of the way. The voices were back, and he felt every bit like a bear on a rope spanning an abyss. Hyperventilation came next, each failed breath striking a blow to the rope, until at last he toppled, tremors vibrating through body, mind, and soul. When he came to his senses he was covered in filth, face down in a ditch. The smell was atrocious, but in that era it was considered par for the course. Sanitation was unheard of, and everything, including human waste, was routinely tossed into the roadside ditch. The ditch was periodically dredged, but on any given day it was laden with all manner of disease-ridden refuse. He immediately ran to the fountain in the center of town, where he washed the stench from his trembling body before returning to his burned-out mansion.

He had no choice but to run for his life. He had heard captivating accounts about life in the Greek islands, and now, in the throes of despair, he clung to his only hope of peace and tranquility. The very thought quieted his mind, allowing a small ray of hope into the darkness that possessed his soul. He traveled on foot, using the collection of coins that had survived the fire for food and lodging. He had just enough gold to make a fresh start, but he would have to be careful, because the lure of riches could cost him his life.

Unaccustomed to the rigors of life on the road, he was pleasantly surprised to find the journey invigorating. He couldn't help but notice that the voices in his head had subsided, that he was sleeping and eating better than he had in years. Whether it was because he had finally rejected a life given over to greed and deception, or because he was totally preoccupied with the daily routine of life on the road, he didn't know. Whatever the cause, he accepted the results. And yet, vigilance remained his daily companion, because the voices could still be heard whispering in the background of his mental amphitheater.

Soon after arriving on the island of Crete he acquired a home overlooking the sea. He took a vow to never again use his psychic faculties and, rather than risk any reoccurrence of past mistakes, he chose a reclusive lifestyle. Celibacy appealed to his nature, given the wanton abuse that had marred his past; and asceticism appealed to his conscience, given his need to atone for past transgressions. Thus he never reached out to the local community, slowly turning their goodwill into casual avoidance, followed by total rejection. If he had integrated into the community, made friends, and perhaps even married and raised a family he might have escaped the torment that awaited him.

Years passed with almost no reoccurrence of the voices. In the end, however, sustained isolation ultimately charged his subconscious mind with inordinate power. Thus did his guilt take voice, attacking with a barrage of withering accusations; while his rage, long suppressed and totally malicious, took up the cudgel and lobbied for his death.

In the final analysis it was guilt that destroyed him. His guilt awakened ancient memories from his karmic past, thereby unleashing a mighty wave of destruction. Thus empowered, guilt rampaged through his psyche with all the paralytic power of an arctic ice flow, ultimately glaciating his will to live. But that wasn't the full extent of his misery. In the depths of his being there burned a fierce rage just waiting for an opportunity to wreak havoc. Thus the frigid waters of unrelenting guilt encountered the flames of hell-born rage, and the resulting mist clouded his mind once and for all. That's when he picked up a table knife and sliced open the carotid artery running down the left side of his neck. Blood gushed onto the floor, splashing and puddling at his feet, dolefully announcing his arrival in the earthbound world.

LIFE ELEVEN
The Solitary Monk

ERCHED ON THE edge of the world, the Solitary
Monk watched the migrating clouds as they slowly
wrapped around the mountain. Birds sailed effortlessly
on the wind, winging and gliding in perfect harmony with
the rhythm of his breath. A gentle breeze accompanied the
hypnotic movement of the flock, rippling his tunic as if
encouraging him to take flight. In point of fact he was saying
his last good-byes to the only home he had known for many
years. He would miss the serenity of the mountain, and he
would miss the old deserted monastery that had given him
refuge. As a young man he had retreated to the monastery in
search of enlightenment, and was now preparing to go forth
in order to share his discoveries.

He grew up in a small Himalayan hamlet, and had grown
accustomed to a slow, uneventful life long before retreating
to the monastery. As a boy he had minimal contact with
the outside world, except during the summer months when
trade caravans sometimes detoured through his part of the
world. The men who worked the caravans generally stayed
to themselves, but occasionally stopped and shared their
adventures in exchange for food and shelter. That, however,
was not his only contact with the outside world.

His family was related to a Lama who resided in a not
too distant lamasery, which is how he became acquainted

with the ascetic ways of the Himalayan monks. The old Lama recognized his potential and, despite the hardship of the journey, had made an effort to occasionally visit the family. Trapped in the village one winter by any early and unexpected storm, the Lama passed the winter instructing the boy. The boy felt a natural rapport with his teacher, and soon demonstrated a capacity for long hours of meditation. When the snow melted and the passes were once again safe to travel, the Lama promised to return, and upon his return he promised to reveal the location of an abandoned monastery suitable for retreat if ever the need arose.

Suspended amongst of the clouds, the Solitary Monk tried to remember how many years it had been since he had last seen the Lama. The old Lama no longer resided among the living; however, the memory of his teacher had never failed to carry him through those times when loneliness invaded the top of the world. True to his promise, the Lama had introduced him to the abandoned monastery, perhaps sensing, even then, that the day would eventually arrive when his student longed for solitude.

During his formative years he had been prone to anger and frustration, followed shortly thereafter by bouts of depression. Back then he had little patience for people who demanded love and understanding, but offered little of the same in their daily interactions with others. He expected everyone to aspire to their highest potential, and therefore judged others harshly when they failed to meet his lofty expectations. Eventually he came to the realization that he too had failed to live up to his highest potential, expecting as he did, only the highest and best from himself. Consequently, whenever love and understanding eluded his grasp, he struggled with the contradiction between his aspiration and his behavior, which ultimately drove him to the mountaintop retreat.

Not unexpectedly, life at the monastery presented its own problems. The isolation charged his subconscious mind with an unusual intensity, sometimes manifesting as auditory aberrations. It wasn't at all unusual for him to hear voices emanating from the environment, disconnected phrases wholly unrelated to his state of mind. Because he was an experienced meditator, he was familiar with incursions upon the sanctity of his mind, and therefore rarely attempted to analyze their content. It happened, however, that the voices occasionally gave expression to thoughts and feelings undoubtedly his own. So he ultimately took the matter into meditation, intent on discovering their source. Little did he know, but the ego itself is a mental construction, consisting of a complex network of lesser identities. Therefore, tampering with the ego's infrastructure, especially within the context of meditation, necessarily threatens its stability.

Despite weeks of meditation exploring the connection between his auditory hallucinations and the content of his mind, he arrived at no meaningful conclusions. Nothing changed, except perhaps his relationship with the mountain. Its quiet splendor, its soothing rhythm, and its gentle pulse no longer lifted his spirits. So he abandoned his enquiry into the nature of his auditory hallucinations, resuming instead the practice of meditation upon the nature of the Buddha.

Meanwhile, mesmerized by the billowing clouds, he momentarily forgot that he was precariously perched on the edge of the world. Temporary disorientation had never really concerned him, because he had always been able to quickly reorient himself. Still, he couldn't help but recall the time he had ignored the fall of night upon a moonless sky, and had consequently succumbed to the effects of disorientation. It was an error in judgment that had nearly cost him his life. Despite the clarity of that frightening memory, he quickly transcended any sense of danger, slipping effortlessly into deep meditation. It would be his last meditation before departing his mountaintop retreat.

One might think that meditation upon the Buddha could only be uplifting; however, it sometimes happens that the Soul meditates upon something entirely different, invariably catching the personality off guard. In this particular case the Solitary Monk was presented with the image of his own dead body. He was dead, his body displayed in an old, battered box. His yellowed skin was taut and strangely translucent, while his hair, wild and unkempt, did nothing to lessen the shocking specter of his decaying flesh. A ripple of despair suddenly corrupted the placid surface of his awareness, threatening to wreak havoc upon his inner world. But then it occurred to him that the image of his dead body was undoubtedly symbolic, portending not death, but personal transformation. In fact, images of death do sometimes herald fundamental changes in consciousness; however, more often than not their only function is to alert the personality to impending disaster.

Truth, having found a willing receptacle, was not yet done with the Solitary Monk. Once again images of death assailed his meditation, only this time he was confronted with a throng of corpses. As if that wasn't enough, they were pointing directly at him, all the while whispering in concert. The actual words escaped his comprehension, but their meaning was all too clear. They were chanting a dirge meant just for him. He immediately terminated his meditation, focusing instead upon his bodily sensations, thereby reclaiming his hold on physical reality.

It was a strange, unnerving experience and it shook him to the core. The vision depicting his death was almost certainly symbolic, but the whispering dead somehow made death a tangible reality. The whole experience made no logical sense, so he decided to once again enter meditation in search of an explanation.

Seeking to activate the power and presence of his Soul, he imagined a stream of Light descending into the crown of his head. Almost immediately his breath assumed a deep, rhythmic pattern, relaxing body and mind while at the same time banishing fear and confusion. Next he briefly pondered the meaning of the whispering dead, certain that guidance would follow. And so it did, revealing the truth concealed within his vision. The meaning, he discovered, was unrelated to his life as a monk, but related to a previous incarnation. Chanting the Om, he consciously directed Love and Light to the source of the problem, thereby releasing the whole affair into God's hands.

Upon concluding his meditation, the Solitary Monk said good-bye to the mountain and began his descent to the world below, fully expecting to spread the Buddha's message. The Buddha had walked amongst the common folk, and he intended to follow in his footsteps. He could see it all in his mind, but what he could not see was his karmic past slowly approaching the light of day. The karma of the Whispering Dragon was coming to the fore, trailing disaster in its wake.

Enlightenment was his goal and service to humanity was his method. So he set out in search of pilgrims toiling upon the Path, fully expecting to encounter travelers of similar temperament. He was a man driven by a mighty purpose; a man who never contemplated the possibility of failure. Nor did he anticipate the chain of events that would ultimately cost him his life.

It wasn't very long before he came upon a caravan of traders intent on reaching their base of operations before the onset of winter. They were hardened men who never looked kindly upon strangers, men who expected the worst from everybody they encountered. Still, they gave the monk no mind when he fell in at their side, because he obviously presented no threat. Besides, they were behind the season, and intent on making up time; hence, it was only natural that the monk should bear a share of the load.

The Solitary Monk found it hard to accept his newfound friends. Their manners were non-existent, their habits disgusting, and their dispositions sour to say the least. And yet he remained undeterred, repeatedly chanting the Om, constantly reaffirming his commitment to share his enlightened state of mind. Nevertheless, he had to acknowledge that the task before him was more difficult than he ever could have imagined. Ruffled, but undaunted, he was a determined man, wholly intent on discovering the true pilgrims amongst that band of smelly folk.

Truth be told, he would have rendered a greater service had he remained on the mountaintop chanting the Om. The Om carries power when sent forth with a loving heart; however, when confronted with scoundrels it's best to send that love from afar. His new companions were loveless men, and loveless men usually resent the imposition of goodwill. Ever the earmark of civilized humanity, goodwill threatens the uncivilized brutes of the world, seemingly casting a spell over their evil intentions. They prefer a firm grasp on reality, and therefore find goodwill nearly impossible to comprehend, because the more it's shared, the more it spreads, until it's completely out of their control.

There were no lambs amongst that motley crew of misfits. Truly, there were no pilgrims in that collection of dullards. They were loners by nature, and they wanted to remain in harmony with their natures. They tolerated him as long as he packed a load, and if he packed it in silence so much the better. Unfortunately for the Solitary Monk, he never comprehended the fact that, despite repeated warnings, he was endangering his life by constantly meddling in their affairs. If that band of misfits feared anything, it was someone who failed to recognize impending danger. It was completely unnatural, and could only mean one of two things. The monk was either completely witless, and therefore a liability they could not afford, or he was so cunning as to be an immediate threat to life and limb.

The Solitary Monk had one last penetrating insight into the temperament of that strange cast of characters; one last glimpse into the sturdy resolve of men working in concert towards a common goal. At the end of the day they caucused and promptly arrived at a unanimous decision.

He knew that something was wrong, because he had never before witnessed them standing around with idle hands. And yet, there they were, whispering secrets. He couldn't hear what was being said, but he certainly paused and considered the fact that whispers had recently touched upon his life. Those whispers had reeked of death, and something about the mood of his companions carried that same scent. He wasn't the least bit surprised when they seized him about the limbs and flung him off the mountain.

He passed the gate in a state of shock, not because his traveling companions had tossed him to his death, but because he had lost his voice somewhere between the fall and his arrival on the other side of the gate. As a result he could only whisper. And whenever he whispered his spirit guides couldn't help but wince, knowing as they did, that in another time and place he had exhibited more than a passing interest in whispers.

LIFE TWELVE
The Hardheaded Disciple

WHEN STILL A boy he was accepted as a disciple by an itinerant guru, and together they wandered the land, keeping to the forests, rarely entering the villages that dotted the countryside. They lived off the land, but also depended upon the kindness of strangers for life's necessities. His guru differed from other teachers in that he neither taught nor practiced the extremes commonly associated with asceticism. Rather, he respected his body, eating only fruits and vegetables, while carefully attending to his hygiene. His teacher traveled without encumbrance, carrying only a few cherished possessions, most notably a sacred amulet depicting the likeness of the Buddha. One might therefore conclude that his guru was a Buddhist; however, he did not adhere to any particular religion. In point of fact, he worshipped the Creator, and taught, as the Buddha had before him, that everything in the universe was a manifestation of God.

Due to his lineage the guru had received an unadulterated version of the Buddha's message, completely free of the distortions that have corrupted His Wisdom down through the ages. For example, modern Buddhists deny the fact of reincarnation, the uninterrupted flow of consciousness from one life to the next. The Buddha had no quarrel with the physical evolution of the body; however, he also taught that the evolution of consciousness was the product of the Wheel of Rebirth.

After each lesson imparted, the guru required his disciple to take the lesson material into meditation until its meaning was adequately assimilated, followed by a discourse on his findings. The guru did not accept halfhearted effort, nor did he allow his disciple to terminate his meditation before demonstrating the required level of understanding. Even that was no reprieve, because the guru invariably returned to the same lesson at a later date, requiring still more meditation.

With the passage of time the Disciple gradually mastered the basics of yogic philosophy, only to become totally enamored with his intellect. That's when he started arguing with his guru, asserting his right to disagree with his teacher. The guru, rightfully dismayed by his student's disrespect, adopted the practice of whacking him over the head with his walking stick each and every time he went too far. Much to the guru's surprise his strategy had no effect upon the Disciple. Whenever he whacked him over the head he simply continued arguing as if nothing had happened. There was nothing to do but whack him harder, and to do so immediately upon the first sign of disrespect.

Striking students was an accepted, time-honored tradition in ancient India. When properly applied by a wise and loving guru, the blow, whether by hand, foot, or stick, carried with it the spiritual power of the guru, thus serving to awaken the consciousness of the recipient. The strikes applied to the Disciple, however, carried no such power, because only teachers and students sharing significant karmic history were able to invoke the ancient practice of guru strikes. The practice is no longer necessary, because the inner bodies of modern students are more refined, and therefore more receptive to the influx of spiritual energy.

The Disciple knew full well that his guru intended a lesson when he struck him with his walking stick, so he rarely took it personally, but viewed the practice from his own peculiar frame of reference. It seems he sought a collegial relationship with his guru, and in his inflated self-appraisal imagined that he was imparting a lesson by silently ignoring the whacks to his head.

Determined to earn his guru's respect, the Disciple periodically redoubled his efforts, sometimes increasing the frequency and duration of his meditations, sometimes trying his best to listen and learn without starting an argument. Upon recognizing his student's resolve, the guru always responded with lessons designed to elicit yet higher levels of awareness.

In many respects the Disciple's progress under the tutelage of his guru was nothing short of spectacular. He was, after all, becoming an accomplished practitioner of the Yogic arts. There was, however, a major flaw in his development – he continued to rely upon his intellect no matter the situation, completely overlooking the importance of love and understanding. He valued the intellect over the heart, and therefore saw no reason to stop arguing with his guru. He did, however, make one concession. First thing each morning he wrapped his head in a towel, lest he accrue yet another lump before the last one had healed.

Lest you imagine that the Disciple's granite-like head rendered him incapable of any emotion, you should know that his emotions sometimes got the better of him. On those occasions when his feelings cut anchor, he invariably found himself floundering in the uncharted waters of his ego. Consequently, old karmic patterns emerged, and his guru became the father who had failed to recognize the worth of a dutiful son.

Determined not to inflame the situation, the guru made a practice of ignoring his angry outbursts as unworthy of comment. He fully appreciated the distinction between his disciple's generally disputatious nature, and the meanness that characterized his outbursts. One stemmed from his ego's natural resistance to discipline, while the other stemmed from a difficult karmic condition. To be sure, every psychological dynamic contains karmic components; however, only those that result from either traumatic events or repetitive occurrence are considered karmic in nature. In this particular case the Disciple's problem was rooted in another lifetime, and was so powerfully cathected that the guru had no choice but to stand clear. Fortunately for the Disciple, the guru always forgave him. It made for quite a contrast in styles, because when the Disciple argued with the guru, he received a whack to the head; but when he attacked his guru as if he were a neglectful father, the guru always responded with love and forgiveness. The guru saw no contradiction and the Disciple saw no reason to change his behavior.

It happened that the Disciple fell into one of his funks, only this time, rather than berate his guru he collected his belongings and departed rather smartly, thereby signifying that he had arrived at a momentous decision. Predictably, he didn't go far, but hid in the forest and waited for the guru to call him home. Hours later, having discerned no visible change in the guru's routine, he returned, ardently announcing his intention to leave and not return. Never one to argue, the guru agreed that perhaps the time had come for him to set out on his own.

In the end the Disciple experienced a change of heart, although he saw no reason to change his behavior. There was, however, one notable development. Towel in hand, he approached the guru and asked why, despite years of study and meditation, he had failed to attain enlightenment. The guru reminded him that the answer to his question could only be found within, that he should take the matter into meditation.

Retreating to a secluded spot, the Disciple first relaxed his body, followed by his favorite breath technique. Focusing his attention upon the sacred center located in the brow, he soon reached that place where the inner dialogue subsides and total concentration upon the object of meditation is achieved.

While contemplating the essence of enlightenment, a disagreeable scene unexpectedly appeared upon the inner screen of his mind. His meditations had always been peaceful, if not uplifting; therefore, he never expected an image capable of evoking fear and revulsion. And seeing himself lying at the bottom of a ditch, covered in filth and half out of his mind, certainly qualified as both terrifying and repugnant. Something had gone seriously wrong. What else could possibly account for such a ghastly scene?

Utterly dismayed, the Disciple recounted his vision and confessed his total lack of understanding. The guru responded by guiding him through several rounds of alternate nostril breathing, thereby calming his emotions. He explained that the cells of the body harbor countless memories, many of them stemming from other lifetimes. Furthermore, when awakened those memories were capable of imposing their burden upon the present.

Revealing a method for removing unwanted memories, the guru explained that powerful emotions, whether deeply etched through constant repetition, or through a single traumatic event, were extremely difficult to purge. Nevertheless, it was possible to remove them by sending Love to the source of the problem. So the Disciple entered meditation and, having reached his usual state of heightened awareness, he visualized a beautiful beam of Ruby Red Light raying out from the sacred center located in the middle of his chest, directing it to the man he had once been, the man lying at the bottom of a ditch. There was nothing else to be done.

It was a compelling experience, so compelling in fact, that the Disciple thought that he had completely purged the negativity associated with the image. Little did he know, but one application, no matter how powerful the energy, rarely purges deeply imbedded memory patterns. The Soul lives in the eternal now, and when the personality undertakes to purify the past, the Soul understands that only so much can be achieved in any given moment.

The years peeled away and, even though the guru no longer whacked him over the head with his walking stick, and despite a lifetime of study and meditation, the Disciple never stopped arguing with his guru, until the day finally arrived when his guru passed over to the other side. Never one to become overly attached, the Disciple accepted the death of his guru with equanimity, and immediately departed for the Himalayas in search of a new teacher. Once there he discovered men not unlike himself, men enamored with their intellects, and therefore wholly unfit to teach. Pondering this unexpected revelation, he realized that his guru must have been a Saint, because he had actually lived the principles that he taught.

Asking for guidance, the Disciple entered meditation, thereby drawing his recently departed guru to the scene. Communicating telepathically, the guru gently guided his disciple's meditation, encouraging him to meditate upon the Inner Silence. Not unexpectedly, the Disciple at first resisted the suggestion, but after mulling it over for several minutes decided to follow his guru's advice and began contemplating the Inner Silence. Unfortunately, every time his inner dialogue faded into the background he immediately engaged his intellect. Needless to say, Inner Silence can not be achieved until the inner dialogue subsides and the intellect is put to rest.

Having failed to attain Inner Silence, the Disciple decided to continue his quest at a higher elevation, somewhere closer to God. He ascended alone, and in due course discovered a mountaintop retreat, abandoned and long since overrun by Mother Nature. Ignoring the howling wind and freezing cold, he assumed the lotus position and entered meditation. The story goes that the guru once again communicated with his disciple and advised him to go back down the mountain before it was too late. The story further goes that the Disciple argued right up until his last breath.

LIFE THIRTEEN
The Champ

L ONG BEFORE THE Romans became a militarized force in the world, the Greeks nurtured the flame of civilization, legitimately laying claim to a special place in human history. They borrowed much of their inspiration from India, just as India borrowed much of her inspiration from Atlantis. India preserved the spiritual essence of Atlantis, but never fully embraced the Atlantean passion for democracy, passing that particular legacy on to the Greeks, who fell in love with free speech, individual rights, and representative government; and who were endlessly fascinated with the portrayal of those democratic ideals through the medium of the dramatic arts. They were, after all, concepts that engendered powerful reactions, both capturing the imagination and challenging the traditions of the past. They loved the playwright, and they loved the dramatist who depicted the challenges confronting everyday citizens. Not surprisingly, their love of drama extended beyond the stage to include the realm of professional sports.

Their athletes were supported by wealthy benefactors, men who deluded themselves into believing that the young men they supported were manifestations of their own egos. The athletes themselves accepted and maintained the illusion, not only because they depended upon their benefactors for financial support, but because they too were products of their culture. They competed as a way of life, and accepted the fact that others were viewed as the source of prowess behind their achievements. When it came to actual competition, however, they competed not for their benefactors, but for the glory of personal victory. Accordingly, they exhibited the same commitment and dedication as the modern athlete, only they never had an off-season.

The most popular sports were of the track and field variety, although for many enthusiasts wrestling was the only sport that truly measured the heart of a champion. Their style of wrestling was similar to the modern version, but with fewer rules, and a number of holds unknown in today's world. With few rules to control the violence, and holds that attacked the integrity of the body's joints, the sport of wrestling was undeniably vicious. A great many competitors were seriously injured, while others were killed in the arena.

The men who rose to prominence in the sport of wrestling received the highest accolades, and therefore attracted the wealthiest benefactors. Because the sport was prone to serious injury, careers were generally short-lived, and once a career was over the limelight was lost forever. The Greeks loved their athletes, but cared little for anyone past their prime. You were either a shining star, or a meteor plummeting to earth. Popularity rested not upon the laurels of the past, but on the hope of a glorious future, and athletes past their prime had little enough of either.

Every age produces its heroic figures, those who transcend the benchmark of past accomplishment, attaining heights that so inspire the imagination of the society in which they live that they are forever immortalized. Every athlete aspires to such greatness, but only a few realize the fulfillment of their dreams. This is the tale of such a man, a wrestler who achieved immortality during the Golden Age of Pericles.

He was the greatest wrestling champion of all time, and until his recent loss he had gone undefeated in 44 brutal bouts.

It was an unheard of achievement, and as far as the record book went, no one else had ever come close to winning that many consecutive competitions. He was a natural born athlete with an incredible physique, almost from the day of his birth, although long years of training in the gymnasium had certainly added to his enormous bulk. In point of fact, he trained with a vengeance that could only be rooted in the depths of his karmic past. His training methods, like his holds, were noted and copied, but the aura of invincibility that emanated from his presence could not be replicated.

He was returning to the arena not only as the ex-champion, but as the underdog for the first time in his career. He was 27 years old and his body was already showing signs of abuse, ever the harbinger of deteriorating skills. For years he had been the most popular athlete in all of Greece, and even now, anticipating his arrival in the arena, the crowd was going wild for the legend of the sport. His one and only loss had not relegated him to the realm of the forgotten, because he had risen to the very pinnacle, and his fall, unlike that of the lesser gods, would be long and slow.

When the Champ was undefeated his benefactor had enjoyed celebrity status, but now that the Champ's career was coming to a close the benefactor was preparing to drop his support. This represented no small concern for the Champ, for the simple reason that years of dedication to the sport had created a void when it came to marketable skills. He had begun his training at an early age, embarking on his wrestling career before the age of seventeen, never anticipating his inevitable departure from the sport. The years had passed quickly, leaving behind a host of aches and pains, including the specter of diminishing prospects. Consequently, when he lost his last match, it seemed that he had lost everything. Fortunately, his brother, a brilliant politician and man about Athens, came to the rescue. He knew that the Champ could never leave the sport with his tail between his legs, and therefore encouraged him to reacquire the crown. So the Champ went into seclusion, determined to train harder than ever before, but also determined to come up with a plan that would give him an edge, and once again place the laurel of victory within his grasp.

The Champ had a glorious past, not only because of his physical prowess, but because of his unique fighting style. His most famous move was a jujitsu-like charge to the feet of his opponents, but instead of grappling his opponents to the ground, he lifted them off their feet and hurled them through the air. Strength and quickness alone were not enough to make the move a success. The correct placement of the hands and feet was essential, as was the proper alignment of the spine. When properly executed according to the laws of physics the Champ exploded up off the ground as if launched from the netherworld. Not a few of his adversaries finished the match the moment they landed, because the Champ could hurl a man six feet into the air. If, at that point, they refused to submit, the Champ wrapped his massive hands around their skulls, viciously twisting their necks into obscene contortions. Permanent neck injuries were not uncommon, and purple bruises encompassing the skull served notice that the Champ had been there.

He was the prototype, and his success had bred a generation of clones trained to beat him at his own game. They trained harder and they trained smarter, until finally one of the young bucks embarrassed him in the arena. Had he been in his prime the Champ would have undoubtedly defeated his challenger. Instead, for the first time in his life, he was forced to endure his opponent's insults.

Casting his gaze upon the crowd, the Champ caught the eye of his benefactor, and noticed that his usual look of pride was absent. When the Champ was winning the benefactor was revered as the heart and soul of a champion who had dominated a generation of talent. Now that the Champ had lost his crown, the benefactor's self-esteem had plummeted along with the adulation he had enjoyed. The benefactor would have to find another champion. It seems he was addicted to the glory of athletic prowess, even if someone else expressed it for him.

When the Champ entered the arena the spectators cheered and shouted until they were hoarse; then they stomped their feet on the stone slabs that encircled the arena. The slabs were arranged in tiers and were not, as is commonly thought, meant for seating, but for standing. They stomped their feet until they ached, honoring the man who had attained the eerie heights of the gods. They weren't ready to resize the image, because the man so closely fit the icon that they could barely comprehend the fact that they had lived in his lifetime.

Momentarily overwhelmed by the pandemonium, the Champ was carried back in time, back to the early years of his career, a time when the taste of victory magically splashed his palate whenever he stepped into the arena. It was a familiar taste, and just then he longed for the reassurance it afforded. He would not be disappointed.

It's hard say for certain whether it was the mood of the crowd, or the memories of past glory that enflamed his already palpable desire for revenge. For whatever reason, he knew then that he was about to unleash a lifetime of pain upon his opponent. The man had forfeited any possibility of a normal life when he swaggered around the arena after their last match. The Champ had never belittled an opponent, but the man had mocked him in public, unwittingly choosing the life of an invalid.

When the umpire signaled the start of the match the Champ charged across the arena like an enraged bull protecting its turf. His opponent was ready and, with impeccable timing, leapt into the air at the last possible second in order to avoid the Champ's famous 'dive and toss'. Unfortunately for him the Champ had anticipated his countermove. Instead of diving at his opponent's feet, the Champ struck a mighty blow, driving his massive fist deep into his opponent's abdomen. The impact was awesome to behold; all the more so because his adversary's feet never touched the ground. He landed on his back six feet from the point of impact. Phase one of his new strategy was an indisputable success, so much so that it stunned the crowd into total silence.

Approaching the semi-conscious casualty, the Champ initiated phase two, a bellowing roar that echoed through the stadium, sending chills up every spine within its vibratory range. It was an astonishing replication of a lion's roar, a sound that awakened frightening memories from man's ancient past. It was the roar of the jungle beast passing benediction upon its prey, a sound that filled the spectators with paralytic dread, leaving them utterly fixated upon the scene playing out before their eyes.

Dazed and defenseless, his opponent somehow managed a four-point stance. There was no way of knowing for sure whether he was trying to launch a defense, or simply trying to crawl out of the arena. The Champ wasn't going to allow either course of action. His blood was up, and the only question that remained unanswered was whether he would kill his adversary or cripple him for life. The truth be known, the Champ just wanted to administer a beating that would discourage the man from ever mocking another human being.

Before his opponent could collect his wits and concede the match, the Champ clapped his enormous hands together, striking his quarry with enough force to explode both of his eardrums. Hovering over his victim, the Champ watched with dark, pitiless eyes. All the while his vanquished foe whimpered like a wounded dog, which only served to enrage the attacking beast.

Never one to tolerate a coward, the Champ grabbed his victim by the arms and, beginning with small, stuttering steps, rotated in a circle until his opponent was lifted up off the ground. He swung the howling fiend in an arc from high to low, and when he couldn't hold on any longer, he released his grip on the upward arc, sending his opponent sailing into the crowd, knocking a dozen or more to the ground. When it was over the crowd didn't know whether to cheer the resurrection of their hero, or turn their backs on the most vicious attack they had ever witnessed in the arena. The benefactor, on the other hand, had regained his honor and reasserted his status. Dumbfounded, the Champ's brother couldn't help but wonder just what planet his brother was from.

Believing that he had administered a well-deserved beating, the Champ was totally satisfied with his performance, no matter what his detractors said about his violent behavior. It was a feat that would never be surpassed - the perfect time to retire as a champion. It was almost unheard of to go out a winner, but the Champ wasn't the type to linger past his prime, nor was he the type to coach the younger athletes. He truly loved the brutality of the sport more than he loved the sport itself. It was only by the grace of God that he had found an outlet in the arena and not on some field of battle. Life, however, is a continuing saga, and even then the vital threads of his next incarnation were being woven into the fabric of a warrior's life.

Besides the spectacle of his grand finale, the closest the Champ ever came to killing a man occurred a few months later when a political adversary assaulted his brother, breaking his nose with a service tray. The Champ seized the perpetrator by the throat, effortlessly lifting him up off the ground. He never acknowledged the onlookers' pleas for mercy, but steadily applied his massive strength until his victim's face turned blue, his lips dark purple. The Champ stared directly into the eyes of his prey, watching his life slowly ebb away, totally oblivious to the crescendo of pleas pelting his ears. Just when it seemed his victim would surely succumb, the Champ eased his grip and waited for the light of consciousness to once again flicker in his eyes. Then he struck a mighty blow to the malefactor's head, crushing every bone in his face.

The Champ had disfigured others in his time, but he had never before reduced a man to the reclusive life of a social outcast. The victim's larynx was permanently damaged, resulting in a squeaky, feminine sounding noise whenever he spoke. What's more, besides the damage done to his nose, his cheekbones were shattered, his facial features distorted beyond recognition. He never regained his former appearance, his countenance permanently resembling an actor's death mask - somewhat suggestive of a human face. No longer active in pubic affairs, he rarely left the family home, and never made another public appearance.

The victim's family members thought to hire assassins, but were quickly persuaded against such an extreme course of action when the Champ visited their home and presented his wrestling crown as compensation. Once they got a look at the Champ they realized that it would take an army of assassins to avenge the family's loss of honor. Obviously, it was best to leave well enough alone. If their attempt failed no one in the family would ever again be safe. Making a gesture to ensure closure, the Champ's brother brokered a deal that proved to be extremely favorable to the family. The family grew accustomed to their disfigured member and eventually came to view the trade-off in a positive light.

The brother, though troubled by the Champ's violent outburst, never rebuked him. Instead, he began tutoring him in the nuances of cultured society. When the time was right he introduced him to the elite of Athenian society, which naturally included the Golden One.

Those who revered him referred to him as the Golden One, but to all who truly knew him, he was simply Pericles. Quiet and reflective in private, he was affable and outgoing in public. He enjoyed sketching and painting, and on occasion donned the role of playwright. It happened that he was also a great lover of sport, so that when introduced to the Champ the spark of camaraderie ignited their souls. He grilled the Champ with endless questions, but was especially interested in the now famous lion's roar. Such is the way of friends, striking at the heart of the matter without warning. Good friends sense the inner map, and always travel the shortest route to the buried treasure within; prompting the Champ to share a story he had never shared with another person.

The story goes that while praying to the gods the Champ had a vision that featured a large black lion stalking its prey. When launching its attack the lion unleashed a deafening roar. To the Champ's way of thinking his dream was sent by the gods, so he practiced for months until he had mastered every nuance of the lion's thunderous roar.

Known only to a few at the time, and not at all to the modern world, Pericles was descended from an Indian Yogi. He discovered his lineage quite by chance and, except for a few trusted friends, kept the secret. He made the discovery while traveling in India, visiting the sacred shrines that dotted the land. It wasn't, however, in a shrine that he discovered the truth of his heritage, but in a small, nondescript village located on the shores of the Ganges River. In was there that he met a man who was himself a teacher of some repute. When the time was right, the teacher tapped him on the brow, and in that tap came the revelation of his heritage.

While in India, Pericles mastered the art of meditation, thus learning to free his mind from its incessant chatter. That was the real source of his wisdom, because the ensuing silence magnetically linked his consciousness to the higher mind of the Soul. Beyond that, he supplemented his meditation with the little known art of subconsciousing, routinely instructing his subconscious mind to first analyze and then offer creative solutions to the challenges he faced.

It wasn't until several years later that Pericles began instructing the Champ in the ways of the Ancient Wisdom.

He started with the fundamentals of breath control, thereby demonstrating the connection between breath and mind. Next he emphasized the importance of mental training, how thought shapes the reality of daily life. Finally, he taught the art of meditation, how sustained concentration opens the door to wisdom and knowledge. The Champ found meditation life sustaining, but failed to understand the true source of his well-being. It was then that Pericles introduced him to the concept of One God. It was an idea that contradicted everything the Champ had ever been taught, but he listened, and he reasoned.

He reasoned that an ordered universe presupposes a Master Planner. He further reasoned that if the universe was ordered according to Plan, then he too was a part of the scheme for the simple reason that he was necessarily a part of the universe. His reasoning confounded the conventions of Greek society; nevertheless, it felt right because it validated the sense of renewal he experienced while meditating. Thus did he learn to trust his intuition, just as he had learned to trust his instincts when competing in the arena.

When Pericles died the people of Athens lined the streets, paying tribute to the man who had influenced an entire generation. There was, however, one notable absentee. On the day of the funeral the Champ fled Athens. He simply could not bear the pain. The wisdom of Pericles had struck a familiar cord, and his death struck yet another, this time producing the discordant note of self-destruction.

The Greeks respected suicide, so there was no inhibition from that quarter. The only thing that prevented him from repeating an ancient mistake was the image of Pericles repeatedly appearing upon the inner screen of his mind. There he was time and again, smiling as if all was well. Just as Pericles had intended, his love crossed over the divide and saved his friend from a death born of despair. Somehow Pericles had survived the grave, and that knowledge eased the Champ's pain.

With the help of his brother the Champ entered the world of business, thus awakening skills long since abandoned to time. He had a way with people, and when disputes overheated his leonine roar silenced even the meanest temper. He never forgot Pericles and he never disclosed the true nature of their relationship, that of teacher and student. Nor did he ever reveal the secret study hidden beneath the home of Pericles.

The Champ passed the gate a grateful man. He had achieved legendary status in the arena, and had studied under one of history's greatest men. He died quietly while vacationing on the island of Crete in the study of an ancient home overlooking the sea. He could not have known, but once before he had occupied that same house and had passed the gate in that same room. This time he departed the world a happy man.

The Warrior Monk

THE GREAT WALL of China has had a long and storied existence. The original wall was constructed from mud and rock and has all but disappeared, except for those sections constructed from quarried stone. The original wall required several generations to build, taking a terrible toll on human life, only to be abandoned centuries later when a bigger and better wall was conceived. By the time the final version of the wall was completed nearly one million people had sacrificed their lives. Most died of exhaustion, some died of disease, while others were crushed under the weight of rock that just wouldn't go where it was supposed to go. Still others were executed for lackluster performance, thereby serving as an example to others.

The original wall was the brilliant idea of an emperor who loved extravagant projects. From his point of view the wall represented the crowning achievement of an otherwise lackluster reign. Determined to create a legacy that would live forever, he sought immortality through the creation of a national symbol. Accordingly, he directed his scribes to painstakingly record every step of the project, hoping that history might look kindly upon his reign of terror. The truth be known, he did manage to create a legacy, because the wall eventually became a symbol of national unity. At the time, however, only the daft saw it that way, because who but the deranged would build a wall that served little or no purpose in the middle of nowhere? The barbarians who observed its construction laughed and roared for hours on end at the folly of it all. And no wonder, because the original wall was a haphazard affair, providing little or no protection. Centuries of construction made no difference, because the Mongol horde either dismantled strategic sections of the wall, or built ramps over which tens of thousands poured.

From the point of view of the Chinese people the project was a national scandal. People were taken from their homes and whole villages were shanghaied to work on the wall. Taxes were raised in order to pay for the exorbitant cost of construction, and those who protested either the taxes or the enforced labor were summarily executed. Hence the wall crept along year after year, while everyone knew it to be a shameful waste of resources. Better they had taken the money and manpower and built a network of roads.

A warren of cesspools followed the point of construction, its residents dedicated to exploiting conditions at the wall. Drugs, alcohol, and women were available at minimal cost, because the government encouraged the proliferation of carnal desire in order to discourage defections. The overseers demanded a long, hard day of grueling work, but during the night the workers were free to indulge all manner of addictive behavior. They smoked opium, locally grown and processed, and they surrendered their wages to professional gamblers, but when it came to alcohol they made their own. They drank to forget and they drank to soothe their aching bodies, but whatever justification they gave, the underlying reason was always related to the emptiness of their lives. Many died and many more suffered from the effects of poisonous brew, but that never slowed the rate of consumption. Thus were the sinister seeds of serious karma strewn about the fertile fields of life, and even now many struggle to overcome the effects of deeds long since sown.

Few ever left the wall alive, which explains the popular slogan, "Once on the wall, forever under the wall". The foundation of the next section under construction was routinely filled with the bodies of the dead, making it the permanent resting place for everyone who died at the wall. Even the camp followers were buried under the wall. It seems the wall accepted all contributions, no questions asked.

One of the men conscripted to work on the wall happened to be a Tibetan monk renowned for his mastery of the ancient art of Kung Fu. Being young and eager for adventure, and having heard the tales spun by itinerant monks passing through his parish, he abandoned his temple and embarked on a journey across China in search of the famous wall.

He sometimes lingered for days, and occasionally weeks in the villages through which he passed, invariably attracting students anxious to learn the art of Kung Fu. Because he incorporated the teachings of the Buddha, his approach to Kung Fu was somewhat unique. That combination, spiritual discipline and martial arts technique, awakened his chi to unheard of dimensions of strength and prowess. Chi imparts superhuman strength to the skeletal structure of the body, affecting the connective tissue much more so than muscle. When used appropriately chi manifests no harmful side effects; however, when combined with negative emotions and questionable motives it can have a deleterious effect upon the body, sometimes resulting in serious damage to the nervous system.

When the monk arrived at the wall he was totally bewildered by what he found. A small city surrounded the point of construction, while thousands of conscripts labored from sunrise to sunset. The nighttime revelry was unparalleled, ceasing only at dawn when work on the wall resumed. The shock was overwhelming because what he saw represented the antithesis of everything he held sacred. He had dedicated his life to a code of conduct founded upon the principle of universal brotherhood, and what he saw at the wall was anything but the expression of brotherhood.

It was only a matter of time before he was spotted by the authorities and conscripted into the labor force. The work was debilitating, while decent food and sound sleep were nearly impossible to come by. Being worked to death was not the adventure he sought, so he decided to lend a guiding hand to the fate that awaited him.

He waited for the right opportunity, fully intending to flee into the northern wilderness. It was an avenue of escape few ever attempted, because the northern territory was controlled by the barbarians. Nevertheless, he was not deterred by the thought of a chance meeting with the infamous horde that roamed the north of China. Besides, it seemed a good strategy to plan his escape in the direction most feared by his captors.

He made his escape during the night, crossing a section of the wall where new foundation was being laid. He never planned on killing anybody, but as it turned out, he was more than surprised to discover a bona fide Warrior Monk hidden beneath his temple robe.

While negotiating the terrain he came upon a platoon of six soldiers armed with pikes and swords. Spotting a lone man creeping amongst the decomposing bodies adorning the newly laid out foundation, the soldiers rejoiced at the opportunity to torture and kill an unarmed man. It seems the sight of blood never failed to stimulate their gonads, while cries of agony aroused them until they were as hard as their pikes.

Savoring the power that stems from an overwhelming advantage, the soldiers taunted their prey, thereby drawing to the scene a small crowd of onlookers hoping to see the death of anybody but themselves. Like the soldiers, the crowd found the display of brute force sexually stimulating, a rare achievement for those living a life of dissipation. The night promised riches for the camp prostitutes, who were well aware of the existing connection between sex and violence. Violence stimulates the instinctual brain, and violence in the form of conquest and submission is ever the nature of animal sexuality. The crowd's delirium was made all the more intense by the alcohol that coursed through their veins. And no wonder. When taken in large doses, alcohol anesthetizes the brain, leaving the door to consciousness wide-open, and therefore receptive to the baser instincts.

Eager to initiate the attack, the captain of the guard lunged at the seemingly helpless monk. Much to his chagrin, the monk easily disarmed him, taking possession of both his pike and his sword. The Warrior Monk struck with lightning speed, eviscerating the captain and two others in one coordinated movement. Thinking to overwhelm the Warrior Monk, the remaining three soldiers launched an all-out attack. They were dead before they knew what had happened. By the time they hit the ground the Warrior Monk was gone. The battle lasted but a moment; consequently, the witnesses were unable to agree as to what had occurred. It had all happened faster than the eye could record, thereby inviting the subconscious mind to fill in the blanks, which is why they gave varying accounts as to what had happened.

He knew that walking away was now out of the question, that the authorities would launch an organized pursuit. He would have to outrun them, and that required a new plan of action. He decided to head south, back the way he had come.

While making his escape, three more soldiers riding horseback and armed with broadswords attacked the Warrior Monk. Instead of running for cover, the Warrior Monk charged the lead horseman at a dead run, seemingly intent on ramming heads with the man's horse. Just when a collision seemed imminent, the Warrior Monk leapt high in the air, passing directly over the head of the oncoming rider. Reaching down, he plucked the rider's sword right out of his hand and, still in the air, brought his newly acquired weapon to bear on the next approaching rider. The second rider's head toppled to the ground, his headless body still mounted on the horse. The Warrior Monk landed gracefully on his feet, the tip of his sword piercing the underbelly of the next oncoming horse. The unseated rider never had a chance; the Warrior Monk lopped his head before he could get on his feet. By then the first rider had wheeled his horse and was intent on riding the Warrior Monk down. The Warrior Monk sidestepped the horse, and with one powerful slash cut the rider's leg off at the knee, disemboweling another horse in the process.

Two battles lasting perhaps a few minutes each had resulted in nine dead soldiers. The bounty on the Warrior Monk's head was growing by the minute. Gathering what weapons he could, he mounted the only surviving horse, its headless rider having recently disembarked. Driven by desperation, he rode the horse hard until it started showing signs of impending collapse. Knowing that its life held the promise of his own, he dismounted and continued on foot until the horse recovered its vigor. Again he rode hard, but this time the horse showed no sign of fatigue while eating up the miles at a rapid clip.

The following day he spotted what appeared to be a blotch on the horizon and knew at once that he was being pursued. On day three the blotch became a pack of horsemen riding with grim determination. On day four he counted twelve riders coming on strong. They rode with practiced ease, and like most men riding down prey, they came with extra mounts, which accounted for their relentless pace. Unfortunately, the Warrior Monk's horse was ready to drop from exhaustion. It was time to go to ground.

It was early afternoon when he spotted the redoubt he was looking for, a rock-strewn hill with a panoramic view of the surrounding terrain. Best of all, it was steep enough to prevent a mounted charge. The soldiers would be forced to attack on foot, and that was enough to change the odds in his favor. Leaving his horse at the foot of the hill, he climbed to the top, lugging weapons and provisions on his back. Up on the hill he discovered an assortment of large boulders strewn about as if dropped from the sky.

Satisfied for the moment, he assumed the standard pose for seated meditation, legs crossed, palms face up on the knees. However, rather than enter a state of meditation, he undertook a series of deep breaths, mentally summoning the chi residing at the base of his spine. Thus empowered, he went to work manhandling three oversized boulders into place, thereby creating the semblance of a defensive position. Next, having assessed every angle of ascent, he started gathering rocks suitable for tumbling, stacking them in a heap at the head of the most likely route up the hill.

Once again he assumed a cross-legged pose. The soldiers were closing in for the kill, but the Warrior Monk was busy visualizing the upcoming battle, carefully creating a mental blueprint of the victory he intended. A few minutes later the soldiers arrived and immediately began their ascent.

Straight into the path of an avalanche, they charged up the hill and met with disaster. Those who survived reassembled at the foot of the hill before once again braving the bloody slope. When they finally crested the hill they expected an immediate confrontation with the Warrior Monk, but instead discovered an array of gigantic boulders. Deep furrows in the ground bore witness to the fact that they had been recently moved, and for one brief moment in time their fierce determination waned as they considered the kind of man capable of such an extraordinary feat.

Suddenly, from out of the sky, the Warrior Monk dropped into their midst, sword to the right, knife to the left. Two men died before the whirling tornado ever touched ground, one by the sword and one by the knife. Before the others had time to react, he was back in the air, simultaneously lashing out with both feet. One foot stopped a heart, while the other crushed a windpipe. Both men were still standing, dead on their feet, when the Warrior Monk hit the ground running.

Grasping the desperate nature of their plight, the dwindling band of assailants turned and ran for their lives. They stumbled and then tumbled out of control back down the rocky hillside, creating such bedlam as to bring tears of laughter to the eyes of the victorious Warrior Monk. He watched the melee for several minutes before realizing he didn't dare leave any survivors, lest they return with reinforcements.

He ran down the hill, but arrived too late to prevent their hasty retreat. The tattered, defeated remnants of the strike force had fled on horseback. Tracking them down was out of the question; he simply could not afford the time required to run them to ground.

He rode for the better part of two days, until he found a secluded spot that afforded some cover. Feeling confident that the Chinese would not mount another expedition any time soon, he made camp. He needed rest, and he needed time to digest the events of the past few days.

Days later, while exploring the immediate surroundings, an unnatural stillness suddenly permeated the air. The familiar sound of wind whipping through the tall grass could still be heard; otherwise, Mother Nature was holding her tongue. Obviously something out of the ordinary had occurred. Searching the terrain, he soon found the source of the interruption. Not a hundred yards away a detachment of soldiers had encircled his campsite. As if by some strange orchestration of nature, the soldiers spotted him just when he located them. The pursuit was on; only this time the Warrior Monk's advantage was measured in minutes rather than days.

Both he and his mount were fit for duty and, sensing the mood of his horse, the Warrior Monk allowed it free reign. His was a powerful steed and, having sensed the gravity of the situation, there was no stopping that horse. Like the wind, it chose the path of least resistance, conveying its master back to the scene of the recent battle.

He rode all day and through the night, arriving at the foot of the hill at the crack of dawn. Up the hillside he went, once again lugging weapons and provisions on his back. Reaching the top, his horse was nowhere to be seen, but the soldiers were clearly visible not more than an hour away.

Once again he gathered an assortment of rocks suitable for tumbling, only this time he amassed a veritable mountain of mayhem, because by the looks of things there were nearly twice as many soldiers as before. Next he collected a pile of throwing rocks, sized to kill, but small enough to hurl at velocity. Satisfied with his preparations, he climbed the nearest boulder, summoned his chi, and then visualized the outcome of the impending battle. This time there would be no levity; this time no one would leave the hill alive.

When the soldiers dismounted and gathered at the foot of the hill, the Warrior Monk's horse suddenly appeared from out of nowhere, running full tilt straight at the enemy. Alarmed, the soldiers scattered out of reach, lest they be trampled under the hooves of a crazed horse. One of the soldiers, however, was caught in the path of the charging mount, and went sailing through the air as if launched from a catapult. It was not an auspicious beginning; however, they were professional soldiers, and therefore believed themselves more than a match for their adversary.

Much to everyone's surprise, the Warrior Monk's horse hadn't yet completed its self-imposed mission. This time, instead of attacking the soldiers, it barreled into the enclosure where the soldiers had herded their horses, dispersing them in utter terror. They would not be easily tracked, prompting more than a few of the attackers to shudder at the thought of having no avenue of retreat. They were on foot in the middle of nowhere.

Just like before, the soldiers met with an avalanche of tumbling rocks, followed by a blistering barrage of missiles that rarely missed their mark. By the time the heartiest members of the attack force had reached the crest of the hill, the slope was littered with bodies, some dead, others sorely wounded. Just when it seemed things couldn't get worse, the Warrior Monk dropped out of the sky, unleashing a blinding volley of lethal blows. It was an awesome display, sword and knife working in concert, and yet wholly independent of each other. Death arrived from all points of the compass, while the sound of gurgling blood provided the dirge.

Coated in blood, the Warrior Monk confronted the last of his assailants, who immediately threw down their weapons in surrender. They died with the sound of clattering metal accosting their ears.

The battle over, the Warrior Monk systematically dispatched the wounded before heading back to the location of his previous encampment. He needed to rest and he needed to clear his head. Soon after the first hilltop battle he had experienced some disturbing nightmares, unwelcome intrusions upon the sanctity of his mind.

Once encamped, he passed his time partaking of Mother Nature's healing balm, right up until the nightmares returned. Nearly a week had passed since the second hilltop battle, long enough for him to have dismissed any possibility of their return, especially since they had struck almost immediately after the first battle. Evidently they had seized the opportunity to rally their cohorts, because this time they attacked in force. He had no choice but to confront the problem, so whenever he awoke with a nightmare he immediately commenced a series of deep, slow breaths. Once fully relaxed he visualized a stream of White Light pouring into the crown of his head, directing the flow down his spine all the way to his feet. Thereafter, he practiced the same technique every night before drifting off to sleep. Within a fortnight the nightmares were gone.

Having tired of the Chinese experience, the Warrior Monk returned to his Tibetan temple; only he wasn't received in the manner that he expected. It seems he had changed in ways that could not be reversed. He was no longer the self-effacing monk who taught the art of make-believe war. He was now the infamous Warrior Monk. It hadn't taken long for word of his exploits to reach the monastery, how he had slaughtered half the population of China. Consequently, his fellow monks no longer looked upon him with respect, but rejected him and his deeds.

So he returned to China, where he became something of a legend, because everywhere he went bodies turned up in alarming numbers. His heroic deeds enraged the emperor, who placed a bounty upon the head of the "vermin monk". At first the lure of gold drew scores of would-be assassins, but when it became apparent that no one ever returned to claim the reward, the seductive power of gold lost its glitter for all but the truly fearless.

One day an outlaw priest showed up to claim the royal bounty. He too was a Tibetan monk trained in the art of Kung Fu, and like the Warrior Monk he roamed the countryside, killing as he went. The showdown took place in a village not far from the infamous hill where the Warrior Monk first earned his reputation.

The outlaw priest sat the saddle well, despite the fact that he rode leaning forward, not unlike an ancient tombstone, its purpose long since eroded by the passage of time. His hooded eyes, dark and foreboding, bore no hint of humanity. Rather, they drilled into a man's soul, leaving behind naught but an empty shell. He was evil to the core and the very sight of him sent brave men running for their lives.

Having spotted the Warrior Monk exiting the local whorehouse, the outlaw priest spurred his horse into a gallop. The Warrior Monk showed no sign of alarm as he slowly sidled up to his horse. Patiently timing the approach, he barked a command just when the charging mount drew near. Ever quick to obey, the Warrior Monk's horse reared up on its hind legs and, flashing its mighty hooves, crushed the skull of the oncoming horse. The impact rocked the trusty steed, knocking him backwards until he toppled over onto his side, seriously injuring the Warrior Monk's leg in the fall.

The outlaw priest was thrown from his horse, but quickly regained fighting form. Seeing his adversary disabled on the ground, he approached the disadvantaged Warrior Monk. The Warrior Monk was not the common ruffian he was accustomed to fighting, but a seasoned warrior whose karmic heritage stretched all the way back to the cave. Compared to the Warrior Monk, the outlaw priest was but a babe when it came to serious killing. And it showed because when he closed for the kill, the Warrior Monk caught a glimpse of passion in his eyes.

Propped on his elbows, sword to the right, knife to the left, the Warrior Monk lay perfectly still as the killer priest approached. He couldn't help but notice the subtle changes invading the man's gait, most notably the loss of fluidity and the upward migration of his center of gravity. He recognized the symptoms as the loss of chi, and understood that passion had robbed the priest of his power. Emotion had rendered him helpless, but he saw only advantage.

Raising his sword in a two-handed grip, the priest paused just long enough to savor the taste of victory before plunging his weapon downwards. In one fluid motion the Warrior Monk parried the blow with his sword, simultaneously driving his knife straight into the killer's groin. The ensuing scream pierced even the coldest of hearts. The villagers, knowing that the danger had passed, reappeared, and immediately began arguing over what they had witnessed from behind closed doors.

With a little help the victorious Warrior Monk clambered to his feet, checked on his horse, now up and prancing about, and then hobbled over to the dying priest. He never said a word to the would-be assassin. Instead, he demonstrated his contempt with one mighty thrust of his sword. The head of the ill-fated priest had barely tumbled a yard when the Warrior Monk's trusty steed, ever timely with his handy hooves, stomped it into a pile of mush.

A few days later the Warrior Monk was forced to mount up and ride out. An army of imperial soldiers had been spotted heading in the direction of the village. It was time to head for home.

He reached the mountains in early winter, barely making passage before the first heavy snowfall blocked the passes. He was tired of life on the run - too many enemies and too few friends had finally taken its toll. He knew that he could never return to his former life as a monk, so he dreamt of starting over in India, hoping to revive the man he had once been.

The Chinese would never see the likes of him again, but the legend of the Warrior Monk was destined to grow. In the decades to come many would claim they had seen his ghost, sometimes at the Wall, sometimes on the hilltop where he had slaughtered so many. Years later that same hill served as headquarters for a notorious warlord. Although the warlord knew all about the Warrior Monk's legendary stand, he laughed derisively every time his subordinates claimed that the slash marks embedded in the boulders at the top of the hill exactly matched the blade of a sword. The warlord met his death at the foot of the hill, the victim of an inexplicable torrent of tumbling rocks.

Soon after his arrival in India, the Warrior Monk was accepted as a disciple by a wandering ascetic. For years he traveled the countryside at his teacher's side, never once questioning the choice he had made. For reasons he didn't understand, reasons rooted in his karmic past, he found the life of an ascetic both familiar and comforting. And while he disagreed with some aspects of his teacher's philosophy, he never debated the issues, but listened carefully to the lessons imparted. When his teacher passed away he felt the loss, but quickly recovered his balance. Thereafter he retired to an abandoned monastery situated high in the Himalayas. Years passed, and still he remained at the mountaintop retreat, bereft of any human contact, ultimately meeting his fate while climbing a nearby ridge. He had ascended above the snow line and, trapped in the path of an icy storm, was unable to make a descent. Being the man of courage that he was, he accepted his fate and welcomed the freezing cold that invaded his flesh, imagining that Mother Nature was gently wrapping him in a shroud.

When he arrived at his celestial home on the upper astral plane he was overjoyed when greeted by friends and family from other lifetimes. While not everyone remembers their past lives, most people recover at least something of their past once they realize that it's entirely possible. The only prerequisite is the desire to remember and the willingness to accept the good with the bad. Even so, some lives are best forgotten for all time, while others shine with the Eternal Light of the Soul.

LIFE FIFTEEN
The Purple Cape

URPLE CAPE FLAPPING in the wind, on bended knee the Commander reached out, pressing his hand firmly to the chest of his fallen adjutant. But there was no life to be found in the man who had served Rome so well. He had given his life for the glory of Rome; a proper ending, the Commander thought, for a Legionnaire. An objective observer might have interpreted the gesture of kneeling over the body of a fellow soldier as an act of compassion; however, that was not the case, because even then he was acutely aware of his purple cape fluttering in the breeze, sounding all the more like the call of Destiny.

As if responding to history's herald, he came suddenly to his feet, unsheathing sword and knife in one fluid motion; sword to the right, knife to the left. He was majestic. He was magnificent. Even his purple cape seemed to radiate an aura of invincibility, as if protecting the Redeemer Himself. He wore it like no other, and in point of fact no one had ever donned the purple with so much pride and passion. And then there was the dreadful manner in which he wielded sword and knife; the Archangel of Death could not have been more terrifying. Last but not least, his eyes, those necrotizing pools of darkness, radiated the indomitable will of a man destined for greatness. Proud, ambitious, and completely self-possessed, he surveyed the field of battle, and where others saw death, he saw the promise of immortality.

There was a war to be prosecuted, and he was determined to reign victorious no matter the cost. Life was not only reasonably cheap, but in his mind it was absolutely expendable. He would appoint another adjutant, another lamb to be sacrificed for the greater good of Rome. The loss of one good man was of little consequence, because Rome trained the best soldiers in the world, men willing to die at his command, no questions asked.

Failure was completely out of the question, because he knew himself to be feted by the gods. To the outside observer his fervor revealed all the earmarks of a typical Roman religious conversion: total commitment based upon nothing more than blind faith. But those who marched to war at his side knew that faith alone could never adequately explain the man or his behavior. Their Commander revered but one god, and his god demanded neither faith nor surrender, hungering only for death and destruction. His god was Mars, the God of War, the most powerful god of all. Mars had called him by name, offering the highest accolades proffered by man, those won on the field of battle. He was chosen not only for his prowess, but for his unstinting dedication; because, like Mars, he reveled in the horrific sights and sounds found only in the blood zone. Thus it was said that he served his god not as a supplicant, but as a favored son.

His Legionnaires deemed him no ordinary man. They knew him to be a special breed of warrior; a battlefield commander capable of dictating the outcome of a battle, not with tactics alone, brilliant though they were, but with sword and knife. They had a word for men such as him, men who fought with reckless disregard for life and limb. It was a word rarely applied, least of all to someone holding the rank of Commander. It was just one little word, and yet it brought chills to the most hardened men on the field. It was a common word for a common creature, and was sometimes used in jest when describing the battlefield conduct of a friend. They applied that word to their Commander, but never to his face, and never in jest. The word was 'mouse'. It was a curious appellation for a soldier, but consider if you would the fact that bloody battlefields invariably attracted meat-eating scavengers, that only the mouse refused to quit the field during the heat of battle. The battlefield was home, and the mouse rarely scurried away to avoid either being trampled to death or hacked to bits. The mouse had no sense, and the soldier who earned the appellation had no sense of danger. Oddly enough, the Commander of untold Roman Legions was known to be a mouse, albeit one who donned a purple cape and applied sword and knife with all the familiarity of dinner utensils.

There was no telling to what heights he might ascend. It was only a matter of time before he crested, perhaps as the Emperor of Rome. He had joined the ranks of the illustrious Senate at a very young age, and already wielded power and influence in the affairs of state. As a military commander he was an unparalleled tactician, and the only one of his station who personally led men into battle. The blood of Caesar flowed in his veins, and today, just like so many other days, he would prove that the blood of the Caesars was still the blood of war.

Standing next to his dead adjutant, twin blades glistening in the sun, the Commander was momentarily mesmerized by the sound of his purple cape fluttering in the wind. He so loved the recollection of the day when the Emperor wrapped his shoulders in his very own purple cape. Purple was the color of the Caesars, and purple was the color worn by the members of the Senate. Purple symbolized power and status, and he cherished his purple cape over all of his other possessions. He wore it on the battlefield, clearly visible to friend and foe alike, so that they might behold the purple majesty of a Caesar.

He knew it in his soul; today's battle would add to the legend surrounding his ascent to glory. Today he would bask in the aura of greatness. On such occasions he truly became the God of War, unknowable and unconquerable. Standing there, alone and aloof, his eyes acquired a look reminiscent of a distant realm, somewhere far from the human sphere. His bearing seemed to announce, if not command, the coming of death. Today would be such a day; today he would become the greatest Caesar of all.

Planting his foot upon the chest of his dead adjutant, he thrust his sword skyward, as if intent on piercing heaven's underbelly, at the same time emitting a battle cry heard throughout the ranks. Not a few Legionnaires later swore that at that moment their Commander underwent an eerie transformation. Those closest to him were evidently suffering from battle fatigue, because they later claimed that bolts of lightning shot from the point of his sword.

Whatever it was, whether the reflected light of the sun or the effect of the lightning that leapt from his sword, something galvanized the Commander's otherwise lifeless eyes, sending an electrical discharge through the Legionnaires, instantly igniting the tinder of their warrior souls. Like a mighty wave carrying a man-of-war upon its crest, they fell upon the enemy from the heights of glory. Hundreds died in a single breath-cycle of the wave; hundreds more lay wounded, but the battle was far from over.

Drenched in blood, the Commander's purple cape no longer fluttered in the breeze, but glistened in the sun as he reformed the troop for one more charge. The blood of the vanquished coated everything, so they quickly threw their weapons to ground. Blood robbed them of a good purchase, and they needed a firm grip on their weaponry for the coming annihilation.

Once again they charged down the middle of the field, but this time they stopped short of the killing zone. The remainder of the army, yet unseen and therefore uncommitted, remained concealed in a ravine, awaiting the signal to charge into battle. When the main body slowed to a stop, they stormed out of the ravine and down the center of the field, growling and snarling like a pack of dogs on a hapless fox. It was a glorious moment, Roman swords glinting in the sun, led at last by the caped Commander as both cohorts joined for the attack. At that precise moment the Legionnaires roared in chorus. It was a roar that froze the blood of its intended victims in the wake of uncontrollable fear. It was a sound that could only emanate from men completely given over to the annihilation of every living thing.

The crescendo stopped as suddenly as it had erupted, and the only sound to be heard was that of leather soles trampling the earth. At the point of contact the dreadful sounds of carnage suddenly accosted the ear: clashing swords, fierce battle cries, and the sound of spent blood. For the victors there was nothing quite like the sound of gurgling blood. And in that particular Roman Legion it was an all too familiar sound.

Wounded combatants littered the field for as far as the eye could see. Some lay where they fell, while others, those familiar with the Commander's wretched practice, tried in vain to crawl away. As a matter of policy the Commander routinely executed the critically wounded, friend and foe alike.

The Legionnaires watched in horror as the Commander, never known for his humanitarian fervor, signaled thumbs down, extending both for emphasis. The double-thumbed gesture was sometimes satirized behind his back, but today there would be no mockery, only the annihilation of their comrades. The seriously wounded, both Roman and savage, were dispatched without hesitation. The executioners offered no words of comfort; rather they went about their loathsome duty with iron-willed determination. The walking wounded reformed with the troop, and those deemed unfit for duty were given leave to make their way home as best they could. Neither escort nor provisions were provided, thereby delivering them into the hands of the savages who preyed upon the castoffs.

The killing of their comrades did not sit well with the Legion. They argued amongst themselves, the bulk of them despising their Commander for his callous disregard for those who had given their all to the fight. The old guard made up his defenders, never doubting that they were truly blessed to fight alongside a Caesar. He was a living legend, one of history's anointed representatives, and they felt privileged to bask in the light of his immortality.

The Commander was a complex man. Heartless warrior though he was, he had come to understand something of human potential. He was particularly interested in the innate power of the human will, but only when yoked to dreams of glory, no matter how improbable. The Legion was the perfect place to test his resolve, because Roman soldiers were nothing if not obedient. They respected authority, rarely resisting the imposition of a powerful will, especially the will of a ruthless superior. And ruthless he was, not only with their lives, but with his own as well. It was only natural that they reflected their Commander's indomitable will.

He told himself that he fought for the glory of Rome, that his personal ambition coincided with the good of the Roman Empire. In the end, however, he served no one but himself. Some judged him the product of a debased Roman aristocracy, while others judged him innately evil, destined to scar the human psyche. Still others held that he was neither evil, nor the product of his culture, but the inevitable result of a cause set in motion in times unknown. The truth be known, he was both the product of his culture and the result of ancient deeds - sometimes motivated by the allure of Roman glory, sometimes driven by a wicked disposition.

The Legionnaires both loved and hated their Commander. He was a man capable of evoking both the high and the low; a man admired by his detractors and hated by his admirers.

Even those who hated him for his inhumanity loved him for the courage and bravado that he instilled. On the other hand, many of his staunchest supporters, men who revered him as a god, despised him for his abhorrent double-thumbed decrees. It was an explosive dynamic that pitted duty and discipline against powerful allegiances forged upon the field of battle.

The men with families were the most affected by the slaughter of their comrades, because they were the most likely to ask the question that weighed upon everybody's mind. It was a simple question, but a question that could cost a man his life if given voice in the presence of the wrong people. What, they asked, would the families of the slaughtered say when they learned that their loved ones had been murdered? In the end many considered it the price of being a Roman soldier. Others, however, were determined to put an end to the practice.

The battle over, glory crowned the day, but darkened their hearts. There was the usual aftermath of battle: grieving the loss of comrades, but also rejoicing in the fact that they too hadn't fallen on the battlefield. But there was something else, some indefinable essence slowly dissipating from within, almost as if each exhalation expelled a portion of their inner being. Had they understood the Law of Karma, that every conflict of conscience sets a mighty force in motion, they might have slain their leader sooner than they did.

Wrapped in his purple cape, thus warding off the sudden chill that contradicted the radiant warmth of the sun, the Commander stood alone on the crest of a hill overlooking the battlefield. He felt neither remorse nor guilt, reveling instead in victory, imagining the effect of his stunning campaign upon the Roman Senate. Everything was unfolding just as he had planned. He would return to Rome, his legendary exploits emblazoned upon the pages of history, ready and able to dictate his will upon the fawning lot of them. Unfortunately for the Commander, Destiny had already whispered in his ear, quietly conveying a message of impending doom.

History invariably places its foulest deeds at the feet of tyrants. Sometimes those deeds are deliberately planned, while at other times they seem to be magnetically linked to the fate of every villain, as if possessing a will of their own. Either way, cause and effect cannot be denied. Whether the cause lies in this life or another is of no consequence to the universe. The Law must be fulfilled, and the only hope of reprieve lies within the scope of Heavenly Grace, and there was nothing heavenly about the Commander. The Law of Karma was about to descend upon the Commander, purple cape and all.

Swayed by the mob, his principal accusers took up their swords and rushed him from behind while he stood overlooking the scene of his crime. They came from behind because they had been warned. Those too cowardly to join the attack had warned them, had even beseeched them to avoid his eyes. It was said that his eyes burned with a flame that consumed the souls of lesser men. And no man ever counted himself anything other than a lesser man while in the presence of those fiery orbs. They believed the tale because they had seen it for themselves, so they came from behind with their eyes cast to the ground.

They came in numbers, silently reeking fear. Could the lamb stalk the lion? They thought not, and yet they persevered despite the mind-numbing fear that claimed their souls. They could hear the revelry wafting up from the camp below, and they could feel the heat of the sun burning into their flesh. They could smell the spilt blood even there on the hill, but the thing they remembered most was the taste of fear, metallic and lifeless upon their tongues.

Unleashing the fury of ancient demons, the gates of hell opened and the Commander stepped through to face his assassins. The wrath of Mars infused his sword, and every blow carried the weight of countless Legionnaires. Some of the assailants later claimed that bolts of crackling lightning leapt from his sword, that they had encountered an impenetrable wall of searing heat and blinding light. When it was over twelve Legionnaires lay dead at his feet.

When the sound and fury had passed there he stood: twin blades of destruction glinting in the sun, purple cape drenched in yet more blood. The remaining cowards, who by some quirk of fate were still on their feet, ran for their lives. Surely, he truly was the God of War. No man could survive an attack like that and live to tell the tale. The old guard, however, expected as much. Everyone knew that he wielded sword and knife in a two-handed style that was but a blur to the eye. They weren't at all surprised when the cowards ran from a true warrior wed to the lore. Surprise came when their Commander staggered, and then tumbled down the hill, all the while clutching his precious purple cape.

He came to rest at the foot of the hill, purple cape draped over his head. Obviously, fate had entered in. How else do you explain both the glory and the folly of Rome in a single pose? He had sought Rome's accolades and had worn her purple, but in the end he had come full circle, blinded still by his purple cape.

He began his transition to the other side with a vision. And what he saw was a man of royal bearing riding in a chair held aloft by eight strong men. The man sat his chair with imperial majesty, occasionally stopping his conveyance so that he might whisper into the ear of a subordinate. By all appearances he was a distasteful man, a man lacking any redeeming quality, except for the purple scarf that fluttered about his neck.

The sound of Roman sandals gathering nearby interrupted his vision, drawing him back to the flesh. His Legionnaires were assembling to witness the passing of their Commander. Most stood stone silent, but others grew bold now that he was forever laid low, and demanded that he be put to death.

Some wanted to finish him off for the sake of comrades long since murdered. Others wanted to honor him, not only because he had fought like a common soldier, hand to hand like the rest of them, but because he had never been defeated on the field of battle. The remainder stood back on their heels and waited to see which way the wind would blow. Would hate dictate revenge, or would the memory of their Commander's valor sustain them? The decision was made by the men who had fought at his side from the first, their allegiance forged upon the field of honor. With impeccable timing born of the blood zone, the old guard stepped forward, swords drawn, feet firmly planted in the earth. There would be no further assault upon the man who had led them to the heights of glory. Had he been any other sort of man they might have stood down, but he was no ordinary man. During their military service they had endured many a leader who could not lead and would not fight. This was a man who had understood war, a man who had brought honor to the field, even if he had tarnished the memory of those who had died under his command.

Later that day, the old guard led the assassins, trembling still from their first ascent, back up the hill to the scene of their infamous deed. Without so much as a word or nod of the head, they executed the traitors, applying their bare hands rather than dishonor their swords. Their cowardly deed would live in infamy, but their gravesites would be forever forgotten, because no markers were erected.

They had assassinated a Caesar. True, the perpetrators had all died that day, but how would Rome greet an army that had failed to protect its Commander? Most of them would never know, because from that day forward they met with disaster upon the field of battle. Defeat decimated their ranks, until only the veterans who had drawn their swords and stood firm upon their allegiance ever made it home.

When the surviving veterans returned from the war they spread the tale, and the legend of the caped commander spread through the streets of Rome. His heroic deeds and untimely death at the hands of traitors inspired a generation of Legionnaires. As if preparing for their time of glory, young boys in every town and village could be found reenacting the death scene, sword and knife in hand, purple cape fluttering in the breeze.

No one could have ever guessed, but at the very end the Commander shed a tear. Not for those lost in battle, and not for those expunged by decree, but because his assassins had tarnished the legend he had brutally chiseled upon the granite face of history.

He passed the gate with no shame, no guilt, and no resolve to make amends. When he arrived on the other side, eyes yet aglow with the bleak and barren light of Mars, he hoisted sword and knife while cursing the darkness that awaited him.

Decades later he was finally released from the realm of the walking dead, only to be admitted into one of the many hospitals located upon the etheric plane. A short time later life once again called him to task. This time he was returning to Africa, where a lifetime of slavery was already beginning to take shape in the karmic substance of his life.

LIFE SIXTEEN
The Lion

H E WAS PRIME stock and, needless to say, the slavers recognized his value the moment they laid eyes upon him. He was easily six feet seven inches with shoulders to match. His gigantic frame was layered with muscle, creating the impression of superhuman strength. In every sense of the word he was majestic. Strange though it may seem, the shackles that adorned his wrists and ankles somehow added to his majesty, even as he glared at the Arab slavers with every ounce of hate his heart possessed.

His father was the village shaman and, being the son of an important man, his disappearance would definitely raise the alarm. Still, the slavers were a clever lot who undoubtedly intended on setting sail before the discovery of their foul deed. He hoped to escape before they sailed, but if that proved impossible, he would do whatever it took to delay their departure until help arrived.

He had never before set eyes on a slaver, but had heard stories of the men with hooked noses and flowing robes who arrived on empty ships, but later departed with their cargo holds filled to the brim. It seems they only snatched the young, the strong, and the healthy. The rumor was that the captives were transported across the sea, where they were sold into a life of misery. He wanted no part of the ordeal, and was determined to remain vigilant through the night, hoping for an opportunity to escape.

When the sun dipped toward the horizon the ship's crew began transferring their prisoners from the meadow out to the ship, a two-tiered vessel that stood well out to sea, except when loading cargo. Rows of iron rings glinted in the fading sunlight as they shackled their captives to the deck. They classified their human cargo according to a predetermined plan, interspersing women and children, thus isolating the bucks. Anyone caught making trouble was hauled to the stern of the ship and tossed overboard, whereupon many a wager was placed as to whether the rejects would drown, or be beaten to death by the guards on shore.

When she sailed forth from her homeport on the Arabian Peninsula she bore no hint of evil intent, but had looked a companionable ship en route to parts unknown. Experienced captains never let their intentions be known, because at that time slavery was outlawed in the area now known as Arabia. But that was only because the Sultan's brother had been kidnapped and sold into slavery.

The Sultan's brother was a man of culture who occasionally traveled to Luxor in search of the splendor that had once been ancient Egypt. He especially loved the ruins, and frequently walked amongst the relics of the past, ever aware of the ghosts that haunted such an ancient city. It was during one of those walks that he was seized, and subsequently enslaved. The Sultan ultimately recovered his brother, although he was never again the man he had once been. The brother finished out his life a shattered remnant of his former self, no longer interested in the affairs of the world.

Back on the ship, the shaman's son sat shackled to the deck, gazing up at heaven's vault, knowing that the stars somehow influenced human destiny. Perhaps the stars would engineer his escape; perhaps they had already arranged for his rescue. Tonight, however, they somehow looked utterly powerless, but he wasn't worried one way or the other, because he had a plan of his own. It would in fact be his last night onboard the slave ship.

When the night sky clouded over, darkness cloaked the vessel, providing the opportunity he sought. Thus he began prying his shackles apart with a piece of root taken from the meadow and concealed in his loincloth. The root was supple but tough, thus allowing both concealment and utility. Winding the root around the shackles, he heaved with all of his might, redoubling his effort upon seeing the progress he had made. The metal rings chewed at his flesh, but still he tugged at the root, never slackening his effort until his legs were finally free. Next, he started working on the manacles that bound his wrists, but soon realized he needed help.

Two captives lay within easy reach - one angry and sullen, the other sound asleep. Holding the gaze of his scowling neighbor, he rattled the manacles that bound his wrists, his intention perfectly obvious. His would-be accomplice clearly understood, but turned his back on any thought of escape. Next he reached out to the female sleeping on the opposite side, pressing a hand lightly over her lips.

At last it seemed that good fortune had found him, because the woman seemed to understand his language. Lowering his voice to the barest whisper, he revealed his plan and how she figured into his scheme. He had either misjudged her grasp of the language, or she simply wanted no part of his suicidal plan, because when he removed his hand she let out an ear-piercing howl. Kicking and screaming, she rolled beyond his reach. Within minutes trouble arrived in the form of a crewman brandishing a nasty-looking club.

As the club arced towards his skull, the would-be escapee, wrists manacled and tethered to the deck, lunged like a lion landing its prey. He seized the crewman by the throat, instantly crushing the life from his body. The crewman died without a sound, until he hit the deck, whereupon the clatter created by his tumbling corpse immediately raised the alarm.

Still manacled and chained to the deck, the renegade slave jumped overboard, hoping that the weight of his body would break the chain at the bottom of the fall. The chain wasn't very long; consequently, he barely made it over the side - just far enough so that he was left wriggling like a fish on a line. He had no choice but to wait for the crew to pull him back up onto the deck of the ship. When the crew drew in their line to see what they had caught, they weren't at all surprised to discover who had caused the commotion. The beast had obviously turned man-killer, but rather than beat him senseless, they turned him over to the Captain, knowing that he would arrange a special show for everyone to enjoy.

The Captain was known for his cruelty, ever the sign of an inadequate personality. His was the type of cruelty born of pain and suffering, and not the kind associated with personal failure. When derived from personal failure cruelty usually manifests as contempt for others. When derived from psychological trauma, such as parental abuse, or some other equally damaging betrayal, it normally manifests as sadistic behavior.

The Captain ordered the slave, now known as the Lion, hung from the mast. He favored dangling men by their feet over any of the other popular methods of hanging, because no other technique offered the same advantages as the path of steady resistance. Necks snapped all too easily, while arms frequently tore away from the body long before the legs even began to tire. What's more, when hung by the feet, it didn't take long for the blood to accumulate in the head, creating a dull aching throb that intensified with each beat of the heart. Through careful observation the Captain had discovered that given enough time the average head turned purple, not unlike a prized plum. Once ripened the best of the lot exploded in a shower of blood and brains when punctured with a knife.

If, however, a needle was inserted in just the right spot, blood sprayed the deck for hours, lending no small amusement to those who enjoyed such things. All in all, it made the Captain quite popular with the men, but only until he turned his wrath upon the crew.

They strung him up early in the morning and left him dangling on a tether with his head ten feet off the deck. Straining his mighty torso to the limit, the Lion studied the leather cord that ran from the spar to his ankles. All the while the pressure in his head was building, causing his nose to drip blood onto the deck below, slowly creating a sinister pattern of impending disaster upon the weathered planking. The situation appeared utterly hopeless.

Meanwhile, the slaves were being taken off the ship to the meadow where they would spend the day under the boiling sun. The bulk of the crew would be going ashore, while those who remained onboard would be busy below deck. He would soon be alone.

Alone at last, the Lion arched his massive frame, quickly generating the necessary momentum to arc his body across the deck of the ship. It was a dangerous plan that risked a deadly confrontation with the mast, but it was a risk that had to be taken. The first ray of hope appeared when the boat shifted with the incoming tide at the precise moment he reached the furthest point of his trajectory, thus straining the tether to its breaking point. When the tether failed to snap, he redoubled his effort, repeatedly braving the perilous sweep of the pendulum. The stars must have worked their magic after all, because the ship rocked and rolled with the tide, aiding and abetting his eventual escape. He landed on his back, thudding onto the deck.

When he came to his senses he was below deck. His wrists were manacled and chained to the overhead structure and his legs were similarly secured to the hull of the ship. But it made no difference to the Lion. Bent at the knees with his feet braced against the ship's frame, he heaved both legs at once, utterly destroying the shackles that bound his ankles. Grabbing the chains attached to his manacled wrists, he ripped the mountings free of the overhead beam, shattering one of the metal rings that fettered his wrists in the process. The other ring held fast, although the chain attached to it was completely free of its mooring.

When the crew arrived on the scene they found the Lion whirling the chain still attached to his manacled right wrist. He was a menacing sight, but he was outnumbered and trapped below decks, so they never thought to devise a strategy. The first crewman to brave an attack died when his head was nearly severed by the whirling chain. Another crewman, having timed the cycle of the rotating chain, ducked and charged. He received a brutal kick to the chest and instantly crumpled to the deck. The rest of the crew backed away and waited for the Captain to arrive and take charge.

Moments later, fully apprised and totally dissatisfied with his crew's performance, the Captain appeared on the scene. Hoping for an immediate resolution, he yanked a knife from his belt and flung it at the Lion. Evidently the stars were still working their magic, because the knife was deflected into the eye of a wary crewmember, giving pause to all who thought wariness a match for sheer ferocity. At that point the Captain went in search of a fishnet. During his absence a crew member tried to upend the Lion by rolling underfoot. Dropping to one knee while still rotating the chain, the Lion pummeled his attacker with his free hand, inadvertently dislodging an eyeball in the process. The next would-be assailant nearly died of fright when he saw his shipmate's eye pop out of its socket. He might have survived the ordeal if he hadn't stepped on the skittering orb and lost his footing, which sent him flailing into the trajectory of the whirling chain.

When the Captain returned with the fishnet the Lion reacted swiftly. Releasing his grip on the arcing chain, he launched his massive frame straight at the Captain. Unfortunately for the Captain, he was on his own, because the rest of the crew leapt from the path of the rampaging Lion. Landing his prey with one mighty surge of adrenalin, the Lion crushed the Captain's skull with his bear hands. The rest of the crew flinched in horror when the sound of crackling cranium filled the air. It was a terrifying sound, and everyone, with the exception of the First Mate, ran for the upper deck of the ship.

The new Captain, and former First Mate, carefully reached beneath his shirt while pointing at the Lion's manacled wrist with his other hand. The Lion could read a man's eyes, and therefore knew that intentions not otherwise stated were sometimes communicated through the faculty of the eye. And what he saw was not guile, but total surrender. So he extended his arm and watched with palpable intent as the newly appointed Captain unlocked the manacle.

Motioning the Captain to stand aside, the Lion hurried up the ladder that led to freedom. Nearing the hatch, he could hear the sound of shuffling feet. The crew was gathering for another attack, but there was no stopping now. Ascending onto the sunlit deck, he let out a bellow that might have been mistaken for a pride of lions fighting over fresh kill. The next sound to be heard was that of bare feet scurrying across the deck, followed by the sound of men splashing down into the water below.

He was free; however, his ordeal was far from over, because the distant shoreline was well beyond his reach. Sensing another eruption of volcanic rage, the Captain quickly motioned the Lion to the port side of the ship, where he pointed to a small boat secured to the hull. He would have to climb down the footholds leading to the waiting craft. Down they went; the Captain first, followed by the Lion.

Once on board the Captain commenced rowing for shore, only to change course, suddenly veering out to sea. Alarmed, the Lion jumped to his feet, clearly intending deadly harm. Pointing to the crewmembers waiting on the shore, the Captain directed the Lion's gaze to a more distant section of the coastline where there were no crewmembers to be seen. The Lion immediately understood.

Once ashore the Lion hit the ground running, crossing a narrow stretch of sandy beach without incident. However, upon entering the thicket that followed the coastline he stumbled upon a squad of slavers escorting a string of female captives back to the ship. The unexpected encounter caught the slavers off guard, providing the Lion with the opportunity he needed. Seizing the two nearest slavers by the neck, he effortlessly crushed the delicate bone structure characteristic of the throat. The others thought to attack in concert, which turned out to be a fatal mistake, because close-quarter battle had recently become the Lion's forte.

The Lion knew there had to be a key, so he searched the dead until he found what he was looking for. Removing their shackles, he instructed the women to follow at a run if they wanted to live; otherwise, they were perfectly free to fend for themselves.

Hours later he allowed a brief rest before resuming their grueling march. As night approached he slackened the pace, but ignored the women's pleas to stop for the night. Traveling at night was not a good idea; however, the racket that attended their flight would almost certainly frighten off any predators. So they marched through the night, and by morning found themselves traversing familiar territory. Nevertheless, the Lion refused to stop and rest. His greatest concern was no longer the safety of the women, but the plight of the captives still shackled to the deck of the slave ship. Their rescue depended solely upon him, and time was running out.

That afternoon they arrived at their destination, and much to the Lion's surprise and relief, he found a war party assembled and ready to depart. Scouts had discovered the ship and knew of his capture. They hit the trail with the Lion leading the way, running all day and into the night before stopping to rest. Several minutes later they were back on the trail without a hitch in their collective step on their mission of mercy.

The meadow was deserted and, rushing to the shore, they saw no sign of the slave ship or its crew. The Lion's mission of mercy had failed, and he took it hard. He had accepted the role of savior, fully intending to liberate the other captives. Many people spend their lives rescuing the downtrodden, seemingly overlooking the other half of the equation, that hardship bestows qualities prized by the Soul. In the Lion's case, however, his mission of mercy was solely aligned with the fight against evil.

The Lion's encounter with slavery ultimately changed him in ways he could not have predicted. With the passage of time his anger gave way to the irrepressible beat of the human heart, creating a rhythm that slowly healed the pain and sorrow of the past. He no longer yearned for the trail, and he no longer resented the guiding hand of his father, who had always insisted that he follow in his footsteps. On the contrary, he accepted instruction from his father, and ultimately accepted the role of village shaman. His most important contribution was the creation of an inter-tribal coalition that maintained a lookout for slavers. He never forgot the harsh reality of slavery, or the feel of iron clamped to his limbs. Nor did he ever forget the men who thought to cage a lion.

He was sound asleep when the end came, his attention riveted upon the lifelike image of a ferocious black lion. It was digging its powerful claws into the earth, seemingly serving notice of imminent danger. Then, as if dispelling any doubt as to its intention, the lion parted its jaws and, flashing a nasty set of meat eating tools, roared from the depths of its animal soul. The sound was not unlike thunder rolling over the land. At that precise moment a man wielding a club crushed the Lion's skull.

The individual wielding the club was none other than the Captain who had granted the Lion his freedom many years before. At the time, freeing the slave had seemed a good idea, but then the Lion had repaid him by liberating six prime catches on his way to freedom, killing an entire squad of slavers in the process. Amongst the dead the Captain had discovered his brother impaled on a jagged stump, the victim of the Lion's rampage.

The Captain had no concept of forgiveness, and had often prayed to god for the gift of revenge. Countless were the times he had imagined the Lion in his clutches, dangling from the foremast until his head exploded in a shower of blood and brains. When the moment of conquest finally arrived, however, he surprised himself when he unexpectedly changed his mind. He had fully intended on taking the Lion alive, but the memory of their previous encounter convinced him otherwise. So he struck a vicious blow to the back of the Lion's head. Death was instantaneous.

Led by the Captain, the slavers descended upon the village under the cover of night, clamping irons and breaking heads until there was nobody left who hadn't fled into the jungle. Then, before the survivors could organize a counterattack, they rounded up their newly acquired assets and immediately set out for the safety of their ship. They were but a few hundred yards from the village when they first heard the menacing roar of a lion somewhere off in the distance. The Captain trembled ever so slightly, but quickly regained his composure; nothing was going to overshadow the happy aftermath of revenge. Halfway through the morning they heard it again, only this time it sounded like thunder erupting from the surrounding terrain.

Terror was sinking its teeth, but before the Captain could formulate a plan of action an enormous black lion leapt from the landscape. It landed its intended prey with a deafening roar, lacerating flesh and bone, rending and shredding the

Captain's spasmodic corpse until it was no longer recognizable. The rest of the slavers fled the scene in utter terror, leaving their captives shackled one to the other. Fortunately, a young man who had studied at the feet of the Lion, and who had managed to escape into the jungle during the first moments of the attack came to the rescue. He knew the legend of the Lion, and therefore knew there had to be a key. Searching the remains he was greatly relieved to find the key hanging from a cord around the Captain's truncated neck. The irony of the situation did not escape the young hero. His teacher, the legendary Lion, had once failed to rescue a shipload of captives, and now his student had rescued an entire village, not only with the help of a lion, but with the help of the Lion himself.

When the Lion passed through the gate he found his father patiently awaiting his arrival. His father was in perfect health, showing no sign of age. His wrinkles had somehow disappeared, and the gray hair that had formerly crowned his visage was no where to be seen. Such is life on the other side of the gate.

LIFE SEVENTEEN
The Death Of A Warrior

A DENSE FOG ROLLED over the terrain, taking no prisoners save those caught in its icy grip. He was accustomed to the haze that frequently shrouded the land, but this time it had somehow assumed a strange and different meaning, subject like it was to his interpretive mind. Strange indeed are the creations of the mind once enthralled with the nebulous aspects of nature's most familiar environments.

His imagination had seized upon the encroaching fog and, by some quirk of fate, had called to life the goblins of his youth. The stories he had been told as a small child, stories intended to frighten, had set the stage for this horrific animation. His parents had hoped that the fright instilled in his fertile imagination might one day protect him; however, the very seeds meant to inoculate him against life's pitfalls were now surrounding him with the specter of hideous prospects. Wounded on the battlefield, at the mercy of the shifting, swirling fog, seeds long since planted in his subconscious mind were coming to fruition.

Terrible sounds invaded the scene, sounds long since associated with the throes of agonizing death. Disembodied voices communicated a range of emotion: despair, rage, and fear, each embodying its own version of human suffering. But, there was one thing they all had in common, and that was their intended destination. Each and every shriek lodged first in his ears, and then in his brain, evoking vivid images of men condemned to a horrible death. It was the unearthly sounds that gave substance to the macabre scenes now forming in the swirling, lifelike mist. It was, therefore, only natural to assume that the gates of hell had opened, that he had arrived at his final destination.

Regaining his wits by force of will, he told himself that he lay wounded on a battlefield, and nothing more; that he was all too familiar with the capricious nature of the fog that rolled in from the sea; that he had long since grown accustomed to the sights and sounds of violent death. Surely he would soon be dead and the nightmare would be over.

His mental faculties somewhat restored, his fear abruptly receded, as if announcing the sudden appearance of new possibilities. And so his mind wandered back and forth, contemplating for a time the possibility of life beyond the grave, and then returning to the terrifying scenes given form and substance by the fog.

Just when his rational mind seemed to be gaining the upper hand, the surrounding clamor assumed a rhythm of its own, as if orchestrated by an unseen conductor. The gruesome sounds of death merged, creating a musical composition audible only to the dying, and even then a tune most difficult to carry. Its message was reminiscent of his life, somehow recalling the intimate details of his past. Old memories came to life and, as if by cue, the fog marched across the field in tumbling waves of seemingly tangible substance, returning him to the one and only warship he had ever crewed.

He found himself back on board that ill-fated vessel, an early version of the warships later developed on the coast of Britain. He had joined forces with a raiding party sailing to the mainland even though he had no experience with the sea. As it turned out, neither did his shipmates. Every sailor knows that the sea demands respect, but he was young, and the spirit of adventure won out over commonsense. Had he shipped with experienced sailors, the end result might have been different. As it was they encountered a violent storm and capsized almost before they got started.

As if by the hand of God, he escaped with his life, breaching the surface just as the hull of the ship was disappearing beneath the waves. There were precious few survivors, and together they swam toward the distant shore. The swim was long and arduous, and one by one the weaker swimmers perished, until he alone remained. Reaching the shore, his pale blue flesh trembling in the frigid night, he made one last decision that saved his life. He burrowed into the sand, which yet held the heat of the day, and slept through the night. By morning the crisis was over.

His attention momentarily diverted, the parade of hallucinations receded, beaching his mind upon the shores of reality. He knew then that the end would come soon, because no one in his condition could survive the bitter cold of late fall without shelter. He had witnessed many a warrior die on cold and desolate fields, some nearly frozen to the bone, others whimpering in a wave-pool of quivering flesh. It was a horrible death by any standard, but an unthinkable death for a warrior, because every warrior expects to meet death in the heat of battle.

His ordeal, however, was far from over. Instead of rolling, crashing waves, and instead of ancient goblins come to life, apparitions of the dead suddenly accosted his faculties. Decayed and well past their prime, the ghosts of enemies past materialized, not unlike emissaries sent from the netherworld. He tried getting on his feet, but his body refused to obey his command. He was paralyzed. Death at least offered a note of finality, and perhaps the promise of a new beginning beyond the veil. Paralysis, on the other hand, offered no closure, leaving him defenseless against the fiendish apparitions.

By his accounting they had no cause to be angry. He had killed most of them on the field of battle, and those he had slaughtered in their homes had been fair game. And yet they blamed him for their incorporeal condition. Like a kettle of vultures claiming its prize, they swooped out the sky, landing on his chest with an audible thump, seemingly intent on driving a stake through his heart.

He nearly died of fright. Once acknowledged as a viable force, fear paralyzes the mind, ultimately usurping the authority of mind over body. The last vestige of reason gradually slides into oblivion, shattering the harmony of life's most sacred melody, leaving only the sound of discordant notes clashing in pointless protest.

Even so, he was no ordinary man, but a man with an extraordinary past. Qualities long since buried in the sea of consciousness were about to surface. Once again the swim to shore would be arduous, and once again a miracle would save him, only this time the miracle would not ensure the body's survival, but that spark of life commonly referred to as the Inner Man.

With the ebbing of his life the Warrior suddenly experienced a stunning revelation. There was a striking similarity between the fairy tales he had been taught as a child and his belief in a warrior's paradise beyond the grave. That's when he realized his life had been a fraud, completely devoid of meaning and purpose, not unlike the toll of an ancient bell long since pounded into submission. Seemingly within his reach, the warrior's paradise he had so ardently believed in suddenly disintegrated amidst the dead and dying on a misty field invaded by apparitions from the past.

Truth flows ever onward, and like a stream that barely trickles during the summer, but floods with winter's first thaw, the frozen shards of his life melted away, depositing what remained of his existence upon life's flood plain. Fear had pillaged his soul, and everything that had infused his life with meaning had been stripped away. His identity disemboweled, there was nothing left to cling to but the prospect of life beyond the grave.

The specter of death offers everyone the opportunity to examine the past, to take a fresh look at what's truly important in life. Those fortunate souls who take advantage of that opportunity invariably transition to the other side of the gate ready and able to make the most of their afterlife experience. Truly, death sometimes ushers in the night, but more often than not it announces the dawning of a new day.

Rising to the occasion, the Warrior faced his past, and what he saw sickened his heart. On the one hand he saw a stouthearted warrior, but on the other hand he saw a monster who had relished the taking of life. He had sent many a soul to their heavenly reward, and even though some of them deserved what they got, others had been entirely innocent. Even if there was such a thing as a warrior's paradise, he wanted no part of it, not if it rewarded conduct such as his.

Having traveled the subterranean corridors of his mind, and then back again to lucid thought, he turned his attention to the possibility of life beyond the grave - a subject much talked about by the warriors of his clan. Some believed they were destined to rot in the ground, never again to know the company of man or beast. Others feared the afterlife more than oblivion, because the guilt that attended their savagery did not allow for hope. Some few, however, believed that life would continue just as it had in the world of mortal men.

He believed in an afterlife, but didn't feel worthy of heaven's glory; nor did he feel deserving of damnation. So he imagined an afterlife where people were categorized according to merit. The evildoers descended into hell and the saintly ascended into heaven, while people like him gravitated to various realms coinciding with the purity of their hearts. It was a fairly accurate portrayal, because everyone is destined to pass the gate into a world that accommodates the vibratory rate of their atomic structure. Those whose atoms approach the speed of light ascend into the highest realms of consciousness, while those who resonate to the lower, denser vibrations of the material world are drawn to a wide variety of possibilities, depending upon the nature of their earthly attraction.

Nearing death at last, he began his transition with an unusual dream. It started out like any other dream, but that's where the similarity ended. By the time he realized that something strange was happening, he had already merged into the fabric of his dream. Little did he know, but he wasn't dreaming in the normal sense of the word, but had stepped out of his physical body onto to the astral plane, while retaining a dreamlike consciousness in his brain.

He was standing face to face with his deceased father. Speechless with joy, his father took him by the hand, and together they walked towards a beautiful golden staircase. Stepping onto the ascending staircase, the Warrior paused, then turned and looked back over his shoulder at his yet living, but soon-to-be-dead, body of flesh. That hesitation came with a terrible price, because back he went to the wreckage of his body. Coagulated blood crackled in response to the body's reanimation, sending a bolt of fear right through his heart. Death was instantaneous.

His father at his side, the Warrior approached the staircase for the second time, only this time he did not hesitate, but ascended into the Light streaming down from above. With each successive step his confidence grew, until at last tranquility permeated every atom of his being. In an instant he was fully awake upon the astral plane, even if not fully oriented to his new environment. But that wasn't a problem, because his father was ready and willing to take him under his wing.

He passed the gate under the best of conditions, and soon became an integral part of his community. In time he would experience astral death, and once again take birth in the world of physical form. Strange it may be, but those preparing to incarnate into the world of flesh do not view the transition as taking birth, but as a dream to be lived with every ounce of love and gratitude they can muster.

The Bamboo Garden

THE MORNING SUN anointed the day with its radiant warmth and dazzling illumination. The sound of foliage quietly bantering in the breeze could be heard throughout the bamboo garden, while the melodic tune of a nearby brook added to the peace and tranquility of the setting. There was absolutely no reason to suspect that Death stalked the garden that day, but as surely as the sun rises and sets on the horizon, Death was indeed making his rounds. He hadn't yet claimed his victim, but there in the bamboo garden, bathed by the sun and swept by the gentle current of a lazy wind, sat a man with death on his mind.

Surely, Death comes to all of us, but just as surely we never know when his beckoning hand might summon us to another realm. His arrival may seem premature; nevertheless, he invariably arrives with impeccable timing. He always comes prepared to succor the deceased, ever ready to ease the transition from this world to the next. When, however, he comes for those who have wrongfully taken their lives through despair and delusion, his healing power is greatly diminished. Those poor souls are doomed to walk the earthbound world until such time that their earthly lives would have reached a natural conclusion.

Truly, the quality of life beyond the grave is directly correlated to the good accomplished during any given lifetime. Sincere effort is always rewarded, because effort and motive constitute important aspects of both spiritual and moral development. A life characterized by love and service guarantees countless blessings, whereas a life marred by habitual cruelty guarantees an earthbound existence. Fortunately, the earthbound condition is not permanent, because most people repent their sins rather than suffer indefinitely in a world of unrelenting darkness. Some, however, refuse all help, and remain trapped in the earthbound world, right up until they are reborn in the flesh. The harm they visit upon humanity is a story best left untold; however, there is a certain tale that can be told involving the ancient practice of seppuku.

Long before the modern age, during a period of national and cultural expansion, there was a custom in Japan known as seppuku. Tradition would have it that seppuku was a time honored practice, one that demanded extraordinary courage. True enough, it requires a certain type of courage to disembowel yourself, but the fact remains that seppuku was a form of institutionalized murder. The climate of the times was such that few dared question the moral implications, and even fewer dared resist the order to commit suicide. Besides, not everyone opposed the practice, especially those who coveted the lifestyles enjoyed by their superiors.

Soothed by the comforting melody of the nearby brook, Death's intended victim basked in the warmth of the morning sun. The sound of rustling bamboo added to his auditory delight, further accentuating the all-embracing rhythm of Mother Nature. Somehow, the essence of the bamboo, ever the symbol of strength and resilience, was working its way into his core, fortifying his will to live. Thus his anxiety was dissipating, as if swept away by the same wind that captivated the bamboo.

He was only vaguely aware of his wife sitting directly opposite, balancing a ceremonial sword upon her knees. Not wanting to disturb his mood, she was patiently awaiting his acknowledgment. She revered her husband, not because he was a powerful man, but because he was a good man in spite of the evil system that had ensnared him. He was undoubtedly trapped, and seppuku was the only way out. She had long feared this day, and now that it had arrived she felt totally numb, completely unable to comprehend the inevitability of her impending loss.

He had been highly placed throughout most of his life, but had never dared aspire to the office of Regional Governor. That all changed when his predecessor committed seppuku. His initial reaction to his appointment to the office of Governor had been one of elation; however, it wasn't long before he realized he was in over his head. He served an evil lord and, despite his growing contempt, he had always managed to suppress his rage, knowing that one day the slightest provocation might awaken his true feelings. That day had finally arrived.

Oddly enough, it was because the warlord favored a rare delicacy that the newly appointed Governor was ordered to commit seppuku. The warlord's favorite dish just happened to be a poisonous fish, unless prepared with a specific combination of freshly picked herbs, which were only available during late summer and early fall. The timing presented a major obstacle, because for some unknown reason the fish sometimes failed to migrate on schedule, making its availability unpredictable. Unfortunately, the warlord had no sympathy for the dictates of Mother Nature. When his favorite dish wasn't available, he took his frustration out on the local fishermen. And things weren't much better when the fish was available, because it was too small to net and too quick to spear. The only reliable method was to catch its natural predator, hoping to harvest one or two of the smaller fish. The operation was labor intensive, and the fishermen could not afford to waste time and energy on a project that contributed so little to their welfare.

The situation finally came to a head when the fishermen failed to meet their quota for the second year in a row. The season was over, and once again the warlord hadn't had a single bite of his favorite fish, leaving little doubt as to his position on their list of priorities. And he wasn't far from wrong, because the fishermen never made a serious attempt to catch the fish, having decided they could live with his wrath, but not with the loss of their daily catch. They could not have been more wrong.

Intent of having his revenge, the warlord ordered the total destruction of the fishing village. Every building was to be burned to the ground, every boat destroyed, and the harbor contaminated with pollutants known to ruin the ecological balance of any environment. The Regional Governor argued against reprisal, noting that the loss of the harbor would inconvenience the warlord, that so much destruction would adversely affect the entire province. Surely, there were options to be considered.

No friend to the insubordinate, the warlord went temporarily insane, descending into a fit of uncontrollable rage. Grabbing the nearest object, which just happened to be a beautiful golden goblet encrusted with precious gems, he hurled it at the Governor, opening a gash on the left side of his head. The Governor reacted badly, communicating years of contempt in a single glance. That glance cost him his life because the warlord ordered him to commit seppuku. What's more, his estate was to be forfeited and his family forced to vacate the property. All record of his existence would be erased, his name never again spoken in the warlord's kingdom.

The warlord had long since discovered that a steady diet of revenge helped fuel his quest for absolute power. Little did he know, but when power and position are abused, highly cathected emotions are generated at the subconscious level. Those emotions unleash a flood of hormones into the blood stream, temporarily creating a heightened sense of well-being. Eventually, however, those hormones alter the body's chemistry, ultimately unbalancing the mind, frequently creating a sadistic personality.

Upon hearing the warlord's decree, the Governor's immediate reaction had been one of relief. He had battled his conscience and concealed his emotions for too long. At least he would be free of the guilt that tortured his existence. At least the nightmares would end. He would gladly forfeit his life.

At the moment, however, everything seemed perfectly harmonious in his lovely bamboo garden. The warmth of the sun, the rhythmic sound of the rustling bamboo, and the consoling melody of the tumbling brook filled him with gratitude for the life that pulsed in his veins. He was standing at death's door, and yet he marveled at the surrounding beauty. It was a strange juxtaposition, abundant life and imminent death, and yet one that bestowed peace of mind.

Contentedly ensconced in nature's embrace, it occurred to the Governor that the brook's destination was forever established, but that its route to the sea was subject to change. Mother Nature might one day reorganize her priorities, and the brook might find itself transplanted to another part of the garden. And when that day arrived, as it surely would, the brook would simply continue its journey to the sea. Strange though it may seem, the brook was sharing its secrets with the Governor.

It was a magnificent moment, a rare occurrence to be sure, when life's indignities are forgiven, bestowing instead the blessing of peace and tranquility. Such was the Governor's state of mind, completely unrelated to any rational thought process. It simply was, and that was all the evidence he needed to know that he was an integral part of a Life much greater than his own.

But alas, life inevitably manifests in paired opposites, and his moment in the sun was no exception. Peace and tranquility ultimately gave way to the depths of despair, unleashing the dreaded Four Horsemen. The Four Horsemen always ride at night, ever hiding in the shadows of impending doom, forever shunning the light of day. Man fears them like no other, and when he shuts the door to his heart he might as well send out invitations, because the Four Horsemen always ride to the sound of closing doors. They have been known to sharpen their hooves and lay waste to a life in a fraction of a second, and their names are Guilt, Fear, Sorrow, and Fury.

The Regional Governor's conscience was now armed and dangerous. And it went like this. His wife was going to suffer because he had allowed his emotions to go unchecked. If only he had held his tongue. If only he had concealed the contempt in his voice, maybe then he could have averted catastrophe. Guilt, the most dangerous of the Four Horsemen, had arrived on the scene.

Thus he launched a desperate search for viable options, someway to escape the terrible fate that awaited him. He knew that if he refused to commit seppuku he would be hunted down and tortured. The last person to make that mistake was disemboweled with a garden rake, and then forced to rake up his entrails. Fear, the most deadly of the Four Horsemen, had arrived on the scene.

Suddenly, a single tear streaked down his otherwise impassive countenance. Somehow it had all gone wrong. Sorrow, the most devastating of the Four Horsemen, had arrived on the scene.

He was so startled by that display of emotion that had his kimono not born witness to his disgrace, he would have denied the fact in all sincerity. Furious with himself for having exhibited such an unforgivable sign of weakness, he lashed out at his wife, striking her upon the ear. It was not a mighty blow, but a blow nonetheless. Fury, the most destructive of the Four Horsemen, had arrived on the scene.

Reeling from the impact of the blow, the ceremonial sword slipped from her grasp and fell onto the ground. The sword would have to be cleansed, and the nearby brook would do nicely. She was more concerned with the sanctity of the ritual than she was with the stinging rebuke that now claimed a portion of her ear. He had never struck her before; therefore, she understood his behavior to be the product of extreme duress, and not a thing to be taken personally. She knew her husband, his fears, his follies, and his strengths. She therefore knew that his outburst was not an expression of his character, but a prelude to mental and emotional collapse.

Singing was not her forte, but she could carry a tune, and when her husband was feeling down she sometimes lifted his spirits with a song. So she sang their favorite ballad, the story of an impoverished young girl who had no hope of marriage. She was not very pleasing to the eye, and to make matters worse her father could not provide a dowry. It was by chance that she met a young man of high station, and it was by chance that Mother Nature threw them together. They were caught in a storm and, while working the fields, she happened to look up at the precise moment the young man was thrown from his horse. She rushed to his side and attended to his injuries, sheltering him from the rain with her cloak. The young man fell in love with his rescuer, and insisted upon marriage despite the low order of her station.

The ballad expressed a depth of gratitude she herself possessed, because she too had been born into a life of poverty, and she too had won the heart of a gallant young man who saw past the judgment of the world. Thus did she sing to her beloved for the last time, tenderly imbuing each note with the essence of her love and gratitude. Just as she had intended, the burden of past mistakes slowly dissolved, thus inviting the sights and sounds of Mother Nature to once again soothe her husband's aching heart. The tumbling brook, the chattering bamboo, and the radiant sun all resumed their ministrations.

Intending a quick, decisive end to the ordeal, the Governor gripped the hilt of the sword with one hand, while supporting his abdominal wall with the other hand. He knew exactly how to proceed. He would plunge the sword into the abdominal cavity, severing the aorta as quickly as possible by thrusting the razor sharp blade from one side of the abdomen to the other. There was no science to the art of self-inflicted disembowelment, but there was such a thing as good technique. He had witnessed men agonize for hours because they hadn't thought to stabilize the abdomen. The abdomen required firm support; otherwise, the blade invariably went astray. If he performed as expected, death would immediately ensue; otherwise, his wife would have to finish the job.

Holding the sword firmly to the flesh he paused just long enough to take in the essence of the bamboo garden. He dearly loved his garden, and the garden surely loved him, because at that moment the rustle of bamboo took voice on the wind, sharing a thought that instantly appealed to his nature. He would not comply with the warlord's order to commit seppuku; instead he would completely destroy his home and property. Only then would he take his own life, but he would not commit seppuku.

Strange though it may seem, it sometimes happens that the subconscious mind acts of its own accord, the conscious mind having made no overt decision to act. It's a rare occurrence, but there are those times when the subconscious mind is so highly charged that the conscious mind is left out of the equation. Thus it happened that the Governor unwittingly punctured his abdominal wall with the tip of his sword. The wound wasn't serious, because the unexpected stab of pain immediately prompted him to withdraw the sword.

Jumping to his feet, he hurried out of the garden, leaving his wife in a state of shock. She didn't understand what had happened, but whatever it was it had to be better than seppuku.

Summoning his most trusted retainers, the Governor instructed them to pour lamp oil throughout his magnificent home. Once ablaze, it burned to the ground in a matter of minutes, consuming everything he owned. Then, having assembled the field hands, he ordered them to first slaughter the livestock and then set fire to every acre of grain. Next he turned his attention to his private wharf. Soon the wharf was ablaze, his sailing ship scuttled near the entrance to the harbor. The channel was narrow and not very deep; consequently, the mast of the sunken vessel could be seen extending well above the surface of the water.

Still not satisfied, he climbed to the top of the bluff overhanging the harbor. The sky was filled with smoke, black and acrid; it wouldn't be long before it aroused the warlord's suspicion. He put every available man to work, and within the hour a ready-made avalanche stood perched on the edge of the cliff. Wasting no time he released a lifetime of accumulated rage, jumping back in awe as pure, unadulterated mayhem toppled over the edge. The entire jumble of madness cascaded into the channel, creating an impasse that blocked the harbor.

Mindful of his wife, and anxious that she depart before the arrival of the warlord, he attended to his last official act of destruction. Standing at the very edge of the bluff, he stepped into oblivion without uttering a single word. Unable to bear the weight of her gaze, he never looked up, but waved good-bye as he plummeted to his death. Stricken with grief, his wife immediately followed him onto the rocks below.

The following day, while searching the garden, the warlord came upon the Governor's disemboweled body, ritual sword at his side. His wife's body was found splayed out on the rocks at the foot of the bluff. All of the evidence suggested that the Governor had done his duty, that his wife had destroyed the estate in a fit of rage before leaping to her death. That alone spared the lives of their retainers.

When the Governor and his wife arrived on the other side of the gate they were delighted to discover that they were free to live as they pleased. The astral world is almost entirely shaped by desire, and those who reside upon its upper levels create beautiful environments, completely free of the hardship and drudgery that characterized their former lives. The inhabitants comport themselves with love and respect and live in a world rich with sound and color. Some enjoy a leisurely life, while others undergo extensive training in order to work as spirit guides. Still others enroll in one of the many universities, choosing from a wide variety of studies. The universities are free, and graduation generally earns a promotion to the mental plane.

Still longing for the comforting embrace of Mother Nature, the Governor recreated his bamboo garden down to the last detail. He was content to relax in the warmth of the sun, listening to the soothing sound of bamboo gently swaying in the breeze. The sound of tumbling water could be heard in the background, and next to his place in the sun sat his devoted wife, happy to be at his side.

He never bothered to review the life he had left behind, nor did he see any need to make preparations for his next incarnation. He simply surrendered to the sights and sounds of Mother Nature. It wasn't a bad choice, but had he looked a little deeper, he might have taken advantage of the many opportunities available to him. Had he done so he might have been better prepared to face the karma that awaited his arrival back on planet earth.

LIFE NINETEEN
The Bandit

BORN AS HE was into a family of cutthroats, it was no small wonder that he cut many a throat in the years allotted to him. In his world there was no such thing as the rule of law, and therefore justice was but rarely served. Rather, there was a system of retribution, fiercely applied and jealously guarded by those who claimed the right to judge their fellowman. He grew up believing that violence ruled the affairs of men, so it should not surprise you to learn that he became the embodiment of his ideal. Eventually, he rose in status until he was recognized as the leader of a clan known for its depredations. His comfort zone was such that he felt entirely at home with his band of villains, having been bred to lawlessness and unbridled passion from the day of his birth.

His clan numbered perhaps a few hundred strong and, despite their limited numbers, they were nearly invincible when they restricted their violence to the vicinity of their home base. They headquartered in a section of the plain elevated by tectonic movement, which all but prevented a mounted attack. Additionally, their stronghold was amply supplied with water and grass for grazing their horses, thereby creating a natural fortress.

During the winter they bided their time, content to sit by the fire, but when spring arrived they couldn't wait to slake their thirst for blood. Throughout the summer and fall they raided far and wide, but rarely more than a fortnight's ride from their headquarters. Barbarism was their trade, and while most came to the work through the unabated surge of animal instincts, some arrived at the same place on the evolutionary scale through the need to expiate their guilt.

The latter carried the seeds of self-hate, and that hate clamored for projection onto somebody else. Had they been born into another culture they might have expunged their self-contempt in a socially acceptable manner, but their karma was such that they were denied any advantage. Instead, they found themselves in a world of perpetual violence. Strange though it may seem, they felt somehow cleansed of the evil that lurked within whenever they murdered the innocent.

As for the Bandit, he practiced the art of war with a fervor that both shocked and awakened the impulse to primeval aggression. He routinely rose before dawn, bundled his weapons, and departed camp with the look of an out of work assassin upon his face. He danced and flailed at the sun, enacting various throws and thrusts designed to maximize the destructive power of his weaponry. His entire life was given over to the art of war, although when seen in its application, it might best be described as violent crime.

As a young boy he had consistently bullied the other children, and never missed a chance to abuse the dogs that foraged the camp. His antics were tolerated because no one dared confront his father, who was the sort of man who killed first, and then didn't ask any questions. Not that the bandit horde was mortally offended by the boy's behavior; they simply grew weary of his pranks, and sometimes felt that he went too far when tormenting the women and children. To be sure, everybody beat their wives and pounded on their children, but they generally had the decency to restrict their violence to their own affiliations.

The father considered his son a burden and, while he hated him for the fact of his existence, he tolerated no abuse from any hand but his own. And his hand was not idle, because he routinely beat the boy throughout his formative years. Eventually the boy reached the end of his rope, and murdered his father in his sleep. One little slice of the carotid artery and his troubles were over. The father's death may have put a stop to the beatings, but it also rendered the boy vulnerable to anyone with a score to settle. There were some unpleasant scenes, but when it was all said and done, he had established himself as an accepted member of the clan.

One fine day during the summer of his prime, accompanied by a gang of cutthroats chosen from his clan, the Bandit set out on a great adventure. He and his cohorts traveled farther than was their usual custom, but were ultimately rewarded when they came upon a band of itinerants bivouacked on the bank of a river. They arrived on the scene just in time to witness the departure of a large party of scouts, leaving the camp undermanned and vulnerable to attack. After waiting a decent interval of time, they descended on the encampment like a pack of wild dogs. At first strike blood filled the air like summer rain, and by the last stroke everything and everybody was coated with the mark of Cain. They slaughtered everyone but the women, sparing them for obvious reasons. Next they mutilated the corpses and stuffed their throats with their private parts, thereby commemorating their great victory.

Then they turned their aggression on the women. For the bandits sex was nothing more than animal passion, which made the women who died resisting the lucky ones, because the survivors were in for a night of misery. The bandits had no concept of civility, let alone tenderness; but they knew how to conquer their enemies, and that's just what they did to the women. They ravaged the women until they were exhausted, and then executed them lest they trouble their sleep. Cavemen treated their women better, and had that crew of villains been associated with the Cro-Magnon, they would have been culled from the flock at an early age. Even the Cro-Magnons respected the right of a woman to survive the sexual encounter.

Sexual perversion has its roots in man's ancient past, and anyone sexually aroused by violence is either the product of a tortured past, or has sunk into the depths of sexual depravity one life at a time. Those with tortured pasts are often re-enacting past degradation, unconsciously attempting to expunge their own pain. Those who arrive at the depths of depravity through the avenue of gradual descent are the most incurable of all, because they have learned to love their perversion through constant obsession. Either way, change is doubtful, because it takes decades, if not lifetimes, to eradicate the urge to rape and murder.

Having tired of the festivities, the Bandit retired to a quiet spot amongst the trees. He fashioned a lean-to designed to conceal his location, and soon fell into a deep, but troubled sleep. Entering the world of dreams, he found himself surrounded on all sides by a raging fire. His only refuge was a mound of sizzling corpses. Climbing to the top of the heap, the stench of human flesh caused him to heave the contents of his stomach. But, it wasn't food that erupted from his putrid guts, rather a tangled mass of clattering chains. He gawked in terror when the chains suddenly sprang to life, first entangling his legs, then dragging him down into the flames.

Dreams frequently signify nothing important, reflecting instead the purging of the subconscious mind. It also happens, however, that the Soul communicates through the medium of dreams, employing symbols and awakening memories likely to motivate the personality. In the Bandit's case his Soul was troubled by the life he was leading, and was serving notice that he had forged his own chains, that the gates of hell had opened.

The Bandit awoke to the sound of bloodcurdling screams. Because the screams coincided with his dream, several minutes lapsed before he realized something was terribly wrong. The scouts had returned during the night, and had crept amongst the bandits as they slept on their grog, cutting dozens of throats before someone awakened to the familiar sound of gurgling blood. Had the scouts pressed their advantage they might have slaughtered the entire contingent. Instead, they quickly faded back into the night, having lost not a single man. The advantage now rested with the enemy, and for the first time in their lives the bandits were confronted with the prospect of their own annihilation. Thus they started blaming one another for their misfortune. Understanding dawned when it became apparent that the night watch had been hitting the grog.

Life was hard with precious little entertainment, and even less worthy of celebration; hence, the common practice was to consume alcoholic beverages until rendered witless. They loved their grog, and after the usual run of the mill massacre they routinely drank themselves into a stupor. The sentries were duty bound to remain sober, but on that particular night the women had been especially alluring. Besides, they had endured a long ride followed by a lot of tiresome hacking and piking.

Desperately outnumbered, the surviving bandits hoped that it wasn't too late to hightail it out of there. That hope died a frightful death on the vine of despair when they discovered that the enemy had surrounded their encampment. To make matters worse, diabolical shrieks could be heard piercing the night. The shrieks were unlike anything they had ever heard, and they had heard their share of inhuman sounds. It was an evil sound, not unlike the clangor of ghouls and demons. Not surprisingly, their skin began to itch, as if crawling with insects, ever the sign of ancient memories from the dawn of man. Terror was literally manifesting in the flesh.

The bandit leader experienced no such symptoms. From the outset he had recognized a weapon with which he had no familiarity. He had heard many a battle cry, but never a shriek capable of unnerving the fiercest warrior. So he carefully observed both tone and pitch, taking note of its effect upon man and beast. He soon discovered that the dogs were not the least bit affected. The fact that the shrieks totally unnerved his men, but had no affect upon the dogs could only mean one thing. The effect was purely psychological. What's more, the shrieks reminded him of the neighing of a wounded horse. Horses were held sacred, and the plaintive sound of a suffering horse was just about the worst sound imaginable.

Thereafter the Bandit practiced replicating the sound. When the enemy shrieked, he answered in kind, with one notable difference. He had long since discovered that battle cries were more effective when combined with mental imagery depicting mutilated corpses. Therefore, whenever he shrieked he conjured up vivid images of severed limbs and headless trunks. The scouts were completely stunned. They never expected their secret weapon to be turned against them.

Abandoning his faint-hearted cohorts, the Bandit slipped into the surrounding forest and commenced waging war with the enemy. He was a killing machine, and it began to look as if he might single-handedly turn the tables. Sensing the changing of the tide, the scouts launched an all out attack on the bandit camp. Unfortunately for the bandits they hadn't slept in days, rendering them totally incapable of putting up any meaningful resistance. The end came quickly.

Rather than wait until the scouts ferreted him out, the Bandit stole into their camp early one morning. To his chagrin the scouts were not at all surprised, but had been patiently awaiting his arrival. They beat him senseless and, rather than kill him, tethered him to a post located in the center of their camp.

He hurled abuse. He spit. He snarled. He shrieked at the top of his lungs. Eventually he snapped his tether and charged into their midst, punching and kicking a platoon of onlookers. A blow to the back of the head took him down. This time they lashed him securely in place, tying him to the post with but a yard of tether to spare, thereby restricting his movement.

Later that day, having rigorously debated the sequence of events, they amputated a full complement of the Bandit's toes, followed soon after by all of his fingers. Each and every appendage was passed around for inspection, and then tossed into their nightly stew. They had no intention of letting him die; knowing as they did that systematic amputation could take weeks, if not months to kill a man.

The following morning they cut off his ears and shattered his teeth with an axe handle. The pain was intolerable, but he never begged for mercy. Slipping in and out of consciousness, he plummeted into the realm of dreams and found himself standing on a mountain ledge overlooking a rock-strewn valley below. He was determined to jump, but before he could carry out his plan, a blue-eyed man suddenly appeared and offered a helping hand. The Bandit awoke with a start and, recalling his dream, knew that he would never forget those pale blue eyes sparkling like gems on the moonlit crest of a mountain.

The effect of the dream was remarkable, because now he was even more determined to fight to the bitter end. He wanted them to know the kind of man they were dealing with, which is just what his tormentors hoped to discover when they decided to bore a hole in his skull. They held him down while the camp's only doctor bored a fairly large hole in his head, and then tried prying the contents out with a spoon designed for plucking eyeballs from dead critters. The so-called doctor soon abandoned his quest, because he found the human brain remarkably resilient when filled with blood. But not, as it turned out, very resistant to bacteria.

The Bandit's head swelled beyond recognition, dwarfing his facial features in a sea of mutilated flesh. He was nearly dead, but that didn't stop him from lashing out at his tormentors. Amazed at his continued resistance, the leader of the group decided to pay a personal visit to the man who had bravely endured the unthinkable. When he carelessly stepped into range, the Bandit lunged with every ounce of strength he possessed. Grappling his prey to the ground, he sank his broken teeth into the nearest eye socket and proceeded to suck the eyeball right out of the man's head.

They beat him to death, but not before the errant eyeball twittered away, coming to rest in a pile of excrement before its owner could retrieve it. He tried to stuff it back into the socket, but the fit was all-wrong. He survived the loss of his eye, but not the infection that resulted.

The Bandit was a tragic mess when he crossed over to the other side. Half out of his mind, he refused admittance into the hospital, totally frustrating the spirit guides who had gathered around to help ease his transition. When his Beloved Master intervened and ordered him into the hospital, everyone expected the Bandit, who gave no indication of recognition, to refuse even him. However, when the Bandit caught a glimpse of the Master's pale blue eyes, he recalled seeing those same eyes while standing on a mountain ledge in his dream. Thereafter he agreed to cooperate.

One hundred years later, when the call of the flesh once again reverberated throughout his atomic structure, he was drawn to his heart's desire, a family of his own.

LIFE TWENTY
The Family

BLOOD TRICKLED DOWN his sides while he sat on his haunches, deflecting what blows he could. Head down, eyes tightly closed, he was rapidly approaching the limits of his endurance, almost to the point of passing out. He wasn't afraid of losing consciousness, because he knew that his father would stop once he keeled over, but only if he was unconscious. His father was a determined man, and had found a surefire way to test whether or not he was feigning. If a bucket of icy water straight from the fjord failed to arouse the boy, he knew that he had accomplished his goal.

A lifetime of abuse had accustomed the boy to daily prayer in hopes of deliverance, even though he knew that any mercy decreed by the gods was destined to fail. He had come to believe that the gods had forsaken him, perhaps even hated him. Why else would his father beat him every day of his life for no apparent reason? His father never assaulted his three older brothers, but maybe, he thought, that was because they were bigger and stronger. Maybe when he grew up the beatings would stop, but for now he could expect at least one thrashing a day.

Fists were the easiest to endure, because they were more easily deflected, unlike the lightning strikes of a switch. He hated the switch, and feared for his life whenever it was brought to bear upon his tiny frame. Besides, he had noticed that while punches to the head and body were almost always spontaneous reactions, the switch represented a form of ritualistic torture, requiring a convincing performance for the benefit of those who watched.

His three older brothers were never troubled by the beatings, because like their father they hated him for his diminutive size, and therefore loathed the very sight of him. Unlike the rest of the family he would never attain the stature of the average Viking male, and therefore would never become the ideal man, tall and hardy and capable of enduring a hard life with few frills. What's more he showed no interest in the Viking way of life, making it obvious to everyone who knew him that he would never become an accepted member of society, preferring like he did the solitude of the forest.

Eyes open, the boy stared at the macabre scene taking shape upon the cracked surface of the stone floor. Each new drop of blood added to the emerging terrain, seemingly creating a burgeoning network of rivers and streams, becoming instead the outstretched claws of a hideous monster. Moments later he plummeted straight into the monster's grasp. The monster possessed all the standard features for a creature of that sort, fierce black eyes with claws to match, while breathing fire from a mouth sporting multiple rows of jagged teeth. Not unexpectedly, the monster's razor-sharp claws lacerated his flesh, evoking a blood-curdling scream. Momentarily amused, the beast retracted its claws, whereupon the boy picked up a knife and lunged, cutting and slashing until the blood of the beast coated his skin. Just when it seemed that victory was within his grasp, the monster retaliated, unleashing a blinding volley of deadly blows. When he awoke he recalled the dream, and instantly knew what had to be done. He interpreted his dream not as a warning, but as permission to commit murder.

Clambering to his feet, he leaned against the wall for support, quickly orienting himself to his surroundings.

Nobody was home, so he made his way to the corner of the house where each night he slept on the floor. Sinking to his knees, he swept his bedding aside, revealing the stone slab that concealed his secret cache. It took but a moment to pry the slab loose, and once dislodged he reached for his most prized possession. Removing the gleaming blade from its den, he felt a surge of power infuse his tortured body.

He had discovered the knife deep in the forest on one of his many excursions into the wild, and had kept it hidden from view ever since. It was a hunting knife, the kind used for big game. Its owner would kill to get it back, because knives like that were rare, and the men who plied the frozen north were quick to settle their disputes.

The boy's father was such a man, and yet many years had come and gone since he had last gone to sea with the war parties that raided to the south. His father was proud of his past, and never let anyone forget that he had once sacked and pillaged with the best of them. Not surprisingly, the boy identified with his father's stories, never realizing that when over stimulated, the imagination can awaken karmic conditions best left in the past.

Storytelling aside, the boy nurtured a burning hatred for his father, and felt much the same towards his brothers. He knew that another beating might end his life, so he formulated a desperate plan of action. Hate fueled his plan, unwittingly fulfilling the karma of his victims, while at the same time awakening memories from his ancient past. The Club was coming to the fore, and it was time to cull the flock. This time, however, brute strength would give way to careful planning. The details had to be carefully worked out, and then flawlessly executed; otherwise, he would be the one who ended up dead.

Late that night, clutching the knife to his chest, he patiently waited for the telltale sounds of rhythmic breathing. Once satisfied that everyone was sound asleep, he crept to the hearth and scooped up a bucket of glowing coals. Positioning the coals next to the door, he retrieved a jug of whale oil used for coating the knives and utensils. Jug to the right, knife to the left, he spread oil throughout the one room hovel, dousing his victims' bedding as he went. Where murder was concerned he was both practical and efficient.

Standing next to the door, he recounted his movements, making doubly sure he had accomplished everything according to plan. Then, without so much as one last glance, he flung the glowing embers into the center of the room. Towering flames engulfed the house, igniting the jug of oil in his hand. Shocked and dazed, he staggered outside and thrust his injured hand into the cold, white snow.

When the fire burned out he ventured into the remains and found his brothers still in their beds, burnt beyond recognition. His father had apparently tried to escape, because he lay in the middle of the room, facedown, arms extended towards the door. It was a gruesome sight, but one that inspired his imagination. His father had unwittingly provided him with an alibi. And it went like this. Roused by the fire, he had valiantly tried to save his father, giving up only when the fire threatened to envelop him. It was a believable story. After all, who would suspect a twelve-year-old boy of such a deplorable crime?

The locals considered the boy a hero who had risked his life while courageously trying to save his father. Because of his age and the nature of his loss, several families agreed to share responsibility for his care, offering their resources to the extent that it elevated their standing in the community. After all, the boy was a hero, and their support was deemed almost as worthy as the support given to the families of slain warriors.

Because of the abuse he had endured the boy was incapable of love, so he never formed an attachment to any of the families that raised him. Consequently, when he reached his sixteenth year everyone agreed that it was time for him to make his own way in life. By then he had been plying the forest for years, and had become an expert woodsman, developing skills few possessed. No one was surprised when he severed all ties with the local community, choosing instead the solitude of the forest.

Several years went by without incident, until one day, while trekking through the forest, he came upon two brothers who made the mistake of belittling his diminutive size. Having endured more than his share of contempt, he lashed out with lightning speed, his knife but a blur to the human eye. They fell in a heap, gushing from multiple wounds, warm blood turning the snow-covered ground to slush.

Knowing exactly what had to be done, he applied his knife to the awful task of dismembering the bodies. The whole ghastly mess had to be hauled out of the forest and dumped in the fjord. Choosing an isolated area, he heaved the evidence of his crime into the turbulent sea. Hauling mutilated corpses was one thing, but doing so without leaving a trail was quite another. Even so, he completed his task without leaving a drop of misplaced blood. His crime would never be discovered.

When he returned to the scene of the crime he was immediately confronted with the mess he had created. That's when he realized that removing the bodies wasn't enough, because the bloody aftermath of the assault would undoubtedly prove his guilt. Just when it seemed frustration would get the better of him, he became aware of an ominous sound approaching through the trees. Stepping back into the shadows, he witnessed the arrival of an oversized bear. The smell of fresh blood had drawn it to the scene of the carnage.

Recognizing his cover story, he leapt onto the bear's exposed back, repeatedly thrusting his knife into its flesh, only to be tossed through the air time and again. He was no match for the bear, and soon found himself pinned under its massive weight. Survival seemed out of the question, but then the bear pitched over onto its side and began writhing in the throes of death. He passed out in the snow right next to the bear.

Fortunately for the boy, he was discovered in the nick of time, knife in hand, dead bear at his feet. Despite the extent of his injuries, his recovery was faster than might be expected, and within a matter of weeks he was back roaming the forest. Only now his body bore the scars of battle, furrowed arms and ruined face proclaiming his manhood. He wore his scars like badges of honor, seeing not disfigurement, but proof of his courage. As for the two brothers, they were presumed lost in the wild.

For the next several years he survived by hunting game over a vast expanse of land. On one of his excursions, while trekking into the frozen north, he discovered a trail seemingly left by humans. It struck him odd, because there were no known settlements that far north. He dogged their trail for days before realizing he had ventured out of his element. He was far from home and wasn't prepared for the freezing cold that permeated his flesh right down to the bone. His supplies were nearly exhausted, and the tundra offered little in the way of food or shelter. So he decided to turn back at first light. Bedding down for the night, he burrowed into the snow for warmth and protection. He never heard the sound of encroaching feet.

They were huge and they were hairy. Not one of them weighed less than 300 pounds, and the shortest of the lot would have dwarfed the average Viking male. They wore no clothing and had no need of shoes. When viewed from behind they appeared human at first glance, but upon further inspection they resembled nothing he had ever seen before. That's when he recalled the legend of the Abominable Snowman.

They left him barefoot and bound to a tree. Curiously, they didn't seem the least bit angry. They simply wanted to prevent him from following their trail.

The legend of the Snowman is not a myth. Utilizing thousands of crystals, Atlantean scientists created both the Snowman and Big Foot by combining human genetic material with that of apes. Unlike Big Foot, the Snowman was never transported to Madagascar, but went straight from the lab to the arctic regions of northern Scandinavia and beyond.

Faced with immanent death, he was surprised to discover that he feared whatever it was that awaited him beyond the grave. He had long since concluded that the gods hated his very existence, so the concept of hell was not new to his way of thinking. Given the treachery of his past, having murdered for revenge, the artic cold hardly compared to the avalanche of despair that suddenly overwhelmed the internal fortress he had so carefully constructed.

Lashed to a tree, arms to the back, knees to the chest, he slipped in and out of consciousness, ultimately plummeting into a terrifying nightmare. The hairy beasts had returned, and they were mutilating his flesh. He screamed at the top of his lungs when they sliced off his fingers and toes. He shrieked in horror when they bored into his skull. He begged for mercy, and then he begged for death. He was completely hysterical, and still they continued their depredations.

He awoke in a cold sweat, and immediately understood that something evil awaited his arrival in hell. In reality the repressed horror of his previous life was intruding upon his conscious mind. Had he understood the nature of his dream he might have avoided the nightmare that was about to occur.

When he arrived on the other side of the gate he immediately started running for his life. Ten years later he was still running from his tormentors, a pack of hairy beasts armed with a full array of weaponry. Of course, the beasts, though they had been real in the flesh, were nothing more than figments of his imagination. The situation might have continued indefinitely had it not been for the intervention of his Beloved Master, who persuaded him to stop running. When he finally stopped he promptly fell asleep, a common occurrence on the lower levels of the astral plane. When he awoke from his slumber he was already occupying the body of a newborn babe. Little did he know, but his ordeal was far from over.

The Moon Child

T HERE WAS NO stopping them and there was no avoiding them, because no matter what preventative measures he employed the voices continued their assault upon his brain. Only he could hear the voices that plagued his days and tormented his nights, therefore no one could possibly understand the terror they evoked. Nor would anyone ever comprehend the war being waged between him and his ancient past. He was alone in his misery, and one day soon those voices would drive him to a lonely grave.

He lived in a region now known as the Ukraine on a large, sprawling farm. The farm was owned by a feudal lord, but managed by his family who worked long, hard days for their keep. His family members struggled with his incapacity, but never seriously resented the burden of his disability, except when it interfered with their work. Beyond that, they frequently tired of the extra care and attention he required, but still managed to do what they could to make his life bearable.

His name was Moon. Moon was not his given name, but it was the name most often used by the locals. He had earned the name by virtue of his mental condition, because in their minds he was 'as crazy as the man in the moon'. It was a natural connection given the significance of the moon in human history.

The moon has long been a symbol of aberrant behavior. The source of that wisdom lies in man's distant past, and relates to a time when the moon was ensouled by a race of humans who ultimately succumbed to their lower natures, not unlike the people of Atlantis. At that time the moon held its own orbit around the sun. It wasn't until thousands of years after its civilization self-destructed that the moon fell into the earth's magnetic field. The locals had no knowledge of such esoteric matters, but believed, nevertheless, that the moon exerted a negative influence upon the affairs of men.

The voices first appeared during his late teens, but remitted for nearly a year during his early twenties, only to return for no identifiable reason. The voices were his constant companions, and even when blessed with a temporary reprieve, he spent nearly every waking moment anticipating their return. To be sure, there were those times when they presented as harmless; however, most of the time they were less than cordial. They occasionally offered helpful suggestions, but more often than not they barraged him with threats and accusations. He would resolve not to listen, but sooner or later he would react to their threats. Fear invariably entered into the equation and, once embraced, there was no escape, until utter exhaustion resulted in total collapse.

Moon spent most of his time alone in his room, held hostage by the voices that ruled his world - they commanded his full attention. Whenever he engaged them directly the outcome was always the same. First they flattered him, then they cajoled him, and finally they accused him. He invariably fell under their spell, endlessly defending his right to exist, sometimes demonstrating his usefulness with a flurry of household chores. Hard work bore witness to his personal worth, and he was determined to prove his point. When hard work failed to appease the voices, it wasn't unusual for him to sit motionless for hours at a time, refusing to acknowledge their presence. Beyond that, he tried donning various disguises, which included wearing clothes made from the hides of predatory animals. On one occasion, he even wove a poisonous snake into the fabric of his hat. Nothing worked, not even the amulets he had obtained from the local witch.

His only escape was sheer exhaustion. Only then could he sleep. Sleep came hard, and except for those times when exhaustion overrode his agitated state of mind, he rarely experienced any significant rest. Exhaustion was his friend, which is why he frequently ran for miles, crisscrossing the farm with geometric precision. The tactic worked well enough when he gave no thought to anything but sleep; however, he sometimes fixated on the thought that sleep might elude him despite his exhaustion. And sure enough, sleep was nowhere to be found once he had alerted his mind to the possibility.

And so it happened that he went for a run in an effort to exhaust his body to the point of unavoidable sleep. He ran for hours, never deviating from his chosen pattern. After his last extended run he had slept for an entire day; however, this time he had no such luck, because soon after falling asleep he awoke with a disturbing dream. The dream was impossible to ignore, rendering sleep out of the question.

In his dream he intentionally set fire to the house while the rest of his family slept in their beds. When the blaze got out of hand, he rushed outside, but not before the fire had bitten him on the hand. Ignoring the pain, he watched in fascination as the house burned to the ground. Despite the hideous nature of his crime, he experienced no remorse, and not a shred of guilt.

He awoke to the sound of voices - voices only he could hear. They were taking credit for his dream. According to them, they not only ruled his conscious mind, but controlled his dreams as well. Therefore he had no choice but to obey their wishes, and setting fire to the house while his family slept was precisely what they wanted him to do.

The closer Moon came to acquiescing, the quieter the voices became, until it seemed as though they were literally whispering in his ear. All he had to do was reach into the fireplace and pick up a stick of burning wood. The rest would be easy. A couple of little fires strategically placed, and the house would go up in flames.

Moon knew that his family loved him, but he also knew that they considered him a liability. He knew that setting fire to the house was wrong, but he also knew that they deserved to be punished; otherwise, the voices would not have told him to set the house on fire. He was balancing the books, and the outcome was yet to be determined.

That's when the voices played their trump card, dragging his worst nightmare out into the light of day. The voices claimed to have overheard his family members conspiring to sell him to a band of Gypsies. He couldn't imagine a more terrible fate.

Brandishing a flaming torch, Moon crept into his parents' bedroom where he ignited the woolen fabric adorning the outside wall. Screams of terror assaulted his ears, causing him to forego any plans he had for torching the other rooms. Instead, he rushed outside and stood watch just out of sight. It was then that he noticed something unusual. The voices were gone. Strange though it may seem, catastrophic events can temporarily silence the voices associated with schizophrenia, which is what happened when Moon set fire to the house.

Slowly, he edged out the shadows, and to his dismay he found no evidence of fire. That's when he knew that he had been duped again, only this time he had gone too far. This time he had endangered everyone in the house. This time his antics would surely cost him his freedom, if not his life.

His parents had been feigning sleep, lest he engage them with some of his foolishness. They had heard him enter, but it wasn't until they heard the crackle of flames that they understood what he had done. Fortunately, they managed to put the fire out before any real damage was done. Meanwhile, adrenalin was coursing through their veins, feeding the rage that was now burning hotter than the fire they had just extinguished. In the past Moon had always managed to avoid their ire, but this time was different. This time he would pay with his life.

Fearing the worst, Moon started running, fleeing the wrath of his parents, not to mention the specter of wandering Gypsies. At first he ran in panic, but then he remembered his secret hiding place in the woods. Over the years he had used his hideaway as a safe haven, but never in the middle of winter, and never without first packing in supplies. Nevertheless, it would have to do, because he had nowhere else to go. He had dug it out years before, and while it was nothing more than a hole in the ground, it served its purpose.

He discovered his hideaway buried under a snowdrift, and spent the better part of an hour clearing away the snow. Lifting the hatch, he was relieved to find his hideout ready for use. Jumping into his escape pod, he closed the hatch and settled in for the night. It wasn't long before he drifted off to sleep.

Moon loved his dreams because they always contradicted the harsh reality of his daily life. They sometimes featured a fearless military commander, a man who was both feared and revered by his men. He loved the commander's fierce fighting style, but he especially loved the purple cape that adorned his heroic figure. Then there were the dreams that depicted a solitary monk perched on the peak of a mountain, serenely gazing into space, clearly enjoying the quiet splendor of Mother Nature. Now, however, drifting into his final sleep, he dreamt not of war, nor of mountaintop retreats, but of a beautiful grove of wispy bamboo gently swaying in the breeze. There were no voices to be heard - just the sound of chattering leaves.

Meanwhile, Moon's family was building an ironclad case against his continued survival. The house had sustained minimal damage, but enough to arouse suspicion. The feudal lord, otherwise known as the Baron, was a heartless man. At the very least he would throw them off the land. They would be out of work with no prospect of employment. For all intents and purposes Moon had murdered them after all. The more they thought about it, the more they became convinced that the moon had nothing to do with the voices in his head. Obviously, evil spirits had been whispering in his ear all along.

By morning, rage was the emotion of the day, and the search for Moon was underway. They expected the Baron to act quickly once he received word of the fire, but there was still time to dispose of Moon. With any luck at all, his death would assuage the Baron's wrath.

It was well past midmorning when they found Moon entombed in his self-made grave. Relief was the only emotion that touched their hearts, not because Moon had found his final resting place, but because the burden of his existence had at last been lifted from their shoulders. They never looked back as they tramped away through the cold, white snow.

They were in for a surprise. The house was in flames, and they had arrived just in time to witness the final stages of the inferno. Unbeknownst to them, Moon had tossed his torch beneath the house, thinking to destroy the evidence. The torch had smoldered through the night, eventually erupting into flames. By the time the fire had worked its way through the wooden foundation, it was well on its way to becoming the raging fire Moon had imagined.

All was lost. The Baron lived according to the precepts of the Old Testament, and therefore believed in the age-old principle of an eye for an eye. Death was an absolute certainty. The Baron was a powerful man, and his reach extended throughout the land, virtually eliminating the possibility of flight. Turning to their neighbors for help was out of the question, because the Baron would crush anyone who defied his authority. He would undoubtedly stake the entire family out in the public square, common treatment for common criminals. It was a hideous prospect and they had no intention of enduring such a horrible fate. Their only option was suicide and, except for one last act of revenge, they would settle the matter quickly, if not cleanly.

They salvaged what they could from the wreckage of the house, and then carted it off to the local witch's den, where they traded for enough poison to kill an army. Each in his turn drank some of the brew, saving the major portion for the task ahead. They were bound for the village, but stopped along the way at the Baron's private well, long renown as a source of excellent drinking water. They poured the remainder of the poison down the shaft.

Their diabolical plan was coming together. One by one they dropped dead within minutes of passing through the village gate, their bloated bodies creating the dreaded specter of the Black Plague. The news spread throughout the village, creating mass hysteria, until the local doctor came to the rescue and assured everyone that the deaths were totally unrelated to the plague. Rather, it was an obvious case of mass suicide. As it happened, he had recognized the symptoms at once, having resorted to the same means himself when his wife, now dead and gone, had given every indication of becoming a serious detriment to his happiness.

When the Baron suddenly dropped dead in a puddle of liquid excrement, everyone in the village knew that the doctor had been wrong, that the plague had in fact struck. Pandemonium broke out and a gang of rioters set fire to the Baron's estate, killing everyone who got in their way. Next they went in search of the village priest, seeking an explanation for their misfortune. Obviously, God had forsaken them for a reason.

They found the priest in bed with a child, drunk as usual. They staked him out and left him to die, not because of his sexual perversion, but because he had failed to solicit God's intercession on their behalf. It wasn't long before the priest succumbed to the elements, never having figured out why he had been so rudely treated. The entire village was aware of his taste for alcohol and little boys; therefore, that certainly could not have been the cause. Understanding dawned when he christened the mob 'a bunch of lunatics'. It wasn't an official diagnosis, although it certainly described the whole chain of events.

Unfortunately, the violence did not end with the priest, ultimately claiming anyone who looked the least bit ill. Innocent souls were staked out in the snow, and before the day was over a goodly number were on their way through the gate that knows no return, except, of course, in the form of a newborn babe.

When Moon arrived on the other side of the gate he was met by his Beloved Master, and together they ascended into the realm of the upper astral plane, where he was reunited with friends and family from other lifetimes. When given the opportunity he reviewed the Celestial Record, and was able to identify mistakes he had made in previous lifetimes, mistakes that had shaped the life he had just endured. From that point forward he applied himself to the work at hand, laying the groundwork for his next incarnation. Little did he know, but hard work and diligent planning were about to pay a big dividend.

LIFE TWENTY-TWO

The Golden Life

T HE GOLD WORKER lived in the area now known as the Yucatan during the early years of the Mayan culture. The Mayans had at one time inhabited the heart of South America, where they were exposed to the remnants of the Atlantean culture. Because of that exposure the Mayan race would one day reach extraordinary heights; however, during the time of the Gold Worker, those heights were but distant goals.

The Gold Worker began each day with a visit to the temple of the Sun God. The walls of the temple were lined with gold, creating a spectacular golden hue when captured by the morning sun. He always arrived at dawn, and he always faced the western wall, thereby aligning himself with the Sun God's heavenly journey. On this particular morning he was alone in the temple, a blessing for which he was abundantly grateful, because total silence facilitated his meditation.

Assuming a comfortable position, the Gold Worker commenced a series of deep, rhythmic breaths, all the while focusing his attention upon the rise and fall of his abdomen. It was an ancient technique, one guaranteed to quiet the mind while restoring the body. Wholly alert and totally relaxed, he visualized a stream of Light cascading into the crown of his head, mentally directing the Light of the Soul into the cells of his body. Having achieved spiritual alignment, the Gold Worker next visualized Light radiating from the center of his being, while at the same time affirming God's ubiquitous presence. Incredible though it may seem, having merged with the Light of the Soul and therefore with the Spirit of the Sun God, the Gold Worker stopped breathing, his breath temporarily replaced by a subtle current of energy. The breathless state is very rare, and should never be attempted by force of will, but allowed to manifest as a natural occurrence.

Upon closing his meditation, the Gold Worker returned to everyday awareness feeling remarkably refreshed and focused. His mind was filled with creative ideas and he couldn't wait to start his day. He was a master craftsman and he specialized in custom-made jewelry, as well as other objects of fine art. His method, though ancient, was known to very few, and fully mastered by him alone. Even his tools were handcrafted; otherwise, he would not have been able to produce the threadlike lines that declared his mastery. Beyond that, his method required that he place the gold in the afternoon sun before any work was begun, thereby promoting a natural state of malleability.

Arriving home at the end of the day, the Gold Worker greeted his wife, and together they prepared the evening meal. They ate no meat in accordance with local custom, feasting instead on fruits and vegetables. After eating they gave thanks for the bounty they had received, and then parted company until the sun went down. There was always plenty to do in the village, and they were free to pursue their own interests, but only until dark. After dark no one was permitted outside the confines of their homes. Security was taken seriously, because predators, whether man or beast, invariably prowled the night.

Bandits were not unusual in the Mayan culture, because like any other society they had their share of troublemakers. Some were the victims of unfavorable circumstances, while others were criminally inclined from the day of their birth. The criminal mind is rooted in animal consciousness, and therefore feels entitled to take whatever it wants without reference to the rights of others. That is not the way of every species, but it is the way of the ape, and the ape is the forebear of the human race when it comes to the physical body. The ape as a species longs for autonomy, but also tends to obsession, and obsession combined with autonomy defines the very essence of the criminal mind.

Roving militias patrolled the jungle, apprehending bandits whenever possible. Once caught, they were usually executed on the spot; however, the worst of them were handed over to the local authorities. Thus it happened that a notorious bandit was apprehended and detained in the Gold Worker's village. The bandit's arrival was more of a spectacle than an official event; consequently, when the novelty wore thin, he was tossed headfirst into a pit reserved for just such an occasion. The pit was located near the center of town, right next to the public latrine. The Gold Worker's shop was just around the corner, close enough to draw him to the scene.

Having landed on his head, the bandit lay unconscious for the better part of an hour, ultimately awakening to the sound of beating drums. Jumping to his feet, he became immediately aware of his newly acquired cockeyed neck, not to mention the atrocious odor of human waste. It seems a bucket of waste had been dumped into the pit while he lay unconscious. He begged for mercy, but his pleas fell on deaf ears. When he began shouting obscenities, he was rewarded with yet another bucket of waste. The Gold Worker had little sympathy for the bandit, but when he saw how rudely the man was being treated, he decided to intervene when the time was right.

The Council of Elders fully intended on allowing Mother Nature to have her way, but changed their minds when the high priest in charge of human sacrifice claimed the right to decide the bandit's fate. The priest presented his best argument to the Council, and when he was finished thought he had persuaded the members to his way of thinking. But he was in for a surprise, because he hadn't factored the Gold Worker's opposition into his plans.

The Gold Worker approached the Council of Elders exhibiting the demeanor of a man who refused to take himself seriously. Ordinarily, self-effacement was considered a sign of weakness; however, the members had dealt with the Gold Worker before, and were well aware of his standing in the community. Much to their surprise, the Gold Worker never attacked the practice of human sacrifice, but based his plea for leniency entirely upon the premise of a benevolent God. His God was a loving God, but a God who nevertheless demanded accountability. Amends had to be made - if not to the victims themselves, then to the community as a whole. Everybody, the bandit included, stood to gain. Moved by the Gold Worker's eloquent plea for mercy, the Council ruled in his favor. However, after hearing the crowd's reaction to their ruling, the members thought it best to summon the bandit before finalizing their decision.

Reeking from the stench of human waste, the bandit was brought before the Council of Elders. Appalled by his condition, they sent him away, charging his wardens with the task of getting him cleaned up and suitably attired. The following day he was brought before the Council for the second time. His foul mouth and ugly disposition immediately surfaced, but before he could work up a steady stream of abuse, the bailiff struck him over the head with a mallet. When he came to his senses he was back in the pit, his neck more cockeyed than before.

When next brought before the Council, the bandit was gagged and bound to a chair. He expected to hear his death sentence pronounced; instead, everyone who had ever suffered at the hands of a bandit was given the opportunity to confront him. Those who had been seriously hurt reviled him with vivid accounts of their injuries. Those who had been robbed acquainted him with the terrible consequences that had befallen both them and their families. A woman who had been brutally raped tried to stab him with a knife, claiming that it was him who had attacked her. A family whose son had been murdered unleashed a torrent of animosity before subsiding into a quiet rendering of unrelenting sorrow. The parade of devastated souls lasted for hours, and then the merchants arrived, followed by a bevy of priests.

When the ordeal was finally over they tossed him into the pit still tied to his chair. The following morning they found him lying on his back. His legs partially paralyzed, he was unable to stand on his feet. So they dropped a rope and pulled him out, only to slam him to the ground with all the force they could muster. Then they dragged him before the Council of Elders and left him lying in a heap.

Disabled citizens had no standing in Mayan society, and the usual practice was to abandon the seriously impaired in the wild. Given the bandit's paralysis, there could no longer be any doubt as to his fate. Surely, the Council of Elders would not allow a cripple to sap the resources of the village, especially one such as him.

After summarizing the proceedings from the day before, the Council demanded an explanation from the bandit, but only after he was once again bound to a chair so that they might look him in the eye.

The bandit tearfully explained that he had always taken for granted his right to do as he pleased, if for no other reason than he had always been able to do just that. It was as simple as that. He knew no law but the law of the jungle, and they were asking him to make amends for his own nature. If ever there was a wrong answer that was it. Truthful though his answer was, it did not have the ring of contrition sought by the Council. Angered by the bandit's lack of remorse, they summoned the Gold Worker, whose brilliant plan to rehabilitate the bandit had gotten them involved in the first place.

The Gold Worker advised the learned leaders that he had been talking to the victims, and had discovered that many of them were greatly relieved, having had the opportunity to confront the source of their misery. At least that aspect of the plan had been a success, and well worth the time and effort expended by the Council. As for the bandit's lack of remorse, the Gold Worker offered to interrogate the prisoner.

The Gold Worker began his enquiry by asking the bandit whether or not he was interested in becoming a member of civilized society. The bandit's affirmative reply surprised everyone but the Gold Worker. When asked for an explanation, the bandit responded with a heart-rending story detailing the horrors of his youth. As a child he had longed for love, but instead had been sexually abused by his father, until he ran away and joined the bandits who roamed the jungle. Consequently, he no longer thought of himself as a human being, but as an animal who lived by the law of the jungle. It wasn't until he was confronted with his past that he had come to understand the full extent of his depravity. But, if given a chance to prove himself, he would do everything within his power to make amends. The Council was somewhat mollified, but remained unconvinced.

The following day the Council reconvened. Having taken all of the evidence into account, they sentenced the bandit to death, reasoning that a break with tradition for the sake of a crippled criminal would only sow dissent in the community. The Gold Worker went straight to the pit, and seeing the bandit on his feet, realized his paralysis was no longer an issue. He hurried back to the Council chamber only to discover that the Council had already been informed of the bandit's recovery, but considered his cockeyed neck just as much of an unacceptable infirmity as the paralysis of his legs.

Back at the pit, the bandit stoically accepted the news. He was resigned to his fate, having thought of little else since the procession of victims. Expressing his gratitude one last time, he asked the Gold Worker to honor his dying request. Would he find and care for his twelve-year-old son? Surely he could save the boy if he could transform a wretch like him.

Having agreed to the bandit's request, the Gold Worker ventured into the jungle in search of the bandit's young son. Word of his mission spread throughout the bandit kingdom, and within a matter of days the boy was placed in his custody without a single word being exchanged.

Meanwhile, back in the village, the bandit was taken to the top of a pyramid-like structure where he was publicly beheaded. The priest who performed the ritual appeared solemn and reverential, but on the inside his heart was undeniably black, just like the ceremonial garb that adorned his body.

The Gold Worker adopted the bandit's son and came to think of him as a natural born child of the marriage. The villagers, even though they had clamored for his father's death, saw in the boy the hope of redemption, and therefore accepted him into their community. The boy assumed the role of apprentice, and while he never fully mastered the art of gold working, he became a fine craftsman in his own right. Learning a trade was an important part of the boy's transformation, but not nearly as important as the spiritual tradition handed down by his adoptive father.

With the passage of time the Gold Worker's health gradually declined until the day finally arrived when he fell deathly ill. His loving son, born in darkness, but raised in Light, cared for him night and day. Unfortunately, the more he contemplated the loss of his father, the more depressed the son became, ultimately plummeting into the depths of despair.

Summoning every ounce of his dwindling strength, the Gold Worker entered meditation for the last time. Ascending into the highest realms of consciousness, he offered a fervent prayer. It was a deep and profound request that poured forth from the wellspring of love that resided within his heart. He asked only that his son be helped, for he could not bear the thought of him succumbing to grief and despair.

After completing his prayer, the Gold Worker turned to his son and, with loving eyes and fading voice, promised to walk at his side whenever the need arose. All he had to do was ask for his help while in a state of meditation.

Having done all that he could, the Gold Worker surrendered his earthly obligation. He was ready to shed the mortal coil. Not wanting to alarm either his son or his wife, but convinced they had the right to know, he explained that he was about to pass through the gate of his own volition. It would require but a single breath - the Breath of Death. Neither of them had ever heard of such a thing, and therefore thought him out of his head. What they didn't know was that he had been communicating telepathically with his Beloved Master these past many years, which is how he had learned the well-guarded secret of the Death Breath.

Passing over to the other side, the Gold Worker arrived on the upper mental plane, ever the realm of the Soul. The residents of that world have no form beyond the upper torso, and frequently congregate in groups of shared consciousness. They live the life of the Soul, and when they next incarnate they enter the world magnetically linked to the Soul of Humanity.

LIFE TWENTY-THREE
The Sacred Word

H E DIDN'T KNOW it, but he had entered the world with but one goal in mind - mastery of the Sacred Word. Had he known this to be true in his physical brain he would have found it strange indeed, because who plans a life around the chanting of one little word? It makes no sense to those who believe that man has but one life in which to fulfill his destiny, and even those who believe that man incarnates over and over again find it hard to imagine such a narrow focus.

As it happened he took birth in a time and in a place likely to provide the opportunity he sought, a place formerly known as Siam, now known as Thailand. The wisdom of the Buddha was being taught to the masses, and because of his karmic past it was inevitable that he would find the lessons easy to assimilate. Thus when still a young boy he was drawn to the local temple, where he received food and shelter, but only if he worked, and only if he adhered to a strict code of discipline. It wasn't long before his aptitude was recognized by the head monk, who was himself a teacher renowned for his mastery of the Sacred Word.

The teacher offered regular instruction at the temple, and was well received by the people he served, mostly because of the way in which he simplified the lessons he imparted to their enquiring minds. He was always available to the sick and downtrodden, and whenever he laid his hands upon the ailing, no matter whether the sickness was of the mind or of the body, steady improvement was noticeable over time. He always chanted the Sacred Word when healing with his hands, and he always encouraged others to rely upon the Sacred Word whenever life's challenges got them down. The Sacred Word infused everything he did and, therefore, everything he did reflected the Light of the Soul.

The teacher knew that the boy was somehow different from the other boys, because whenever he observed him going about his daily chores he invariably felt something stir in his heart. Taking the matter within, the teacher ascended into the eerie heights of advanced meditation. Free of distraction and wholly aligned with his Divine Inner Presence, he asked for understanding. The answer arrived bearing neither words nor symbols, rendering its message somehow all the more explicit. He had loved the boy with all of his heart in a previous life, but the precise nature of that relationship would be withheld until he had earned the privilege of knowing.

Needless to say, the teacher assumed full responsibility for the boy's education, schooling him according to local custom until the age of puberty, whereupon he introduced him to the sacred teachings of the Buddha. The boy effortlessly absorbed his lesson material, and in due course the teacher accelerated his instruction, initiating him into the arcane knowledge of advanced spiritual training. Up until that point the boy's meditation had centered upon the contemplation of the divine virtues, but that all changed. Now he simply relaxed, affirmed his innate divinity, and then delved directly into the Sacred Word. Little did he know, but meditation upon the Sacred Word was destined to his change his life, not through the power of the intellect, but through the faculty of Divine Revelation.

The Sacred Word consists of three letters (Aum); however, the modern version has just two letters (Om). Either way the sound remains the same, and its meaning and power remain unaltered. Complete mastery of the Sacred Word requires enunciation at various octaves in ascending and descending order. Each of the various tones must be intuitively selected, and then combined in rhythmic orchestration with the breath. Finally, achieving the correct resonance demands expert control of the chest and sinus cavities. It is a difficult art to master, but once achieved the gifts bestowed make it well worth a lifetime of effort.

For example, when chanted by a dedicated student, the Sacred Word blesses the practitioner, but also radiates healing energy to everyone within its reach, thereby ameliorating a multitude of conditions. When chanted by an advanced initiate, the Aum uplifts world conditions, whereas a Master of the White Lodge can literally accelerate human evolution.

After completing his daily chores, which included sweeping and mopping the floors, the boy practiced chanting the Aum for several hours every evening. No one was permitted to observe, and even the teacher rarely appeared to oversee his progress. He wanted the boy, now adopted son and devoted disciple, to discover the essence of the Sacred Word of his own accord. Nevertheless, some direction was required, so the teacher made good use of his time whenever he appeared, instructing his disciple on the various tonal qualities of the Aum, as well as the proper rhythm of the breath. Eventually the boy discovered the method behind master level instruction, and came to understand why his teacher visited so infrequently. It seems that every time he thought that he had mastered a lesson, he uncovered yet another nuance of truth just waiting to be discovered.

On one occasion, having transcended everyday reality while meditating in the presence of his teacher, a major portion of the boy's identity dropped away, thus creating an avenue of descent for the Light of the Soul. Three separate images appeared upon the inner screen of his mind, each lasting no more than a few seconds. First he saw an angry, disheveled man trapped at the bottom of a pit, shouting obscenities at the people looking down from above. The scene quickly passed from view and was replaced by another. This time he saw a gold worker patiently teaching a young boy his craft. Once again the scene changed. The same man who had been instructing the boy was now holding his fingers to his nose, striking a totally unfamiliar pose. Death instantaneously resulted, simultaneously bringing his vision to a close.

Something was definitely wrong. At first he feared the worst, thinking he had somehow committed an egregious error. However, upon reflection that did not seem plausible, considering the discipline that defined every aspect of his life. Next he lapsed into the standard mystical orientation, and thought that perhaps the vision was entirely symbolic, foretelling not death, but the transformation of his personality. But, upon further consideration, that didn't seem right either, because he had been taught that the personality required elevation, not annihilation. Thus the meaning of the vision remained unclear.

Responding to his disciple's apparent distress, the teacher mentally wrapped him in Light from crown to toe, moving left to right. As the story unfolded the teacher's eyes welled up, ultimately launching a pair of renegade tears. The disciple was now totally confused, because it seemed that even his teacher sorrowed at the thought of his student's fate.

Having regained his composure, the teacher explained that the dreamlike images were in fact karmic memories, memories that involved not only the disciple, but the teacher as well. Beyond that he would have to meditate upon their meaning in order to discover the truth of the matter. Retiring to his private quarters, the teacher entered into meditation; only this time, rather than chant the Sacred Word, he searched the records of the past. Rare is he who can access the Celestial Record in its highest and purest form, but the teacher had long since earned the right to seek help in such a manner. Thus did the Record pass before his inner vision, revealing his past association with the boy who had become his adopted son and devoted disciple.

Life can be exceedingly strange, frequently because the Law of Karma is infinitely complex. For instance, the effects of ancient causes invariably arrive unexpectedly, hence the difficulty associated with connecting them to their source. The dynamic is further complicated because the effects of past causes sometimes appear in reverse order in relation to their causation. Hence, effects may appear in childhood despite having originated in the life of an adult. Similarly, childhood fantasies from one incarnation sometimes reappear in the twilight years of a later incarnation. Additionally, karmic influences from multiple sources frequently manifest in concert. It also happens that teachers and students exchange roles from one life to the next. Such was the case with the boy and his teacher.

In a previous life their roles had been reversed. His adopted son and disciple had in fact been his adoptive father and spiritual teacher. What's more, in that lifetime his disciple had reached the rarefied heights of spiritual attainment, and had summoned his own death with a single breath

Truly, the ironies of life can be as unpredictable as they are undesirable, but it is also true that the Law of Karma sometimes works miracles. Each in his turn had saved the other from a horrible fate. Instead of a life mired in misery, they had each been blessed with the love of a father, and they had each received advanced spiritual training. What's more, their love had survived the vicissitudes of time, totally unaffected by the finality of the grave.

After years of practice the disciple realized that something within his own nature was standing between him and complete mastery of the Sacred Word. So he asked his teacher for help, and together they entered deep meditation, whereupon the disciple was confronted with a disturbing image. Tiny fragments of fear, black and sinister, broke loose from the darkness that was his ancient past. At first the fragments rode the gentle swells of life's great ocean, content to drift with the prevailing wind. Then dark clouds suddenly appeared overhead, and the gentle swells became crashing waves. What was once a collection of scattered fragments was now a frightening mass of destruction. Somehow he had opened Pandora's Box, thereby releasing a tidal wave of fear.

And like all fears, his took the form of the thing he dreaded most, his teacher's inevitable transition to the other side of the gate. It made no rational sense, because he had long since accepted the fact of life beyond the grave. Still, the fear of losing his teacher pushed him into the void, that barren landscape of doom. The Atlantean karma of the boy and his Master had finally found its way into the light of day.

Images of self-destruction continued to intrude upon his meditation, and just when it seemed all hope was lost, a great shining Light illuminated the darkness, revealing the presence of a blue-eyed man, earnestly chanting the Aum. The effect was immediate and undeniably powerful, delivering a mind-altering revelation. And it went like this. When sounded by the Creator the Sacred Word imposes order upon the universe; equally so when sounded by the individual, aligning body, mind, and Soul with the Divine Plan. His meditation over, he returned to everyday awareness, his fear of losing his teacher vanquished by the sound of the Aum.

The following year the teacher's health suddenly and unexpectedly failed and, dreading a prolonged debilitating illness, he asked his disciple to recover the secret of the Death Breath, the same Breath he himself had used in their prior life together. Entering meditation, the disciple recovered the secret of the Breath and immediately shared it with his teacher. The following morning he sat and watched while his teacher consciously expelled the life force from his body.

Much to everyone's amazement the teacher's body did not decompose. Weeks went by, and still the body retained the appearance of peaceful slumber. Finally, the disciple entered meditation, seeking guidance from his recently departed teacher. Because of the love they shared, a telepathic link was easily established, allowing the teacher to communicate one last piece of advice. It was time to inter the body, its unusual condition but a demonstration of the power of the Sacred Word.

The new teacher, and former disciple, served with distinction until the day of his death. His passing wasn't nearly as spectacular as his teacher's had been, but there was a wind, a wind like no other. It swept in from the sea, wrapping everyone within its reach in a loving embrace. Some failed to notice the effect, while others thought it strange to experience love for no apparent reason. Still others recognized an age-old phenomenon, one that announced the passing of a great Soul.

He passed the gate straight into the arms of his Beloved blue-eyed Master. The joy he experienced can not be adequately described, except to say that he never left the side of his Beloved Master.

The Navigator

THERE WAS A time when Arab culture crested the tidal wave of human consciousness. The fire and brilliance of the intellect was alive with ideas, and those ideas were creatively applied to the challenges of the day. It was the era of the Prophet, the true Messenger of God. The Prophet entered the world bearing a message of hope, and the world has profited greatly from the proliferation of ideas that subsequently poured out of the Middle East. But for that contribution to world literature and science, the Dark Ages might very well have tolled the bell on the human race.

That being said, it's also true that when the Prophet entered the world he sought to release his people from the burden of the past, because custom and tradition had become ritualized, and therefore devitalized. Certainly, tradition adds to every society, and in some cases represents the very essence of a culture. Nevertheless, every society sooner or later arrives at that point where it must let go of the past if it is to have any hope of adapting to the challenges of a changing world.

The Navigator grew up in the desert, and when still a young boy, at an age when most children were still attached their youth, he was out plying the desert, learning secrets few ever discovered. He learned firsthand how the desert sustained life even when survival seemed impossible; how it took life even when survival seemed assured. He learned his lessons well and ultimately became a navigator of the sandy sea. He could find a water hole by the configuration of the stars, and when the stars refused to cooperate he relied upon instinct alone. But that wasn't the full extent of his talent. Like many others bred to hazard and hardship, he possessed a sixth sense, the guiding hand of the subconscious mind. The subconscious mind contains a wellspring of knowledge, and because the Navigator welcomed its input he was blessed with an uncanny talent. The members of his tribe considered his skills absolutely essential, not only because of the inherent dangers associated with life in the desert, but because they made their living attacking the caravans that plied the desert.

His little band numbered no more than a couple hundred brave souls, but at that time it was considered large for a group that wandered the desert. They moved about freely, fearing neither the desert's endless expanse, nor the fact that the desert was dangerously unpredictable, because the Navigator could find his way to water right through a desert storm. As a navigator he was flawless, but as a man he was decidedly deficient, and in due course the nature of his flaw would be revealed.

The Navigator's authority was rarely challenged, even though he routinely scoffed at the customs and traditions of his tribe. He charted his own course, not only through the desert, but through the intricacies of tribal life. Because of his skill as a navigator, the tribe had no choice but to suffer both his rudeness and his obvious disdain for their way of life. So he plied the desert, water hole to water hole, caravan to caravan; aloof and unyielding, but always ensuring the tribe's survival.

Plundering caravans provided the tribe with life's essentials, but none more prized or coveted than the camels they liberated. They held their camels in high esteem and thought them to possess individual temperaments. Accordingly, whenever they encountered a disgruntled camel, they separated it from the herd and lavished it with kindness until it finally came around. They identified with its loneliness, and knew from experience that special attention would cure the forlorn beast soon enough. It was a practice that saved both time and resources, and the custom was to appoint handlers whose duty it was to appease the camels.

The Navigator hated camels. When just a boy he witnessed a runaway camel stomp his sister to death, and had never been able to forgive or forget. And yet, he practically lived on the back of a camel, sometimes traversing the desert for weeks at a time. When others extolled the merits of their favorite beast, he invariably objected, citing the fact that camels lived in the desert, and were therefore undeniably stupid. When it was pointed out that he too lived in the desert, he always laughed in agreement, admitting that he too was stupid, not only because he lived in the desert, but because he lived on the back of a camel.

They never took him seriously; rather, they attributed his comments to his quick wit and wry humor. Besides, he rode with the best of them, and always made sure his mounts were fed and watered. Surely, he was all bluster, and perhaps even harbored a secret admiration for the creatures that sustained their lives. Little did they know, but he sometimes tormented the camels with well-placed punches and kicks. He did not, however, make it a regular practice; otherwise, the entire herd would have revolted. Certainly, the camels hated him; however, because the rest of the tribe showered them with love and respect, they went out of their way to avoid open warfare with the Navigator. Nevertheless, the Navigator was playing with fire, because when a camel declares war, a not uncommon occurrence when mistreated, it becomes totally obsessed with the need for revenge, manifesting a general attitude of belligerence, if not premeditation.

The first real evidence that something was amiss turned up when a camel the Navigator had been riding went berserk and charged through camp with mayhem on its mind. Only a deranged camel, or the victim of abuse, would do such a thing. The tribe ruled out derangement for the simple reason that they showered their beasts with love and affection. That left only one possibility, so they suspected the Navigator, recalling in a whole new light the harsh opinions he routinely expressed regarding the nature of camels. After considerable debate the tribal Council summoned the Navigator.

The Navigator was not accustomed to lying, nor was he accustomed to losing face, so he refused to cooperate with the tribal Council. Having no recourse, the Council dogged his tracks day and night in order to discover what was going on with the camels. It was a delicate affair. On the one hand they feared alienating the Navigator. On the other hand they could not allow their camels to be mistreated. It was the oldest law of the tribe.

They lived by the light of tradition, and past practice constituted the very basis of their survival. But, more importantly, they believed in Allah, the one true God. Unfortunately, having received a distorted version of the Prophet's teaching, they thought of Allah, not as a loving God, but as an overseer who looked out for their interests, provided they did not break with tradition. And tradition demanded that they protect their camels.

Strange though it may seem, they believed Allah incapable of seeing at night; otherwise, He would not have created the moon. Therefore, they concluded that whatever occurred on a moonless night was as good as non-existent. Accordingly, they always waited for the moon to wane before sending out their raiding parties. When, however, a daytime raid became absolutely necessary they simply asked Allah to give them credit for those nights when they had remained in their tents.

The Navigator's transgressions took on a whole new dimension when it became apparent that he had been abusing the camels in broad daylight. He was not only endangering the tribe's livelihood, but allowing Allah to witness his criminal behavior. The situation had suddenly assumed nightmare proportions, and they found themselves torn between the vengeance of Allah and the irreplaceable skills of the Navigator.

Things simmered for weeks, and still his watchers hadn't observed anything incriminating. The Navigator was acutely aware of the unfolding drama and made every effort to play the part of the innocent victim. He was evidently enjoying himself, because whenever he happened to spot his surveillance, he began reciting ancient verse ripe with love and gratitude for the camel. Wise to his tactics, his watchers interpreted his behavior as an obvious attempt to lull them into complacency. And yet, despite the fact that he wasn't taking the situation seriously, they ultimately concluded that he had learned his lesson. Nothing could have been further from the truth. The surveillance had no sooner stopped than another camel went berserk; and this time there was no recourse but to put it to death. Killing a camel was tantamount to treason. The Navigator was therefore ordered to stand trial before the Council.

The death of a camel was a cataclysmic event, leaving the Council no choice but to sentence the Navigator to a term of banishment. If he failed to repent he would receive another term, and then another, until he demonstrated remorse. It was a judgment that answered all of their prayers. Allah would be satisfied because they had upheld tribal law. The camels would be satisfied because revenge had at last been meted out. And the tribe would be satisfied because they could rest in peace knowing that both Allah and the camels were happy.

Seething with rage, and hating every member of the tribe as much as he hated their flea-bitten camels, the Navigator stormed out of the tent reserved for matters of law. As for his banishment, he was not afraid of the desert. If anyone had reason to be frightened it certainly wasn't him. Just let them try to navigate the desert alone. Without him they would surely perish. At the very least they would suffer greatly and, because they meant nothing to him, he looked forward to their eventual ruin.

Gathering his belongings, the Navigator strode out to the herd, where he found three handlers guarding the beasts. The message was clear - his banishment did not include the services of a camel. The Navigator was not a man to be trifled with, and there would soon be three unfortunates who would learn that lesson the hard way. He was an accomplished knife fighter and, unlike the rest of the tribe, he carried two blades attached at the waist. Most of the men in the tribe carried but one knife, and that attached to the lower leg, thus allowing easy access on the fly. Sitting a camel, tucked behind its head for protection against wind and sand, naturally brought the lower leg within easy reach of the hand. It was a reliable method that had survived the test of time, but the Navigator rarely used a knife from the back of a camel, preferring to have his feet on the ground when fighting for his life.

Grinning from ear to ear, the Navigator approached the handlers. It wasn't until he unsheathed his knives that his smile disappeared, as if carried away on the desert wind. They might have been forewarned by the glint of the sun, reflecting as it did from the burnished surface of his deadly blades, but they most likely died without ever registering their disbelief. When it came to bladed weaponry the Navigator was a master of the art, not unlike his talent for navigating the desert.

He selected three of the heartiest mounts and then scattered the rest of the herd. They wouldn't wander far, just far enough to give him a decent head start, and that was all he needed. Ready at last, he departed camp on the back of a camel, trailing two extras behind. There was no going back – they would hunt him down no matter how long it took. Killing was serious, but stealing camels was unforgivable. If he survived the ordeal he would become an outcast, a loner plodding the desert, forever in search of his final resting place. Clearly, the desert was not an option.

He traveled at speed all through the night, taking care to alternate camels every few hours. Fortunately, he had appropriated food and water for both him and his beasts. Now that his life was at stake, he treated his camels with respect, taking care not to run them into the ground. Come morning, he stopped to rest, and couldn't help noticing that the camels thought it a good idea as well. And well that he stopped, because when a camel feels overburdened it invariably acts out its resentment, sometimes deliberately slowing its pace, sometimes heading off in the wrong direction. The only thing to do at that point is to stop and wait until the camel lets you know that it's ready to resume work.

His destination was the great sea to the north, but first he would lead his pursuers into the most dangerous part of the desert, an area known for its countless dunes. The dunes were constantly shifting, and were capable of disorienting a man faster than a camel could chew its cud.

He reached the dunes with the sun straight up, and without delay entered the maze of shifting sand. He knew his pursuers would be reluctant to follow, but if they wanted to catch him they would have no choice but to track him into the maze. Otherwise, they would have no idea of his ultimate direction. He knew their strategy, and therefore knew they would station men on the tallest peaks in order to coordinate their search, and also avoid getting lost in the labyrinth of tightly packed dunes. Even so, the Navigator had a plan of his own, and with any luck his pursuers would be trapped in the dunes before they realized what had happened. They were several hours behind, and would undoubtedly wait until morning before entering the maze, which allowed him plenty of time to set his trap.

At the break of dawn the Navigator led one of the camels away from the others. Reassuring the beast, he fed and watered it in a manner that suggested special attention, while at the same time making an incision in its neck, thereby creating a trickle of blood. Once a camel starts bleeding there's no stopping the flow, unless it's taken out of the sun and kept completely still while compresses are applied to the wound. The camel experienced minimal discomfort; however, within the hour it would be howling like a demon. By the time his pursuers rushed to the scene, the Navigator would be leagues away, far enough to prevent the two remaining camels from ever guessing what he had done.

When the camel's heart-rending shrieks reached their ears, the band of pursuers knew they had been right all along. The mournful cries of a dying camel had betrayed the Navigator, and they would soon have him in their clutches. They would show no mercy. They would stake him out and trample him into the sand. As a final insult to his memory they would heap camel dung onto his mutilated corpse. Having worked themselves into a killing frenzy, they charged pell-mell into the trap. They were experienced desert dwellers, but there were certain places even the experienced never went, and that particular expanse of tightly knit dunes was one of those places.

They were lost, and the sudden realization of their predicament only served to feed their fury. Their only chance was to wait for nightfall, and then look to the stars for a way out of the maze. And so they waited, and while they waited they nurtured their hate with thoughts of revenge. Preoccupied like they were, they never noticed the approaching storm coming out of the south, and therefore made no attempt to at least find a safer, more protected location amongst the dunes. As a result they found themselves in the worst possible place on earth to sit out a storm, because high velocity winds can carry entire dunes across the desert like waves rolling over the ocean. It was a perfect deathtrap, and death is what they expected, because death in the desert was an everyday occurrence.

The experienced desert dweller understands that survival is a matter of both skill and endurance. The experienced navigator understands the bottom line - survival is directly related to keeping your head. And emotion does not belong in your head. Granted, it was not the season for storms, so they never expected the terrible tempest that struck that night. Nevertheless, they should have been on the alert, and they should not have entered the dunes without an experienced navigator. Mistakes were made, and the biggest mistake of all was allowing their rage to overreach commonsense. They died for the sake of revenge; therefore, they died for no reason at all.

Free at last, the Navigator made his way to the great sea to the north, following the coast until he arrived at a seaport. Intent on leaving the desert behind, he sold both of his beasts to a camel trader, and then booked passage on a ship bound for greener pastures. A lifetime in the desert had taught him to expect the unexpected, so he had insisted upon the right to buy his camels back if for some reason he changed his mind. It was thoughtful planning, because the night before its scheduled departure his ship was rammed by another vessel, sending it to the bottom of the harbor. That's when decided to reacquire his camels.

The camel trader refused to honor their agreement, ultimately enforcing his right to change his mind by pulling a knife. Never one to be cheated, the Navigator promptly cut the man's throat. Removing his tongue, he positioned it in the middle of his forehead, which explained what had taken place. Having confiscated what goods he needed, the Navigator collected his camels and resumed his journey, traveling north along the shoreline.

The camels hadn't suffered any mistreatment, but couldn't help noticing that their very existence disgusted the Navigator, which explains why they took off at a run at the first opportunity. He tracked them from sunup to sundown, eventually cornering them in a narrow ravine. Sooner or later they would have to come to him for food and water, or so he thought. To his utter amazement neither of the camels approached him. They were trapped, but they didn't seem to care. Finally, the Navigator got the message - they felt the same way about him as he did about them. So he abandoned the siege, thereby acknowledging their victory. For some unknown reason, rather than make good on their escape, the camels trailed along behind him, never more than a few meters away.

He traveled for weeks, always on foot, and always with the sound of camel hooves dogging his steps. He skirted settlements along the way, rarely making contact with another human being. Eventually, he and his trailing dromedaries arrived at the north end of the sea. Weary of his nomadic lifestyle, it seemed the perfect place to settle down. He soon fell into a daily routine, hunting small game and retrieving fresh water from a near-by stream. The two ruminators kept their distance, still refusing to allow the Navigator to mount. Thus he remained a man on foot.

He was a solitary man who had no need of companionship, a man who thoroughly enjoyed time alone with his thoughts. Life was perfect, right up until the arrival of some unwanted visitors. A menacing band of Turks had discovered him trespassing on their land. The Navigator was totally unaccustomed to intimidation, so when the leader of the band poked a finger in his face, he reached for his blades, gutting the Turk like a lamb to the slaughter. Surrounded by a band of cutthroats, and fighting for his life, the Navigator slipped and lost his footing, whereupon he fell flat on his back. Rather than kill him, the Turks trussed him up and threw him over the back of a camel. That was not how he wanted to meet his fate, facedown on the back of a stinking camel. He had to do something, even if it meant sinking his teeth into the hide of the bug-infested beast.

As it turned out, help arrived from a totally unexpected quarter when the two wooly beasts appeared from out of nowhere. Together, they charged the Turks, first one and then the other colliding with the unfortunate animal hauling the Navigator. Failing to knock him free, the two wild and reckless dromedaries paused just long enough to shake off the effects of the collision before commencing the next phase of their attack. Phase two called for biting, kicking, and stomping like the deranged beasts that they were. The Turks, struck dumb by the sight of two crazy camels attacking a caravan of armed men, couldn't help but laugh. Surely, the scene challenged the limits of the imagination, but then people started getting hurt, and it wasn't funny anymore.

Sensing danger, the camels bolted to freedom, only to regroup at a safe distance. The Navigator understood what the camels intended, and for the first time in his life gratitude flooded his heart. Thus it happened that a couple of camels, hated and despised though they were, imparted a lesson in the art of forgiveness.

Hoping to bring the whole situation to an end, the Turks dragged the Navigator into plain view and promptly sliced off his head. The camels went berserk, and now lived to kill. They came on like hell's own fury, and by the time they were finished both the Turks and their camels had sustained a multitude of injuries.

The two camels died trying to rescue the Navigator. They passed the gate in a dream-like state, ultimately merging back into the animal group soul from which they had originated. They returned bearing the gift of forgiveness, and in due course their contribution to the group's collective memory would inform the nature of all camels.

When he passed the gate the Navigator was a changed man, having learned the value of love and forgiveness from two hairy beasts. Nevertheless, when confronted with the light of the upper astral plane, he stopped dead in his tracks. The light reminded him of the sun, and the sun reminded him of the desert. Fortunately, just as he was turning away from the light, he caught a glimpse of the world that awaited him, an unbelievably beautiful world filled with friends and family from his many different lifetimes.

The Camel Driver

T HE MAN WHO actually committed the crime had already fled, never to be heard from again. He had no family, no friends, and no one he could turn to for help. He didn't have to lead such a lonely life, but he was unabashedly self-centered, a quality that never fails to repel others in quick order. He lived in an egocentric world, and consequently exhibited no compassion for others, regardless of their pain and suffering. He viewed his fellowman as he would a common servant, destined to forever serve his needs. Not unexpectedly, he was inordinately suspicious, because extreme self-involvement invariably gives rise to paranoia. In this particular case the wife of the local headman had slighted him, deliberately giving him the cold shoulder. Deluded beyond any hope of reform, he arrived at the illogical conclusion that the insult was more than he could possibly endure.

Thus did his indignation set the stage, quickly transforming his paranoia into an ugly outburst of rage. He picked up a rock and hurled it at his tormentor, striking her on the rump. Striking a woman was not unusual; however, touching any of her intimate parts constituted a particularly onerous affront, and doubly so if she came from a good family. Startled by the blow to her posterior, the victim grabbed her buttocks, closed her eyes, and then screamed at the top of her lungs. Several seconds passed before she remembered to fall to the ground, whereupon she began writhing in pain.

When she opened her eyes the first person she saw was a camel driver who had just arrived in the village after a long, arduous journey through the desert. Scraggly, unkempt, and basically filthy, the Camel Driver extended a helping hand while staring through a pair of eyes that had obviously been overexposed to sun and sand. Seeing no one else in the immediate vicinity, and frightened by his trancelike visage, she immediately accused him. Needless to say, the Camel Driver vehemently denied the accusation, but to no good effect.

The headman wielded unequivocal power, and had never been known to pass up an opportunity to demonstrate his authority. Deeply offended that anyone, let alone a miserable camel driver, would have the effrontery to strike his wife's posterior, he was incapable of making a rational analysis of the situation. Had he been accustomed to first weighing the evidence, and then exercising his reasoning powers, he might have asked himself why someone would assault a woman and then offer to help her to her feet. Had he asked that simple question he would have undoubtedly concluded that any man in his right mind would have fled the scene. But then, the Camel Driver didn't appear to be in his right mind. Consequently, he made no inquiries, and yet knew exactly what had to be done in order to resolve the matter. He called everybody together and promptly incited them to violence.

After pummeling the Camel Driver senseless, they dragged him up the rocky slope of a nearby hill where there was a cave reserved for the likes of him. He arrived battered, bruised, and skinned to within an inch of his life, having remained stone silent throughout the ordeal. They shoved him into the cave and sealed the entrance with a heap of rocks, the same rocks they had used the last time they had imprisoned someone in the cave.

Their mission accomplished, the mob rejoiced, because several years had come and gone since they had last walled anyone in the cave. There was a time when the cave had seen regular use, and legend had it that many a man had either died or gone insane whilst in its confines. Only one man had ever departed with some semblance of sanity, and that was because his brothers had forced their way into the cave barely three months into his confinement.

Taking advantage of a small gap in the rocky barricade, the villagers dropped food and water into the cave every morning. They came and they went, but never uttered so much as a word, because part of the fun was ignoring their victims until they begged for conversation. As luck would have it, the Camel Driver didn't play by the rules. The first sign of trouble appeared when someone noticed that he hadn't attempted to initiate any conversation. In fact, he had yet to utter a single word, which infuriated the villagers.

So they trooped up the hill determined to make him talk. Arriving slightly winded, they paused to catch their breath before implementing their plan. Incredibly, they thought they heard him singing, but that just didn't seem possible, because only a madman would sing in that hellhole, and he hadn't been in there long enough to go mad. Several minutes later they could no longer deny it. He was happily crooning, by all indications quite content in his prison cell. It just didn't seem humanly possible. Outraged by his merriment, they gathered around the mouth of the cave and, according to plan, emptied their bladders onto to the barricade. The smell was horrific and, as the day wore on, the heat only made it worse. The Camel Driver never uttered a complaint.

They needed a new plan, one that guaranteed success, so they decided to withhold his food ration until he talked. For three days he remained stone silent. The battle of wills was irrevocably invoked, leaving them no choice but to withhold his water ration. He would receive neither food nor water for another three days. They knew that withholding water amounted to premeditated murder, because not even a hardened desert dweller could survive three days without water. Nevertheless, by their standards he deserved to die, having violated the sanctity of a woman's arse.

Three days later they trekked up the hill to check on their prisoner. This time they heard not singing, but the gentle sounds of snoring. By Allah, they thought, the man had either miraculously survived, or he was snoring in his grave. Not knowing what else to do, they dropped a few morsels of food and a bladder of water through the hole. The snoring continued for what seemed like hours before the familiar sounds of consumption could be heard emanating from the cave. Having witnessed a remarkable feat, if not a miracle, his tormentors were now well beyond thoughts of revenge, and were growing profoundly curious as to the kind of man they had imprisoned.

Surely, Allah would not have allowed a guilty man to survive. So it occurred to them that perhaps their prisoner was no ordinary man, but a holy man disguised as a camel driver.

In which case, they had spent the better part of a month defiling a holy man. So they caucused, determined to find a way out of their predicament. In end they decided that Allah most likely hadn't detected anything out of the ordinary, because the cave was utterly devoid of light. But, just in case they had it all wrong, they doubled his daily allotment of food and water.

It wasn't long before fear and confusion spread through the village. Some of the villagers believed that the Camel Driver was a saint, while others suspected the work of the devil. On the one hand only a saint could endure extreme hardship and deliberate cruelty in total silence. On the other hand maybe the devil was trying to catch them off guard by mimicking a saint. The only thing they were in total agreement about was that they had to try something different. So they went back up the hill to the Camel Driver's retreat.

Incredible though it may seem, they offered to set him free, but only if he promised to intercede with Allah on their behalf. Needless to say, once released, he could not tell anyone about his ordeal, nor could he ever return to their village. They thought it a deal he could not refuse. All he had to do was forgive them, pray for them, keep their secret, and then never return to hold them accountable. It seemed an easy thing. They were offering him his freedom in exchange for a few simple promises.

The Camel Driver never uttered a sound. His unexpected silence dumbfounded his captors, until someone suggested that perhaps he had lost his voice. It seemed entirely possible, so they implored him to throw something out through the opening to indicate acceptance of their magnanimous offer. Not so much as a fly came out of the cave. Thinking that he must have fallen asleep, they shouted until they were hoarse. Their efforts were rewarded with peels of laughter. That's when they knew he was mad.

Actually, his laughter bore no relationship to madness, but revealed the extent of his relief. The time was approaching when they would truly want him out of the cave, but not yet. They still wanted to bargain, and therefore weren't prepared to set him free. So he decided to wait until they surrendered all hope of striking a bargain, and sought only to be rid of his onerous presence.

Comfortably situated in his cozy little home away from home, the Camel Driver counted his blessings. The cave was really quite spacious - it even had room to stand if he stooped a little. The food wasn't that bad, nor was the heat of the day much of a problem, because late at night the temperature never failed to drop. Things were not as bad as they seemed. He was, after all, accustomed to being alone in the desert, and had long since adapted to short rations.

A lifetime of traversing the desert had taught him that both his mind and his body were susceptible to suggestion. For instance, in the heat of the day he routinely directed his body to lower its temperature. Conversely, during the cold desert nights he instructed his body to raise its temperature. When frustrated with life in the desert he affirmed peace and tranquility. He didn't understand how, but his method worked because the subconscious mind accepts instruction. He soon discovered, however, that practice and patience were required, because the subconscious mind frequently contains contradictory instructions within its storehouse of information.

Given his unusual background, the Camel Driver endured his confinement in the best of spirits, strong and purposeful in all that he did. Each and every day he imagined himself thanking his captors, mounting his camel, and then departing the village a happy, contented man. He basked in the warmth of their smiling faces and savored the essence of their loving glances as they bid him farewell and wished him good fortune. In return he embraced them all with an effulgent smile, offering nothing but love and forgiveness to those who had imprisoned him. He even imagined the stink of camel dung scenting the air, thereby adding an element of authenticity to the scene he had created.

He sometimes questioned his strategy, knowing that he had to be careful, lest he cross over the line and join the ranks of the mentally deranged. Surely, a normal person would consider his situation hopeless and his response entirely delusional. But then he would remember the lessons of the desert, and immediately concentrate upon whatever good he could find in his prison cell of a home. Thus he rejoiced that his jailers had seen fit to feed him at all, let alone increase his rations at a time when he needed it most. In a particularly forgiving moment he genuinely appreciated the discomfort they must have endured while holding their urine all the way up the hill before relieving themselves on the rocks. Every day was filled with challenges, and every challenge was met with a positive response.

His strategy worked to perfection, because the villagers were now determined to kick him out the cave, having endured his insults long enough. So they steamed up the hill and, without stopping to rest, commenced removing the barricade, fully expecting to find a madman dangling from the edge of the world. When at last the barrier was removed, their prisoner was nowhere to be seen. At first they entertained thoughts of a miracle, thinking he had ascended into heaven. That flight of ideas lasted but a moment in the light of day, because when their eyes adjusted to the darkness they found the Camel Driver comfortably propped against the back wall of the cave. Surely, the man was deranged.

Valiantly overcoming his recently acquired stutter, the headman informed the Camel Driver that he was free to go. The Camel Driver immediately responded, shocking his jailers all the more because now he was avoiding eye contact. Eyes closed, he quietly informed the headman that he needed time for his eyes to adjust to the light. The villagers pondered his proposal, and at first refused, only to change their minds when he settled in for a nap.

Several hours later, with slotted eyes and wobbly legs, the Camel Driver stumbled down the hillside. Upon entering the village he found his camel properly cared for and ready to travel. He never rebuked his tormentors, offering instead kind words and polite gestures. He was filled with gratitude for having survived the ordeal, and consequently felt no resentment, no anger, and no need for revenge. He did not count himself a victim, but an observer who had chosen not to empower the mistakes of others.

The Camel Driver had scarcely departed when despair gripped the village. They were now absolutely convinced their prisoner had in fact gone mad, not in the usual manner, but in the strangest manner possible. In his madness he saw only goodness, regardless of the circumstances. He had to be insane. After all, what sane person walked away from a life threatening ordeal with a smile on his face and a fair-thee-well upon his lips? So it seemed they had not only driven him mad, but had given him the opportunity to recover his sanity and then return with reinforcements. Chagrined, the villagers upbraided the headman for allowing the Camel Driver to escape. All the same, just to make sure all of their bases were covered, they began fabricating stories that disallowed any personal responsibility. Others, leaning more towards murder than exoneration, advocated hunting the escapee down in the interest of justice.

In the end they took no action, but waited for something to happen, something that would evoke a suitable reaction. No harm ever befell them; nevertheless, their fear of strangers was heightened, and every sound in the night weighed heavily upon their minds.

The Camel Driver died while still a young man, the victim of a fierce desert storm. His Beloved Master observed from a distance, pleased that all was well with his Son. The day of his Son's final release from the cycle of rebirth was slowly approaching, even if far into the future. Thus did he reinforce the mental blueprint of his Son's final achievement. And so it would be, because the Master had never affirmed anything that hadn't come to pass in the fullness of time.

The Master Warrior

I N THE PURE, clean light of early dawn they attacked. They numbered in the thousands, and they rode astride their sturdy steeds with the ease of men doing the familiar, having no need to consciously attend to the task at hand. They made no effort to control either the stride or the path of their charging mounts, knowing beyond any shadow of doubt that rider and beast were as one. Every nuance was known to the other, every breath taken in perfect unison.

They were Mongols, and they wandered far and wide, lugging their belongings wherever they went. They lived on the backs of their horses, and considered it the natural thing to do. Many societies have loved the horse, but few have ever loved man's best friend as completely as did the Mongols. The horse's pain and discomfort was theirs to endure, while the horse's reservoir of strength and stamina was theirs to draw upon, rendering the line separating man from beast only barely perceptible.

Overwhelmed by the sheer magnitude of glinting blades and thundering hooves, the targeted village had no choice but to prepare for the end. Resistance was pointless. They had long coexisted with the Mongols, but a new leader had recently arrived on the scene, and his name was Genghis Khan.

It had been prophesied by the soothsayers of the day that the Khan, having been born with certain marks on his body, was destined for greatness. If one measures greatness by the fruits of evil, then he certainly fulfilled his destiny. His lust for power first appeared in his early teens, followed soon after by an unsurpassed appetite for total domination.

Throughout his life he was given to fits of rage, and yet he somehow exercised undue influence over better men than himself. To be sure, his hold over others was in no way based upon physical prowess. Rather, his ability to command allegiance was based upon an idea. It was an idea that embraced its devotees with loving hands, only to commence choking and strangling once welcomed into their hearts.

The Khan's great insight was that of the super race. He had always considered himself innately superior, and ultimately projected his delusional state of mind onto the Mongol race, while at the same time sharpening his skills at manipulation and intrigue. He held nothing sacred, not even his cause, because even that served the insatiable demands of his ego. In the end, when he passed over to the other side, he went straight to the fire, and there lost his Soul for all eternity. It rarely happens, but when it does happen, the loss is inestimable. The Soul suffers a setback, and the next incarnation pays the price.

When the Khan came to power it was with a following that included both rogues and warriors. The rogues were not men to be taken lightly. They calculated every step of their journey from obscurity to worldwide menace, repeatedly swearing allegiance to the Khan and his plan for world conquest. They were not taken in by the rhetoric, but followed the Khan because his plan worked both in theory and practice. Like the Khan they lusted after wealth and power, and had long since grown accustomed to experiencing life through the lens of dark motive.

The true warriors, however, revered their leader, and therefore never guessed the depth of his depravity. Believing the Mongols to be God's chosen people, they sought the glory associated with serving a higher cause, even if that cause offered nothing beyond elevating the Mongols above all others. Their lives were hard and, while they never enjoyed the benefits of a formal education, they were steeped in the folklore of the past. They thrived on the legends of Mongol glory and, when viewed from the perspective of the average man, the prospect of becoming a legend was enormously seductive. Hence, they saw not the inherent evil of ethnic supremacy, but the hand of God shaping their destiny. Thus an entire race of people embraced the promise of a special destiny, believing they had enlisted in a noble cause. In such a manner, through the unholy alliance of madness and seduction, was the yoke of a tyrant willingly accepted.

One of the Khan's followers was known amongst his own as the Master Warrior. He was a man to be feared, a man who had never known defeat on the field of battle. He always wore a fierce scowl upon his embattled face, matched only by the look of imminent danger in his cold, dark eyes. His fierce image was enhanced by his choice of horses - always black, just like his hair, his eyes, and his mood. He sat his horse like the veteran that he was, his movement completely synchronized with the rhythm of his charging mount. When he charged into battle, arms flailing the air as if trying to lift his horse into flight, he rode half-naked, wearing nothing but a loincloth. Fierce though he was, he also relied upon the workings of his mind. Before launching an attack, he always visualized victory, imagining every detail of the battle in his mind. He knew not the source of his method, but accepted it as a natural expression of the art of war.

He was considered a fierce opponent when wielding either the sword or the knife, but when it came to two-handed fighting he knew no equal. He couldn't say how he came to the style, but was, nevertheless, a master at wielding both weapons in coordinated, devastating attacks. It was a feat many attempted, but few ever mastered, because each weapon obeys its own nature on forfeit of life. He only knew that from childhood his fighting style had been the most natural thing in the world, and by the age of seventeen he had already earned a reputation as a skilled and fearless warrior.

Led by the Master Warrior, the Mongols fell upon the hapless village, killing every man, woman, and child. Every animal was slaughtered, every home burned to the ground, every field set aflame. Not even the smallest remnant was left as witness to the people who had occupied the land. When the Khan ordered complete destruction, the Master Warrior knew exactly what was expected of him. He felt no remorse and experienced no guilt, because he was a hardened warrior dedicated to the Khan.

Such is the power of belief. If a man believes with absolute faith and conviction, then almost anything can be accomplished, whether for good or for evil. In the case of the Master Warrior, his every resource was dedicated to serving the Khan. His true identity, however, was rooted in his karmic past, and one day soon that identity would be summoned into the light of day.

After his great victory, the Khan rewarded the Master Warrior, bestowing the honor of destroying a hated foe. He was ordered to attack a Chinese fortress located on the border between the two empires. China had so far resisted the Mongol invasion, and the Master Warrior was charged with sending a message, one that would announce the beginning of a new era. Accordingly, the devastation was to be so overwhelming as to strike terror into the heart of China, setting her ancient soul aquiver.

They arrived at their destination just after nightfall, and immediately dispatched scouts to gather intelligence. Within the hour the scouts returned with two Chinese soldiers found prowling the dark. When they refused to provide any useful information, the Master Warrior ordered one of the captives mounted on a horse with his hands trussed to the pummel of his tiny saddle. Grabbing the reins, the Master Warrior led horse and rider to the very edge of a nearby ravine, whereupon he drove the horse over the edge. Rider and mount fell screaming into the night, landing with a sound that chilled the Mongol horde. It seems they couldn't bear the loss of a good horse.

The other soldier was dragged kicking and screaming to one of the many campfires ringing the encampment. Without any warning, with a single stroke of his mighty sword, the Master Warrior sliced the man's arm off at the elbow, catapulting the severed limb into the fire where it sizzled like a hunk of succulent meat. Several moments passed before the soldier's agonizing scream invaded the night, only to be immediately stifled when the Master Warrior once again raised his sword. Realizing the hopelessness of his situation, the soldier revealed all that he knew.

The Mongols assembled their divisions in the predawn light, knowing that they were facing a difficult battle. This time they would not be attacking a community of farmers, but trained soldiers defending a fortress at elevation. The fortress sat on a knoll, which afforded some measure of visibility, while impeding the momentum of hostile forces.

The Mongol strategy was simple: they would overwhelm the fortress. In fact, contrary to every expectation, the knoll's elevation barely slowed the Mongol onslaught. Deeply entranced they crested the rise without having uttered a single manmade sound. The only sound to be heard was that of thundering hooves.

In ancient times seasoned warriors slipped into trancelike states of mind in order to put all distractions aside. Their state of mind was similar to that of meditation, the difference being that one promotes savagery, while the other facilitates communication with the Soul. Even though it produces a dedicated soldier with no discernible conscience, trance is rarely used in modern warfare, because modern soldiers are trained to confront their fear, rather than banish it from the conscious mind. The ancient method produced the superior soldier, because it allowed the subconscious mind to take over for the duration of the battle. The modern method, however, produces the better man, because the soldier learns firsthand as a conscious participant that war is seldom the answer it appears to be.

Breaching the fortress wall, the Master Warrior filled his hands, sword to the right and knife to the left. Charging into the teeming mass of Chinese soldiers, he had no intention of yielding to anyone or anything. Blood coated every inch of his frame, but somehow never affected his purchase on sword or knife. He was deeply entranced, and therefore impervious to all but the prospect of delivering a killing blow. The enemy was powerless before his onslaught, and many died in the face of his wrath.

Near the center of the fortress the Master Warrior encountered an elite cadre of Chinese soldiers. There were perhaps a few dozen defenders and, even though they were hopelessly outnumbered, they were determined to hold their ground. The Master Warrior, still entranced, never wavered. Death looked through his eyes as both he and the men who followed in his wake waded into the thick of the fight. Perhaps he should have allowed his horde to finish off the remaining defenders, but reason hadn't yet been restored to his mind. It was then that the improbable happened. In the thick of battle an errant blade found its mark, opening a gash at the base of his neck.

The dirt and dust of the plain infiltrated everything and, being infected with dung like it was, open wounds frequently led to infection, followed soon after by death. The Master Warrior knew that it might spell the end, so he gathered his lieutenants and gave them their final instructions. There would be no survivors, no indication that man had ever occupied the land. It would be a mighty undertaking, one that would require weeks of labor. Meanwhile, the Master Warrior fevered.

For the better part of a week he burned, sweat soaking completely through his night rig. He felt death lingering nearby, but refused to surrender his hold on the body. Taking a page from his book of war, he visualized victory, not on the battlefield, but in the cells of his body. With dogged determination he imagined perfect health, willing his body to recapture its former strength and vitality. For some unknown reason, using his mind to facilitate his body's recovery felt natural, almost as if he had done it before. It wasn't long before his fever subsided.

Weeks later, arriving at the Khan's prized golden tent, the Master Warrior regaled his liege with an account of the battle. The Khan was pleased until he learned that his loyal subject had returned bearing neither gold nor silver. He suspected treachery and therefore confronted the Master Warrior, accusing him of not properly interrogating his prisoners regarding the location of the fortress' treasure. The Master Warrior was deeply offended, but maintained his composure while quietly informing the Khan that he fought not for fame and fortune, but for the glory of the Khan.

That's when the Khan revealed his true nature and announced that the quest for wealth and power was the only glory the Mongols would ever know. That enlightening bit of treachery on the part of the Khan stunned the Master Warrior - right up until he erupted like a volcano. Breaching the barrier standing between him and his ancient past, rage overwhelmed his rational mind, instantly erasing years of misplaced devotion. Like a bolt of lightning from out of the sky he struck a mighty blow, cracking the Khan's sternum as if it were an eggshell. Without a moment's hesitation, so fast in fact, that in far less time than it takes for the eye to focus, the Master Warrior unsheathed his weapons and began decimating the inner guard.

It was a knife in the back that brought him to his knees, and a walloping blow to the back of his skull that dropped him to the floor of the tent. Some said he was lucky, that surprise had been his biggest asset. Those who had witnessed the carnage firsthand, however, insisted that surprise had nothing to do with it, that the outcome wouldn't have been any different had he publicly announced his intentions. Those who had fought at his side laughed at such wild speculation, and claimed that if the Master Warrior hadn't lost his temper, and therefore his fighting edge, he would have undoubtedly killed every last man, the Khan included.

Uncovering the truth represents one of life's crowning achievements; however, when it involves the destruction of a major belief system, caution is advised. The Master Warrior came to his truth in a sudden flash, and it cost him his life. Slow, meticulous transformation is nature's way, because sudden awakenings sometimes deliver a severe shock to the nervous system. Most people are content with nature's pace, but some people strive mightily, unaware of the fact that momentous insight can either bless its recipient or unravel its victim.

They strung him up with a piece of rope. He was suspended in the air, hung by the wrists, a public specter on display, all the while dripping blood upon those who dared approach. Some in the crowd were happy to see him pared down to size, while others were shocked to see the very essence of Mongol manhood hoisted on a rope like a common criminal. Death seemed imminent, but the crowd, sensing a strange quality permeating the air, guessed that something unusual was about to happen. So they waited for the next act to unfold. They would not be disappointed.

Dangling from the rope, but somehow fully alert, the Master Warrior denounced the Khan, revealing the truth for all to hear. And it went like this. The Khan was a tyrant, an evil lord who had deceived his people with empty rhetoric. It was wealth and power that motivated the Khan, not the glory of the Mongol nation. The crowd jeered with their tongues, but in their private thoughts wondered if it could in fact be true. After all, everybody knew that the Khan loved the sparkle of precious gems as much as he loved the glitter of gold, not to mention the vast treasure hidden within his exquisitely embroidered tent.

The Khan received a full report from his spies, and for the first time in his miserable life was struck dumb with humiliation. So he ordered the immediate execution of the Master Warrior.

The executioners took up their positions, pausing just long enough to acknowledge one of their own before riddling his body with a swarm of arrows. Some of the eyewitnesses later claimed that when it was all over the Master Warrior still lived, hanging from the rope in total silence. Others asserted that dozens of arrows had found their mark, enough to kill any man.

In the end there was no mistaking exactly when the Master Warrior died. During the night a desert wind, out of season and completely unforeseen, blew through the camp. It began as an ordinary gust of wind, but quickly turned into a savage tempest. The Khan's tent was blown end over end, rending its precious fabric in so many places that it was never adequately repaired. The camp was in a state of complete disarray, but then, as suddenly as it had arrived, the wind departed, leaving behind the mystery of its meaning.

With the wind at his back the Master Warrior embarked on the fabled journey across the River Styx to the land of the dead. He passed the gate in total silence, brooding like he did before an impending battle. Not only had the Khan betrayed him, but he had betrayed himself, having dedicated his life to an evil cause. In the days to come he would learn that unfettered belief can unbalance a life; that belief systems, no matter how sacred, are but stepping–stones to higher realms of consciousness. In the end, however, guilt overrode the Wisdom of the Ages, shrouding his mind with memories of past mistakes. His guilt would shape the life to come, and mar the next as well. Such is life, whichever side of the gate you call home.

LIFE TWENTY-SEVEN
The Flagellant

SWEAT DRIPPED FROM his body, causing his hand to repeatedly slip from the rail he so desperately clutched. In his right hand he held the vile instrument of self-mutilation. It looked rather harmless when seen on the shelf, worn leather handle with multiple strands of tattered rawhide streaming forth. Upon closer inspection, however, the dark red stain that permeated its fibers shouted for an explanation.

Pausing just long enough to catch his breath, the Flagellant struggled to regain his composure. Muscle tremors were affecting his concentration, preventing him from attaining that glassy-eyed look so often associated with hypnotic trance. Obviously, he had to try harder, so he tightened his grip and resumed his penance with renewed determination.

Flagellation was required at the abbey; however, unlike the Flagellant, the other members of the monastic community had more sense than to mutilate their bodies. Instead, they flagellated until an impressive array of superficial welts appeared, stopping before causing serious damage. From the Abbot's point of view anything less was unacceptable, while anything more was completely unnecessary.

The Flagellant wholeheartedly embraced the practice of flagellation, and blessed the Catholic Church for the opportunity to cleanse his soul. He judged his sins beyond any hope of redemption, and therefore willingly exceeded the limits of obligatory discipline. He was a devotee of the art who needed no exhortation. Nor did he need any reminders of his past.

He had endured seven long and lonely years at the abbey, and before that he had soldiered for a local tyrant. He had been pressed into service, only to find the life of a soldier much to his liking. The war itself had been meaningless, fought not to preserve the sanctity of the home, but to assuage the honor of contentious nobles during the time of the Crusades. He soon discovered, however, that there were advantages to military service, not the least of which was the propagation of unfettered passion.

As a soldier he had participated in many battles, but now, after years of reflection, he judged his conduct more akin to savagery than war. Undefended villages had been destroyed, children had been indiscriminately slaughtered, and countless women had been raped and murdered. He had committed heinous crimes in the name of war, not because he didn't know right from wrong, but because he was addicted to sex.

He had enjoyed many alliances, some consensual, others acts of violence against helpless women. At first it was the sex that drove his passion, but eventually it was the violence that fueled his sexual appetite. Behind his unholy obsession lurked the ghostly apparition of his mother, which he unknowingly projected onto his victims. His mother had been a domineering woman who constantly humiliated his father; consequently, he detested women with every ounce of his being, but at the same time desired the pleasure of their bodies.

Initially enticed by the delights of the flesh, it was inevitable that he would become addicted to the violent images that attended his depredations. At first they were but fleeting glimpses, but eventually those images intruded upon everyday reality, ultimately eclipsing the joys of sexual union.

Staring at his reflection, the Flagellant stood perfectly still, his gaze fixated on the polished metal pot hanging from the wall of his cell. What he saw was a miserable, contemptible retch, a man destined to suffer with no hope of redemption. Church doctrine demanded that he pay for his sins, and flagellation was the coin of the realm for the seriously wicked. Thus he mutilated himself with the same grim sense of reality.

The sight of his odious visage had apparently restored his zeal, because he gripped the rail with surprising resolve. Then, lest he falter during the administration of his penance, he secured the whip firmly to his wrist and began flailing his naked back as if intent on murder.

His wounds generally healed within a week or two, but this was turning out to be no ordinary thrashing. Death was not beyond the realm of possibility; however, suicide was a grievous sin in the eyes of the Church, and he knew that he didn't dare precipitate his own demise. It was a delicate balance, but he had long since grown accustomed to approaching the threshold without falling over the edge. Just now, however, he was fast approaching the brink of deadly penance.

His flesh was throbbing and twitching, his skin peeling away, but still he flailed with all of his might. It wasn't long before his nervous system staggered, forcing his heart to surrender its natural rhythm, carrying him to the very brink of unconsciousness, a state of mind sometimes associated with sexual arousal. In fact, he had on occasion masturbated while in that peculiar state of consciousness. Oddly enough, severe trauma numbs the nervous system, signaling the brain to release a flood of chemicals known to heighten sexual orgasm. Unfortunately, masturbation represented one more evil that had to be scourged from his system. Little did he realize, but masturbation serves a purpose when associated with the natural rhythm of the body. Celibacy certainly wasn't the answer he sought, because sustained abstinence restricts the life force, adversely affecting both the body and the mind.

Determined to launch one more assault upon his crumbling body, he ignored the warning signs and unleashed a mighty stroke intended to please God. A ball of light consumed his brain, not the Light of Illumination, rather the light expelled from his dying brain cells.

He fell, not just to the floor, but into the void that attended his sudden loss of consciousness. Hours passed, bleak and devoid of any form of stimulation, until at last he awakened to find his body locked in painful spasms. The cold, hard floor upon which he writhed felt cruel and unforgiving, having crushed his nose and both of his cheekbones. He had no way of knowing, but the disfigurement that would result was the effect of an ancient cause set in motion during his life as a Grecian wrestler.

Ever so slowly and ever so painfully, he struggled to his feet. Agony cloaked his every step, while each and every breath launched rivulets of pain through the wreckage that was once his face. Legs aquiver, he staggered off to the abbey's doctor. A lesser man would have been devastated by the havoc wreaked upon his body, but the Flagellant was no ordinary man, hence the pride that swelled his chest.

Believing he had atoned for at least one major sin, the Flagellant briefly considered the Abbot's reaction, knowing he would disapprove of his conduct, but convinced, nevertheless, that God would approve, and therefore reward him on Judgment Day. Such are the workings of a deranged mind, forever balancing the budget, only not in the usual manner, but through the application of tortured logic.

The abbey's doctor despised the practice of flagellation, and viewed the body, not as a whipping post, but as a wonderful instrument with which to serve God. Despite his vow of obedience, he openly defied the Abbot, and refused to take the whip to his own back. Because he was the abbey's only doctor, the Abbot allowed him to care for their bodies, but not their Souls.

The doctor, seeing the extent of the Flagellant's injuries, correctly surmised that only a deranged mind could believe that God would condone, let alone reward, the practice of self-mutilation. Nevertheless, he steeled his nerves and held his tongue while calling forth the natural healing power of the Soul. Applying those herbs and salves commonly regarded as medicinal, he silently affirmed health, vitality, and a full recovery. Next he visualized a stream of purple light descending from above, penetrating every cell of the Flagellant's body. When it came to spiritual healing, the doctor was an adept of the art; nevertheless, he took great care to keep his talent a secret. Surely, a revelation of that magnitude would invite the wrath of the Abbot. The Abbot considered spiritual healing the devil's domain, whereas flagellation was unquestionably God's work.

His work completed, the doctor broke his silence and shared his diagnosis with the Flagellant. If he continued to practice self-mutilation he would risk severe disability, and possibly death. He had already suffered irreversible damage, evidenced by the muscle spasms that continuously wracked his body. As for the damage to his face, there was nothing he could do beyond recommending a painkiller. Seeing no sign of agreement, only the blank look of the doomed, he ordered rest and sent the Flagellant on his way.

The Flagellant was utterly miserable, but determined, nevertheless, to bear the pain, lest the doctor's elixir steal salvation from under his nose. He appreciated the doctor's kindness, but didn't trust anyone who refused to do penance. The doctor was either inviting damnation, or he truly was a Lamb of God, completely free of sin. The very idea seemed blasphemous.

Several days passed before he ventured a look into the reflective sheen of his metal pot, whereupon he was suddenly confronted with the face of a stranger. His nose had the look of a winding staircase, turning this way and that, but always ever onward. The rest of his face was quite another matter altogether. Unlike the nose, which at least resembled something he had seen before, his overall appearance brought to mind the work of a deranged potter. Fear began to seep through the cracks and crevices of his seemingly impenetrable façade, and for one brief moment in time he nearly lost his nerve.

At first the Flagellant quietly went about his daily routine, but with the passage of time he grew bolder, and began encouraging others to take up the whip in earnest. The vast majority judged him mad, although a few lost souls seeking redemption for past transgressions saw in him the hope of salvation. Unfortunately, one of his followers succumbed to the whip, generating no small debate amongst the brethren. Had one deranged monk extended the practice of flagellation to absurdity, thereby causing the death of another? They arrived at no conclusions beyond what was already common knowledge - flagellation worked best when taken in small doses.

Upon hearing of the monk's death, the Bishop summoned the Abbot and demanded an explanation. Somehow things had gotten out of hand, and the practice of flagellation was suddenly under scrutiny. Incredibly, the Flagellant was ultimately granted an audience with his Holiness the Pope. He arrived at the Vatican in a state of terror; however, comfort was near at hand, because all the while he clung to his scourge, lest he disappear into one of the seismic faults that characterized the contours of his face.

While awaiting the monk's arrival, the Pope gave some thought to the case, but could not for the life of him understand how anyone could beat himself with a whip. It seems he had no concept of expiation, but related to life in terms of gains and losses. And yet, when it was all said and done, who was he to interfere? Especially since flagellation had in no way impeded his own pursuit of carnal bliss. Nevertheless, he savored a keen interest in the monk's sordid past. He too had ravaged many a young maiden, not in the field as the monk had, but in his Holy Robes for the sake of Christ.

His interest piqued, the Pope questioned the monk regarding his sexual encounters, relishing every detail of every act of depravity. While the Pope was rejoicing at having at last found someone who understood the complexities of sexual relations, the Flagellant was experiencing more pain in the retelling than he ever had while doing penance.

Strange though it may seem, the Pope was an atheist. His family members wielded enormous power and, because the papacy promised untold wealth, they used their power to have one of their own seated at the head of the Church. Many were bribed, while others were kidnapped and tortured. Still others were murdered, not at the behest of the future Holy Father, but with his tacit consent. When he passed the gate he found himself completely severed from his Soul, and to this day can be found wandering in agony as he slowly dissipates into free floating atoms. Eventually, the papacy was restored to its intended elevation, not as an infallible mantle, but as a Guiding Light for those lovers of God known as Roman Catholics.

The Flagellant was thoroughly repulsed, but didn't dare reveal his contempt. Unfortunately, concealing his emotions was not an easy task, because they invariably launched rolling waves of flesh and bone, constantly altering the shape of his face. By some miracle he survived the Pope's interrogation, but not without reawakening the lust that had once consumed his every thought. In desperation he reached for his only source of comfort, applying his scourge in a frenzy of violence that rivaled the very episode that had resulted in his being shipped off to the Vatican in the first place. Blood flowed freely, first down his back, then down his legs, and finally onto the Holy Father's exquisite handcrafted carpet.

In the end, still reeling from the sight of his blood-soaked carpet, the Holy Father issued a Papal Decree that required flagellation to be administered in such a manner as to not ruin any decent furnishings. More to the point, the Decree noted that flagellation was obviously useful, because the monk hadn't raped or pillaged since the onset of the practice. He neglected to address the original controversy, namely the propriety of flagellation unto death. Ever the consummate politician, he saw no advantage to be gained by inflaming one side or the other. The middle ground was the safe ground, and there he would make his stand, once again proving himself capable of rendering hard decisions.

When the Flagellant returned to the monastery he was teetering on the edge of a nervous breakdown, totally shaken by the resurrection of his past. Had he been willing to accept God's Love and Forgiveness he might have discovered the salvation he so desperately sought. Unfortunately, God's Love was out of the question, because the Church had conditioned him to believe that suffering was the only cure for the sins of the flesh. Thus he resumed the work of redemption, applying his scourge with unflinching determination. Gradually at first, and then with ruthless persistence he masturbated while doing penance, repeatedly traveling down that ancient pathway linking pain and pleasure. Once the connection is made it's only a matter of time before disaster strikes, and that's exactly what happened to the Flagellant when he sliced off his penis with a kitchen knife.

He passed the gate into a sea of darkness, where he remained for decades until once again called to the flesh, never having recovered from his delusional state of mind. There was a lesson to be learned and his next incarnation would bear witness to that fact. Truly, when Love is denied, when Grace is spurned, the Law of Karma is all that remains.

LIFE TWENTY-EIGHT
The Love Child

FROM THE MOMENT of birth his mother knew that his life would be hard. He was born with a rare deformity that crooked his legs, rendering him unable to walk, but able to scoot around on the ground. Unfortunately, the society into which he was born believed physical imperfection to be a manifestation of evil. Lacking any formal education, and having no understanding of karmic conditions, the locals relied upon the Church for guidance in such matters. Not unexpectedly, according to the local priest the boy was in league with the Devil.

His mother saw neither deformity nor the work of the Devil, but a child deserving of love and attention. She viewed his deformity as a mistake of nature, and the boy but one of nature's unwitting victims. To her way of thinking God would never deliberately inflict such a painful condition upon a child. And she was right. The boy's affliction was not ordained by God, but was karmic in nature, and therefore the effect of an ancient cause.

They were a poor family, and yet the one thing the mother consistently provided was priceless beyond all comparison - she showered her son with love and affection. She toiled in the fields during the day and tended to her household chores after dark, rarely allowing fatigue to interfere with her commitment to her son. She loved the boy dearly and demonstrated her love daily; although, being human, she occasionally lapsed into bouts of depression brought on by exhaustion. Like so many others dedicated to service, she overlooked the importance of maintaining a healthy balance between duty and self-preservation. She desperately needed rest and relaxation and the boy desperately needed to learn self-reliance; however, whenever she encouraged the boy to work harder at meeting his own needs, she invariably cursed herself in retrospect. Had she understood the purpose of disability in the human family, she would have demanded more from her son, knowing that disability only claims the illusion of a conventional life, and not the opportunity for a meaningful existence.

It happened that the Law of Karma intervened, and the boy's mother was killed by a band of marauding outlaws. They found her walking the fields, relishing the warmth of the morning sun while remembering fonder days when her husband was alive. They were strangers to the area out to make a quick score, knowing there was little chance of detection provided they did their evil far from home. They ravished her until they were spent, and then trampled her to death with their horses.

After several days of anxious waiting, fearing that his mother had met with misfortune, the boy was obliged to seek help from the local church. He had been to town on several occasions, but only with his mother, and only in the back of a cart. He was deathly afraid, but knew that he needed assistance; otherwise, he would certainly perish. Crawling on his belly, he somehow managed to reach the center of town, drawing to the scene a crowd of onlookers. When, despite their prayers, God refused to strike the boy dead, the crowd turned ugly. They were determined to drive him back into hell, straight into the arms of Satan.

The local priest was a heartless man who felt no pity for the boy. Rather than rush to his aid, as Christ Himself would have done, he summoned the counsel of elders. Together they debated the boy's future. The mother's body had been discovered days before, and they had already decided against helping the boy. As far as they were concerned his fate rested with Mother Nature. They never imagined him capable of dragging his twisted frame all the way into town.

The only question that remained, now that he had made his way into town, was the manner of his demise. Some favored hauling him into the woods, in the general direction of a known wolf lair. Others, not wanting to take the time required to travel that far, recommended that he be carted off to the town dump. Still others, desirous of community participation at the grass roots level, suggested that the citizenry be allowed to stone him to death.

One man alone voted in favor of aiding the boy. He had originally sided with the others, but now offered to escort the boy back to his home. He had no love for the boy; however, having had loving parents himself, he couldn't help but experience some degree of compassion. He therefore disagreed with his brethren, reminding them of one very important fact: when the boy died his evil spirit would be unleashed upon the town. Everybody knew that evil spirits haunted the living, especially the people they hated. That was all they needed to hear, because they wanted no part of a vengeful ghost. That settled, the boy's lone supporter volunteered to act as his guardian, ensuring his continued survival while making certain he never again aggrieved the good citizens of the town. Seclusion was the only viable option.

Meanwhile, frightened by the mob, the boy crawled under the church, which provided protection from the rain of debris, but offered no shelter against the threats and insults hurled his way. They railed against his very existence, totally convinced he was evil to the core. It was common knowledge that evil manifested as bodily imperfection, that disease and disability bore witness to that fact. Surely, God had abandoned the boy for a reason, and that reason undoubtedly lurked within his anatomy.

Assuming custody of the boy, the guardian dragged his terrified charge out from under the church, whereupon he heaved him into the back of a broken-down cart. The townspeople followed them all the way out of town, heaping abuse every step of the way, causing the guardian to regret his decision. But it was too late to turn back, because he had already raised the terrifying specter of the boy's rampaging ghost, and the brethren would not look kindly upon a change of heart. Having resolved to go forward at any cost, the guardian was surprised to discover a burgeoning sense of pride. It seems he had somehow managed to rise above the din of public outcry while escorting his little lost lamb back to the safety of his home.

Once a week the guardian delivered food and necessities, but never anything more than what was needed to ensure the boy's survival. Initially, the boy resented the many tasks required of him, but eventually learned to appreciate the true value of his growing self-reliance. With appreciation came gratitude, and with gratitude came love. In such a manner did the boy come to love his guardian, not as a friend, but as he would a father.

Not surprisingly, given the boy's growing attachment, the guardian's attitude underwent a radical transformation. The more time they spent together, the more apparent it became that the boy not only possessed a kind and generous heart, but was also extraordinarily intelligent. Thus for the second time he altered the course of the boy's life when he willingly accepted responsibility for his education. The boy was eager to learn and welcomed the opportunity to read and study, ultimately becoming an avid reader of the New Testament. As time passed, the boy, having studied the words of Christ, became enamored with the concept of unconditional love -

a concept rarely understood, and still more rarely put into practice.

Thus it happened that the boy and his guardian frequently debated the nature of love. The guardian held that only the worthy were deserving of love, while the boy advocated the practice of love and forgiveness regardless of merit. The guardian had a good heart, but a heart conditioned, nevertheless, by the notion of a punitive god. Therefore he was utterly and completely astonished when he realized the boy had actually forgiven the townspeople who had treated him so cruelly. Hated and despised as a cretin, the boy was teaching him, a church elder, the meaning of love. It was a lesson the guardian would never forget.

When the inevitable day of the guardian's passing finally arrived, the boy had no choice but to return to the town that had so violently rejected him. He wasn't, however, the least bit worried. Surely, the mood of the town had changed. He himself had changed in ways he could not have predicted. It was a classic case of projection, and like all projections his did not coincide with reality, but reflected the content of his mind.

Crawling to town on his belly posed a difficult challenge; however, as it turned out his journey proved more daunting than ever he could have imagined. The closer he got to the center of town, the more townspeople he encountered, and they weren't happy to see him. To the contrary, they pelted him with rocks and beat him with sticks, shredding his clothing and lacerating his flesh. He might as well have been a snake in the road.

He arrived at the church covered in blood, his face battered and bruised, his teeth shattered beyond repair. His condition was dire, and yet, despite it all, he clung to his faith. Fervently praying for strength and courage, he planted himself in front of the church, as if declaring his innocence for all to see.

Thus began his final ordeal, not unlike a certain crucifixion in another time and place.

He maintained his vigil with pride, determined to endure whatever came his way with a loving heart. The first few hours were the worst, right up until his tormentors noticed that his gaze was perpetually turned skyward, as if communicating with the heavens. His behavior was not the usual reaction, so it occurred to the townspeople that perhaps he wasn't in league with the Devil, after all. It fact, by all accounts, he had remained in prayer throughout the ordeal. The diehards, however, insisted he was undoubtedly evil; otherwise, he would not have shamed them in front of God's house.

No matter how they looked at it, they had a problem. On the one hand, if the boy turned out to be a saint, they were in serious trouble. On the other hand, if the boy really was the spawn of Satan their troubles were just beginning. In the end they rushed over to the boy bearing food and medicine with every intention of asking his forgiveness. They found him dead, his gaze still lifted to the heavens, but dead, nevertheless. In his hand they found a tiny carving of Christ the Savior.

Thinking him a saint, the townspeople carried his broken body to the morgue, intending that he receive a stately burial. Even the densest amongst them acknowledged his saintly countenance, while some went so far as to compare his death to the Crucifixion of Christ. Hence they took pride in their accomplishment, because surely the boy could not have ascended to Glory without their assistance.

Positively frantic at the thought of having lost control of his flock, the priest rushed to the morgue and claimed the boy's body for the Church. Being the sole arbiter between man and God, he was the only one qualified to examine the body. He alone was capable of identifying the insidious presence of evil. Having thus established his credentials, he ordered everyone out of the morgue before beginning the dissection. He began by removing the internal organs, but failed to discover any evidence of putrefaction, ever the most reliable indication of evil. Nor did he find a single trace of decay when dissecting the brain, even though it was suspiciously larger than normal.

As it happened the priest had a consuming interest in anatomy, based like it was upon his karmic past, a past he shared with the boy. Whereas in the past he had sought to discover the essence of a warrior by boring a hole in his skull, he was now determined to uncover the evil lurking within the boy's body. Despair was closing in when the truth unexpectedly dawned - the evidence he sought resided in the blood. He had conducted dozens of makeshift autopsies, but had never thought to suspect the blood. It was a mistake he would never make again. In the future he would drain the blood first.

Having completed his task, the priest meticulously sopped up every drop of misplaced blood. Tossing the blood-soaked rags in with the mutilated corpse, he nailed the coffin shut, sealing each plank with a heavy layer of wax. Later that day the coffin was removed to a secret location where it was interred under a mountain of stone. Serious precautions to be sure, but the priest breathed a little easier, having trapped the boy's spirit beneath the formidable weight of earth and stone. Safety was his concern, and safety seemed assured.

When the congregation next assembled the story unfolded with all the drama of a Greek tragedy. The priest, having worked himself into a state of rapture, riveted the crowd with all the gruesome details. Saving the best for last, he revealed the horrifying truth - every organ in the boy's body bore the mark of Satan. Conducting autopsies was dangerous work, and who, he asked, was better able to combat the foul vapors and acidic poisons emitted by Satan's followers. It was a grand story, and it worked its intended magic upon the crowd. Grown men howled in terror, while women and children lapsed into hysteria, running into walls and pulling clumps of hair right out of their heads.

In the end they thanked the priest for having saved them from the Antichrist. Had it not been for him they would have been taken in by the boy's saintly pretense. They had long suspected the motives behind good intentions, and now they knew for certain that piety was the work of Satan. Surely, the wise kept to themselves, shunning anyone who gave the appearance of goodness. It was a valuable lesson, and they would be eternally thankful that the boy had died as he had, alone and despised.

Several years later a man claiming to be the husband of the boy's mother inquired as to her whereabouts. He had been away fighting the infidels, and had just returned to find his home deserted. He knew nothing of a son. He and his wife had never been blessed with children; otherwise, he never would have joined the Crusade. Counting up the years on his fingers, the priest quickly determined that the husband had abandoned his wife long before the time of conception. Alas, the answer to the question he had pondered for so long. The boy was a bastard.

Never one to shirk his duty, the priest vowed to uncover the truth. Somebody had fornicated with a married woman, and somebody was going to be punished. It wasn't long before several suspects were rounded up and subsequently detained in the basement of the church. When one of the detainees died under interrogation, the two remaining suspects immediately confessed to being the boy's father. Nobody challenged the priest's findings, because two biological fathers certainly explained the boy's deformity, not to mention the abnormal size of his brain.

The priest died a happy man, blindly trusting in the virtue of his anatomy. It seems his body exhibited no sign of abnormality. He was therefore assured of a place in Heaven, or so he thought. His satisfaction was such that he never looked back; although, had he looked ahead, he might have had a change of heart. Little did he know, but the Lords of Karma had already mapped out his future. Karma inevitably returns with a punch, but never more so than when the innocent have been unjustly maligned.

The boy passed over to the other side in a state of grace. He arrived in perfect health, totally lacking any indication of abnormality.

The King

AND SO THERE was in distant times a king who ruled a small city-state, a thriving community in the area now known as central Europe. He lived and ruled during an era that predated the great nations of the modern world, a time when family and culture dictated allegiance, and skillful political maneuvering formed the foundation of every society.

He was unlucky in that his father died soon after his birth, but because his mother was the daughter of a wealthy merchant, he was afforded every advantage, and eventually rose to a position of leadership in the community, ultimately becoming the people's choice for king. He seemed the logical choice, if only because he lacked any semblance of raw ambition, exhibiting instead a sense of duty to the city that he loved.

Throughout history the rich and powerful have manipulated the masses, routinely maneuvering into positions of authority with no intention of serving the public interest. Even well-intentioned leaders become adept at the art of deception, for the simple reason that the pursuit of power invariably evokes the very worst in man. Unfortunately, the King did not prove to be the exception to the rule.

Having ascended to the throne, the King thought it only right and proper that he wear a golden crown upon his head and, for the sake of aesthetic harmony, he ordered the jeweler to craft yet another to bedeck his hand. He preferred a traditional crown, one that sported a series of peaks and valleys, much like life itself. The ring was likewise cast in the shape of a crown, duplicating the original in every detail. He was especially fond of the ring, if only because he could wear it in public and catch the eye of those who admired a stylish king.

Needless to say, it was common knowledge that every king required an official residence. Once constructed, the royal palace both celebrated his status and embellished his ego, making it clear to even the dimmest of lights that appropriate furnishings were absolutely essential. No king could properly entertain the rich and powerful while ensconced in a dingy palace. Before very long he was the proud owner of a fabulous palace, custom-made furniture, fine furs, dazzling jewels, and a nifty crown with matching ring.

He surrounded himself with the rich and powerful, and from their ranks appointed both the members of the royal court and the commander of the newly appareled army. Those stalwart members of the kingdom soon realized their own palatial needs and set to building. Naturally, the army had to be enlarged to protect their holdings.

The budget, like all budgets devised by the ruling class, was loaded onto the backs of the common folk. At first the people protested, because not only were they burdened with higher taxes, but many of them had lost their sons to the army. But, they were reminded, they had demanded a king and, having had their wish granted, did they now prefer a shabby sovereign? They most certainly did not, leaving but one conclusion. They wanted a king who commanded respect, a fashionable sovereign who looked every inch the monarch they deserved. Surely, the benefits were well worth the costs incurred.

Wrapped in furs and shielding his eyes against the winter sun, the King surveyed his domain, but not without experiencing a compelling need to undertake major improvements. He had a natural talent for planning, and when contemplating the many possibilities, inspiration dawned, setting his imagination ablaze. First he would fortify the outer wall. Then he would extend the city's network of cobbled streets, which would undoubtedly attract more people to the city, thereby revitalizing the local economy. He knew then that he would not be an ordinary king, but a king long remembered for his public works.

Just as he had planned, the King's projects created new opportunities for both workers and merchants, gradually elevating the city's standard of living. What's more, the newly expanded army all but eliminated the criminal menace, making the streets safe at night for the first time in the city's history. By anybody's view, the economy was booming and the city was thriving - and it was all because of the King.

Riding the crest of ongoing prosperity, and concerned that his genius might fail to reach every nook and cranny of his kingdom, the King concluded that his authority needed to be broadened. Accordingly, his power and presence soon permeated every level of society, creating divergent lines of thought concerning both his motives and his accomplishments.

On the one hand his supporters reckoned him amongst the elite of the Greek pantheon of gods. He had, after all, revitalized the city while at the same time modernizing the army, thereby protecting the interests of the rich and powerful. In short, he had made them all very wealthy. On the other hand his detractors criticized every aspect of his life, both personal and public. They decried his abuse of power, claiming that he used his position corruptly, serving not the welfare of the common man, but the interests of friends and supporters. They condemned his extravagant lifestyle, citing unwarranted expenditures, not to mention illicit sex. His allies countered every attack, claiming, for example, that he never really had sex with the women in his harem, because everyone knew that sex was something that transpired between a man and his wife. Needless to say, the King was not married. And then there was the ultimate defense of his extravagant lifestyle. No King could possibly love his subjects in grander fashion than by attiring both himself and his household in the very finest furs and jewels. Only an ungrateful king would comport himself as if he were unworthy of a well-appointed lifestyle.

Indeed, he was a complicated man, whatever view one took. How thought he on the subject? Insight, it seems, had not yet illumined the shadowy recesses of his mind. He was accustomed to justifying his behavior, and was apt to spend long hours reflecting upon his accomplishments. To that end he summoned the local woodworker's guild and ordered the construction of a den befitting a king, one that boasted the rarest woods and finest craftsmanship. Once constructed, he frequently sought refuge within its walls so that he might quietly ponder his many achievements. A daily dose of self-examination might have tempered his pride; however, self-reflection was not one of his accomplishments. Little did he know, but everybody creates their own reality one life to the next, whether as an unwitting member of society, or as an independent actor upon the stage of human drama.

Most people would probably agree that sooner or later greed and corruption return to their source; however, the fact that they return bearing greater mass and velocity is seldom recognized. That's what happened to the King. One of his edicts went awry, adversely affecting a very powerful adversary, an influential family known to oppose his every decree. It happened that their eldest son accepted a commission in the army, only to perish under suspicious circumstances. Steeped with intrigue and fueled by thoughts of revenge, the aggrieved family members hatched a diabolical plan. The King would suffer an irreversible loss. He would share their pain.

Thus it happened that the King's only child, a boy of twelve, met with an untimely death at the bottom of a well. Several witnesses claimed that it was a freak accident, because they had never before seen anybody fall into a well while standing ten feet away. Others disagreed, asserting that it was really quite common to fall into a well no matter where you happened to be standing if your time had come. Still others, with a notably different bent on perception, thought that witchcraft was afoot, that the King would do well to investigate anyone suspected of Satan's work. Those with their wits about them, however, reported seeing three men toss the boy headfirst down the well. What's more, the boy had been standing ten feet from the well just prior to his fall. They further reported that the men responsible bore an uncanny resemblance to Satan's minions. Obviously the boy's time had come.

The King wanted to avenge his loss, but didn't know who to accuse, because there was no trail leading to their lair. Rage and despair clouded his mind, totally eclipsing the light of reason. The mind is a wonderful thing, but when it pitches its tent in hell's domain, demons are sure to gather. And sure enough, it wasn't long before the King was careening down hell's corridor, straight into the grasp of his ancient past. A mighty wave of emotion, black and scarlet to the eye, swept him away, depositing him upon the barren shores of self-destruction.

Suicide was rare, but when it did occur it was generally associated with either grinding poverty or debilitating illness. As a result the King's suicidal ideation was perceived as nothing more than posturing. Misjudging the seriousness of the situation, his friends and advisors ignored his threats and, rather than console his aching heart, encouraged him to repress his feelings, until the day arrived when he was ready and able to avenge the death of his son.

Then one day they found him on the roof of his palace, fully intending to jump. He was out of his head, and by every appearance Satan's brigade had taken full possession of his sanity. It's a shocking thing to discover a stranger inhabiting your body, especially one harboring thoughts and feelings universally abhorred by humanity. The King had set his mind to self-destruction.

It wasn't until they saw him teetering on the edge that his advisors grasped the full extent of the problem. This time they tried reasoning through his deluded state of mind. And it went like this. He had lost his son, but surely the boy had gone to a better place. Might not his son be watching even now? Surely his son would encourage him to resume his duties if only for the sake of the realm. Despite his past errors in judgment, the people needed him at the helm.

Given his condition, it didn't seem possible, but the voice of reason somehow anchored his mind in reality. His recovery was slow at first; because once the body's chemistry has been altered by severe psychological trauma only time can restore the natural balance of the organism. Had he been treated by the standards of modern medicine he most likely would have been prescribed antidepressants. The drugs would have undoubtedly accelerated his recovery, but the unseen damage to his nervous system would have eventually manifested a variety of symptoms. As it happened he made a full recovery, benefiting from the knowledge that he had survived a terrible ordeal with the help of his friends.

Thereafter the King underwent a transformation of character, becoming both a better man and a better king. Determined to rule his kingdom wisely, he embraced the practice of daily review, first identifying those behaviors requiring modification, and then amending them in the light of understanding. Thus he resumed his duties with renewed vigor, and before long a new vision for the city manifested in his fertile imagination. He recalculated the budget, reduced his personal income by half, and rescinded funds previously earmarked for the rich and powerful. He rallied support for a wide variety of civic projects, and then turned everything over to a bevy of newly formed committees. He was a new man, no longer driven by the pursuit of fame and fortune.

The King's transformation evoked a wide range of reactions. The skeptical scoffed, believing that guilt alone was responsible for his conversion. The rich and powerful thought him a fool intent on destroying the kingdom. The poor and dispossessed, won over by his new policies, proclaimed him a saint dedicated to the downtrodden. Others wisely concluded that he was neither a fool nor a saint, but a man who had cast off his personal demons, only to discover that society sometimes applauds the reprobate while denouncing those worthy of admiration.

Wrapped in his favorite blanket, a fine woolen fabric interwoven with golden thread, the King was alone in his bed when Death came calling. The light of the moon danced across the surface of the blanket, creating a magical mood of hopeful expectation. Slipping beneath the threshold of consciousness, he suddenly realized he was no longer sleeping in his bed, but was fully alert and surrounded by four walls of burnished gold. However, it wasn't the glitter of gold that held his gaze, but the man who stood in the center of the room, as if patiently awaiting his arrival. He was a becoming man of exceptional height, dressed in white and wearing a smile that eclipsed the gleam of the gilded walls. His features were universal, and yet somehow uncommonly distinct. His hair was the color of straw, his eyes the palest blue he had ever encountered. A strange but reassuring clarity radiated from his countenance, a single glance communicating everlasting love and devotion.

The King's last earthly tear coincided with his last mortal breath. His tear was in no way ordinary, bearing witness as it did, not to the grief he had known, but to the joy that awaited him. He passed the gate fully conscious, straight into the loving embrace of his Beloved Master.

The Guillotinist

THE GUILLOTINE WAS developed as a means for slaughtering pigs, and was first used in Europe over a thousand years ago. The pigs were drawn into a chute and their heads were lopped into a bin, which was then hauled to market. It was the custom to roast the heads and eat the brains, a delicacy enjoyed by the poor, but good food, nevertheless.

During that era people routinely ate meat without the benefit of refrigeration; consequently, serious illnesses developed without anyone ever suspecting that spoiled meat carried bacteria. They went by smell, and if it didn't smell too bad, they ate with no regard for health or safety. Many people died, while many others developed a tolerance for bacteria, quickly recovering from what would have otherwise been a terminal illness. Thus was the guillotine associated with human misery long before it was ever applied to the human head.

The first official use of the guillotine as a means of human execution remains lost to historians; however, a review of the Celestial Record reveals that a handful of villages started using it approximately 500 years ago in France. It gained popularity not only because of the ease with which it severed the human head, but also because the townsfolk considered it especially gruesome, and therefore perfect for disposing of society's castoffs. Beyond that, the severed heads sometimes uttered sounds, leading the observers to believe that the victims remained conscious despite decapitation. The heads did occasionally gasp and groan immediately after beheading, but only rarely did they utter discernible words. Besides the auditory delights, the heads sometimes grimaced and glared, thereby reinforcing the impression that life lingered on. It wasn't long before people were traveling from town to town in order to witness the spectacle of the talking heads.

The notion that the personality momentarily survived decapitation was not far-fetched. In fact, there was some truth to the matter. Once the heads were severed, the victims were most assuredly dead; however, it sometimes happened that the subconscious mind took voice, emitting the occasional utterance. The subconscious mind was also responsible for an array of facial expressions, making it impossible to tell the difference between muscular contraction and emotional expression. Be that as it may, the people of the day had many a lively argument about what it all meant. Some suspected the work of the Devil, while others feared the reanimation of the dead, which is why the heads were almost always buried apart from the bodies.

The Guillotinist lived with his wife in a small but comfortable dwelling on the edge of town. The carpentry shop where he constructed his platforms and the smithy where he forged Madam Guillotine's notorious blades were both located behind the family home. He took great pride in his work, not only because he believed in sending evildoers to hell, but also because he believed in human kindness. Long experience had taught him that not everyone introduced to the blade was a villain. Some were totally innocent, while others were guilty of nothing more than acts of desperation.

It was the victims of circumstance, and not the rogues and villains, who motivated him to carve beautiful designs into the framework of his platforms. He especially wanted to give comfort to those in need of a small reminder that their misdeeds were not so grave as to strip away their humanity. As for the others, the thieves and murderers who preyed upon society, he had no sympathy, and therefore cared little for their comfort. They were despised and feared by the people, and whenever they were caught they were executed without the benefit of a trial. The common folk, on the other hand, appeared before a magistrate, and in the interest of justice the court sometimes spared the innocent.

His wife frequently worked at his side, but never at the block, and never in public. Construction was a labor of love, and when they sanded and polished together they often laughed and sang as they worked. Under the circumstances, joviality might seem inappropriate, but the fact remains that any work is God's work so long as the intention is good. There were those times, however, when his wife succumbed to the tragedy of it all, imagining who might die, and how awful it must feel to be the object of public derision.

Afflicted with doubt, she couldn't help but wonder whether or not her husband was truly doing God's work. So he would remind her that because of Madam Guillotine many a villain would never harm another person. As for the others, he did what he could to make the experience bearable. The truth be told, many a man and many a woman climbed the stairway of doom comforted by the fact that their suffering would soon be over. Unbearable hardship was a cruel fact of life, and for some the Angel of Death was a blessing in disguise. It sometimes happened, however, that even those who welcomed the sweet slumber of the grave faltered while standing in the shadow of Madam Guillotine. The fear of death had been drummed into them by the Church, and they fully expected to suffer unthinkable horrors. Little did they know how foolish they were, and yet how were they to know the truth, that erroneous belief creates pain and suffering beyond the grave? If only they had received the unadulterated teachings of Christ, then they would have known that a better world awaited their arrival.

The Guillotinist genuinely believed that those last few moments spent gazing upon his artistry somehow comforted the condemned as they waited their turn at the blade. But woodwork wasn't the full extent of his ministry, because it wasn't unusual for him to dedicate a few minutes to those who awaited death. Knowing their deepest fears, he promised to do what he could to have their heads buried together with their bodies, or at the very least to say prayers over their graves for the safe keeping of their souls.

Early one summer morn, while constructing a new platform, the Guillotinist's brother, who was also his assistant, stopped to rest in the shade of some nearby trees. The brother, besides being lazy, was not a skilled worker; and yet, despite his brother's shortcomings, the Guillotinist never found fault, either in the moment, or upon reflection. And so when his brother went off to rest, he paid him no mind, even though it was too early in the day to be taking a break from work. Hours later when the Guillotinist looked around for help his brother was nowhere to be found.

The Guillotinist had no choice but to head out alone in search of wood. He was running low on lumber and needed to replenish his supply, knowing that the wood had to be cut and dried before it could be sawn into planks. Steady use of the blade rendered the platforms unstable, and the last thing he wanted was for either the blade or the platform to topple over during an execution.

Rolling out his cart, the Guillotinist hitched up his horse and departed with plenty of daylight to spare. An hour later he was contentedly trundling along when he heard riders coming his way. They were riding hard, and they had a man trussed belly down on the back of a horse. It was a pack of vigilantes who had taken somebody into custody. The Guillotinist didn't intend on stopping; however, one of the vigilantes grabbed his horse by the bridal. There was no mistaking the action. Their business had something to do with him.

His voice rigid with authority, the leader of the group inquired as to his brother's whereabouts. The Guillotinist at first demurred, but finally acquiesced, and revealed that his brother had disappeared from work earlier in the day, that he too was concerned for his welfare. The vigilantes erupted in laughter. There was something unnerving about their merriment, because theirs was not the type of laughter that dispelled an awkward situation. Rather, it was the type that alerted its victims to impending danger. Something sinister was being concealed within the sound of their laughter.

Tiring of the game, the leader of the vigilantes abruptly pulled back the hood that concealed the head of their trussed-up captive. The Guillotinist was totally unprepared for what he saw. His brother was unconscious, and appeared to have suffered a severe beating at the hands of the vigilantes.

Vigilante justice certainly provided a much needed service in those lawless times; however, it also happened that innocent men died for reasons totally unrelated to lawlessness. The Guillotinist was therefore certain the vigilantes had made a mistake.

Collecting his wits, the Guillotinist leapt from his cart and hurried to the aid of his brother. At that point his brother came to his senses and immediately denied having done anything unlawful. Once again the vigilantes burst into laughter, this time sounding all the more like hell's own choir. Regrettably, some people enjoy the suffering of others, but never more so than when that suffering is deemed warranted. In the case of the brother, he had been apprehended in the act of committing a robbery.

Drawing upon his dwindling reservoir of self-restraint, the Guillotinist suppressed his anger, or he too would have been judged a highwayman before the sun went down. There was nothing to be done except offer support and encouragement until the vigilantes led his brother off to town.

By the time the Guillotinist returned home his wife had already heard the news. The word had spread: the mighty Guillotinist would lop his brother's head before the end of the week. Had he been a religious man he would have dropped to his knees and commenced praying for his brother's life. As it happened, he had no use for prayer, having long since abandoned the Catholic Church. He scoffed at the Church's rituals, especially those that promised absolution. He knew from experience that the wicked routinely exploited the confessional with no intention of making a fresh start on a better life. Rather, they sought to continue their hardhearted ways with a clear conscience.

The following day, having tossed and turned through the night, the Guillotinist beseeched the town council to spare his brother's life, arguing that the vigilantes had made a terrible mistake. When his plea fell on deaf ears, he couldn't help but notice that when he spoke the council members listened with glassy-eyed indifference, while those same eyes burned with conviction when denying his request. Listening to their rationale, he grew increasingly frustrated, slowly stoking the embers of his slumbering rage. Recognizing a familiar pattern, his wife grabbed him by the sleeve and pulled him aside, quietly rebuking him for adopting the same attitude as the vigilantes. Had they not believed themselves undeniably right? When his temper cooled, he reappeared before the council and asked only that justice be done. By all appearances he had come to his senses, and everyone rested easy when he calmly withdrew and headed for home.

Having first constructed a magnificent platform, the Guillotinist labored for two whole days carving a beautiful pictorial into the framework of Madam Guillotine. His wife was at first concerned, until she observed how tenderly he caressed the wood, as if breathing life into his brother's corpse. When his work was done he slept for an entire day.

It was now the fourth day since his brother the highwayman had been taken into custody. With time running out, he made one last appearance before the town council. This time he remained composed in the face of rejection. Later that afternoon he lopped a few heads, steadfastly displaying his customary courtesy and concern. After the remains were carted off, different carts for different body parts, with different destinations to be sure, he tore down the platform. At this point he altered his routine and started digging where once the platform had stood. The townsfolk paid him no mind. After all, what mischief could he get into with a shovel?

After completing the initial preparations the Guillotinist returned home to finalize his plans. The blade and its frame, the platform, and even the steps were all stained blood-red, making it unlikely that anyone would ever detect the absence of his brother's blood. Additionally, the platform would not rest upon the ground as it had in the past, but would be sunk into the earth, creating a space large enough to conceal his brother. Of course, the execution would be a hoax, allowing him to spirit his brother away, alive and unharmed.

Knowing that he would have to put on the show of his life if he were to have any hope of convincing the wariest observers, the Guillotinist practiced his deceit. He began by wrapping himself in a shroud of despair, masking his visage with the look of the deranged. Next he practiced sleight of hand until he could perform his deception faster than the eye could follow. The trick never fails to succeed, because the eye needs time to refocus. That brief moment in time opens the door to the subconscious mind, allowing it to fill in the gaps, effortlessly creating a seemingly uninterrupted sequence of events. Rarely does the observer discover the nature of the deception, because he himself has created the illusion.

While awaiting his appointment with the Angel of Death the brother was held incommunicado. He was housed in a building originally used for winter storage, but at some point in time had been converted into the local jailhouse. There were no windows or furnishings, just four walls of stone. At first the brother scorned every attempt at intimidation, believing he was more than a match for his jailors' diabolical designs. Much to his surprise, he started cracking after just two days of lonely isolation.

The brother had committed a number of robberies in his time, but had never come under suspicion. And no wonder. He had taken advantage of the perfect cover: he had a reputation for ducking work, while his brother the Guillotinist commanded the town's respect. Furthermore, he had concealed his ill-gotten gains, having buried his plunder in the depths of the forest. His plan was to one day disappear, never to be seen or heard from again. Instead, he was trapped in the depths of despair, confronted with the villainous deeds of his past. He had preyed upon innocent travelers and, on one occasion, had even murdered a man for his gold. And now he would pay the ultimate price. There was no escaping Madam Guillotine.

Unable to accept the fate that awaited him, thoughts of suicide pummeled the brother's brain, urging him to cheat Madam Guillotine, after all. Removing his shirt, he ripped it into strips and then knotted the pieces together to form a rope. Next he fashioned a noose, securing it to a large hook suspended from the ceiling. Lacking a platform to stand on, he leapt into the air while at the same time drawing his knees up to his chest. The weight of his body unexpectedly snapped the makeshift rope, sending him sprawling onto the stone floor. Frustrated, he pulled off his pants and ripped them to bits in order to reinforce the rope. This time the rope held firm.

They found him alive, but critically injured. His neck was cockeyed, his breath conspicuously irregular, so they sent for the local physician. The physician applied what techniques he knew, but with no discernible change in the patient's condition. Unfortunately, his neck wasn't the only thing cockeyed, because his mind was gone, forever beyond the realm of everyday reality.

Informed of his brother's condition, the Guillotinist rushed to the jailhouse, where he found his brother writhing in pain and completely incoherent. His brother had joined the ranks of the totally unhinged. His plan to fake his brother's death was now out of the question. His brother couldn't possibly dive through the trap door quickly enough, nor could he be expected to remain silent while hidden beneath the platform. At least now he could bury the head he had surreptitiously appropriated from the last execution. It was no longer needed.

That night, the Guillotinist sat staring into the fireplace, totally entranced by the rhythmic dance of the flickering flames. His mind was totally blank, and therefore susceptible to impression. Prolonged staring can be harmful, rendering the mind passive, and therefore vulnerable to intrusion. However, despite the inherent dangers, passive states of mind do occasionally bestow something of practical value. And that's exactly what happened to the Guillotinist. Incredible though it may seem, the fluttering flames somehow assumed the substance of tangible reality, creating a scene that shocked the Guillotinist. He saw his brother committing murder.

His wife found him staring blankly into the fire, his flesh aquiver despite the proximity of the hearth. He was obviously on the verge of a breakdown. Her gentle touch and reassuring words soon restored his faculties, enough so that he had no trouble relating the details of his vision. Then he listened carefully to her words of wisdom. She validated his experience, but warned that visions were sometimes unreliable, especially those originating in the nether regions of the mind. And yet, it was entirely possible that he had witnessed an actual event.

He couldn't say exactly how or why he changed his mind, only that the vision had somehow opened his eyes. He now believed that his brother deserved his place on the blood-soaked platform of Madam Guillotine, where departure was guaranteed, but the destination uncertain.

He received word early the next morning. The execution would take place at noon, and he was the only one qualified for the job. Lopping heads could unbalance a man, rendering him totally unfit for polite society, but in the case of the Guillotinist, a lifetime of care and concern had saved him from that fate. Even so, he felt woefully ill-equipped for the coming ordeal. He had once lopped two young boys caught stealing food from a priest, but that atrocity was rectified when, years later, he lopped the priest for stealing money from the Church. This time Madam Guillotine would resolve the matter in one fateful swoop.

Kneeling in the shadow of the Angel, his brother showed no sign of recognition - not a shred of comprehension. The significance of what was coming had completely escaped his conscious mind, having declined, as it were, the invitation to its own execution. It was a painless departure, but that in no way portended glad tidings when he arrived on the other side of the gate.

The Guillotinist had dedicated his life to public service; however, after the death of his brother he no longer found satisfaction in his work. So he trained a local lad to take his place on the platform. His replacement had neither the flair nor the heart for the work, but exhibited, nevertheless, an aptitude for the observation of severed heads.

Within a year's time the Guillotinist passed away in his sleep. Bone tired and in need of rest, he arrived on the other side of the gate thinking only of the poor souls who had died by his hand, wishing with all of his heart that he had never been introduced to Madam Guillotine.

The General

THE SOUND OF pounding hooves clashed with the stirring tempo of the drums. The drummers were executing the same rousing beat that always preceded a major battle, but the General didn't seem to notice either the sound of the approaching horse, or the roll of the drums. Diminutive though he was, he sat secure in the saddle, emanating an aura of self-assurance. He somehow knew that the upcoming battle would unfold exactly as he had planned. He could feel the truth of it invading his solar plexus, giving rise to a common sensation, the juxtaposition of two competing emotions. Despite the effects of both nervous tension and glad anticipation, he welcomed the feeling because it invariably preceded victory upon the field of battle. Had he ever discovered the link between breath and emotion, a few complete breaths might have released his tension, while preserving the joy of expectation. A small thing to be sure, but proper breath control might have softened the abruptness that braced his personality.

As the sound of thudding hooves grew louder, the General's horse shuffled its feet, thereby releasing tension through its stuttering steps. The General, however, was deep in thought, and barely noticed the disruption. Having mentally entered the battle zone, he was totally absorbed with preparations for the upcoming engagement, and was therefore impervious to all distraction. When he finally turned his attention to the approaching rider, he watched with pride as one of his junior officers reigned in hard. The lieutenant had been out on a scout, and was intent on making his report. But first he shouted a greeting to Sir William. His men invariably addressed the General by his title, knighted as he was by King George.

The lieutenant delivered his report with customary brevity, while Sir William listened with obvious interest. It was just as he had suspected, the Colonial Army held the advantage in both field position and numbers. Even so, the General was not the least bit concerned. Forget the high ground and forget the numbers. He had worked out a winning strategy, and in his mind the battle had already been won. The General's victory was entirely mental in construction, but that in no way invalidated his effort, because reality itself is but a thought in the mind of God. And like all thought, reality is amenable to change, ever responding to, and ultimately reflecting man's desire.

Having created a blueprint for victory, and having accounted for every conceivable possibility, the General fully expected events to follow the script he had prepared. There was no magic to his method, simply the inevitable effect of a powerful will released upon a malleable world. The enemy invariably sensed his resolve, feeling the iron-fisted grip of defeat long before the battle had begun. The effect was real enough, but seemed all the more real because of the notorious reputation attributed to the General. The Colonials knew him to be utterly fearless, highly skilled, and entirely ruthless.

Despite his stunning victories in the field, Sir William was a controversial figure. He had many admirers, men honored to serve at his side; but he also had his detractors, men who were more than willing to undermine his command. It wasn't his bravery or his tactical genius that they questioned, but certain practices that had come to the attention of the General Staff.

Sir William valued good military intelligence. He therefore experienced no compunction when it came to mistreating prisoners of war in order to obtain reliable information. It became a point of contention with the General, because his superiors, as did one or two of his junior officers, considered the practice barbaric. Needless to say, as far as the General was concerned the Colonials got what they deserved. They had taken up arms against the King of England, and duty dictated a zealous defense of the Crown. He harbored no doubts on the matter, and often proclaimed that any clear-thinking soldier would have to agree that brutality defined the very nature of war.

Having thanked the lieutenant for his report, Sir William turned his gaze upon the terrain. A fresh blanket of snow was covering the field, while a cold, unforgiving wind was blowing out of the north, sending shivers through the men. It was the kind of weather that tended to shred a soldier's resolve, unless of course, you took the field with Sir William in the lead.

Ready for action, the fearsome mask of the warrior descended over the General's visage, claiming every last shred of his identity. His icy stare encompassed the field, and he could sense the chilling effect it had upon the fainthearted enemy waiting off in the distance. The enemy's fear was palpable, calling to mind images of wholesale slaughter, as if foretelling the outcome of the battle long before a single shot had been fired.

The General knew fear to be a physical thing that left its own unique taste upon the tongue, a taste the Colonials would soon find familiar. The seasoned soldier knows the taste, and stands all the firmer whilst in the blood zone, determined to never again know the taste of defeat. It was rarely discussed, but those who had seen action knew its metallic flavor to be strangely familiar, never realizing that it tasted of blood. Fear extracts iron from the capillary blood, typically depositing its residue upon the tongue. The loss of iron promotes fatigue, thereby robbing the body of strength and stamina. The General understood that victory would forever elude an army with the taste of fear upon its tongue.

The General's plan was coming together. The Colonials had overlooked a natural source of protection, even though their salvation lay but a short distance from the outcropping of rocks where they awaited their fate. The rocks offered a seemingly impregnable defense, so they never thought to take up a position amongst the maze of trees that crowned the hill.

Their tactics confirmed the General's opinion. They were nothing but a collection of misfits who had unwittingly chosen the means of their own demise. In the woods his men would have been at a significant disadvantage, because most of them hailed from the streets of London and Liverpool, not from the country, and certainly not from the woodlands. They were typical British soldiers of that era, and as such they were totally unsuited for guerrilla warfare, preferring instead coordinated troop movements. They fought their best on an open field, and the woods promised nothing but chaos and confusion.

Positioned at the head of his army, the General once again envisioned the battle from beginning to end. He imagined his soldiers advancing, fearless and single-minded. He witnessed their unflinching gait, anticipation growing with every step, foretelling the defeat of their hapless foe. How he loved the potency that hummed through the air during that moment of stillness just before the explosion of opposing wills.

Next he turned his fertile imagination upon the enemy. Wide-eyed stares met his gaze, replete with dilated pupils and quivering brows. Sweat trickled down their faces and dripped from the ends of their noses; their throats contracted as if choking back the impulse to scream. Tremors invaded their flesh, lodging first in the legs, and then throughout the bodily frame. Finally, the officers hesitated, craning their necks as if seeking an avenue of escape. He created it all with his imagination, and once satisfied with his creation, he stored it away in his subconscious mind.

Some of the newer men mistook the General's state of mind, and thought him so relaxed as to be daydreaming his way right onto the battlefield. The veterans, however, knew their commander, and therefore knew that he was different from other men, that both his methods and his tactics were wholly unassailable. Beyond that, they marveled at his courage, because he always rode at the front of the action. Even those who despised him couldn't help but experience a chill in their bones when the General entered the blood zone, because he never flinched in the face of the enemy.

According to those who judged him cold and ruthless, the General's worst attribute was his apparent indifference to the loss of life. They had to acknowledge that he mourned for the dead and attended to the wounded, that he said all the right things, but only after the battle was long over. Both during and immediately after a fight he was like a man possessed, not by demons, although that was certainly a possibility, but by a caveman mentality that waged war for the sake of brutality.

Little did they know, but the General harbored a secret, something he rarely acknowledged even to himself, and never to another. Deep in his core, somewhere off the beaten path, he had discovered a place inhabited by some lost portion of his being, a place long since surrendered to the grave. It was in that place that he first encountered the warrior who lived in the depths of his soul. That warrior was not Sir William, but someone bred to the ancient way of war. Had he not been exposed to the strange but wonderful ideas coming out of India, the theory of reincarnation would never have occurred to him. As it was he sometimes thought that perhaps the concept of multiple lives wasn't far from the truth. Perhaps he too had lived before, in another time and place.

Advancing on the enemy position, the General could see that his men were aching to fight. Their rifles were primed and their bayonets were attached. They had already entered the crescendo, and would soon pass into the silence. For some unknown reason, men about to enter battle reach a mighty level of sound and fury, but once beyond the point of no return, fall into absolute silence as they collect their wits for the ensuing struggle.

Silence cloaked the field just when the General and his army reached their launching point, a small hillock just left of center. The drummer boys knew their craft and immediately struck up a marching rhythm, thereby announcing the impending charge. Sir William knew not how or why the drum had become an indispensable ritual of war, but understood that the roll of the drums prepared men for war. Drums have long been used to awaken the cells of the body, inviting soldiers of every race and nationality to forsake all manner of sense.

Given the difficulty of the terrain, and the fact that his army was outnumbered, one might suspect that the General had finally bitten off more than he could chew. But that was not the case. The General had deployed his troops in Roman fashion, hiding a portion of his army in a ravine directly behind the main force. His plan was to give the enemy a false sense of hope, only to surprise them with a crushing blow. Truly, every moment in time possesses limitless potential, and the General intended on using his moment to strike a killing blow.

Totally relaxed, the General cantered towards the enemy position. Bullets began taking their toll, humming through the air like angry hornets. Men fell all around him, some silently, others screaming in agony. On they went, until at last he led the charge up the hill towards the enemy's rocky redoubt. The General's plan was already manifesting in physical reality, because the first taste of triumph announced itself upon his tongue, a taste not unlike the taste of fear, but recognizably distinct to the seasoned veteran. And well it should, because rather than iron residue, elation bestows the slightest hint of lithium.

At last Sir William gave the signal, the wave of his scarf, deep purple in color, and worn around the neck. It was a keepsake from his wife and, for reasons unknown to him, but obvious to anyone familiar with his karmic past, he cherished his purple scarf. Responding to the signal, the remaining force exited the ravine and charged into battle with bayonets attached. All told, many hundreds of the enemy perished, and another hundred or more were taken prisoner, most in no condition to resist. The seriously wounded were left on the field to die, while the rest of the prisoners were escorted down into the ravine to be interrogated.

The interrogators were anxious to apply their trade, and it wasn't long before they had acquired a treasure trove of military intelligence. Most, but not all of the Colonials survived the ordeal, only to be released into the harsh winter climate without provisions or adequate clothing. Horrid though the practice was, the General felt no compassion for the traitors.

Despite the growing opposition of his superiors, Sir William held firm in his belief that the Colonials had forged their own fate. He had no intention of changing his method of interrogation, and if he had his way more of the same would ensue. The matter was resolved when destiny informed Sir William that he too had chosen his fate. The Lords, in all their suspect wisdom, relieved him of his command and ordered him back to England. The letter was succinct. His mistreatment of enemy prisoners had embarrassed the Crown.

The General was astonished. He had been cashiered from the army by a pack of fools. They obviously didn't appreciate either him or his accomplishments, or the fact that he had done it all in service to the Crown. Name one other general officer undefeated in the field. Name one other field commander who was both respected by his men and feared by his enemies. Many similar thoughts intruded upon his mind, and while in a state of rage he thought to change sides. It was only a momentary impulse, but an impulse, nevertheless, that threatened the very foundation of his life. He was not a traitor, but a man with a score to settle in London, especially since the accusations leveled against him applied to others on the General Staff as well.

Back in London the General was highly regarded as someone who wielded power and influence with dignity and propriety, but someone, nevertheless, capable of misdirection when protecting both his own interests and those of his friends. Loyalty was important to the General, and he both gave and received allegiance with unquestioned alacrity. Consequently, no one was surprised when he dedicated his every resource to ferreting out the source of his downfall. Whoever they were, the General would hold them accountable.

Beloved though he was by the bulk of his army, some few were genuinely relieved when they first heard of the General's fall from grace. He wasn't anything like the other commanders they had served under. The others waged war with commonsense. They knew when they were outnumbered and out maneuvered, and therefore knew when to cut and run. Most of the men, however, loved and respected the General, and therefore wept for their commander, not just for the loss he had endured, but because the man himself had become something of a mystery. Everybody knew that even the meekest soldier was capable of unleashing a monster when faced with extinction, but in the General's case the alteration seemed more transfiguration than transformation, because he literally became the monster, wielding sword and knife with breathtaking speed. And not just on one occasion, but every time he set foot on the field of battle.

Years later, when the officers who had served under his command returned to England, they were surprised to discover that the General hadn't changed. They wondered that he had never reverted to his former self, but had remained the warrior-general who had crushed every foe.

He never commanded another army, his genius for war all but forgotten by his country, creating a deep and lasting sadness that gnawed at the very fiber of his being. Some thought him embittered, having never come to terms with the loss of face he had suffered when removed from his command. At least one old friend believed that he had lost his mind, that his conduct during the war had sentenced him to eternal damnation. Still others, recalling the fact that he had always tended toward the morose, thought that the war had simply exposed his true nature. The simple truth was that the General was an ordinary man possessed of an extraordinary skill. And that skill would never again know expression. It is that and that alone that drives the genius mad, and it was that knowledge that wrapped Sir William in a shroud of melancholy.

In his later years, while in failing health, and sensing the end at last, the old warrior confided in his friends. He talked about the mysterious place he had discovered in the depths of his soul, a place where ancient moods and motives dwelt. He no longer considered that place unfathomable, but was now convinced it contained the history of his soul. He was certain he had lived before; that he had been a warrior many times in the past. Strangest of all, he believed himself bound in service to the God of War, that his God would once again call him into service, albeit in another time and place.

When the end finally came he was alone in his private study, as was his custom during the final years of his life. With a great sigh of relief he crashed to the floor and tumbled down the stairs leading up to his study. Once through the gate, the sound of approaching leather sandals accosted his ears, and he suddenly found himself surrounded by a cadre of Roman Legionnaires. At first he thought it a dream, but then he recognized the grizzly veterans standing vigil over his transition. Truly, it was not a dream, but the eternal bond of love and loyalty that had summoned old friends only too happy to don the garb of ancient days. It was a rare reenactment, accurate to the last detail, except this time the old veterans wielded not broadswords, but flaming sheaths of brilliant White Light.

Thus he passed through the gate into the embrace of old friends. They too longed for the taste of victory, but not with the sword. Rather, they now sought victory in the realm of heavenly splendor. The General thanked them for their kindness, declined their offer of assistance, and then marched off to the sound of rolling drums. The God of War was calling the roll, and his name was vividly etched somewhere near the top of the list.

LIFE THIRTY-TWO
The Major

T HE CRIMEAN WAR, like so many other wars, was
fought for no reason. Nevertheless, there is a certain
story that can be told. The story concerns a little known
brigade of British marauders known amongst themselves, and
to those who knew of their secret existence, as the Crimean
Legion. These so-called Legionnaires fancied themselves cast
in the mold of the Roman army. They operated behind enemy
lines, and therefore rarely resorted to firearms, but fought
hand-to-hand with swords and knives. Because of their heroic
exploits, they were admired and respected by everyone who
knew of their mission.

The Crimean Legion was led by a British Major who
himself became something of a legend during his prime. His
family enjoyed the patronage of the Crown, and therefore
wielded considerable clout. They lived on an elegant estate
outside of London, and by the standards of the day were
considered quite wealthy. From the day of his birth, status
and privilege beckoned the Major; however, soon after the
completion of his studies he accepted a commission in the
army, and immediately became the black sheep of the family.
For reasons unknown, both to him and his family, he longed
for the life of a soldier, and cared not at all for the life of an
aristocrat. When he joined the military he chose neither the
cavalry, as was all the rage, nor the navy, long considered

the pride of England. His dream called him elsewhere, to a position less glamorous and infinitely more dangerous. The Major longed to lead men into bloody battles fought hand-to-hand with ruthless determination.

As a young boy he was exceptionally athletic, and consequently participated in all the popular sports of the day. As he grew older he became increasingly interested in military history, which naturally included the exploits of the Roman Legions. After completing his studies he spent an entire summer combing the ruins in Rome, frequently imagining that in another lifetime he had been a Legionnaire. It was a fanciful idea, but one that pleased him to no end, because to his way of thinking life was but a flickering flame upon a sea of fire. And so he became convinced that he had flickered there, in the very heart of the Roman Empire.

For the Major the Crimean War was an unexpected delight, not unlike a songbird heralding the dawn of a new day. It was in fact the sound of Destiny exhorting its progeny to once again march to the cadence of war. The Major wasted no time, and immediately obtained the necessary authority to establish his own command. He was determined to create a special unit of soldiers, men trained to fight behind enemy lines. He personally oversaw every detail of the unit's formation, including the selection of the finest soldiers he could find. He was meticulous in his selections, choosing men whose eyes reflected hell's inferno, men capable of heartless slaughter on the field of battle.

The call to war echoed through the Major, and many a man recognized his duty while standing in his presence. Many thus awakened swore to their comrades that they had known him before, even though they had met him for the very first time during their interview. Little did they know, but when the God of War summoned the Major, he also summoned those who had fought at his side in other times and places.

While studying Roman military history the Major developed an appreciation for tactical surprise. Surprise is a formidable weapon, mostly because of its impact upon the mind, which is almost always rendered passive when confronted with the unexpected. That moment of abrupt passivity renders the mind susceptible to the will of another, whether the projected will of an opponent, or the supportive intent of a friend. It was in that moment of frozen shock that the Roman army achieved its greatest victories, and it was in that timeless moment that the Major and his Legion struck.

The Major was not a vain man, nor was infatuated with his ego, despite his growing reputation as a fierce two-handed fighter. His exploits were legendary and, if rumor had it right, he was destined to wear the cherished epaulettes of a General officer. And yet, it wasn't power and position that enchanted the Major, but the call to glory. For the Major there was but one road leading to true glory, and that road was soaked with the blood of his enemies. Whenever he sensed the slightest moderation in his resolve, he immediately recalled the day when he first received orders for the war in Crimea. Through the constant recollection of that joyous occasion the chant of war grew louder by the day, until at last it possessed his soul, permanently silencing the competing rhythms of his life.

And so it came to pass that the Major led his Legion of Valor on one last mission. He didn't know it would be his last foray behind enemy lines, nor did he know it would be his last command.

The Major and his Legion rode with stealth and cunning all through the night before sighting an enemy encampment. Concealed in a wooded ravine, the Legionnaires immediately commenced preparing for war, caring for their horses and refreshing themselves with a few morsels of food. The battle would be fought hand-to-hand, but first they had to close the gap lying between them and their intended victims, who were encamped amidst a tumble of rocks close by the bank of a lazy river.

Exiting the ravine they merged into the grassy terrain, slithering on their bellies until an alert sentry raised the alarm. Weapons drawn and reflecting the morning sun, they charged the enemy stronghold, but not before the Major's rallying cry broke the silence, signaling his Legionnaires to take up the chorus. The sound carried over the rocks to the bank of the river, where it found a reflective body, creating the illusion of an overwhelming force.

The battle nearly over, sword and knife in hand, the Major was proudly poised on a jutting rock assessing the overall situation. Just when it seemed that victory was assured, at the very peak of exhilaration, the Major sustained a deadly blow. An enemy soldier, armed with a sword and determined to strike, broke lose from the fray and crept up behind the Major. The Major never saw it coming. The ill-fated blow caught him low in the back, scoring the pelvic crest from one hip to the other. He tumbled from the rock, landing with a gasp heard throughout the ranks.

His Legionnaires gawked in horror at the sight of their invincible commander waning into oblivion before their eyes. They knew that he was dying, and yet not a word was spoken. Shock had rendered them speechless, shrouding the reality of the Major's untimely demise. Fully conscious and expecting death, the Major valiantly tried to console his men. And it went like this. He wasn't afraid to die. He had lived his dream and therefore had no regrets. He was ready for the final chapter of his life.

Fear arrived without warning, camouflaged like it was by the taste of victory upon his tongue. It entered through the solar plexus, but quickly took possession of his facial features, announcing its presence for all to see. Some thought it pain, but the veterans knew the look, and understood what it was that had struck such a pose upon the Major's face. He was paralyzed from the waist down. The possibility, even though remote, that he might survive, not as a whole man, but as an invalid, terrified the Major. Death was his only hope. Many a soldier has welcomed an honorable death, but rare is he who blithely accepts the incapacitating wound.

They had no choice but to abandon the Major; however, before departing the scene they made one last show of respect. They wedged his sword into the rocky terrain, thereby creating a grave marker, even though he yet lived. Had they the time they would have waited until he passed through the gate, and then built a monument to consecrate the ground upon which their fearless leader had met his fate.

Alone and resigned to his fate, the soothing sound of the nearby river slowly penetrated the Major's awareness. Thus he drifted with the current, content to leave the world behind, as if disembarking from a dream. When he awoke he was lying in bed. Excruciating pain welcomed him back to the world, serving notice he was no longer paralyzed. A beautiful young woman was attending to his wounds, wrapping his torso with a clean, white sheet that had been torn into strips. Taking in the look of surprise upon his face, she explained what had happened.

She had moved him to the safety of her home, which stood but a few hundred meters from the scene of the battle. She had come upon the scene quite by chance while searching the woods for edibles. Corpses lay everywhere, and the scavengers had already begun their work when she found the Major clinging to life.

His recuperation was slow but steady and he eventually made a full recovery. By then he had come to terms with his destiny, and had fallen in love with his nurse. They had a child together, a beautiful daughter who was the spitting image of her father. He adored them both, and the thought that he might one day return to England never crossed his mind.

And yet, he awoke one morning longing for home, for the friends and family he had left behind. His wife refused to follow him back to England, even though she could not bear the thought of losing the love of her life. She instinctively knew that she would never feel at home on the streets of London, that their relationship would end badly if she denied what she knew to be right for her and her child. Their parting was heartbreaking, rending the bond of love that had linked two hearts as one. Despite her anguish, she granted the Major his freedom so that he might reclaim his past. He left with no small shame, but he left, just the same.

His return to London, unannounced and unforeseen, both delighted and puzzled his friends and family. Happy though they were, they wanted to know where he had been. Two years was a long time, certainly enough time to send word of his whereabouts. He knew they would never understand, so he made up a story, claiming that he had been a prisoner of war, that he had only recently been released. They never questioned his story.

At first he made the necessary adjustments, quickly reclaiming his status as an English gentleman. For a long time there was no hint of melancholy, although he increasingly yearned for the family he had left behind. He sometimes entertained the notion of returning, but feared the consequences should the truth of his past ever be revealed. Still, he often thought of hiring an investigator, but the burden of guilt prevented any inquiry into their fate. And what a terrible fate it was. Both mother and daughter were burned alive while they slept in their beds, the innocent victims of the Major's karmic debt. It seems they had agreed to lend him a helping hand, a rare occurrence to be sure, one that can only be undertaken with the permission of the Lord's of Karma.

Incredible though it may seem, despite every indication to the contrary, the day finally arrived when the cathedral of the past slowly crumbled, creating an avenue of descent for the approach of the Soul. Long since ready to end the Cycle of Rebirth, the Major joined forces with his Beloved Master, and together they got busy clearing out the past, expunging guilt and sorrow, erasing fear and anger, while at the same time awakening memories of past achievement. And it all happened during the hours of sleep. Dazzling lights intruded upon his inner vision, while his dreams were filled with mysterious conversations, sometimes revealing secrets long since forgotten, sometimes offering advice on how to live a meaningful life. Mercifully, the God of War no longer whispered in his ear.

When the Major passed over to the other side he was immediately reunited with his wife and daughter. It was a joyous reunion, one that seemed to go on forever, until one day, several years later, his Beloved Master knocked at the door. Once again the Major bid farewell to his family, only this time he knew that he would be able to return whenever the need arose. Meanwhile, there was work to be done and plans to be made. One more incarnation and the cycle of rebirth would finally be over, but first he had to pass the final test, the same test that had destroyed him on the continent of Atlantis so many thousands of years before. This time the test would be more difficult, but he wasn't the least bit concerned, because his Beloved Master had promised to walk at his side, not in the flesh, but from the world spirit. Together they would serve God's Plan for Humanity, and together they would walk in the Garden of Life.

About The Author

The author is a student of the Ancient Wisdom and lives with his lovely wife in the Pacific Northwest. He has a Masters Degree in Social Work from the University of Washington and is now retired after twenty-five years in the field of corrections. *This Side of the Gate* is his first novel.

Printed in the United States
58972LVS00001B/19

9 781420 888652